John Carl Roat, Martin L. Strong, Larry Bailey, and Rick Bremseth—all former SEALs. You've always been there for me. None of these books would have existed without your generosity.

And to all SEALs who have ever served or who serve now.

This one's for you.

Prologue

If our soldiers are not overburdened with money, it is not because they have a distaste for riches; if their lives are not unduly long, it is not because they are disinclined to longevity.

—Sun Tzu, *The Art of War*

BRILLIANT LIGHT BECKONED. GARTH REFUSED TO LOOK AT it. He concentrated instead on the hot, earthbound smells of blood, of blasted rock, of explosive residue, and helicopter exhaust. He knew what the Light was. He knew what happened to guys who let themselves go toward it.

"We gotta load you now, Lieutenant," the medic checking the straps that held him in the basket said. This medic wasn't *his* medic. His combat medic, the SEAL platoon's hospital corpsman, was MIA somewhere in the dun-colored, dry, rocky hills surrounding the mud-walled Afghan village.

"Can't… leave." Garth put as much force of command as he could into his voice. It wasn't much. "Have to… find Doc… first."

"They're looking for him. You're bleeding bad, Lieutenant. The pressure bandage isn't slowing it down much. I promise you, as soon as there's word, I'll find you and tell you."

Garth knew what the medic was thinking: there might not be enough left of Doc to find.

Doc hadn't been with the rest of the platoon when they were ambushed. Thinking he could be spared, Garth had sent him to another village to give medical aid. If not for Doc, they all would have died. Doc had called in air support, then had bought time with a one-man counterattack. His courage had put him in the kill zone of the friendly fire that had saved everyone else.

The searchers might not believe Doc was alive, but as long as Garth refused to be transported until Doc was located, they would try harder to find him fast. After what was called the Golden Hour, chances of survival dramatically decreased. If by some miracle Doc *was* still alive, he had the same Golden Hour that Garth did—and maybe needed it more.

The Light crept a little closer. With his vision darkening at the edges, it was harder not to look at it. He was conscious—the most conscious he had ever been—but his leg didn't hurt as much. Which probably wasn't a good sign.

"Wait," he whispered. "Just a few more minutes. Wait."

The Light came closer. Suddenly it flooded down from a sky so blue that his heart lifted in joy just to look at it. Fast-moving, perfect cottony clouds sailed the sky. They trailed shadows from one side of the meadow to the other. The shadows played tag and raced across the forest-covered encircling mountains.

There was something wrong with the way the aftermath-of-battle scene looked. Who cared? This was the prettiest meadow he'd seen in Afghanistan. A fresh breeze rippled lush green grass into satiny-looking waves. The grassy knoll Garth leaned against fit his shoulders and supported his head as if designed for him. The meadow was the perfect place for horses, and sure enough there were two—a black one and a brown one, their coats gleaming in the sunlight, grazing on the other side of the shallow stream that gurgled through the grass.

"It's nice here." He looked over at Doc who was propped against his own grassy knoll. Finding him hadn't been hard at all. "Good choice of rest area."

"Listen to the quiet. The sun is warm. The air is cool. I smell flowers and pine trees. Pine trees! Can you believe it? This place looks more like a high meadow in the Rockies than Afghanistan."

Now that Garth thought about it, the area looked like his grandfather's small horse ranch in Colorado. His grandfather had always called it a slice of heaven.

We're losing him, Garth heard someone say. *We've got to transport now.*

"Okay. Time to go back." Garth stood and dusted off his camo. The desert gray and tan looked out of place in this verdant spot.

Doc didn't move. Garth looked down, surprised. He narrowed his eyes and let a snap of impatience into his voice. "You coming?"

Doc squinted up at him. "I don't think so."

"What?" He hadn't issued an order or anything close, but the correct answer was *Yes, boss*. Insubordination wasn't Doc's style. Garth gave him the benefit of the doubt. "We can't stay," he explained.

Doc hooted as if he'd said something absurd. "Why not? I like it here. After I rest up, I'm going to ride the horses." He gave the intervening area the thorough perusal of a man used to sizing up territory. "I'll have to cross the stream to get to them. No cover, but I guess that won't be a problem."

"Doc, *Davy*," Garth switched to the more personal name, hoping to make the point that he wasn't just Doc's commanding officer. "Listen to me. Come back. Now. They think you're dead."

Davy angled an eyebrow in an excessively patient look. "I am."

Garth never lifted his voice, but his men knew to look out when it became more gravelly. "I say you're not."

Davy sighed. "You know, Darth Vader, old pal—" Davy knitted his fingers together over his stomach. "You are seriously messing with my mood. If I don't have a problem with it, I don't see why you do."

His men sometimes called Garth "Darth Vader" behind his back. It had probably started as a joking reference to his deep bass voice as well as a play on his name, but Garth had also earned it. He respected his men; he demanded their best; and he was fair in his praise and unflinching in his discipline. He watched out for them and kept careful track of their needs for food, for the comfort of a hot shower, and for rest. But he was not their pal. The more he had become what he needed to be to lead a SEAL platoon, the more permanently a mask of dark and dangerous implacability had set on his face.

The nickname wasn't disrespectful. Vader, after all, was the consummate warrior—he just gave up much of his humanity to become so. Still, Garth's men didn't call him Darth Vader to his face. Davy's mild impertinence chilled Garth; it showed how far from the real world Davy had already drifted.

"Get up. Now. That's an order."

"Go to hell, Lieutenant." Davy smiled to show he meant no offense. "Go to *Hell*—get it? Funny, if you think about it."

"They're searching for you right now. I can't keep them searching for long. We're losing light."

Davy shrugged. "They'll find me come morning."

Garth knelt and shoved his face close to Davy's, determined to win through the sheer force of his will. "Listen up. Nobody saw you get hit. You might be alive."

Like one of the scudding clouds, gentle pity crossed Davy's face. "I told you, I'm not."

A hollow feeling of unreality opened up in Garth's chest. Unbelievably, Davy acted like the fight was already over. SEALs didn't give up, dammit. SEALs never gave up as long as there was a chance. Nonplussed, he demanded, "How can you be so *sure*?"

"I never wanted anything but to be a SEAL. I couldn't have gotten luckier than to die doing what I loved, serving my fellow SEALs. I fulfilled my destiny."

"So you're letting yourself die."

Davy's eyes shone. "I think it was the Plan. You know. What I was born to do."

"Bullshit! There is no destiny except the destiny we make by making choices."

Davy shrugged. "Fine. I chose to die. Happy now? I knew I wouldn't survive before I took the first shot. You know how the instructors always used to tell us, 'A man alone in battle will not survive'?" His brown eyes twinkled with gleeful understatement. "Turns out they were right."

Guilt twisted in Garth's gut. It was his fault Davy had been alone. He tried another tack. "Isn't there anything you want to live for?"

"To be a SEAL. I've done that."

At last Garth understood why Davy was content to die. He even envied him. He wished he could feel as complete and at peace. Like Davy, once upon a time all Garth had wanted to be was a SEAL. Now he was one. He just wasn't sure the SEAL he had become was the SEAL he had wanted to be.

The SEAL he had wanted to be was willing to take on the hard jobs and ready always to defend his country, a man who fought for liberty, for justice. A man of compassion who would use his strength in service of others.

The SEAL he had thought he would be was the man who went behind enemy lines and struck at the heart of a terrorist organization. He would not only protect his country; he would also spare society the chaos and destruction of a direct attack.

The SEAL he had had to be was callous. The SEAL he had become focused on the mission's objectives and ignored the screams of women and the wails of children. The SEAL he had to be was as unmoved by the pain and suffering he caused as by the pain and suffering he endured. His shell had him retreating in horror from his own self. On the inside he had contracted tighter and tighter.

He couldn't change Davy's mind, but that didn't mean he was quitting. He had come here to find Davy because he had to make something come out right from the debacle he had led his men into. Davy was the best of them. He couldn't allow Davy to be the only man he lost.

Nobody called *Davy* "Darth Vader" behind his back.

He was not going to let Davy die alone on some unnamed hillside. He couldn't. Davy's death would inflict deep and lasting grief on everyone in the platoon. Garth had the trust and respect of his men. Davy had their love.

"I won't leave without you. You *will* come back with me. You don't feel like walking? I'll carry you."

Doc's brown eyes glittered with challenge. His lip curled. "You think you can handle me?" He looked Garth up and down. His eyes widened in shock when he saw the dark blood that soaked Garth's camo pants from his hip to his knee—funny, until now Garth hadn't noticed it either. "Whoa. That doesn't look good, Boss. You've lost a lot of blood."

Garth would use any leverage he could get. He piled on the guilt. "Hell, yeah. Every minute I stand here arguing with you, I'm losing more!"

Doc scrambled to his feet, all medic now. "Where are you hit?"

"Hip, top of the thigh, something. Doesn't matter. Come on, we gotta get out of here."

"It's okay," Doc slung Garth's arm over his shoulder. With his other arm he supported Garth's back. "I've got you. We'll get you out."

The rumble of helos battered the peace of the meadow. "How's the pain, Lieutenant? Need something for the pain?"

"It was bad at first." Garth was grateful for Doc's arm. "I don't feel it much now. I can walk—only a few more steps—we can make it. Just don't let go."

I won't let go. A warm hand clasped Garth's icy fingers. Compared to his, the hand felt almost hot.

"Corpsman, up!" Despite the heavy whoomp of helicopter blades, Garth heard the radio call for a medic. *"Tell the lieutenant we've found his man. Tell 'im, it's good news."*

———— ∞ ————

The light dimmed. Garth couldn't see the meadow anymore. His eyelids were too heavy to open. He smelled blood and dust; hot oil and plastic smell of machines; the occasional clean, sharp whiff of antiseptic.

Hot fingers… the hot fingers were still… there. Garth squeezed them. Finally found the word he was trying to say. *"Hurt."*

"Morphine coming up."

The Light was gone. Garth felt more comfortable in the dark.

Chapter 1

*It is said that if you know your enemies and know your-
self, you will not be imperiled in a hundred battles; if you
do not know your enemies but do know yourself, you will
win one and lose one; if you do not know your enemies
nor yourself, you will be imperiled in every single battle.*

—Sun Tzu, *The Art of War*

EVERYTHING WAS OKAY UNTIL BRONWYN SAW WHITE SATIN
wedding decorations draping the curved staircase in the
entry hall of her friend's ancestral home—and if not pre-
cisely okay, then manageable. She wasn't sure she ever
expected to be *okay* again.

Although to tell the truth, even *manageable* was
an overstatement. JJ, Bronwyn's best friend, wanted
Bronwyn at her side when she married, reason enough
to come to North Carolina at a moment's notice, but on
her best days, Bronwyn was a white-knuckle flier. The
doctor, whose ability to remain calm in the ER was leg-
endary, became one quivering nerve the second she felt
the plane's cabin pressurize.

To get here, she had had to pull back-to-back shifts—
the only way she could get another resident to trade with
her on a Thanksgiving weekend—packed an overnight
bag, arrived at the airport only to find out the flight was
delayed, and survived a flight so rough the seat belt sign

had never turned off and even the flight attendants had stayed buckled in for the entire trip from Baltimore to North Carolina.

Still, she'd been hanging on. She had gotten through the flight without breaking down by promising herself she could relax when she got to JJ's grandfather's great big mansion because the wedding would be small, and her part miniscule. No big deal. All that was expected of her was to stand beside JJ while a judge read the wedding ceremony and then shake hands with a few people afterward. And since there was about as much romance in her friend's decision to marry a Navy SEAL as there was in the average car rental agreement, Bronwyn hadn't thought there would be any reason to brace herself against an onslaught of emotion.

But then she had blown through the front door— literally—pushed by a wet gust of the same tropical storm that caused the rough flight.

In the soaring, classically proportioned entry hall, where the Waterford chandelier was already lit to dispel the gloom of the day, the elegantly curved staircase had been embellished with white satin swags caught up at intervals with nosegays of burgundy roses interspersed with tiny tea light roses and delicate baby's breath.

The newel posts were flanked by towering arrangements of the same flowers in priceless Limoges vases. Branches of candles on tall stands waited to be lit. The staircase, the whole entry, had been decorated to frame a bride's dramatic descent.

The setting spoke of tenderness and elegance and gaiety and so much damn hope.

She wasn't braced. The bottom dropped out of Bronwyn's stomach. Her knees threatened to buckle.

She loved JJ with her whole heart. She would do anything in the world for her. But she was very afraid she had just run into the one thing she could not do—act the part of the happy bridesmaid.

Still, she was here for JJ, and somehow, despite exhaustion that made her feel like she was trapped in quicksand, despite thoughts of Troy and what might have been, she had to keep hanging on.

"Was the flight horrible?" Beautiful JJ excused herself from the teenaged boy she had been talking to and rushed forward to envelop Bronwyn in a hug, the scalloped lace train of her white wedding dress belling behind her. "I'm so glad you're here, but I'm so sorry you had to fly in this weather."

Bronwyn and JJ didn't do air kisses, and they didn't do hugs where no body parts came into contact. When JJ's arms came around her, Bronwyn allowed her head to be pillowed by JJ's breast. JJ was as tall and voluptuous as Bronwyn was tiny and delicate. She and JJ had decided years ago that they could either live forever feeling awkward about hugs, or they could decide they were complete equals, the discrepancy in their size notwithstanding.

"Don't be silly." Bronwyn's eyes went hot with unshed tears—she was *that* happy to see JJ. This was the first time they'd been together since Troy's funeral. They had phoned and emailed, but it was not the same as being able to touch. "I would have come no matter what."

And she would have. When Bronwyn's fiancé died, her parents and brother had sent flowers and called to express their sympathy, but they hadn't been able to get away on such short notice. JJ was as busy as anyone since she was CEO of a large car dealership, but she had dropped everything to be at Bronwyn's side.

JJ had stayed with Bronwyn through the funeral and for several days afterward, putting food in front of her and telling her to eat it. Holding her through the nights.

"Oh, JJ." Bronwyn pulled away a little to look her friend full in the face. "You do look beautiful." She fingered the demure, white georgette with lace inserts on the old-fashioned wedding gown. "This dress is exquisite. Where did it come from? I thought you were going to wear a suit."

"You've heard me mention Mary Cole Sessoms?" JJ waved over a slender, sixtyish woman in a silvery dress. "Mary Cole, this is Bronwyn Whitescarver, my BFF and my maid of honor." JJ turned back to Bronwyn.

"Mary Cole convinced me that I couldn't let the wedding look furtive—like I was ashamed of marrying a man no one's ever heard of. I'm not. I'm doing what's in the best interests of the most people. She wore this dress in 1967 at her own wedding. It's my 'something borrowed.'"

That explained the about-face on the subject of decorating the house as well as the dress, which was exquisite—even though it was *not* JJ's taste. It was the first *demure* thing Bronwyn had ever seen JJ wear. It worked, though. On JJ's voluptuous curves, the innocent sensuality of a long-sleeved, high-necked dress that covered the arms and the dress's underlying décolleté with see-through georgette made *restraint* look regal.

"You look lovely in it. But my pantsuit…" Bronwyn indicated her gray slacks and jacket, the slacks rain-darkened from the knee down where her raincoat's protection had ended. "This is all I have to wear."

Mary Cole held out a hand. "Come upstairs with me. I've brought several of my daughter Pickett's dresses. She's petite like you. Now that I look at your beautiful dark red hair and white skin, I think I have the perfect dress for you."

Judging by the dress JJ was wearing, Bronwyn doubted it. Large, wide-set eyes the reddish-brown color of fine cognac dominated her face and made people assume she was much younger than her years. But even when one took time to look closely, her straight little nose and sweetly shaped lips that hooked upward at the corners made her look heartbreakingly innocent and benign. She despised being described as waif-like, but with the weight she'd lost in the last several months, her eyes seemed even huger, her pale skin looked even more colorless. The small bones stuck out at her elbows and wrists. The truth was, these days waif-like fit her. If Mary Cole wanted her to wear a dress like JJ's, she would look about twelve. At least in the gray pantsuit she looked like a grown-up.

JJ caught her in another quick hug. "I'm so glad you're here." She used the hug to put her lips against Bronwyn's ear. "Trust Mary Cole. You can talk to her," she whispered. "She knows everything.

Chapter 2

It pays to be a winner.

—SEAL saying

"You arrived in the nick of time," Mary Cole said over her shoulder as she led Bronwyn up the stairs. "The best man—he's a SEAL, too—he's already given up part of his leave to go home to see his family. He has a plane to catch—being the holiday and all, it was the only flight he could get when he changed his tickets—and we were wondering if we'd have to start the ceremony without you. JJ asked me if I'd fill in, but I'm so pleased you arrived—I know she really wanted you."

Mary Cole's tide of social patter floated Bronwyn up the stairs and into the guest bedroom that had been set up as a changing room, smoothing Bronwyn's awkwardness at being the last to arrive while gently and skillfully filling her in on all she needed to know.

"I didn't expect to need a bridesmaid dress," she told Mary Cole as soon as the guest room door closed. "Being out of touch for the last forty-eight hours seems to have put me completely out of the loop. What's the game plan?"

"I'm sorry you were caught unawares. Blame it on me. I persuaded JJ that her plan to be married with no frills at all was a mistake. People are going to talk about anything she does. She needs to set the stage for them to say what she wants them to. That being the case, there wasn't time to arrange a big, important wedding, so we're going for intimate, elegant simplicity. With the emphasis on family, rather than social relationships."

"All right. And what is the official story?"

"JJ and Davy felt an instant attraction when they met a year ago—at my daughter's wedding—but their careers came between them. When they accidentally met again—this time at my daughter's best friend's wedding—they realized their feelings hadn't changed. Davy's injury has taught them that life is short. They shouldn't put off being together any longer.

"But his mother recently died, and he's still recovering from his wounds—a great, big weeklong affair with an unending succession of parties isn't something he's physically or emotionally up to. They only want to be married in the company of their loved ones."

"Wow. That's really romantic! And touching." But it didn't sound like JJ. "Who came up with that?"

"I did."

"From what JJ's told me about you—what a clear-eyed businesswoman you are and how much she values your opinion—I wouldn't have figured you for a romantic."

Mary Cole accepted the implied compliment with an inclination of her skillfully tinted blonde head. "Mentoring JJ has been incredibly rewarding—she has the right instincts, and she's had good training. She doesn't need someone to teach her how to succeed in business. The main help I can offer her is that I see the big picture."

"Okay. Just so I don't get tripped up, who knows the other story?"

Mary Cole's eyebrows rose in polite puzzlement. "There *is* no other story. *You* are not surprised because you, being JJ's closest friend, thought all along that they were perfect for each other."

Mary Cole's revisionist history was a little hard to swallow. In point of fact, Bronwyn had advised JJ not to marry anyone and instead to tell her grandfather—the one pushing the marriage—to shove it. "Oh. Then you think she's doing the right thing—to get married just to save the business?"

"A mentor guides. She doesn't choose the path."

Having a mentor was one of the few things about JJ that Bronwyn had ever envied. Her own path would have entailed less floundering and fewer costly mistakes if she had had a guide. Bronwyn had become a doctor in spite of all the advice she had received.

Bronwyn jerked her thoughts from contemplating the difference a mentor, rather than naysayers, could have made for her. She and Mary Cole both had roles to play in supporting JJ, and there was a wedding to get under way. "What do you need me to do?"

Mary Cole went to the closet. She came back with a slim, empire-waist, evening dress of deep forest-green. "I brought several dresses. Do you want to try them all on, or in the interest of time, will you trust me?"

"I'll put myself in your hands." Bronwyn tossed her raincoat on the bed and began to shuck her suit jacket. "I don't have much fashion sense. In college, JJ took me in hand, but I'm afraid I have backslid. I wear scrubs at work and jeans the rest of the time."

Mary Cole managed to frown in disapproval and keep a pleasant smile going at the same time—a trick Bronwyn would love to master. "A professional woman needs to know how to dress. Times have changed, but women still need every edge to get ahead. I thought JJ told me both your parents were doctors. Didn't your mother teach you?"

"She didn't have a lot of time. She had a personal shopper who came to the house with preselected clothes for both of us." Bronwyn had already been on such thin ice with her mother that, rather than demanding the chance to express her own taste, she had accepted whatever the shopper chose. And for a person who had as much trouble fitting in as Bronwyn did, clothes that expressed little individuality were probably for the best.

Mary Cole forbore to comment on what she obviously thought was parental neglect. (Bronwyn guessed that Mary Cole's daughters had felt her guiding hand in *everything*.) Instead, she changed the subject. "JJ tells me you've almost finished your residency. When you're done, do you plan to stay in the Baltimore area?"

"I don't know yet. I have a provisional offer from one of the busiest inner-city hospital ERs. The experience I would gain there would look great on my curriculum vitae."

"You sound lukewarm."

"It gets harder and harder to be enthusiastic. The more successful I am at getting patients in and out in a hurry, the less I'm the kind of doctor I want to be. If I had another way to pay back the money I borrowed to go to med school, I'd quit."

Bronwyn unbuttoned her blouse. When she was down to her panties and camisole, she thought of a possible snag. "Am I going to need a bra for that dress?"

Bronwyn's small, firm breasts rarely needed a bra, and she certainly didn't have a strapless one with her.

"No. The bra is built in." Mary Cole held out the green dress. She discreetly averted her eyes while Bronwyn pulled the camisole over her head. "Hold up your arms. I'll drop the dress over your head."

The cool silk of the dress slithered over Bronwyn's torso and legs to the floor. She lifted the skirt. "This is beautiful. Please thank your daughter for letting me borrow it."

"I brought this, even though the deep olive green is difficult to wear, because it's the least formfitting. You're about the same height as my daughter Pickett but much more slender. She said if you liked it, you could have it. She's pregnant and doubts if she'll ever wear it again."

Mary Cole moved behind Bronwyn to do up the lacing of the bodice. "I've lost trust in medicine as it is commonly practiced, myself." Expert tugs accompanied the older woman's words. "My youngest daughter, the one who donated this dress, suffered—she essentially lost her teenage years—because no doctor listened to her or observed her long enough to get down to the cause of her symptoms. She had celiac disease. We spent thousands for tests that all came back negative until—despite the evidence in front of our eyes—even *she* believed nothing was really wrong, and if she'd just try harder she could be better. Doctors either told me not to worry or implied I caused her problems by expecting too much."

"How's she doing now?"

Mary Cole's lips twisted in a wry smile. "*I'm* the one with the problem now. She says she's fine, but after ten years of being anxious about her, of feeling like I was failing as a mother but not knowing what to do, I can't stop worrying about her. I drive her crazy. She tries not to let it show, but I can tell she avoids me."

"And now she's pregnant and you worry even more," Bronwyn guessed. "That must be hard. I can tell you love her very much."

"I do." Mary Cole's eyes narrowed as if she was deep in thought. "And I'm beginning to understand what JJ has told me about you. If you could be the doctor you want to be—if you had a way to practice the medicine you want to and pay off your medical school debts, but it meant leaving Baltimore—would that tempt you?"

Bronwyn's knees nearly buckled. She rarely told anyone about the hundreds of thousands she owed. People assumed that because both her parents were well-known doctors, her tuition had been taken care of, and explaining that her parents had put her brother, Landreth, through med school but not her took too long and left her needing to explain more of her family dynamics than she cared to reveal in casual conversation.

JJ knew everything, of course, and she must have told Mary Cole. Bronwyn appreciated Mary Cole's interest, but trying to act like there was hope, when she had none, exhausted her. "No offense, but I don't think there is a way. Any practice I join, it will be the same story—"

"Don't answer yet!" Mary Cole cut her off. "It's just an idea, and we don't have time to go into it now. We'll talk later." She stood back and looked Bronwyn up and down. Her eyes widened, and her lips rounded in surprise. "Oh, my."

"Can I come in?" JJ stuck her head around the door and caught sight of Bronwyn. She sucked in a breath. "Oh, my."

Bronwyn allowed herself to be turned to face the full-length mirror on the closet door. "Oh, my," she said.

The dress was one of those deceptively simple affairs, its only ornamentation the diamanté straps. It needed none, however. In some way Bronwyn couldn't have defined, the dress made *her* into its ornamentation. Her figure, easily dismissed as unendowed, looked fairy-like, delicately made but in no sense fragile. Her skin gleamed satin-white, yet glowed with rosy warmth within.

The woman in the mirror in a flowing gown the dark, deep green of magnolia leaves wasn't her. *She* crackled with power and authority as if her small stature concentrated all the qualities found in ordinary mortals. Every movement of the ethereal fabric, the color of woodland mysteries, excited whispers of secret wisdom. It spoke of the power of earth and water met in secret shady pools that had led people through the ages to worship in grottoes and seek healing in their waters.

The woman in the mirror refuted Bronwyn's every claim to ordinariness and denied her every hope that she would ever be the kind of doctor her family admired or respected.

She shivered deep in her bones as if a gong had been struck.

Outside in the hall, something fell with a heavy thud, releasing Bronwyn from this vision that had the power to destroy her.

"What on earth was that?" JJ flung open the door. Bronwyn lifted her long skirts to follow her at the same time that heavy male footfalls could be heard pounding up the stairs.

"Let's let the others deal with it," Mary Cole inserted a note of prosaic calm, catching Bronwyn's shoulders and turning her toward the vanity, "while we put the finishing touches on you. Time is marching on."

While Mary Cole dabbed and brushed her cheeks with cosmetics, Bronwyn heard JJ, out in the hall say, "Did you hear that, David?"

"The whole house heard it," a dark, velvety masculine voice answered. "What happened? Are you all right, JJ?"

"I'm fine. I don't know what it was. Looking around, I don't see any damage anywhere. It's a good thing you came upstairs, though. Bronwyn will be ready in a minute. Since you're here, I might as well introduce you. Where's Garth? I can introduce him, too."

"Bringing up the rear," another deeper, rougher male voice replied, "slowly. Running up stairs isn't in my repertoire yet."

Behind Bronwyn in the mirror, JJ reappeared flanked by two well-built young men, starched, pressed, and polished with military exactitude, though they both wore civilian sport coats and slacks. One was tall and dark, but you wouldn't call him handsome.

The other man, of more medium height, Bronwyn recognized from cell phone pictures JJ had sent. He was David Graziano, JJ's soon-to-be husband. Before the injury that had left one side of his face slashed with red scars, he had probably been very handsome.

For one brief second, Bronwyn could visualize the

structures that lay under the scars, the bones that had been shattered, the muscles torn, the brain bleeding from hundreds of pinpoint hemorrhages caused by violent shaking. It was almost like watching a movie of the explosion from the point of view of the tissues that had been injured and then following the story of how the body had worked and was still working to heal itself.

It was a miracle that he was alive and a double miracle that he hadn't lost the sight in the injured eye. It was no wonder he was still in pain, with that much edema and inflammation at the points where the bone was still knitting. She knew better than to let herself feel the pain, but even shielded, she could trace its path over his face.

She wondered if he was aware of just how close to death he had come—but what did it really matter? Experience in an ER had taught her how easily a perfectly healthy young person could die of *nothing* and how tenacious life could be in the face of massive trauma.

He had undoubtedly been saved by very good care, possibly better than if the trauma had occurred in the States. The specialty of emergency medicine had been born during the Vietnam era when returning army doctors had realized that civilians were dying of injuries soldiers routinely recovered from. Today, once again, trauma care was taking a leap forward as technology and procedures developed for Iraq and Afghanistan came home.

"Bronwyn," JJ began, "I want you to meet—"

"Don't move!" Mary Cole tightened her grip on Bronwyn's chin to prevent her from turning her head. "I don't want to put out your eye with this mascara wand."

"This is David," JJ told her.

"Hi, David."

"And this is Lieutenant Garth Vale, his best man."

Bronwyn shifted her eyes to the reflected image of the taller man. She had an impression of a dark countenance tanned to the color of oak and so impassive that it looked carved.

He wasn't handsome. Composed of broad, hard planes and sharp angles, his face was more about masculine strength and indomitable will encased in an armor of cool control than about pleasing proportions. His thick, black hair was ruthlessly cropped to lie close to his skull. The only mobility his face showed was in his almond-shaped eyes that burned with a hard, blue flame.

"Pleased to meet you," he rumbled in a voice the color of midnight.

Bronwyn suspected he was anything but. In fact, except as an item to be catalogued along with the rest of the room's contents, she doubted if he saw her at all. She could almost see him classify her as human—female—small—unarmed and then move to the next item. He wasn't cold so much as disconnected.

Because she had seen it before—her fiancé Troy had been an undercover cop—she recognized the look of a man caught up in the dark thrill of his job's dangerous demands. The ordinary world was a stage on which he acted a part, but it was no longer real for him. People had become a concept to him. She averted her eyes while she tried to pull air into lungs that were suddenly a couple of sizes too small.

When she could look at Garth again, to her surprise she realized that he was in pain, too, though why she hadn't noticed before, she didn't know. That his leg hurt should have been obvious—he was leaning on a cane. JJ had told her both men had been wounded in the same action in Afghanistan.

Bronwyn felt a little guilty that she hadn't sensed the pain until now, and guiltier still that she had been caught up in her own visceral reactions to a past she had no desire to revisit. She sought for something suitably polite to say.

"Wave," Mary Cole instructed, stroking lip gloss onto Bronwyn's mouth. "Y'all can chat later. I'll be done here in a minute. JJ, stay here and we'll put your veil on. You boys, go and supervise setting up the chairs in the entry hall, please, like we discussed."

In the mirror, Bronwyn watched "the boys" exchange amused glances. The smile the lieutenant gave his friend was surprisingly full of warmth. David, she concluded, was still *real* to him.

As if they had communicated telepathically, they snapped off salutes and left the room.

Mary Cole put the finishing touches on Bronwyn, then had JJ sit at the vanity so she could anchor the fingertip Alençon lace veil to JJ's hair with bobby pins.

At last Mary Cole said, "I'm going to get everyone into place and start the music. Are you sure you don't want Lucas to walk you down the stairs?" she asked JJ. "He's your grandfather."

JJ rose, her habitual grace marred by cold stiffness. "I am sure. If I'm getting married, I will do it on my own and on my own terms. He has *given me away* quite enough."

Mary Cole nodded and let herself from the room.

Bronwyn wondered what she should say, could say.

You don't have to do this sprang to mind, but she'd already said that, more than once. There was no point in reiterating; JJ knew it. JJ had looked at all her options and decided marriage to a man she hardly knew was her best choice. JJ would go to any lengths, accept any sacrifice to care for those who depended on her. But JJ wasn't this cold automaton Bronwyn saw before her.

"JJ, is there any chance you can be happy married to David?"

"You want me to be happy?"

"You know I do!" Except, apparently, JJ didn't.

Guilt rocked Bronwyn. JJ was her best friend, and she had failed her. She had been so wrapped up in her own problems she had offered JJ little in the way of emotional support.

She grasped JJ's hand, willing her to feel her sincerity. "I love you, and I don't care what you do or who you marry. I kept telling you, you had other choices. I should have told you to choose what would make you happy."

"But, it won't bother you…?" JJ let the fact that Troy was dead and Bronwyn's happiness destroyed trail away unspoken.

"If you can be happy, I can be most sincerely happy *for* you. In fact, I'd love it if you would be happy enough for both of us."

JJ's lips crumpled. She looked down at their clasped hands while she gave a jerky little nod of assent. Emotional scenes were not JJ's style.

In the past, Bronwyn might have backed off in the face of JJ's discomfort. But in the past she hadn't been following her heart. Now she knew she was going to.

Wherever it took her. She squeezed JJ's cold fingers tighter. "JJ, how do you feel? About him?"

JJ looked down, almost shyly. "He's a good man. I, uh…"

Bronwyn couldn't have said where the sudden insight came from—maybe from years of knowing her friend. "You *trust* him, don't you?"

The smile that curved the perfect bow of JJ's lips was a little surprised, a lot thoughtful. "I do." She cocked her head, listening. "Mary Cole has started the music. That's our cue—oops, our bouquets!"

"Wait. We might not get another chance to talk today, and there's something I want to say. Even if Troy had lived, we wouldn't have made it as a couple. I think that's why my grief has been so hard. Not only was he taken away from me violently, I also feel like I've been through a breakup.

"You have found a good man—one whom you trust. That's a very good start."

Chapter 3

All war is based on deception.

—Sun Tzu, *The Art of War*

GARTH SCANNED THE SKY AND CHECKED HIS WATCH. THE plane was two hours late. In the southwest, liver-colored clouds massed. He studied the orange windsock sticking up from the peak of the small, blue sheet metal hangar. The sock's tail still angled downward indicating gusts in the negligible, four- to six-knot range.

Garth wasn't reassured. Despite the rain earlier, the late-May afternoon was hot again. The air was thick with the smell of moisture and the sharp, green odor of soybeans in the flat fields adjacent to the runway. Another thunderstorm was coming. The sooner the plane touched down the better.

And not just for the safety of the pilot and passengers. He didn't know how much longer he'd be able to take Henry MacMurtry's smirking interest in how he ran the airfield before he decked him.

Last November when Garth had been offered a temporary attachment for a couple of months to a counterespionage outfit that "consulted" with the CIA, he had jumped at it. An officer who intended a naval career always strategized two promotions ahead.

Limited duty while he waited for his leg to finish

healing wouldn't have advanced his career at all; proving himself in a different arena would. SEALs worked closely with the CIA in many corners of the world. Garth could demonstrate that he could operate solo and get himself noticed in a way that could lead to plum assignments later.

Noticed? What he'd gotten was buried. Performing duties an E-4 enlisted man with the right technical skills and security clearance could have managed. In fact, maintaining an airstrip where small planes could land unobserved was the kind of job done more and more by private contractors, companies hired to provide the support structure that military and intelligence agencies had once provided for themselves. He was cleared for active duty now. He'd asked for reassignment. Any time he tried to find out what was keeping new orders from coming through, all he got were stalls and runarounds.

Briefly, Garth had been glad to see MacMurtry. He had seen no one he knew for months, and at first, any familiar face had been welcome.

MacMurtry was killing time while he waited to pick up passengers on a flight that had most likely originated somewhere in South America. The passenger list wasn't part of Garth's "need to know." VIPs must be aboard, if they rated an officer escort.

Like Garth, MacMurtry was a lieutenant in the navy, a SEAL, and like Garth he was in civvies, but that's where the resemblance ended. MacMurtry was a ring-knocker, a Naval Academy graduate.

The fit of MacMurtry's summer-weight blue business suit on his stocky frame announced familiarity with world-class tailoring, while Garth's khaki cargo shorts and brilliant orange-and-red aloha shirt told the world, if the grease on his hands didn't, that he was a working man.

The cotton Hawaiian shirts were Garth's uniform these days. They had been issued when he took this job—someone's idea of what would make him blend with the populace of South America—and were tailored with the left armhole larger than the right to disguise the presence of a weapon. To date, he hadn't been sent to South America. He no longer thought he ever would be. The loose cotton shirts were comfortable though, so he wore them.

Once he had realized that MacMurtry, under the guise of "catching up," only wanted to needle him, Garth had deliberately kept MacMurtry—and his business suit— outside in the heat while he made preparations for the incoming flight. Call him petty, but watching droplets of sweat bead under MacMurtry's cold-coffee eyes satisfied him immensely.

"Hey, you caught the marriage curse yet?" MacMurtry drained the last swallow from his Coke can, crushed it, and lobbed it into the trash barrel outside the hangar.

Marriage curse. Garth snickered a little. Talk about a stupid gambit! Watching MacMurtry jump through hoops to get his attention satisfied Garth even more than watching the ass-kisser sweat. "What are you talking about?"

"The marriage curse." MacMurtry laughed, showing large white teeth. "You've been in North Carolina so long, I figured it had you for sure." Despite the bonhomie, MacMurtry's eyes coldly assessed Garth's reaction to his taunts.

Garth shrugged. "I've been stuck down here in Podunk, aka Sessoms' Corner, NC. Guess I didn't get the memo."

Garth knew he was smarter than MacMurtry and a more able operator. But he had to admit MacMurtry probably had more of what it took to be promoted up the chain of command. Garth had proved his ability to lead operations, but those who rose higher than lieutenant had to win the acceptance of the officers above them.

In theory, Academy graduates were not given preference at promotion time. In reality, they had an edge. Academy graduates had been bred by the very people they had to fit in with. They understood how every string attached to every favor and knew exactly how to pull those strings. Garth had worked hard to learn those things, but they didn't come naturally to him.

An idea for how he could find out what was holding up his requests for transfer bloomed in Garth's brain, though he allowed no trace of the sudden surge of hope to show on his face.

If anyone had his ear to the ground, knew the score, and had an inside line on everything the brass was up to, it was MacMurtry. If anyone might have a line on why Garth had been stuck in Podunk, it would be MacMurtry. Knowledge was power; no one exploited that maxim more than MacMurtry.

But Garth knew MacMurtry from way back. If MacMurtry's strength was that he was always in the know, his weakness was that he loved to use insider knowledge to lord it over others. He had always felt intensely competitive with Garth. MacMurtry could probably be induced to spill, if given an opportunity to dig at Garth in the process.

Garth decided to give MacMurtry all the opportunities he could.

"There's a curse on North Carolina weddings?" Garth feigned interest in knocking the sandy, gray mud off his boots. "Is that what they're saying?"

"Not the weddings. The curse is on any SEAL who attends a wedding in NC. He's likely to find himself married within a year."

Garth snorted. "Come on!"

"Some guys are seriously spooked. Look at the evidence. It all started when Graham got married down here. Dulaude was best man at Graham's wedding. He was married within a year. David Graziano was at that wedding and at Dulaude's, and damn if he wasn't a married man in twelve months' time. You, you were at Dulaude's wedding and the best man at Graziano's." MacMurtry turned his orthodontically perfected smile to high. "You know what they say: 'Once is an accident. Twice is coincidence. Three times is enemy action.' You're a goner."

MacMurtry was definitely feeling triumphant—exactly the setup Garth intended. But it was important not to let him win too soon. Not until Garth had set his own hook. He smiled a little dismissively. "You are so full of it, MacMurtry. It's no wonder your eyes are brown. Lots of SEALs were at both Graham's and Dulaude's weddings. Are they all married now?"

"It's like the flu. Not everybody catches it. But you still want to be careful about who you hang around with."

Who he hung around with—was that a veiled warning? Or was MacMurtry looking for something to taunt him with? Garth was no damn good at cat-and-mouse games. He stuck with his purpose of frustrating MacMurtry. He made himself smile and laid on his Western drawl. "Hell, if I could find the right woman, I'd get married in a heart-beat. Be nice to have a wife, home, kids."

He wasn't bullshitting. He should have listened when Commander Kohn had visited him in the hospital and urged him to take a desk assignment. While Garth was on LIMDU, stuck in one place, he should find a nice girl and get married, according to the commander. Kohn had had lots of good reasons, not the least of which was that the right wife was a huge career asset.

But the thought of yielding his choice of wife to his ambition hadn't set well. Garth had always assumed, without giving it much thought, that the woman for him would just be there one day. He would recognize her, and that would be that. It's what had happened for his father and grandfather.

And he had another problem. No SEAL had to go without sex, but he'd never been a ladies' man. Women looking for a walk on the wild side frequently told him they loved what one had called his "dark aura." But women he could imagine as the mother of his children? Those he couldn't get to first base with.

Still, he knew the commander's advice was well intentioned. Setting aside all the ways a wife could en-hance a man's career, if an officer hadn't married by a certain age, the brass wondered why.

Of course, he wasn't going to say any of *that* to MacMurtry. "You ought to be thinking about giving up bachelorhood yourself," he told him instead. "At promo-tion time, the Chain of Command likes to see a man married. You know what they say, 'A solid marriage makes a good SEAL a better one.'"

Confident he'd frustrated MacMurtry enough to have

him ready to snap at any bait, Garth set the hook. "If there is a marriage curse, I say, bring it on. My problem is, how am I going to meet eligible women stuck here?"

"That's not your problem."

"No?"

"Your problem, my man, is you've been iced." MacMurtry didn't bother to hide his triumphant smirk. "Word is, your last operation embarrassed higher-ups when your platoon was ambushed."

"We were following up on intel that the Taliban was using the village."

MacMurtry tsk'd. "That's what you're bound to say, isn't it?" His head wagged in false commiseration. "Bro, you ruined a lot of people's day when you got out of there alive—but too bunged up to be sent back down range." *Down range* meant sectors where bullets were flying. "Better for everyone if you're put somewhere you can't ask questions."

Chapter 4

"For God's sake, be careful out there!"
*"If I were going to be careful, I would have joined the
Coast Guard."*

—From the movie, *Navy SEALs*

GARTH WAS GRATEFUL FOR THE IMPASSIVE COUNTENANCE
he had cultivated until it was a habit. Without it,
MacMurtry would have seen that the bottom had just
dropped out of Garth's world.

When Garth tried to see where he had gone off track,
his mind always went back to Afghanistan. Everything
had been fine until that day. He and his men had distin-
guished themselves; and a field promotion to lieutenant
commander had been a real possibility until, because of
bad intelligence, he had led his platoon into an ambush.
The surrounding mountains had blocked radio transmis-
sion. Only the fact that he had sent the platoon's medical
corpsman to a different village on a mercy mission had
saved them.

Bad intelligence happened. There was no reason to
think it had been anything but an operation in which
Murphy's Law had reigned supreme. Though Garth
had gone over and over that day, trying to see the decision nodes at which he could have taken different
action, he hadn't considered a perspective from which

what had gone *wrong* was that he and his platoon had survived.

That was over a year ago. A SEAL officer's career was built on distinguishing himself on operations. For months, on paper, Garth had done nothing. If MacMurtry was not just pulling his chain, Garth's career hiatus wasn't a snafu. It was part of a plan to marginalize him, and it had worked. His career wasn't stalled; his ambition to serve his country by leading Special Operations, and all the hopes he had pinned to that ambition, were dead in the water.

Clear-eyed cynicism was necessary to gain enough rank to institute his vision, and Garth had worked hard to acquire the armor of distrust that fit so easily on men like MacMurtry that they didn't even feel it. Even so, Garth had suffered "a career-limiting event"—the kind of colossal mistake that guarantees an officer will never be promoted again—but the mistake *he'd* made was failing to recognize he was being screwed by someone on high.

When he'd come close to dying, Garth had questioned if he had been the kind of SEAL he wanted to be. Now he didn't know if he was a SEAL at all. On paper, he wasn't even in the navy anymore. His background had been scrubbed. Anyone who checked him out would learn he had retired on medical disability. His checks came from a dummy corporation.

If someone had deliberately diverted him away from the Teams, then he couldn't be sure what he was doing or for whom. And when you came down to it, he didn't know who MacMurtry was working for either.

Everyone is potentially under opposition control according to a list of precepts for spies, the so-called

Moscow rules. The story that the CIA had developed the list during the Cold War specifically for agents operating in Moscow was probably fiction, but the rules themselves were real. Every secret agency, every group that operated undercover had some version of them.

Spies trusted no one, but a SEAL team couldn't operate at all, unless the members knew they could trust each other, even if they trusted no one else. For the first time, Garth looked at a fellow SEAL and wondered if he could trust him to have his back. The answer was no.

Welcome to the world of black ops.

Garth was thinking more like a spy than a SEAL.

The cold truth almost knocked the breath from his body.

Garth thought his mask of inscrutability had held and MacMurtry couldn't tell how much damage his little bombshell had caused. Garth preferred to keep it that way. He didn't know whether MacMurtry had been unable to resist the chance to deliver the coup de grace or if he was a messenger for someone higher up.

MacMurtry was a snake, but he was a company man, which could make him a useful snake. If MacMurtry had only been a messenger—albeit one who enjoyed his work—there would be another move shortly. He might yet have information Garth could use to pull himself out of this black hole he'd been sucked into.

It was time to help MacMurtry out a little, but Garth wasn't good at looking sympathetic, and MacMurtry wouldn't believe it anyway, so Garth sneered. "Down here, it gets hot in May. I doubt if that business suit is rated for a heat index of 110. Why don't you go wait for your VIP in the air-conditioning—before you die of heatstroke?"

MacMurtry looked doubtful.

Garth clapped him on the shoulder. "Don't worry. You can still look like an eager beaver. You'll hear the plane in plenty of time to be standing on the runway when it touches down."

Thinking hard about MacMurtry's revelations, Garth went to the garage. His eyes fell on the red canoe on the wall rack he'd built and the seventeen-foot bass boat— toys he'd bought to entertain himself.

He bypassed his four-wheel drive '99 blue Chevy pickup and the nondescript black sedan MacMurtry had arrived in and got into a white van. The van was fitted on the inside with six passenger seats and the means of restraining those passengers, if necessary. Not that those restraints were ever used, of course.

He backed out the van and parked it on the gravel road leading away from the airstrip. The gravel road meandered through soybean fields until it met up with the two-lane blacktop. After skirting a cypress swamp, the blacktop would access I-40 about ten miles from tiny Sessoms' Corner. Where the van would go after that was none of Garth's business.

Next, he walked the entire length of the runway. The tough crabgrass that bordered it was wet from the previous rain. He noted with satisfaction that the ground was firm and no puddles had formed on the runway. A slight narrowing of his almond-shaped eyes and a tiny twitch of lips sometimes described as sensual, sometimes cruel, were the only outward signs of the pride he felt. The drainage system he had designed and built in his spare time, of which he had a lot, was functioning well.

But in his heart he was a SEAL. No matter how he

felt about it, he had a mission objective, which was to see the plane land safely and send its passengers on their way. And one thing SEALs and spies had in common was a belief in Murphy's Law. Even when everything looked fine, he believed with all his heart that anything that could go wrong would go wrong, and *that* meant he checked and rechecked and then checked again.

Black clouds had turned afternoon to dusk, and gusts from the fast approaching storm slapped at the tail of the C-37 Gulfstream when it finally touched down. Garth admired the pilot's skill but shook his head. He was glad he hadn't had to attempt it. Taught by his pilot father, he'd been flying a plane since he was sixteen. Garth had taken to heart his father's admonition that there were old pilots and there were bold pilots, but there were no old, bold pilots. Garth rushed forward with wheel chocks as soon as the plane came to a stop.

As Garth helped the pilot unload the baggage, he saw MacMurtry question each of the passengers and realized that whomever MacMurtry had been sent to collect, that person wasn't aboard the plane. Garth heard someone say, "Renfro didn't make it."

Renfro? Garth had heard about a SEAL named Renfro, but he didn't think he'd ever met him. Ordinarily, Garth might have heard more since the travelers usually took turns using the head, stretching their legs, and chatting with him before they piled into waiting vehicles. Today, the threat of downpour didn't encourage them to stand around chewing the fat.

In minutes, the plane was unloaded. Garth helped one of the passengers, a man with a battered face who needed to be more than half carried, to the waiting van. The others piled in.

After a couple of worried cell phone conversations, conducted well away from the group, MacMurtry departed in the sedan, alone.

Garth waved everyone off and jumped into the pilot's seat to taxi the plane to the hangar, intent only on getting it under cover. Even tied down, a plane this size would be no match for the winds associated with this latest storm cell.

Inside the plane, he was reaching for the starter switch when a waft of latrine smell hit him. Before he was nicknamed "Darth Vader," the guys had occasionally called him "the bloodhound" for his sensitive nose. The odor wasn't strong, but it was unmistakable. The man with the bruised and swollen face had obviously been beaten, maybe tortured. He must have crapped his pants. It happened.

Garth usually cleaned the cabin after performing a plane's routine engine maintenance—given the weather, he would have waited until tomorrow. An odor like this would only get worse with time, though. As soon as he had the plane inside and the hangar doors shut, he switched on the lights and searched for the source of the stench.

The interior of a C-37 Gulfstream isn't very big. It didn't take him long to locate a sturdy, ventilated, white cardboard box with a fitted lid. It was wedged under a rear seat where the flotation vest should have been. He approached it with caution. Any suspicious package had to be presumed to be a bomb until proved otherwise.

To get a better look he squatted, ignoring the way the scar high on his thigh protested the movement. In red ink the box was stenciled, *Bananes: Produit du Ecuador*. In English, it cautioned: *Perishable. Store at Room Temperature*. On the box's side, a wide, black arrow pointed *up*.

He leaned closer and sniffed. The bad news: The box did not smell like ripe bananas.

The good news: Bombs didn't smell like shit.

Usually.

Assume nothing. He kept his movements slow and easy as he dislodged the box, pulled it into the aisle, and lifted the lid.

Someone had carefully padded the interior with a knitted pink blanket.

On the blanket lay a baby.

Wispy tufts of hair, the tentative gold of corn silk, framed the tender, translucent shells of pink ears. Twin fans of impossibly long eyelashes lay on the baby's pale cheeks. If not for the stink, it could have been a doll—it lay so still and looked so perfect. His heart squeezed to a standstill. He had found it too late. It was dead. Irrational guilt and grief burned the back of his throat.

Then wide blue eyes opened and blinked in the sudden light. Seeing him, the baby's rosebud mouth turned down, but the baby didn't cry. Slowly, with a shuddering sigh that shook its little chest, the baby closed its eyes again.

Being a SEAL was dirty work. It wasn't the stink that made Garth's eyes water and caused the Nabs and Coke he'd snacked on to rise up in his throat. No trace of fastidiousness survived SEAL training. SEALs did what the success of an operation dictated, uninfluenced by what they felt. Weighed against the success of a mission and the safety of his men, distaste for filth and stench, even moral repugnance for the ruthlessness sometimes required of him, had no place.

Still, in the back of a plane looking at the contents of a box, Garth fought the urge to throw up.

Being a SEAL was dirty work, but it wasn't dirty enough to keep him from feeling outraged to find a baby, stinking and too quiet, in a cardboard box aboard a spy plane.

He had the overflowing diaper and saturated shirt stripped from her—the baby was a girl—and pitched into the crabgrass edging the runway before he was halfway to the trailer that doubled as the airstrip's office and his living quarters. Once inside, he set her in the tiny lavatory of the miniscule bathroom and ran warm water over her.

She whimpered when the water touched her. In the cold blue light of the fluorescent fixture over the sink it was easy to see why. Her skin, from her armpits to her round little knees, looked like raw meat. Her bottom was the worst. Huge blue eyes fringed with long, pale gold lashes widened momentarily, then resumed their strange sunken, unfocused look.

He turned the baby over to let the water stream over her little behind. He'd call her medium-sized if he had to guess how old she was. Not a newborn but not able to walk. No matter her size, he had a gigantic problem on his hands.

The number of laws smashed beyond recognition, the number of regulations bent, the sheer number of things that had gone wrong with someone's plan to smuggle a baby into the country—he was looking at the kind of snafu that sent people to jail and ended careers.

He hadn't been told to expect a delivery, but when it came to black ops, there were wheels within wheels, and the left hand frequently didn't know what the right hand was doing. Hell, sometimes the left hand was out to get the right hand. It was possible that whoever had hidden her on the plane had nothing to do with the agency at all.

All he knew was that this tiny scrap of humanity was the only innocent party.

In theory, he should inform his superiors and shift responsibility to them. In fact, shit always rolled downhill. Part of his job, and he understood it well, was to shield the people above him from association with the darker aspects of intelligence gathering. If he let higher-ups know, his only directive would be to "take care of it." That would mean, *Make the problem go away by any means necessary, and don't tell me what you did*.

They only wanted plausible deniability—to be able to disclaim all knowledge—and to swear the head of the responsible party would roll. *That* would be the person in authority who was lowest on the totem pole. That would be him.

The decision of what to do with the baby was his and his alone. Before he did anything, he wanted to talk to Clay. Clay was a retired SEAL living in Wilmington who had done some contract work for the agency while he got his fledgling sea tow operation off the ground. Garth wouldn't have to explain that from the agency's point of view, the baby's very existence was a liability. He turned the water off, wrapped her in a towel, and carried the little one over to his bed.

He went to his closet where he kept several prepaid disposable phones.

"You want me, you got me." Clay's voice came over the wire.

Garth described the situation. "If I can figure out where she came from," he concluded, "I can return her to the only people who have a right to her."

Clay snorted, not unkindly. "Look, we can speculate about who put her on the plane and why, but it's not going to get you anywhere. Once a screwup is this big, it doesn't matter what the mission objective was. There's no fixing it. All you can do is make it go away."

"I can't do that. She's come into my hands. It's on me now."

"Are you crazy? You want to kiss any hope of promotion good-bye? This is someone else's pile of shit. There's no reason for you to step into it. This is the kind of shit that sticks forever and never stops stinking. What you should do is bury it as deep as you can and never, never admit knowing anything about it."

"Except it's a baby."

"Hell, man, I know. Don't you think I know? I love kids, too." Clay had moved to Wilmington to be close to his two children when he realized his ex-wife was not going to cooperate in any way to help him keep a relationship with the kids. "But you got to look after yourself. Think about your objectives. You hope to make it to the top of the food chain. You want to be where you can make a difference. You want to make Special Operations more proactive about taking the fight to where the terrorists are instead of waiting for them to bring the fight to us."

"Yeah, well about that, I got MacMurtry to shoot off his mouth a little. Getting back on track is going to be more complicated than showing up for duty once I'm transferred."

"What did he say?"

Garth summarized MacMurtry's implication that his platoon had been sent into a known ambush.

"A goat-fuck?"

"Yep. Except according to MacMurtry, the Taliban were supposed to win."

Civilians assumed *goat-fuck* was slang for a messed-up situation. In fact it was also military jargon for a strategic use of troops. The jargon arose from troops likening themselves to a goat that has been tethered out in the open as bait to draw wolves into an attack in the open. No matter what happens to the wolves, the goat is fucked. It doesn't stand a chance.

The strategy had to be employed sparingly since it didn't inspire troops' confidence in their leadership. It had its uses, though, and had been employed by generals and elected officials alike.

A military purpose of the strategy was to draw the enemy into action in the place of one's choosing. A political purpose could be served if the attack provided motivation for a war that might otherwise be unpopular. It could make an enemy look stronger, more aggressive, and more merciless. Conspiracy theorists argued that the military's flailingly inefficient response on 9-11 indicated that the attack had been not wholly undesired by those in power in America.

Wiping out a whole platoon of SEALs would make the Taliban look fierce indeed. There would be calls for more troops, which would mean more matériel and more support. More matériel and more support meant more power to the upper echelons and more profit for the private contractors who provided goods and services.

There was money to be made in war and reason to pursue victory as inefficiently as possible. Every time the Taliban destroyed a school, a road, a power station, or a hospital that had already been rebuilt once by contractors, the contractors made even more money rebuilding it. Again. There were those who had incentive to make the war last a long, long time.

"What do you think?" Clay wanted to know. "Is it possible MacMurtry's right?"

"All I know is, if sending my platoon into ambush was deliberate, then the orders had to come from far above my pay grade. They've had all the time they needed for a complete cover-up. One that quietly implies I'm unfit to command."

"You're washed up."

"I'm not accepting that. Not until I know more." Garth stared at the closed blinds behind which lightning flared white. The storm had broken in full force. "Anyway," he went on, "straightening it out will take time. For now, this baby has fallen into my lap. My superiors don't want to know about it, so I can't *win* any points no matter how I handle it. But I can lose them if I don't keep it under wraps. I've got to figure out someone who will take her for me. I can't keep her here."

"You're damn right you can't. In a four-room trailer, you can't keep her out of sight. Give it up. Take her to an ER—a big, busy ER. You can be in Raleigh in eighty minutes. Better still would be somewhere a large percentage of the population is always transiting—Norfolk, Charleston, even Myrtle Beach. Leave her some place she will be found and walk away."

"If I do that, she *will* disappear. There aren't any birth records in this country to be found. She'll be untraceable."

"That's the point."

"No. She may be a pawn, but she's not a throwaway. Somebody loved her." Something about the little pink blanket the box had been lined with and the cloth doll tucked beside her made him think that whoever had hidden the baby on the plane had cared what happened to her.

"*Somebody* who screwed up six ways from Saturday!" Clay roared.

Garth rubbed his neck. "That person might deserve whatever they get, but she doesn't."

"Are you getting soft? Think, man. Think of yourself."

"Look, the only person who knows she's in this country is whoever put her on that plane. The only other person is whoever was supposed to pick her up at this end. All I want to do is stash her somewhere for a few days. Someone is either going to come looking for her—or not. If they don't, dropping her off at a hospital can still be Plan B." Although privately he knew Plan B would never happen.

If no one to whom he could, in good conscience, turn her over ever showed up, well, he would cross that bridge when he came to it. All he knew was he was not going to deposit her into the system and walk away. No institution could care for a child. Its rules and needs would always come first. He'd find a family that wanted to adopt her and manufacture the papers that would make it possible. "You've got contacts with civilians. Who can I take her to now?"

"All right," Clay conceded reluctantly. "A girl I know runs a day care. Sometimes she keeps kids overnight for people who do twenty-four off, twenty-four on shifts. I'll call her, but I'm warning you, she's a stickler for paperwork. You'll have to tell her you're the baby's father."

Chapter 5

It is the rule in war: if ten times the enemy's strength, surround them; if five times, attack them; if double, divide them; if equal, engage them; if fewer, be able to evade them; if weaker, be able to avoid them.

—Sun Tzu, *The Art of War*

GARTH MEMORIZED THE NAME, ADDRESS, AND PHONE number of the sitter. He thanked Clay and clicked the phone off.

When he judged the baby was dry enough to uncover without fear of chilling her, he peeled the edges of the towel back. He didn't know much about babies, but he did know chafed, raw skin, shriveled from being wet too long.

"Surf torture" was a fundamental part of SEAL basic training. Recruits were made to link arms and sit where ocean waves would break over them. The first thing a man learned, when they finally let him up, was that the crotch of his uniform and underwear had filled with sand. Sand he was given no opportunity to get rid of.

Once thoroughly wet and cold, recruits were ordered out of the surf and told to make "sand cookies." That meant roll on the beach until coated with sand head to toe. Then it was on to the next exercise: running, jumping, vaulting, and pushups, endless pushups, while sand relentlessly scraped in every skin fold and was ground into every orifice.

Oh, yeah, he knew raw skin. Now that the soaked diaper and shirt had been removed, and her skin cleaned, her legs already looked less red. He dried her carefully, patting creases behind her knees and under her arms. He didn't see any sores, blisters, or breaks in the skin. If she could be kept clean and dry for twenty-four hours, she would probably heal up just fine.

Nevertheless, ignorance of babies aside, she didn't look right to him. What alarmed him was her lethargy. Although she roused and looked at him from time to time, her eyes would almost immediately close again, which didn't make sense. He'd handled her enough to have woken her up by now.

"Wake up, baby," he told her as he shaped her little arms and legs under the towel to finish drying her. Her condition, whatever it was, went beyond the first aid he'd been taught. Before he could take her to the sitter, he would have to get her medical attention.

At the sound of his voice, her droopy eyelids raised slightly. For a second her eyes searched his. Her wispy eyebrows angled in an ineffably sad look of disappointment.

He'd never spent much time—okay, none really—looking into baby's faces. But something about her disconsolate gaze pierced his chest right in the very center. His heart softened. He felt it happen.

"I'm not the person you want me to be, am I? But I will take care of you." Hot determination filled his chest. She was no longer a duty to be discharged, a problem to be overcome. Protectiveness and hypertrophied accountability were part of his nature; he would have done his best no matter what, but for the first time in a long time, what he wanted to do and what was unquestionably the right thing to do lined up. "If I'm going to tell people I'm your daddy, we need to get acquainted. What's your name, little one?"

He picked up her tiny right hand between two fingers and shook it. It wasn't a fifth the size of his, but like his, the fingers were long. "Until you or someone can tell me different, your name is... Julia Vale. Julia is my mother's name." His heart squeezed, and his eyes went unaccountably damp. "She'd be happy to let you use it. She has long fingers, too."

Security issues kept him from being able to tell his mother specifics about his life when he was operating. These days his mother believed he managed Coastal Air, a small airfreight company whose primary clients were exotic floral importers. Mostly, even if he could tell her, he wouldn't. He didn't want her to know. He did what he did so she would never *need* to know.

He'd never tell her about the baby he had named Julia, either. But he felt good to be pursuing a goal that his mother would think—without reservations—made the world a slightly better place.

He opened a new package of T-shirts and wrapped the baby in one in lieu of any clothes.

Chapter 6

The only easy day was yesterday.

—SEAL motto

"LOOK AT IT THIS WAY, MILDRED," BRONWYN TOLD THE big, shaggy dog panting beside her in the dark. "Now you can write a book like Snoopy's that begins, 'It was a dark and stormy night.'"

Mildred didn't laugh.

Okay, as jokes went, it wasn't very funny. It had been a dark and stormy day as well, and they were both hot, tired, and on edge. Once a cold front passed, the hot mugginess oppressing the tiny town of Sessoms' Corner, North Carolina, should abate, but the collision of hot and cold air masses had created a line of slow-moving thunderstorms. Renewed rumblings promised another was on its way.

Bronwyn pulled up the hem of her T-shirt to wipe sweat from her face. The house's ancient air-conditioner had rumbled without letup but still had fallen further and further behind the heat index. A damp 78 was the best it could do.

Despite the heat, Bronwyn had spent the day sorting her belongings into the beginnings of order in the old house. Mildred had supervised.

Now a fuse had blown; the air-conditioner was off;

and the old house was *really* dark. Dark such as Bronwyn, child of the city, had never seen. This dark wasn't just a concept; it was a thing. It had substance, thickness, weight. Being afraid of it didn't seem all that silly.

Mildred pressed her rough head against Bronwyn's thigh, looking for—and giving—reassurance.

"Get a grip, Mildred," Bronwyn told her, feeling her way around the kitchen and trying not to stub her bare toes on open cartoons sitting everywhere. "We've never been afraid of storms, and we are not going to start now. And we're not going to let our imaginations get the best of us."

She saw no reason to remind the dog that they had abandoned making the bed upstairs when the encroaching clouds had blotted out the last bits of daylight. The storm wasn't really the problem—what had her unnerved was the persistent way the house shifted and creaked. The house constantly made her look over her shoulder to see who was there. Which was ridiculous. She was a woman of science, a doctor, an ER physician noted for her ability to stay cool.

And she wasn't going to second-guess herself about her decision to move here. One day about six weeks after JJ's wedding, she hadn't been able to get out of bed. No matter how she told herself to *keep on keeping on, you can push through this, put one foot in front of the other,* her body refused to get up and get dressed.

She had wished she could go to sleep and never wake up.

A doctor had the means to make that happen.

But she had a dog, and the dog had to be fed and taken for walks. Mildred got her moving again. So she was saved by something even deeper than her love of medicine. If she couldn't hang on any longer, she would have to change. She began to recover from her exhaustion—the exhaustion of both grief and an ER doctor's inhuman schedule. Hope put out tender green leaves again.

She had called Mary Cole Sessoms.

All she and Mildred needed was some light, and they would be fine.

Bronwyn fumbled through a kitchen drawer, searching by touch for her flashlight. She was sure she had tucked it in one of the drawers when she had unpacked, but which one?

Massaging the German wirehaired pointer's shaggy neck with one hand, Bronwyn tugged at the next drawer down with the other hand. The humidity-swollen wood refused to budge. Whatever was in it was as lost as whatever was in that room upstairs with the door stuck tight in its jamb.

Lightning filled the kitchen with white glare. Bronwyn was alternately blinded by light, blinded by dark.

The dog pressed herself more tightly against Bronwyn's leg.

Overhead, renewed downpour drummed on the kitchen's tin roof. Booming thunder rattled the windows. The whole house creaked and swayed under the impact of a sudden gust.

This was the kind of thunderstorm that produced tornadoes. Tornadoes weren't as frequent on North Carolina's coastal plain as they were in the Piedmont, but they weren't unheard of. This house actually boasted a storm cellar. "Boast" being the operative word. Bronwyn hadn't explored it yet, but the more she had explored the rest of the house, the more work she saw to do. And really, she'd be happy to let the cellar stay unexplored. Dark underground spaces creeped her out.

When she'd seen the stately house, she'd fallen in love with its wraparound porch, one side of which was enclosed, and its high-ceilinged rooms, a fireplace in each. But what had stolen her heart was a view of the river from the upper stories. At a more practical level, the arrangement of the rooms would make dividing the house into living quarters and a doctor's office simple.

Best of all, she could live there rent free. If she stayed for five years, the house would be deeded over to her.

Mary Cole Sessoms had introduced Bronwyn to a group of citizens of Sessoms' Corner who were concerned that their town was dying. Even young people who saw the opportunities the area offered—and who desired a simpler, slower lifestyle based on enduring values—bypassed the town for communities where medical services were more readily available. Mary Cole's group hoped the whole town would benefit if they could make it economically feasible for a doctor to live there.

Bronwyn was wondering if she should take herself and Mildred to the cellar, no matter what its condition, when she felt Mildred go on the alert beside her. The dog sounded the deep, baying *Aaarrooo!* that was Mildred's way of saying, *Someone's at the door*. Only then did Bronwyn realize that, in addition to the drumming of the rain, she could hear pounding coming from the front door.

Another flash of lightning showed Mildred's shaggy eyebrows raised in a *What are* you *going to do about it?* look. That was the kind of watchdog Mildred was. She was intelligent, curious, and determined to be in on all the action, but she only *reported* intrusions; she left dealing with them to Bronwyn.

The thing was, Mildred knew as well as Bronwyn did that they had heard someone at the front door several times today and answered it, only to find the deep porch empty. Bronwyn didn't know what was causing the noise. At first it had seemed odd, then mischievous, then mysterious, then downright eerie. Neither woman nor dog hurried to the door any longer when they heard what sounded like fists thudding on the thick oak.

Tonight, in addition to a reluctance to feel her way down a pitch-dark hall on a fruitless errand, Bronwyn was conscious of a deeper dread. Unsettling as it had been to turn on the porch light and see no one, it would be even creepier to be *unable* to turn on a light and thus *unable* to tell if anyone was there.

The pounding came again. Mildred's toenails clicked a doggy Morse code of excitement on the bare wood floor.

"You *want* to answer the door?" Bronwyn asked the dog.

Expecting a reply might be irrational if the dog were anyone but Mildred. Mildred was a cartoon character of a dog who defined "body" as a language. She could speak paragraphs with just the slant of a tail.

Mildred had been a present—a fat, fuzzy, gray puppy with floppy, chocolate-brown ears and too-large skin that made her look like she was wearing some other dog's hand-me-down flannel pajamas—given to Bronwyn by her fiancé, Troy. The puppy had quickly grown into her skin to become eighty pounds of stubborn, impulsive, half-grown dog. Not an ounce of meanness in her, but destructive in her heedlessness.

Bronwyn and Troy had argued over the insanity of trying to keep such a dog in an apartment. She was already impossible to control. What would she be like at her mature weight?

And then one day, the miracle. Mildred had realized that the sounds Bronwyn made were words and that she could understand them. Bronwyn had been looking right at her; she had seen the moment it happened.

Mildred's legs had stiffened, and her ears had flown straight up when she had had her *Eureka!* moment. Bronwyn could read the exclamation as clearly as the letters on a theater marquee. Electrified joy had blazed from Mildred's liquid acorn-brown eyes. *I have discovered interspecies communication!* In that moment, it was like a chrysalis had burst open and Mildred had emerged a transformed dog.

The clicking accelerated, and Mildred jingled her tags for emphasis.

"You're right, Mildred. Since the power is out, the doorbell isn't working. This time, there really might be someone out there. Okay."

Okay. Mildred loved *okay*! *Okay* meant she got what she wanted! (Mildred thought in exclamation points. Anything that wasn't worth an exclamation point probably wasn't worth getting off the floor for.) There *was* someone human at the door and something else. Though the door was closed, Mildred had detected one of the most intriguing, most promising scents she'd ever picked up.

Mildred dashed down the hall, her large, web-toed paws thudding on the bare wood floors. In no more than three bounds, she realized Beloved wasn't right behind her. Eager as she was to find out what was on the other side of the door, duty came first.

Humans were handicapped. Having only two legs made them unstable—real easy to knock over—and *sl-l-o-ow*? With ridiculously small ears and noses, they had terrible hearing and a worse sense of smell. And they could stumble into things in their own house—just because it was dark! Unimaginable, but true.

Mildred skidded to a stop. She padded back to Beloved. She positioned her head under Beloved's hand and led her to the door.

Chapter 7

Subtle and insubstantial, the expert leaves no trace; divinely mysterious, he is inaudible. Thus he is the master of his enemy's fate.

—Sun Tzu, *The Art of War*

THE BIG, WHITE HOUSE'S GIRTH WAS INCREASED BY WIDE porches on the first story, topped by a narrower second story and a cupola with a widow's walk on the very top. Illuminated by flashes of lightning and lashed by silver sheets of rain, the house looked like a gigantic wedding cake gone terribly wrong. Garth positioned his truck so that his headlights lit the porch and left them on while he dashed for shelter.

When he bounded up the shallow steps, a huge black shadow suddenly loomed in front of him. His heart lurched and then resumed its steady rhythm. His own shadow, of course, but still. A SEAL wasn't the kind of man to let his imagination run away with him, but it didn't take much imagination to think he'd wandered into to a SyFy Channel movie.

Once upon a time, he would have laughed.

Garth pounded on the door. His first priority had to be medical attention, and the closest source was this new doctor. Though he didn't mix with the locals, everywhere Garth had been for the last couple of weeks, he'd overheard the buzz that a doctor, the *first* doctor in the area since 1967, was moving into this old house on the edge of Sessoms' Corner. The house was dark, but that might not mean anything. The whole town had plunged into darkness just as he'd approached the outskirts.

The porch offered little protection from rain driven sideways by 50-mile-an-hour gusts. He shifted the too-still bundle he had tucked under his poncho. Garth pounded on the door of the doctor's house again. If the doctor wasn't in, Plan B was to drive sixty miles to the closest hospital ER. He'd take her there if he had to, but a brush with the medical establishment would leave a paper trail as wide and easy to follow as I-95.

Under his slicker, the infant whimpered—a weak mewing sound. What he wouldn't give to hear her cry like a baby—like his nieces and nephews did, howling their dissatisfaction anytime they didn't have exactly what they wanted. He shifted his hold so that she was sheltered from the rain while he pulled her diaper up.

When he'd gone back to retrieve the box she came in, he'd found two diapers tucked under the pink blanket—more evidence she hadn't been someone's throwaway. But apparently there was more to getting a diaper to stay on than met the eye. Reinforcing the little tabs with duct tape hadn't helped.

Somewhere within the house a dog barked. Good. He had someone's attention. He pounded the door again.

Mildred snuffled ecstatically at the cracks around the front door while Bronwyn struggled with the knob of the old-fashioned lock. It wouldn't turn to the right so she twisted it to the left, but the door still wouldn't open so she turned it back to the right. This time when she pulled on it, the door opened on hinges that shrieked their need for oil.

After the dark of the hall, Bronwyn was almost blinded by the brightness of headlights shining directly into her eyes. She threw up a hand to shield them. Squinting through her fingers, she was able to make out the huge, dark shape before her as a man in a poncho. She couldn't see his face. His features were lost in the deeper darkness of the raised hood.

"Are you the doctor?" a voice like oiled gravel demanded. His tone implied that she had better have a damn good excuse if she wasn't.

The hair stood up on the back of her neck. Who the hell did he think he was to come pounding on her door demanding to know if she was "the doctor"? She was a doctor. Period.

She took a deep breath and told herself to get a grip. If there was a grain of fairness in her, and there was, she could admit she was sensitive on the subject, having already met too many times with people's disbelief and their suspicion that she was a kid playing a trick.

Snapping at him wouldn't deal with a problem that was essentially hers. She was tiny and deceptively, *very* deceptively, fragile looking. Ridiculously young looking, as well. Her mother assured her the day would come when she'd be glad. That day had not arrived, although she would be thirty in a couple of months. She never wanted to hear another Doogie Howser quip as long as she lived.

And to be fair, she couldn't blame him for wondering

about her. Barefoot, in an ancient T-shirt and shorts, she didn't meet anyone's standards for professional appearance. Even worse, without a stitch of makeup, with her slippery hair coming down from its ponytail, and with her less than impressive height and chest development, she looked about sixteen.

"Do you have a medical emergency?" she countered in her most businesslike voice. "If so, you should go to the ER in Burgaw. The rescue squad will transport you if you can't drive."

"You *are* the doctor. I have a sick baby. You have to see her." His dark tone didn't project threat so much as determination.

At Bronwyn's side, Mildred waved her nose in the air, wagged her tail madly, and all but cavorted with joy. The dog's obvious welcome made it hard for Bronwyn to match the stranger's imperative tone with steely determination of her own. She restrained the dog by her collar while she tried reasonableness.

"Please understand, it isn't that I'm trying to turn you away. I'm not equipped to handle patients—I'm not even moved in."

What she could offer was a long way from *standard of care*. An agreement to help would be a malpractice suit waiting to happen. Needing to think such a thought made her insides twist in disgust. She hated to practice defensive medicine, thinking first of lawsuits rather than the patient's needs.

"Even if my office were set up, if you have a genuine emergency, an ER can help you more than I can."

"My problem is I don't know much about babies. It could be nothing, or it could be life threatening. The nearest ER is an hour away—if the storm keeps up, maybe two hours."

Bronwyn wished she could see his face to read his expression. She squinted. "The light's in my eyes. Where *is* the baby?"

He drew aside the poncho with one hand and brought forward a bundle cradled like a football in the crook of his elbow.

Seeing the baby, Mildred lunged forward. Bronwyn tightened her grip on the dog's collar. In the headlights' glare, Bronwyn could make out nothing but a silky halo surrounding a little round head and a tiny bare foot dangling. In the headlights, it glowed translucent pink, the tiny toes edged in deeper rose.

Bronwyn's heart squeezed at the sight of the vulnerable little foot. She forced herself not to react. It changed nothing. "My power has gone out. I'm sorry. I really am. I can't examine what I can't see." She felt for the doorknob behind her. She pushed the door open while trying to make her tone final. "Take her to a hospital. That's my best advice."

Lightning flashed. A strong gust dashed rain across the porch and billowed the man's poncho behind him. The house exhaled a cold draft and slammed the door on Bronwyn's heels.

Bronwyn jumped out of its way and lost her grip on Mildred.

Mildred was a good dog, but Bronwyn knew very well that she controlled her only because Mildred preferred for her to. Right now, Mildred, unrestrained at last, preferred to sniff their visitors. Dogs saw with their noses. Mildred wanted a good look. The man calmly stood his ground while the big animal sniffed his feet and then his crotch.

She hated to turn her back on the man, but Mildred was between them. She turned around and wrestled with the knob with both hands. It didn't budge.

Chapter 8

Technology will always let you down.

—The Moscow Rules

SOMEONE SHOULD TELL HER, *"TECHNOLOGY WILL ALWAYS LET you down."* Garth watched her struggle with the door, unsurprised it gave her trouble. Calling a door mechanism "technology" wasn't really a stretch. When Murphy's Law was in control, anything with more moving parts than a toothpick constituted technology.

Garth often reminded his men that every operation went to shit thirty seconds after it got on the ground. God knows this one had the second she stepped through the door. Wouldn't you know, since it was crucial *not* to leave a trail that led from the plane to wherever he took the baby, then the first person he approached would be an acquaintance?

A good memory for faces was a longevity-enhancing attribute in an operator. In the harsh white glare of the headlights, he'd recognized her. He'd left the truck's lights on only to see his way to the porch. It was sheer dumb luck that the light had been in her eyes and she hadn't recognized him the instant he recognized her.

He'd felt the ground shift under his feet. Hoping he couldn't believe his eyes, he had blurted out, "Are you the doctor?"

He couldn't remember her name; he'd only met her once. They'd been introduced, and that was all. Nobody had said she was a doctor.

Watching her struggle with the door, Garth felt a certain dour amusement. Murphy was dangling *him* like a puppet on a string. If Murphy had to screw up everything, at least he was being evenhanded. She had wanted to ditch him, and now Murphy wouldn't let her. His head told him to take her refusal and get out. But going with his gut, he didn't get an overwhelming feeling that he should abort.

The doctor's little grunts of aggravation crescendoed. He couldn't help himself. He grinned. "Can I help you?"

"This door! The latch is broken or something. It seems to have a will of its own when it comes to opening and closing." She rubbed her brow and visibly recovered her dignity. "No," she corrected herself, "that's a ridiculous thing to say. In the dark, I must have put the night latch on, instead of taking it off."

"A night latch? Don't you know it's practically worthless? Any burglar with a pocketknife can jimmy it."

"Well then, I hope a burglar will come by soon! But if he wants to rob the place, he'd better bring his own flashlight!" She whirled to face him. She crossed her arms under her breasts. Smallish, high, round breasts that her T-shirt, thin from many washings, did little to hide. Nice. She cocked an eyebrow. "*Do* burglars go out in thunderstorms?"

Garth grinned, partly because he appreciated the snappy comeback, partly because he saw an opportunity. The game might not be over. She hadn't recognized him so far. If he could stay in control of the light, he could keep his face in shadow. He might just brush through this. "You don't have a flashlight?"

"Of course I do. Somewhere. I was looking for it, so I could go looking for the fuse box, when I heard you knock."

"Your problem isn't a fuse. The power is off all over town, not just here. I'm not a burglar, but I do have flashlights. Let me try the door."

She acknowledged his humor with a smile while she thought it over. After a second she shrugged and patted her thigh. "Mildred, come here."

She needn't have called the dog. Despite the dog's size, he could see the animal was a pushover. With unhurried confidence he forced the dog to give way just by walking toward her. Reaching past the doctor, he thumbed the lever and pushed. It definitely wasn't locked. The mechanism must have been jammed when she was trying it. The door swung open with the lightest push.

"Oh, shoot. How did you do that? I'm telling you, it would not open for me." Bronwyn grasped Mildred's collar and sidled into the doorway. "Well, um," she told her visitor, "thank you."

"Wait. I'd take it as a favor if you'd just give me your opinion of whether I have a real emergency on my hands or not. Let me go get my lights. We can set one up for general illumination, and I'll direct the other wherever you tell me to. If you say she needs attention she can only get in an ER, I'll get her there."

And he would. Bronwyn knew it beyond a shadow of a doubt. Though the medical profession was known for unassailable egos, she had never heard anyone speak with more confidence. At the same time, there had been no hint of inadequacy in the way he had said, "I don't know much about babies." That, too, was a simple statement of fact requiring no elaboration.

Every intuition she had developed as an ER physician said there was more here than met the eye. She wished she could see his face, though she'd bet it would give away no more than his voice did. She had experience with men like this. Troy had been one. They could be damn unstoppable once they had taken on a task.

Bronwyn took the baby, and with Garth holding the flashlight, she led the way to the kitchen. Examining patients in her kitchen formed no part of her plan to convert part of the house into a medical office; however in its present shabby state, the house offered no other room that was remotely suitable.

Once there, the baby's father placed flashlights on the counter that were so huge and bright that they could have been used to signal the moon. One he turned on end to bounce light off the ceiling. It gave surprisingly adequate light—enough, anyway, to keep them from stumbling over the packing boxes everywhere. Bronwyn hastily extracted a towel from the dryer, spread it on the butcher-block table in the center of the room, and laid the infant on it. Once the baby was in place, the man switched on the other light and aimed its beam directly on her.

Mildred was quivering with curiosity, so Bronwyn motioned her to come forward. "This is a baby," she told the dog, while keeping one hand firmly on the infant. "You've never seen one before, have you? You may smell, but you need to be respectful."

Mildred passed her nose over the little one, not, Bronwyn was proud to see, crowding the baby's space. Wuffling softy, Mildred sniffed the child's breath, her ears, her crotch, her tiny feet. She lingered over the top of the baby's head, returning to it several times as if something about it puzzled her.

"All done?" she asked, when Mildred began to lose interest.

"You're real patient with her."

"She's a good dog, but she's very curious and very determined. It's really better if I let her get it out of her system. She is a dog, after all." Bronwyn chuckled wryly. "If I command her to do what she wants to do anyway, it helps us both maintain the illusion that she's obedient."

The man huffed softly—an almost silent laugh. Bronwyn relaxed slightly. "I just wish she could tell me all she just learned. Dogs can be trained to be better than the most sensitive diagnostic equipment at detecting cancer and at anticipating seizures. All right, Mildred, go lie down now."

Attuned to her dog as she was, Bronwyn could tell without turning around to look that Mildred was lying down but still alert and curiously watching everything. Mildred was sensitive to atmosphere. Bronwyn felt reassured to know that Mildred apparently found her visitors interesting but unalarming.

After the wild wetness of the storm outside, the kitchen felt stuffy and airless.

Keeping the light trained on the baby, the man pulled off his poncho. It was like the top had been lifted from a jar of scent. Essence of young, healthy male, a little sweaty from being enveloped in waterproof fabric, bloomed through the kitchen. In the way of odors, it bypassed the cerebral cortex and zoomed straight to the older, emotionally driven, more primitive parts of Bronwyn's brain.

She had to grab the counter to stay on her feet when her knees went weak with sudden sexual hunger. Hunger she hadn't felt since Troy's death. In the middle of a storm with the power out and a strange man in her house was a fine time for her body to assert its interest in joining the living.

Without the poncho, he didn't seem quite so huge, but he was still a large man—over six feet, with broad shoulders and muscular arms revealed by his short-sleeved, flower-patterned shirt. Cargo shorts exposed calf muscles as clearly delineated as in an anatomy diagram. The pockets and loops on the shorts drooped as if they had actually been used to carry things. This was a man who not only worked out but also worked *with* his body.

An incongruous note to his casual look was provided by combat boots with socks turned down over the tops just so. Again, he reminded her of Troy. Troy had been a Marine before becoming a Baltimore cop and similarly would don bits of military gear when mowing grass and doing other off-duty chores.

There was something familiar about this man, but she couldn't place him. Neither light skinned nor dark, his features—what features she could make out in the dim light—were hard to categorize by either race or national origin. Maybe he had come through some ER when she was on duty. She dismissed the question, and with a will developed by years of staying focused even though her body clamored for sleep or food or just a chance to pee, she stifled her libido's untimely awakening.

Bronwyn unwrapped the baby from the man's T-shirt that had swathed her and touched the material wadded and bunched around her hips with the aid of duct tape. She'd never seen a worse diaper job. She would pursue the questions raised by the child's lack of even the most basic clothing in a minute. First she needed to establish rapport.

She extended her hand. "I'm Dr. Whitescarver."

"Garth Vale." He reached across the table to shake. Their hands met in the air over the baby. His hand was a workingman's, hard, calloused. The outer edges of the palm were calloused, too—characteristic of martial arts training, something else she knew about because of Troy. A strange energy, like hundreds of tiny threads snapping, went through her when their hands connected.

"I feel like I've heard that name before, but I can't place it. Have we met?"

"Hard to see how." He spoke in an uninflected Western drawl. "You just moved here, didn't you?"

"Yes. I haven't had a chance to meet many people." She shook her head. "I guess it's one of those mysteries. Let's see what's going on with this little one. What's her name?"

"Julia."

"A pretty name for a pretty little girl. Why don't you stand there," she indicated a place at her left shoulder, "and hold the other light for me?"

Bronwyn's initial visual impression was of a well-nourished infant, around eight months, with no obvious abnormality. Bronwyn gently spanked the soles of the tiny feet to rouse her. "Wake up, sweetie. Let me see your eyes."

Her eyes were dull, the pupils not as wide as Bronwyn would have expected, given the dim light. The most striking finding was the deeply sunken look of her eyes. Coupled with her apathetic air and lack of drool, it suggested dehydration.

In children this age, dehydration following vomiting and diarrhea was potentially serious but common and easily treatable. Bronwyn had seen it frequently enough to be sure of her diagnosis, but as one of her teachers used to say, "The road to hell is paved with snap diagnoses." She needed to make sure she wasn't missing anything life threatening.

"I need my stethoscope to listen to her heart. I'll be right back."

"All right." The man's stance didn't change.

"Put your hand on her," Bronwyn instructed him. "Don't let her roll off the counter." He obviously had spent very little time with his daughter not to know something so basic. He really didn't know much about babies.

Chapter 9

What the ancients called a clever fighter is one who not only wins, but excels at winning with ease.

— Sun Tzu, *The Art of War*

GARTH RESTED HIS HAND BESIDE DR. WHITESCARVER'S on the baby's rounded belly. The doctor's hand was tiny, the unpolished nails trimmed ruthlessly short. As tiny as it was, and as obviously feminine in its covering of smooth white skin, there was something strong, mature, and competent about it. It was a hand made to touch people, full of a latent power that wasn't physical strength but something else.

He allowed his hand to settle, the way hers did, weightless and yet in firm contact. He was surprised to feel the gentle rise and fall of the baby's respirations, the movement of willowy ribs. The baby's skin—he'd noted the condition of her skin before, but now he *felt* it. It was... perfect. That was all: perfect.

A funny sensation filled his chest and made his eyes suddenly moist.

Julia's eyes opened and focused on him in limpid trust, went to half-mast, and then opened again, as if she wanted to look at him and was trying to stay awake.

"It's okay, sweetie." He tried to make his voice a soft, slow rumble as befitted addressing a person her size.

"I've got you. You rest now. The doc's going to make you all better."

He heard an exasperated huff from the doctor and looked around. She was turning in a slow circle, hands fisted on her hips.

"Looking for something?"

"My medical bag. I unpacked it and put it right there on the counter—I know I did."

He shone the flashlight in the direction she pointed.

"It's not there. What did I do with it?"

"What does it look like?"

"It's an old-fashioned, black Gladstone bag, like doctors used to carry." She moved a box to look behind it. "It was my great-grandfather's. It came to my brother, Landreth, when he got his MD, but he gave it to me. He said if I was going to be a country doctor, I needed the bag to help me look the part."

"Your great-grandfather was a doctor?"

"And my father and grandfather. There's an unbroken line of doctors dating back to the Civil War. Where *is* it?"

Garth played the light over the counters. "Maybe you're mistaken about exactly where you put it." The dog sneezed and jingled her tags. He swung the light in her direction. Beside the dog's bed rested a dark shape. "Is that it?"

"Yes!" The diminutive doctor knelt beside the large leather satchel and opened it. "It was all I could do to heave it onto the counter. Mildred, how on earth did you get it off the counter? And why?"

The dog lifted a hind leg to scratch behind her ear.

"She's a tall dog," Garth objected, "but do you really think she could have taken it?"

The doctor frowned at him over her shoulder. "Well, I know I didn't move it. And it didn't move itsel—" her words trailed away. She sighed and shrugged. "I don't know… maybe I did put it here. With the house so disorganized, I can't seem to find anything where I think I put it."

She extracted the stethoscope and rose, warming the chest piece between her palms. "All right. Let's see what's up with this little one."

The doctor finished listening to the baby's chest. The way doctors do, she draped her stethoscope around her neck. Why was it that women looked so graceful when they performed movements like that?

If Garth had met her in an ER, swathed in scrubs and a white coat, he might have looked past her essential femininity, interested only in her professional competence. He still needed for her to be a doctor, but in the dim kitchen, dressed in an old T-shirt and shorts that revealed the exact sort of plush derriere and smooth, strong thighs he liked on a woman, no way was he going to fail to react to her.

She had won his trust almost instantly with the soft-spoken command she had over her spirited dog, which probably weighed more than she did. When she'd run her hands over the baby's limbs, gently palpating, learning with every touch, he had wanted her to run such intelligent hands over him.

Now she smoothed her palm over the infant's head in a gesture that looked like affection and smiled when one of the baby's flailing hands latched onto a finger and brought it to her mouth.

The baby's arms and legs were moving more now than when he'd first found her. More than when the doctor first started to examine her. Her gaze was not so distant and unfocused. He didn't know if she was better, but it made her *look* not quite so sick.

The doctor gently reclaimed her finger and turned to face him. "Her heart and lungs sound good. The main thing is that she looks dehydrated. The question is, how did she get that way? Has she had vomiting? Diarrhea?"

There had been a lot of what looked like wet yellow clay in that loaded diaper, but he hadn't taken time to examine it. She hadn't done anything since. "No. Not in the last hour."

"How about before…?"

He already knew his story wouldn't stand up to any official probing. That's why he wanted to avoid hospitals. He needed to stop mooning over the doctor's womanly attributes and remember she was still a doctor who would have questions. His task now was to feed her the right information so that she would ask only the questions he wanted her to.

"You're thinking I'm not much of a dad, aren't you?"

She didn't deny it. "I'd rather try to help you than judge you. This child lacks the basics. She doesn't even have on a shirt. Where is her mother?"

"No telling." God knows that was the truth. Now for the part he needed her to buy into. "She left. She said since I was the father, I could have her."

She assessed him with a long look. "*Are* you the father?"

"Yeah… Probably… I could be." A certain amount of acting ability was part of a SEAL's skill set. The heat that rose to his cheeks was real, though. Garth didn't have to dig deep to find the shame he would feel if his carelessness had resulted in a child he didn't even know about. He jammed his hands in his pockets. The doctor would have more questions about the baby's condition so he had to stick as close to the truth as possible. "I didn't find her until an hour ago."

"Find her? You mean the mother just left her—without even telling you? That's reckless endangerment of a child—not to mention abandonment. Crimes. She needs to be reported."

"I don't want to get her in trouble. She wasn't careless about it, not deliberately. I would have found Julia sooner if I hadn't been delayed by the weather. The important thing is I have her now. I want her, and I'm willing to take care of her."

"You want her." The doctor lifted one of the baby's feet and pressed her palm against it. Smiled when the baby pushed back. "Where did you find her?"

"In a hangar." *Close enough*.

"Hangar, as in 'airplane hangar'? There's an airport around here?"

"I run a small airfreight service."

"What do you do there?"

"Log flights in and out. Load planes and accept deliveries. Maintain the physical plant. Routine maintenance on the planes. Stuff like that." True. All too true. He also sometimes took a boat past the three-mile limit, where he met fishing boats and occasionally dove to retrieve particular bits of hardware that had been dropped off. And, of course, helped spies into and out of the country.

"How long was she unattended before you found her?"

"I'm not sure." How long would the flight have been? "Maybe as long as six hours. Maybe more."

"Six or more hours as hot as it's been today? If you hadn't found her, she would have died." The doctor's eyes widened in shock and horror even though her voice stayed low and controlled. It did him good for someone else to react as he had. It validated him and formed a connection between them.

"All right," she said, moving on. "We might not need to look any further for the cause of her dehydration. We'll start with fluids. She'll perk up pretty quickly if that's the problem."

"She's just dehydrated? That's a relief." If she had been really sick, he would have had no choice except to take her to a hospital and leave her there. If there was any hope at all of saving his career, there could be no official records of a connection between them.

He would have relinquished the baby to save her life, but for the rest of his life, abandoning her would have weighed on him. He had taken responsibility for her, and until he could return her to whomever she belonged to, he would trust no one else to be in charge. "Does she need an IV?"

"No, you can give her a rehydration formula, like Pedialyte—not water or milk. If the baby is strong enough to suckle, rehydration by mouth is really better. The trouble is I don't have any nursing bottles." She gave him a dry look. "I'm betting you don't, either."

"There was one with her. I didn't bring it."

The bottle had been in the box with her, covered with feces like everything else. Knowing it might be the best source of fingerprints, he had bagged it, feces and all. It might offer the best chance of tracing her origins and returning her to whomever she belonged to. He would lift the prints later and have a contact run them through Interpol AFIS, the automated fingerprint identification system. "I'll get some bottles. Do I need a prescription for the Pedialyte?"

"It's over the counter. You should be able to find it anywhere that carries diapers and baby food."

"Good. I appreciate this, doc." Making sure he had his back to the light aimed at the ceiling, he thumbed off the flash he had been holding and hung it on his belt. He reached for his wallet. "We'll get out of your way now. What do I owe you?"

She flung out a hand, as if she could keep him from reaching for the baby. "Owe me? You're not leaving!"

When he had made his plan to avoid tangling with the establishment, he'd been thinking about all the security cameras at a hospital that would record his and the baby's presence, the number of people he would have to interact with, and the very real possibility that someone would see the condition of the baby and turn him over to a welfare worker.

He'd neglected to factor in the personal responsibility. It was well known that people were more likely to rush to a rescue when alone than in a crowd. In a group, faced with a difficult choice, people could justify their disinclination to get involved by telling themselves it was someone else's job. Whereas if they knew that if they didn't act no one would, they sometimes surprised themselves with their courage.

Now the tiny doctor was standing in front of him,

feet planted like she thought she could bar his way. Something about it made him smile. Physically, she was no match for him. He could take the baby and leave anyway. She couldn't stop him, but she didn't seem to know that.

She was kind of cute, believing that delicate-boned hand could hold him. Just out of curiosity, to test her mettle and see what she would do, he went under the slender arm, fingers curved as if he intended to scoop the baby up. "Thought I would."

Chapter 10

Don't bother running. You'll only die tired.

—SEAL saying

"THINK AGAIN!" BRONWYN GRABBED HIS ARM.

She hadn't wanted him there, and she ought to have been relieved to get rid of him, but she wasn't in the ER anymore, and she didn't have to play by ER rules.

She had decided to open a medical office here so she could practice the kind of medicine she believed in, instead of the "treat 'em and street 'em" philosophy driven by a need to see as many patients as possible to make a practice profitable.

She wanted to get to know patients, to understand what they needed. To understand the environmental influences that were producing their symptoms. Too many of the problems she saw in the emergency room didn't need to be emergencies at all. They were chronic conditions that weren't being managed. Instead the patients went from crisis to crisis.

She wanted to do more than dispense drugs. She wanted to deliver health care—to see patients get healthier and help them stay healthy. She wanted to be part of her patients' world and have them be part of hers.

No way was she letting her first patient disappear in what was obviously a crisis, never to be seen again—not until she had addressed some of the conditions that had put the child in crisis to begin with. At the very least she needed to see, with her own eyes, the baby's recovery.

Still, Bronwyn might not have been so determined to stand up to him if his lips hadn't curled in that slightly dismissive smile with his laconic, "Thought I would."

Her heart pounded. She lifted her chin. Now that she was in a confrontation with him, she was not going to back down. "I'm not releasing this baby. I don't have an adequate history, much less any tests. I'm only guessing she's dehydrated. Until I've seen how she responds to some fluids and electrolytes, she's not going anywhere."

Bronwyn dug her fingers into his forearm, determined to make the point that she would stop him by whatever means necessary. Except for that one brief moment of visceral awareness of him when he had pulled off his poncho, she had been happy to look at the baby more than at him. Now, having thrown down the gauntlet, she tried to read his expression. And discovered she couldn't.

Her heart stumbled and banged against her breastbone. From the beginning, he had positioned himself so that the light was always behind him, his face in shadow. In fact, she hadn't seen his face clearly at any time since his arrival—*by his intention,* she suddenly realized.

A chill went up her spine. She looked at her hand on his forearm. Her fingers didn't go even halfway around and in the dim light looked impossibly white against his darkness. Despite her size, she rarely felt small or delicate. Suddenly she did. She felt small and delicate and soft and feminine and vulnerable. Not her own strength, but his held him back.

Her whole body shook with the force of each heart-beat. She breathed deeply, aware she was close to gasping. Unable to decide if the mix of sensations flooding her was fear or sexual thrall, she withdrew her hand and lightly clasped the baby's round little legs, needing to anchor herself, to remember it was the baby's well-being she was fighting for.

"Let's talk about this a minute." Touching him had been a mistake, but Bronwyn wasn't about to give up. She strove for a tone of reasonableness. "If her symptoms aren't caused by not getting enough fluids in this heat, we could be looking at anything from a stomach virus—to name the most likely—to ingestion of drugs, to serious or even fatal diseases. Do you really want to be off by yourself somewhere when you realize the fluids aren't making her better?"

"Are you trying to scare me?" She couldn't really see his expression, but she could see the white flash of his teeth, as if he was grinning at her. *And aren't you just the cutest little thing to think you can?*—that's what his inflection said.

Jerk. She ignored his provocation. "I want you to understand that I consider this baby's condition serious. I'm hoping we're both on the same side—hers. She can't speak for herself. I have to be willing to go to bat for her." Bronwyn wished with all her heart she could see his face. She couldn't tell whether she was getting through to him or not.

Just then, the ancient fluorescent tubes in the ceiling flickered into life.

Three things happened. The baby began to cry and flail her little hands in front of her eyes.

Mildred *woofed* softly in surprise and scrambled to
her feet, snapped out of her doze by the sudden retreat
of darkness.

And, finally able to see the man's face, Bronwyn
slapped her cheeks in surprise and laughed aloud, more
purely relieved than any time since she had first heard
the pounding at the door.

Chapter 11

Never go against your gut; it is your operational antenna.

—The Moscow Rules

IN THE SUDDEN LIGHT, GARTH SAW THE MUD-GREEN appliances and yellow countertops of a kitchen unchanged since the sixties. It not only hadn't been remodeled since then, it looked like it hadn't been painted or cleaned many times, either. Brown shipping boxes covered most of the floor.

His attention was all for the doctor, though. He had thought her hair was dark brown, but it was actually deep, mahogany red, and her skin was the smooth matte cream that sometimes went with hair like that. Her cheeks were delicately tinted by her laughter, and her eyes, sparkling with humor and surrounded by starburst lashes, were the rich, transparent red-brown of perfectly brewed iced tea, like his mother made. He thought she was flavored like tea, too. Brisk, clear, refreshing, uncomplicated.

He understood now why he hadn't known, and would never have guessed, she was a doctor. If he didn't already know she was strong, decisive, and brave enough to stand up to a man who intimidated a lot of people, he might have thought she looked like a kid with smooth, round cheeks and a round chin—a kid too young to wear cosmetics. She wasn't beautiful, but God, she was pretty in a fresh, innocent way he found enchanting and guessed she probably hated. She had no armor at all.

He wanted her. Wanted to cup those delicious little muffin-top breasts and run his tongue over their sweetness. Wanted to let his hands overflow with the generosity of her tush while plunging into her wet heat.

He wanted her courage and tenacity. Wanted the true grit that would make her take on a man trained in lethal arts who outweighed her by ninety pounds. Wanted the dedication to selfless values that made her do it. Wanted the tenderness she showed the baby and the gentle authority with which she managed a strong animal.

Wanted her now and beyond a shadow of a doubt, he wanted her forever.

The sense of completion, of trust, of sheer rightness he'd had since he'd handed her the baby to hold while he went back for the flashlights suddenly made sense. She was the one. His mate. The woman he would marry. The woman who would bear his children.

Was this what falling in love at first sight was? He'd always imagined something sweeter, milder than this bone-crushing certainty that he had to win her. Something terrible beyond his capacity to imagine would happen if he failed. Some glue that held the world together would fail, and everything he cared about would be destroyed.

He looked down at the whimpering baby. This was so not the time to have a cosmic awakening. This was not the moment to crash into portentous thoughts he only half understood.

And holy shit, if this wasn't the worst possible moment to fall in love at first sight, he didn't know what was. He had a baby to care for until he could return her to those whose she legitimately was. He had to keep her off the radar until he could do that, both for her sake and because he could kiss his career good-bye if the powers that be found out he had gone off the reservation—and once he had her squared away, he had a career that had to be gotten back on track before he had anything to offer a woman.

Why he hadn't understood that Bronwyn was his *forever love* the first time he saw her, he didn't know. Probably it happened *now* because Murphy was still screwing with him. He couldn't have looked more like a loser.

She thought he was an unwed father, and a neglectful one at that. And he couldn't even start over once he had the baby stowed in a safe place. He couldn't appear with a baby in his arms one week and come back without her the next.

It didn't matter what the obstacles were. This might be the wrong time and the wrong place, but she was still the right woman. He focused on the present. "What are you laughing at?" he asked her.

"Not at you." She brushed away his concern with a wave of a tiny hand. "Mostly I'm laughing at myself. I'm just so relieved. I *know* you!" She tsk'd at her own denseness. "Garth Vale. *Of course*. You were at JJ's wedding. I'm sorry I couldn't place your name when you introduced yourself, but if it helps, I kept having a feeling there was something familiar about you! I'm Bronwyn Whitescarver," she beamed expectantly.

Garth nodded slowly. Davy's wedding the previous Thanksgiving had been a spur of the moment affair.

When Davy had asked Garth to be his best man because all Davy's real friends were either operating in far-flung corners of the world or had holiday plans already scheduled, Garth had done it, even though he'd had to give up part of his leave and delay his trip home to see his folks. Here was the proof, if he needed it, that no good deed goes unpunished.

Now, when it was way too late to undo anything, she remembered him. She was waiting for a reply, but what the hell was he supposed to say? *I recognized you instantly and have been trying to duck you?* Oh, yeah, that would win a girl's heart.

Bronwyn picked up the crying baby. "You don't remember me at all, do you?" She slanted him an amused glance. "I'm not surprised. We weren't in the same room more than twenty minutes. Besides, who would look at me if I were standing beside JJ?"

She said it with a twist of humor and without any touch of self-pity. JJ was phenomenally attractive, movie-star beautiful. She was also tall and voluptuous. She would make two of this elfin-looking creature. But God, he hated to think Bronwyn believed she was insignificant beside her. It was too late to correct her mistaken impression that he didn't remember her. If only he could go back and do the whole thing again… either leave the second he recognized her or use their acquaintance to further his mission.

No. Knowing what he knew now, he couldn't wish he had done the first, and knowing what he did now, he didn't really want her mixed up in this. He wanted her safe, set apart, untouched. If there was one thing a SEAL wouldn't do, it was second-guess himself.

Hanging around had been a calculated risk. The possibility that he would jeopardize his future happiness had been unforeseeable.

The only time he could do anything about was now. "How did you recognize me?"

"JJ hauls out wedding pictures every time we're together. You're in a lot of them."

"You and JJ are good friends?"

She smiled happily. "Since college. Do you see a lot of David?"

"Not much." Garth went with his civilian cover story. When an operator's background was scrubbed, he could tell no one what he was doing or who he was working for. It was best not to hang around people who knew him before and who could make educated guesses.

"I got out of the navy not long afterward." His tone was final, dismissing the subject. In fact, he hadn't seen Doc since that day. After getting married, Doc had taken some of the leave he had saved up. Before he had returned to duty, Garth had accepted the TDY assignment.

She narrowed her eyes. "You don't want to talk about old times, do you?" Her shoulders twitched in a tiny shrug of acceptance. "We do have more important business to attend to. We don't have to talk right now. I'm just relieved I don't need to call social services."

Garth's stomach grew cold. "You were going to call?" he asked in his most level voice.

"Well…" A sweeping glance encompassed the condition of the baby. "Yeah. I saw serious neglect—whether it was your fault or not. Based on what I saw—or didn't see—I didn't think you were in any way prepared for a baby."

"But you're not going to call the authorities now."

"Not as long as you do what I say." There was no mistaking the steel in her voice.

While Garth made a run to the shopping center out on the highway for the most basic baby supplies, Bronwyn stirred the rehydration formula developed by the World Health Organization—a mixture of water, sugar, salt, and potassium chloride salt substitute—in a hastily unpacked saucepan and set it on the monolithic avocado range to heat.

She needed a few minutes to regroup and reorganize her thoughts. She had been massively relieved when the lights came on because she finally understood how she could be so suddenly attracted to him.

It wasn't flattering that he didn't recognize her, even after she reminded him, but she couldn't blame him.

Except for a "Nice to meet you" when they were introduced, they hadn't spoken. She'd made sure of it. She'd turned away and made sure their eyes hadn't met again. Not because he wasn't attractive, but because he was. Even through the gray fog of her grief, she had been able to see that he was exactly her type. Tall. Dark. Dangerous.

If she had to have a type, why couldn't it be neatly dressed bankers or scholars with kindly eyes behind their glasses? But no. What made her heart go pitty-pat was a man like this one. She'd already paid the price of loving one of them. Never again.

Troy had come into the ER, a Baltimore cop needing stitches, laughing and flirting despite the blood dripping down his face from a scalp laceration. It was love at first sight—or something close. They had dated for six months. Being a cop, he understood crazy hours. They had breakfast dates, dinners in the hospital cafeteria, and softball dates, extracting minutes together from whatever free time they had. They got engaged. He got killed.

Shot. In the head.

Paramedics had brought him to her ER where the staff recognized him. Another doctor handled the intake. Someone was sent to get her but missed her because she had stepped into the restroom. Bronwyn didn't know until she overheard nurses who came in say her name and something about a GSW and a cop in Trauma Room 3.

She had had nightmares for months afterward in which anonymous fingers dug into her arms and dragged her backwards, and anonymous voices urged, "Don't go in there."

Well, now she knew how she could feel attraction while every intuition she had told her to have nothing to do with this man. And she was better off if it was all one way.

She had remembered the formula, which could be made from ingredients found in kitchens anywhere in the world—and far more cheaply—even before she had sent Garth to get Pedialyte, but she didn't tell him it could be made at home. She wasn't sure she trusted he would always have the ingredients. If he was like Troy, who had rarely fixed so much as a cup of coffee at his apartment, she was pretty sure he wouldn't.

She believed he meant his child no harm. At the same time, she didn't believe he was an adequate caregiver, and that concerned her. He was not a parent she'd give a prescription to and send home with instructions to return if the child didn't improve.

She knew about adrenaline junkies. She understood well what thrilling lovers they could be, but a child did not need a thrilling father. She needed one who could be trusted to arrive on schedule. She needed one who was as likely to notice her if she were too quiet as too rambunctious. She was judging Garth by her experience of Troy, which might not be fair. Even if they weren't the same, Garth still was unprepared to add a child to his life. But ready or not, she was here—and he would have to step up fast.

While she readied and heated the homemade formula, she glanced over her shoulder at the large, roomy box she had cushioned with a folded blanket and laid the baby in. Bronwyn wasn't happy with her homemade baby bed, but infants Julia's size could roll. Many were beginning to crawl. The box would confine and keep her safe. Mildred looked dubious, too. She had stationed herself beside it. Occasionally she raised up to peer over the side and sniff.

Julia was moving her arms and legs more, squirming and fussing a little. More than ever, Bronwyn suspected that some of the baby's lethargy was due to having been given a sedative, and the drug was now wearing off. Anyone capable of dumping a child without putting her where she would be easily found was surely capable of drugging her to keep her quiet.

Of course, she had no evidence that any of Garth's story was true. And again there was the awareness that if he had been a complete stranger, and if she hadn't recognized him when she did, she would have insisted the child be taken to an ER and, if necessary, escorted there by the police.

Bronwyn drew her cell phone from her pocket to check it. She'd feel on firmer ground, more sure she either was or wasn't doing the right thing, when she talked to JJ. She'd left two messages, but her friend still hadn't called back. She flipped the phone open to call again and saw the battery symbol flashing. She blew out her lips in exasperation. She'd already charged the phone once today. For some reason, it wasn't holding a charge. She found the charger and plugged it in.

For the present, she was on her own.

Bronwyn doubted Garth's baby-care abilities, but she wasn't much surer of her own. Knowing how to doctor a baby wasn't the same thing as knowing how to raise one. And really, she didn't know all that much about doctoring them. Babies were not the same as adults except smaller. Their little bodies had quite different requirements. In the ER, if a child came in with anything but the most routine complaints, he or she was passed on to a pediatrician.

Fortunately, she had easily found the food thermometer. She could be sure she heated the solution to the right temperature. Bronwyn removed the pan from the stove and inserted the thermometer. Seventy-four degrees. By the time she transferred it to a bowl, it would probably be the recommended seventy degrees.

She carefully covered the butcher-block table with paper towels and set a notepad and pencil, the bowl of sugar-salt solution, and a 3 cc medicine dropper on it. She drew a ladder-back chair up to the makeshift feeding station and picked up the baby.

The infant didn't seem to know what to make of the medicine dropper. She flailed at it with a tiny fist and fussed. Bronwyn carefully put a drop of sugar water on Julia's tongue. In a second she put another. A third and the baby's interest seemed to be caught.

The next time she brought the dropper to the little rosebud lips, the baby tried to suck on it. She gave Bronwyn an accusing look.

"It's not what you're used to, is it?"

It would be easy to question, as her parents had repeatedly, if she knew what she was doing. Bronwyn had already tried a teaspoon. The baby had opened her mouth eagerly when she saw the spoon as if she knew what it was and was hungry. Eagerness had turned to wails, though. Bronwyn couldn't seem to time tipping the spoon with the baby's tongue movements. There was more solution on her than in her, and they were both sticky from spills. What did people do before the invention of baby bottles and plastic nipples when a breast wasn't available?

Experimentally she dipped her pinkie into the solution and carried the droplet that adhered to the tip to the baby's mouth. Julia latched onto it eagerly.

If only she had anything the baby could suck.

Sugar teat. The thought whispered into her mind, so clear, yet so different that it could have come from somewhere else.

"Was that you, Mildred?" The dog raised shaggy brows in inquiry. Silly. The dog hadn't spoken. Wherever the idea had come from, it was a good one. A sugar teat was what people had used once as a pacifier. A lump of sugar would be knotted into a cloth and given the baby to suck on.

She could do the same thing, but instead of a sugar lump she could use a sponge. Her eyes fell on the blue sponge on the rim of the stainless steel sink. She shuddered. Not that. It had been used with God knew what kinds of chemicals and had developed God knew what bacteria. She was on the right track, though.

If she were in the ER, she would just ask a nurse to get her one. On the other hand, if she were in the ER, she wouldn't have this problem at all. Her mouth twitched in wry contemplation of her predicament. In the ER, she would have handed the baby off to a nurse, and Bronwyn would have hurried to the next patient.

Bronwyn looked around the dingy kitchen. This was her new life. *This* was what it meant to handle patients completely on her on. But frustrated as she felt to be unable to produce even something as low tech as a sponge, she was enjoying having this one tiny being to focus on, and already the challenge of calling on her own resources was making her feel renewed.

"I know, Mildred! Where did I put the box of medical paraphernalia?" At medical conventions, pharmaceutical companies passed out every sort of freebie from ballpoint pens and notebooks advertising the drug du jour to samples of supplies. She had been given some super-absorbent sponge swabs. Her only hesitation was that the tip might come off in the baby's mouth.

In a few minutes, the baby was happily sucking away at a scrap of sterile gauze that held the swab. A bulky knot prevented the cloth from being drawn into the baby's throat and causing her to choke. The baby had grasped the possibilities as soon as the soaked bit of cloth was put to her lips, and thirst had taken care of the rest.

She howled when Bronwyn withdrew the swab to dunk it again. Which made Bronwyn realize she had a use for the medicine dropper after all. She used the dropper to drip the solution onto the fabric protruding from the baby's lips and let capillary action draw the liquid into the baby's mouth.

She estimated the little one had taken about three ounces when the sucking slowed and Julia's head lolled against Bronwyn's breast.

Bronwyn gently pulled the sugar teat from lips gone slack. She noted the time and amount on the yellow legal pad she was using for a chart then carefully carried Julia to the sink where she wet a paper towel and gently washed the stickiness from the petal-like cheeks and tiny curled fists. Julia looked better already. Her lips and eyelids looked shinier. Her skin was dewier. The soles of her feet felt less papery.

Bronwyn considered returning the baby to the box-bed she'd made for her—and getting back to unpacking—but she couldn't remember the last time she'd held a baby purely for the pleasure of it, and she didn't know when she would get another chance. Beyond the kitchen was a small den, a more recent addition than the kitchen, judging by the more modern-looking hardware and light switch plates.

Bronwyn planned to make the den into her "sitting room" and turn the front rooms of the house into her office. The den was as grimy and cheerless as the rest of the house now, but with its river-rock fireplace and large windows, she thought it could be a pleasant room. Among the odds and ends of furnishings that had been left by the previous owners was a platform rocker.

Leaving the light on in the kitchen to provide illumination since there were no lamps, Bronwyn carried the sleeping baby, wrapped in a towel, into the den and settled her on her lap.

Mildred came over and sniffed the baby again, thoroughly and with the same attention to detail. She seemed to approve. She settled at Bronwyn's feet with her head resting on her paws.

Chapter 12

If it don't suck, we don't do it.

—SEAL saying

THE REFRIGERATED AIR OF THE WALMART—LADEN WITH odors of popcorn and new tires, Cheetos, plastic, and humanity—blasted him as soon as the electronic doors whooshed open. The chill that went across the back of his neck wasn't entirely from the cold air hitting his damp neck and shoulders. He wondered if he would ever feel comfortable in places like this again.

Bronwyn had thought he could find most of what they needed at drugstores or supermarkets. However, he had reasoned that he could find everything here in one stop and, more important, far enough away that no one would recognize him or remember him. Generic. He had taken the superhighway thirty miles east to avoid being recognized buying baby things. He needn't have bothered. The place was as anonymous as anywhere in the country.

He used to love to visit the Walmart in Durango with his mother. While she shopped, he would zoom to the toy section when he was little and later to the sporting goods. He hadn't come as often with his dad, but when he did, Garth was more likely to stick to his dad's side. His dad knew the function of every tool in the hardware section and would take time to explain each one.

In those days, Garth had never thought about how easy it was for someone to get behind him, unheard in the constant babble overlaid with cheesy classic rock Muzak. He'd known being a SEAL would require sacrifices. It just hadn't occurred to him that one would be Walmart.

In the baby section, he worked his way down the list of baby supplies Bronwyn had given him. Bottles, glass like Bronwyn had insisted. The funny-shaped nipples didn't look much like the real thing to him. Diapers. Who knew there were that many kinds and sizes? There were cuddlers, cruisers, and Pampers but no poopers— which he would have thought more accurate. Diaper rash ointment.

He cruised into the next aisle. Baby wipes—needed those. He dumped a large package into the shopping cart. Baby soap. Did babies need their own? They must. He tossed in a bottle. On the shelf next to the soap was lotion to help put them to sleep. Julia didn't seem to have a problem with sleeping, so he rejected it.

Ah, there was the Pedialyte. Now formula and food. Bronwyn said to get cereal, but did Julia like rice or whole grain? He tossed one of each into the buggy. He was a Frosted Flakes man himself.

He steered his cart into the "Infants and Toddlers" clothing section. Bronwyn said, for now, Julia only needed a couple of shirts. He found a table of tiny shirts, all of them smaller than handkerchiefs. The tag on one read 12T; on the next was 3M. Neither looked large enough to get his hand inside, much less a baby. He finally found a size chart and selected a couple. He even made himself put back the one with a truck on it and instead pick up a yellow one with butterflies.

On the way to the checkout, he passed through the toy section. Julia needed toys! On a shelf right in front of him was a cool enemy alien robot. Talk about a great toy! And there was a football shaped for little hands. He'd had one just like that! Sadly, neither looked right for a baby girl—and he wouldn't be keeping her long anyway.

A few minutes later, he wheeled the cart into the warm, muggy night. The air hadn't cleared at all, which meant another storm was coming. He stuffed one large plastic bag after the other into the back seat of his truck. He didn't know what had happened. He'd only come to get a couple of things.

He had driven out of the rain by the time he had reached the shopping center. On the return trip to Bronwyn's house, he drove back into it.

Between one moment and the next, the windshield wipers went from squeaking on the barely perceptible drizzle to being unable to keep up with the deluge. He could see only a silver blur punctuated by the red smears of taillights on the car ahead.

He tapped his brakes gently to slow the truck and felt the ABS system feed power to one wheel and then another. The highway's roadbed was built a couple of feet higher than the low land through which it traveled, with deep drainage ditches on either side, but runoff couldn't keep pace with the speed at which the rain was coming down.

Thank God, the ABS had warned him of the danger of hydroplaning even before he felt the loss of traction. He took his foot off the gas and let the truck slow while he guided it to the emergency lane, hoping no fool was coming up fast behind him.

The bleary taillights of the car in front of him suddenly bloomed brighter red. They swung wildly back and forth as the car fishtailed. Then, almost gracefully, the car slid backwards off the pavement and the emergency lane, and rolled backwards down the long embankment to the drainage ditch.

Even in dry weather, water stood in the ditches—the cattails attested to that. After a day of rain, the ditch would be full.

Grateful the baby wasn't with him but safe and dry with Bronwyn, Garth switched on the caution blinkers and angled the truck's headlights to shine on the clump of crushed cattails where the car, an ancient gray Pontiac, rested tail down, its headlights aimed up into the rain. Its position put the driver's seat above water, but it wouldn't be for long.

Garth plunged into the downpour. He could hear a woman and a child screaming.

He opened the Pontiac's driver's side door. As he had guessed, it was above water, but the rear of the car was rapidly filling with black water. The driver had her back to him as she leaned over the seat, wrestling with the harness of the child's seat. Hampered by a pregnant belly and her short stature, the woman's arms weren't really long enough to reach her son, and terror made her fumble. Her voice shook as she tried to reassure the flailing child.

With Garth standing waist-deep in the water, they were almost eye to eye. "Are you hurt ma'am?"

The woman turned at the sound of his voice, eyes

blank with incomprehension. In the light from the dash, her brown face was a mask of terror. "My baby—"

"I see him. Is there anyone else in the car?"

"No, just my baby—"

"Let me help you out of the car, ma'am. I'll get him for you."

"Him first."

"I have to move you to get to him. It's going to be okay. Put your arms around my neck." When she didn't comply, he put her arms on his shoulders. "I'm going to lift you up to the bank. Hang on."

He set the mother on the ditch bank and knelt on the driver's seat. The car was full of the smell of brackish water. Water had risen to the seat bottom. In the greenish light of the dash, he could make out a little boy flailing his arms and legs.

"Mommy! Mommy!" The child's screams escalated when he realized his mother was gone.

"Hey, buddy." Garth made his voice smooth and casual, trying for the tone his dad had always used. "Your mom is safe and waiting for you. Time to get you out of here, don't you think?"

He felt along the straps, trying to determine by feel which ones kept the child's car seat in place and which ones restrained the child. When he found the catch, it took him two heart-stopping seconds longer than it should have to work the mechanism. *Note to self: study how the catch of every child restraint works.* There it was. He pressed the plastic knob and felt the straps go slack.

"Got you now. Come on, big guy." He lifted the sturdy little boy.

"Hand 'im here," a deep voice over Garth's shoulder said. A man in a fluorescent yellow slicker banded with reflector strips held out his arms.

After passing over the child, Garth backed from the car. He dropped into water that was now almost chest deep. He hauled himself up the ditch bank that was slick with mud and algae and saw a large closed truck equipped with spotlights trained on the wreck. More cars had stopped. Beside the highway, clumps of people stood under umbrellas.

His helper in the slicker passed the child to other waiting hands, and in seconds, mother and child were reunited. "Anyone else in the car?" the man asked Garth.

"She says not, and I didn't see anyone. Have you called 911?"

"I *am* 911." The big man's blunt features split in a huge grin. "EMT with the Black River rescue squad," he explained. "Highway Patrol and the squad are on the way. I was passing and thought you might need a little help. Doug Cruikshank," he introduced himself. He stuck out a palm as wide and as thick as Garth's granny's Bible.

Garth wiped his hand on his shirt—for all the good it did. He grinned at the futility of the gesture and offered his hand anyway. "Garth Vale." The man's simple, open pleasure and pride in being a rescuer were touching. He was exactly what he appeared to be.

Once upon a time, Garth might have felt a little superior, a little patronizing, knowing he was stronger, faster, tougher. No longer. Doug had probably met up with people he couldn't save but damn few he couldn't help because he had somebody he needed to kill first.

"You from around here?" Doug asked.

"Near Sessoms' Corner."

"I'll be. You the chap running the CIA drop-off?"

"CIA?"

"Yeah. The landing strip. E'erbody 'round here says Coastal Air's a front for the CIA."

So much for keeping the airstrip's purpose a secret. The real agency operating the tiny airport was too secret to have a name. He'd seen the looks, some speculative, some wary, when he announced he worked for Coastal Air. Doug, apparently, didn't believe in beating around the bush. Garth faked a chuckle and shook his head. "CIA. That's a good one."

"Hey, I know you can't say nothing. Listen, you handled yourself pretty good. No money in it—we're an all-volunteer organization—but we can always use another man on the rescue squad. Come around and talk to us sometime."

"Maybe I'll do that," Garth answered easily. Not that he really thought he was going to. Unfortunately, he wasn't exactly what he appeared to be, and he hoped to be gone from this area as soon as possible. Still, if he was going to stay here, Doug Cruikshank would be a man he'd seek out. "Well then, you've got it handled. I'll be on my way."

"Wait, are you okay? Sometimes it hits you hard—after it's over—even when everything turns out okay. 'Specially when there's a kid involved."

Doug meant the cold shakes or the jacked-up high that went with a brush with danger. Garth could feel a reaction, but it was more a sudden feeling of lightness and expansion. "I'm all right. I feel… um, good…" He nodded toward the woman he had rescued who, sheltered under umbrellas held by bystanders, continued to hug her little boy while crying tears of joy. "You know?"

Doug's thoughtful smile and short nod told Garth he did know. After a moment of wordless communication, Doug pointed to Garth's thigh. "Looks like you're bleeding."

Garth glanced down. His soaked shorts leg had a long, ragged tear. Blood mixed with dirty water ran down his leg. "Shit. I liked these shorts," he groused as he lifted the edges of the tear to check the skin underneath. "No real damage; just a scratch."

"Blackberries," Doug observed wisely. "They love ditch banks. Wicked thorns. I've got a first aid kit in my truck. Let's get you out of the rain, and I'll clean it up for you."

"Not much point in worrying about getting wet now. I'm pretty well drenched." Rain streamed down his face and ran down the neck of his shirt. It was cold, but he was just as glad to let it wash off the rotten-vegetation stink of the ditch water. More to the point, he could hear sirens. He'd just as soon not draw the authorities' attention, even for the most benign of reasons. "I'll put something on it when I get home."

"You got somewheres to go besides that trailer beside the runway? The National Weather Service has issued a tornado watch. You know how tornadoes are." He shook his head in mock sorrow at the phenomenon's perversity. "They're gonna head straight for any trailer they see."

Garth grinned. It wasn't true that tornadoes sought out mobile homes, but it *was* true that trailers were more likely to sustain wind damage than other structures. "I guess you've seen what the wind can do to one."

"Seen more'n I want to. That's a fact."

Garth suddenly understood Doug's reluctance to let him go. Doc—Davy Graziano, Garth's hospital corpsman in Afghanistan—was similarly driven by the same sort of nurturing, protective instincts. He considered letting Doug tend his leg, just because Doug needed to do something, but then had a better idea. "I need to get moving. My girlfriend's going to jerk a knot in my tail if I'm not back soon. Can you stay for the mop-up?"

"Girlfriend, huh? Gotta keep 'em happy. A pissed-off woman can make a man's life a misery. You go on, I'll stick around."

Garth waved and climbed in his truck. He had a girlfriend to keep happy. Wonder how she'd take it when she found out.

Chapter 13

SEALs don't eat their young.

—SEAL motto

T HE HOUSE WAS DARK EXCEPT FOR A DIM LIGHT AT THE BACK, Garth saw as he approached it on foot, large plastic sacks slung over his shoulder. He had hidden his truck in some brush on a side road and hiked through the woods to the doctor's house. The fewer people who saw him come and go from there, the better. Trees still dripped, but the rain had ended. Nevertheless, the night was still hot and humid. So it wasn't a chill in the air that made chills prickle at the back of his neck. The front door stood wide open.

The door's lock was undependable; it might mean nothing that the door was open. He clamped down on his imagination that made him see women and babies, their blood mingling and soaking into the rough stones paving the courtyard.

He made his way through the dark and silent house, down the hall to the kitchen. From the dim light that had been left on over the stove, he could see that it too was empty.

A board squeaked when he stepped on it. From the room beyond the kitchen came the scrabbling and scraping of dog toenails. Finally Mildred was sensing an intruder. *Some watchdog.*

"What is it, Mildred? Is it the baby?" Bronwyn's voice, fuzzy with sleep, also came from the darkened room.

"What's going on? Why is the front door unlocked?" Garth demanded, his voice sharp with the sudden anger of relief.

"Don't *do* that!" Bronwyn, who had been sitting in a chair, her tiny frame hidden by its high, upholstered back, jumped up. She planted her fists on her hips. "You know what? I have had it with hulking silhouetted figures."

She was his woman. Already standing up to him, giving him what-for. Now that he knew she was okay, the relief made him almost light headed. Garth chuckled. *"Hulking silhouetted figures?"*

"Yes." She pointed an accusing finger. "You. With the light behind you and those sacks on your shoulders, all I could see was a huge black *thing* with legs. You scared me."

Garth thought of how large he must have seemed with sacks adding to his bulk. "Hey. I'm sorry I scared you. It scared me, too, when I found the door open."

"Well, don't do it again! I don't *need* it. This house already creeps me out enough." She stalked into the kitchen, rubbing her face. She suddenly cocked her head. "Did you say the door was unlocked?"

"Unlocked and wide open."

"Now I *know* there's something wrong with the catch. I was sure I had locked it."

"Wrong. Anybody could have walked right in." He slung large, white plastic bags onto the yellow-topped counter. "It's locked now."

Bronwyn flipped a wall switch to turn on the overhead lights. She blinked in the brighter light. More of her hair had lost its battle with gravity, leaving her with only a silly little spout of a ponytail sticking straight up, while the rest hung in a silky mahogany curtain. She shoved her hair behind her ears, still clearly sleepy, still trying to get oriented.

She looked adorable. He wanted to pull her close, to nestle her, to rub her back and let her come awake in his arms. God, he wanted *her*. The intensity of desiring not just with his body but with his whole being left him tongue-tied. Soon, he promised himself. Soon.

Unaware of the direction his thoughts had taken, she squinted at him, taking in his appearance for the first time. "Whoa. You're soaked. Is it still raining that hard?"

"Out on 42, I was caught in a cloudburst. A car hydroplaned and went into a drainage ditch." He couldn't think of anything else to say about it. "How's the baby?"

"She's asleep. She's okay," Bronwyn informed him shortly, not willing to be diverted from her line of questioning. "You've been in a *wreck*?"

"Not me. The car in front of me went off the road. I had to stop and help." He opened one of the three large plastic sacks. "Here are the bottles, the formula, and the Pedialyte stuff."

Bronwyn frowned. She made no move to examine his purchases. Instead she looked him up and down. "You said you weren't in the accident, but your shorts are torn. Is that blood on your leg?"

Garth had forgotten the rip in his shorts. The ragged V-shaped rent opened them all the way to the crotch. "I tangled with some briars when I was getting the woman out of the car. Got a scratch, that's all." It burned like fire. Now that he was in the light, there was more blood than he had thought.

"Let me see." She bent forward to lift one edge of the tear.

He stepped back out of reach. "It's a scratch."

"I want to see it." Her eyes twinkled up at him. "Come on, I'm a doctor."

Garth's face got hot. "I'm—uh—commando." He couldn't believe he was blushing. Modesty wasn't a trait found in many SEALs. But images of being naked with her notwithstanding, exposing himself to his future wife without any preliminaries didn't feel right.

Her grin widened. "And I'm still a doctor. Here. Take off the shorts and cover yourself with this." She handed him a towel and, keeping her back to him, went to the sink where she washed her hands. "Sit up on the counter so I can see. Tell me when you're ready."

"You can turn around now," he told her when he had draped the towel over his lap.

It was torture of the very sweetest kind as she stepped between his knees to look closely at his thigh. She was so close he could feel the warmth of her body. He breathed deeply to take in the fresh, herbal smell of her shampoo and her enticing woman scent. He refused to let that thought go where it wanted to—not with her standing almost eye level with his crotch.

Laying her hand on his knee, she positioned his leg to catch the light. He'd never felt anything like the warm buzz that radiated from deep within his flesh when she touched him. He was so captivated that the sting instantly decreased.

The zigzag, red wound had black, coagulated droplets

of blood beaded along its length, but it really was just a scratch. Tough to figure why it had bled so much. It hardly needed the scrutiny she gave it before snapping on plastic gloves and cleaning it with a moistened, antiseptic-smelling pad.

"That's some amazing stuff you're putting on me," he told her.

"This? No, pretty standard. Why?"

"Look at the scratch. It looks better already."

She made a noncommittal sound. "You probably heal quickly."

"I do. In B/UDS—the SEAL basic training—I could be pretty much a wreck one day and healed up enough to go on the next."

"Injured? How?"

"Skin gone from large sections of my hide, bruises, blisters, sprains, concussion. The instructors are diabolical in their ability to think of exercises that will elicit maximum pain while doing minimum permanent harm."

"Why do they do that?"

"They need to find out which trainees will quit and which will keep going."

Bronwyn leaned away from him to look into his face, her brows drawn together in a scowl. "Is SEAL training some kind of macho test? So you can join the man-of-steel club? Making you ignore pain doesn't sound like good training to me. If an exercise causes pain, you *should* stop. People who ignore pain might look tough now, but they're going to pay later."

"If a man isn't going to stick, the sooner they can get rid of him, the more time they have to spend with the ones who will make it."

Bronwyn snorted, unimpressed. "It sounds very survival-of-the-fittest. Like societies that deliberately expose babies to hypothermia. If they live, they are hardy enough to be worth raising."

"In a way it is. A man who will give up won't survive in battle. Even worse he'll be a liability. He'll reduce the other men's chances of survival."

Bronwyn's eyes widened in horror. "But to make you endure pain without complaint in order to prove you're worthy? It's the ultimate abuse paradigm! The abuser tells you he's treating you harshly 'for your own good.' If you stay in the situation, you have to identify with your torturers and invalidate your own feelings."

How had this discussion gone to shit so fast? Some people thought SEALs were nuts for going through the toughest training in the world, but he hadn't expected an argument from the love of his life.

"It isn't about inflicting pain. It's not about proving you can tolerate more pain. It's about when you have come to the limits of your endurance, will you find another source of strength? It's about, even if you're hurting and tired, will you reach back to give another man a hand?"

Bronwyn tilted her head, listening. Another clump of mahogany hair slid from her ponytail. "See," Garth went on, "they don't really take you to where you're physically at the end of your rope. They're watching very carefully to make sure you don't die and are not going to come to permanent harm. But they will take you to where you *think* you're at the end of your rope—and see if you'll go on anyway."

Bronwyn opened another antiseptic pad. "Go on."

"Okay. Let me give you an example. On the last day of Hell Week, the last evolution—what you might call an exercise—was a four-mile run. Well, you have to understand that by the last day of Hell Week, nobody is capable of *running*. You're too tired. You've only had about two hours of sleep in five days. Your coordination is way off, your joints are swollen. The best you can do is hobble along on the dregs of energy you have left.

"My knee was the size of a basketball, but I wasn't going to quit. Two other trainees say, 'All right, we'll carry you.' They sling my arms over their shoulders and they're trying to run, and I'm doing what I can with my one leg, kind of like a five-legged race, but it's not long before we're a good mile behind everybody else, with two instructors following us in a jeep.

"They're playing mind games with us, saying stuff like, 'Don't you want to DOR?' That means drop on request. 'Say the word, Mr. Vale. Just think about how nice a hot shower would feel. We'll let you sleep for a week if you want to.'

"Sometimes they worked on my buddies. 'It's going to take the two with good legs until midnight. They should leave him behind. Look after themselves. After all, they're hurting, too.'

"Of course, we could hear them—they meant for us to—but we just kept trudging. So then one of the trainers says, 'I'm worried if we let Mr. Vale finish this run, he's going to do permanent damage to his knee.' The other says, 'It would probably be okay with some rest. We could roll him over to the next class, but if we do, he'll have to repeat Hell Week.'

"And the first one says, 'Well, I don't want to be

responsible for letting him continue—limping like he is.
Tell you what. So-and-so is a really good medic. We'll
ask him to evaluate Mr. Vale's condition. If he says it's
okay, we'll let him finish.'

"So they put me in the jeep and they take me to the
medic who is like five yards from the finish point. And
they sit there shooting the breeze, and the medic looks
at my leg, and about the time my two buddies catch
up to us, they ask the medic, 'What do you think? Is
the knee too bad, or can we put him back in?' And the
medic says, 'Yeah, I think it'll be okay to let him finish.'

"And so they wave my buddies over and tell them
'Mr. Vale can finish.' So the guys come over to the
jeep and help me down, and the lead instructor gets
this big grin on his face and says, 'You are all secure
from Hell Week.'"

"What does 'secure from Hell Week' mean?"

"It meant we had successfully completed it, and Hell
Week was now behind us."

Bronwyn was silent while she thought his story over.
Her eyes narrowed. "The instructors helped you. Was
what they did breaking the rules?"

Garth waggled a hand. "More like a creative interpre-
tation. They couldn't actively help me, so they made the
guidelines they had to follow work to my advantage."

—◆◆◆—

When she was done treating his scratch, she looked him
over for other wounds. Her eyes narrowed when she saw
the long scar on the outside of his thigh, near the hip. It
was darker than the surrounding skin and fresh enough
to still be shiny and raised.

He tried to imagine what it looked like to her. Until this moment, he'd never given a thought to its appearance. For her, he wanted everything perfect; *he* wanted to be perfect and knew he wasn't. He sighed. It was what it was. They would have to work with what they had. She was a doctor; she had probably seen worse.

At length she stepped back. "It looks clean. No permanent damage." She tossed the used pad in the trash, then stripped off the gloves and tossed them in behind it. "That's a bad scar on your thigh," she observed in a tone so casual it made every nerve in his body go on alert. "Do you have any loss of function?"

She was fishing for something, but he couldn't guess what. "It aches sometimes if I have to stand for long periods. Squats aren't as much fun as they used to be."

She didn't smile at his tiny joke. She crossed her arms under her breasts and leaned against the butcher block. "All right. What's the real story about where Julia came from? You're not this baby's father."

Chapter 14

There is no "I" in Team.

—SEAL motto

"YOU'RE NOT THIS BABY'S FATHER," BRONWYN TOLD THE big man perched on the kitchen counter. She fought sick disgust at herself for letting the situation come to this. She'd had her doubts from the moment she'd seen him—at least she'd sensed there was more than he was saying. Still, she'd let the feeling that, regardless of appearances, everything was okay—coupled with the fact that she *had* met him—keep her from doing what she should have done in the first place: turn the whole situation over to the authorities.

But she didn't know enough about him to know what he was capable of—not really. And as for the elusive resemblance to Troy, she couldn't trust it. Police officers and, she suspected, navy SEALs were forced by their jobs to see the world differently than ordinary people did. They made choices that kept them on the right side of the law, yes, but they had some of the same qualities and had learned to think in the same ways as those they hunted. It would be a mistake for anyone to assume that all SEALs or all cops were, by definition, good guys.

Even now she wasn't handling the situation right. When hospital staff realized a child's illness or injury was inconsistent with the parent's story, they were supposed to make an excuse to get the child out of the room and then call the authorities. They weren't supposed to confront.

But there had been the disorienting shift in reality a few minutes earlier when she'd understood the hulking silhouetted figure was Garth. With her heart still pounding from the jolt of adrenaline, she had nevertheless been sure that *everything was all right. Finally.*

The feeling that he was familiar—that he was in some way known to her—had been so strong that the concern she had felt when he had returned wet and muddy and bloody had been effortless; she had treated him like a friend. Slipping into banter had been the most natural thing in the world. And now she was paying the price. She didn't intimidate him one bit.

In his bronze face, his teeth shone white in a smile full of challenge. "Her mother says she's mine. How can you be so sure she's not?"

The smile made her stomach flutter and her knees get weak. That was bad. She fisted her hands on her hips. "Simple deduction. I'm certified in emergency medicine. I've seen plenty of scars like that." She pointed to his thigh.

She tried not to think about the masculine power and beauty it encapsulated. She tried not to remember how she'd been able to see the pain in it when she first met him. She tried not to get sidetracked by her intuition that some inflammation needed to be addressed.

"I'd guess it's more than six months and less than a year old. The baby is about eight months old. Add nine months gestation, and you get seventeen months. Ergo, you were nowhere near this baby's mother when she was conceived. You were in Afghanistan."

He didn't deny it. His face registered no emotion she could read.

"If I'd been able to reach JJ," she added, "I would have already put all the facts together and called the police."

His smile didn't change. "What facts?"

"What facts?" Bronwyn's voice was rising, but she couldn't help it. His dead-level calm questioning of the obvious made her see red.

"Yes. What facts necessitate bringing in the authorities?"

"Fact," she spat. "You are in possession of a baby who is not yours! Fact: she was drugged and allowed to get dehydrated!" Bronwyn took a cleansing breath. When she spoke again, she managed a more judicious tone. "The simplest explanation is that you kidnapped her, accidentally overdosed her, and became alarmed."

She reached into her pocket for her cell phone but remembered she'd plugged it into the charger. She crossed her arms under her breasts. "Start talking. And you'd better include all the reasons I shouldn't report a kidnapping."

The house creaked in the silence that ensued as they faced off. He sat absolutely immobile—immobility she had no doubt he could maintain for hours.

His intensely blue eyes were the only life in his face. On an Alaskan cruise, Bronwyn had seen icebergs breaking off a mountain of a glacier and dropping into the sea. The deep, clear aqua of ice that had been under pressure for eons had been exactly the same color.

Deep inside she shivered. The color thrilled her now as it had then with its beauty and with its message that she was in the presence of immense forces. Her heart pounded. Her nerves stretched tight. Still she refused to look away. She had already yielded to the force of this man's presence too many times today.

At last the brilliance of his eyes faded slightly—almost sadly—but his eyes didn't waver. "I can't."

"Huh?"

"I can't tell you." He elucidated.

"Why not?"

"I can't tell you that, either."

Bronwyn huffed in disbelief. "Not good enough! You really don't think I'm going to let you walk out of here with her, do you?"

"I don't know," he responded gravely as if he hadn't understood the rhetorical nature of her question. "I want to tell you more than I've ever wanted anything in my life. More than I've ever wanted anything at all," he repeated in the same gravelly, uninflected tone. "Except to kiss you."

Chapter 15

Anyone can just go in there and kill someone, but you can't get information from a corpse.

—SEAL saying

GARTH WATCHED BRONWYN'S CHEEKS FLAME HOT AS THE full import of his words sank in. He had spoken without thought, something he never did, but this was his mate, dammit. Every second he was around her, he became more convinced that was what she was. He'd been instructed by Kohn to go looking for a wife, and, by God, he had found her.

But this was so not the way to go about courting the love of his life.

They weren't supposed to be squared off. They were supposed to stand together, side by side. He had already lied as much as he could to her and more than he wanted to. He had wanted so much to tell her the truth—if not the truth about the baby, then truth about *something*—that he'd blurted out what every cell in his body, every scrap of his soul, wanted.

Thank God, he hadn't used the verb he really had in mind. He'd switched to the more acceptable "kiss" at the last possible instant.

Now the atmosphere between them was weirder than ever. She backed away from him. It took every ounce of self-control, but he let her.

"Um. Put your shorts back on." She held his gaze, but she seemed to be talking more to herself than to him. "I need to get my phone from the charger. I'm calling the cops."

When she turned aside to retrieve her cell, he tossed aside the towel and pulled up his shorts. The sound the snap at his waist made was loud. "Wait. Please."

She whirled around. "What should I wait for? For you to tell me what's going on? Or maybe you think you're sexy enough to make me forget all my questions if I'll just give you a little time to soften me up."

Sexy enough, huh? He liked the sound of that, but he didn't think this was the moment to tell her so.

Her voice rose with exasperation. "*Explain* something. Anything! Just one tiny little thing."

A whimpery protest came from the darkened room beyond. Out of the corner of his eye he saw Mildred get to her feet. She peered over the side of an open carton, sniffed, and then trotted into the kitchen to bump her nose at the back of Bronwyn's leg—just as if she were trying to set Bronwyn in motion.

Garth knew he had seconds to make his case. "Okay, listen. Calling the police is a bad idea. I'm trying to keep her safe."

For a long tense moment Bronwyn's clear, tea-colored eyes held his. "That's *all*?" She stared in disbelief. "You don't think that's adequate, do you? What kind of danger is she in?" The dog bumped her again. "What *is* it, Mildred?" The dog's toenails clicked rapidly on the oak floor. "Okay, I'll go get the baby."

Bronwyn went over to the large box Mildred had sniffed. "Hey, sweetie," she cooed, reaching into the box. "Are you awake and thirsty? You're in luck. Your da—you have bottles, and—"

"A box?" Garth demanded in the steely, dead-level calm tone that let his men know they had better account for themselves. He had thought he'd pushed that first sight of Julia after he lifted off the box top far, far away. Who knew that revulsion could rise up in his throat at the very suggestion it had happened again? "You put her in a *box*?"

"Just to sleep when I got too sleepy myself to hold her—so she'd be safe—if she's not crawling yet, she will be soon—" Bronwyn straightened with the baby in her arms and stared, transfixed by the expression on his face. "*What*? What's the matter?"

Garth ran his hand over his face. *Tired.* He jammed his hands in his pockets, fighting now to keep his control. *Shake it off. Breathe.* Bronwyn was innocent of any wrongdoing. She'd only been using her best judgment under the circumstances. She deserved to understand why he had overreacted.

"I found her closed up in a box," he explained.

Bronwyn's white skin grew whiter as understanding dawned. Her arms tightened on the baby. "You mean it was a complete accident that you found her? She was *hidden*... in a box... in the hangar?" Her eyebrows pushed a little pleat into the area over her nose. "How much more is there to this story?"

"Not much more. I wouldn't have found her if I hadn't smelled her dirty diaper. She was in—" He cut himself off. He had already said too much. Bronwyn had amply demonstrated she could put together every crumb of fact she obtained. Before she could formulate the next question, he said, "I don't think she had been left there to die. There were diapers and a cloth doll in the box. I think someone left her there thinking she was somewhere she would be better off."

"Did the note say her name is Julia?"

At last, an easy question. He smiled his relief. "I don't know her name. Julia is my mother's name. I borrowed it."

"Oh." Bronwyn jiggled the baby while holding his gaze as if she wanted to read his mind. "Get the bottles out, please," she said at last, "and wash one so we can give her something to drink."

When the baby was on Bronwyn's lap and making contented sucking sounds as her pursed lips pulled at the plastic nipple, Bronwyn raised her eyes to his, trying to read the truth in them. She asked sadly, "Was there really a note from the child's mother?"

"No."

"Do you know, or think you know, whose child this is?"

"Honestly, I don't." He willed her to believe him. "I will return Julia to her mother if I can."

"Despite the condition you found the baby in, you would let the mother have her?"

"I don't think she was trying to get rid of her. I think she was trying to save her."

Chapter 16

Build in opportunity, but use it sparingly.

—The Moscow Rules

BRONWYN SHIFTED THE CHILD ON HER LAP TO EASE THE pressure of the amazingly heavy little head on her arm. The baby felt subtly better, less floppy. Her hands grasped at the bottle with more coordination. She lay with one leg cocked. Her tiny foot, with its delicate, translucent pink toes, was propped on Bronwyn's chest.

When, from time to time, she raised her eyelids to look up at Bronwyn, her pupils were more normal, her slate-blue gaze more focused. That confirmed Bronwyn's diagnostic impression that no disease underlay the infant's dehydration—she had simply been drugged and given nothing to drink. Bronwyn noted how angry such neglect made her but filed the emotion away. Responding emotionally to what had been done to Julia would not help her sort out the truth now.

The fact was, the improvement in the baby's alertness as the drug wore off lent subtle credence to Garth's story—what little he had told her. Drugging a child to keep it quiet made sense if the child was to be hidden for any length of time in a box.

And if there was one part of his story she didn't doubt, it was that Julia *had been in a box* and Garth *had been appalled* to find her there. Though controlled, Garth's surprise and fury at learning that she had let the baby sleep in a carton were so disproportionate that for a second she had had a direct glimpse into the shock and horror he had felt when he found Julia.

Something within Bronwyn that had been squeezed tight to the point of pain unfurled as she concluded that *he* had had no part in how the infant came to be neglected and abandoned.

He was nothing to her; the sooner she had him out of her house, the sooner she could reassemble her fragile peace, but she didn't want him to be one of the bad guys. She could report a case of child abandonment to the police without getting him into trouble.

"Look," she told him, "I believe you didn't kidnap Julia. I even believe you found her in a box—and you had nothing to do with how she got there. But it doesn't matter what I believe. Legally, I have to report child neglect. Actually everyone does, but because I'm a doctor, responsibility for failing to act would fall heavier on me than it would on you."

Garth jammed his hands in his pockets. "What will happen if you don't?"

"I'm not sure what the penalty would be, but even if I wouldn't go to jail, I could lose my license." Bronwyn heard her own words as she spoke them. Was she practicing defensive medicine again? Did she believe turning the child over was the right thing to do, or was she covering her ass? "Why do *you* say calling the police is a bad idea? Can't they find out where she came from and who should take her better than you can?"

"I found her on a plane. The flight didn't originate in the States. When the cops try to find out where she came from, they'll need to involve the FBI. The FBI will question where the plane came from and why, but they won't get far before they are told for 'national security reasons' to stop the investigation. Someone will be sent to take custody of her, and she will disappear—without a hope of tracing her—finally and forever."

Bronwyn noted the sudden inclusion of the plane detail. Put together with the secrecy that surrounded everything, his explanation almost made terrible sense. Sick, cold dread made it hard to breathe deeply. "They would kill her?"

"Maybe not." But the way he said it made her know he thought it was a real possibility. "No one would ever know what happened—but if her mother is looking for her, she would never find her."

Impatience with his evasiveness welled up again. She wasn't going to fall for a bunch of paranoid non-sense. "This does not compute. What are you leaving out? Why would federal agents clamp down on an investigation of a baby stowaway in the name of 'national security'?… Do they really make people disappear never to be heard of again? *Give me a break.* Your story sounds like you've been watching too much TV. It isn't real—is it?"

"Bronwyn, I know how these things work."

"Because you used to be a SEAL?" He was silent. "Where did you plan to take her after you left here?" She gave him a warning glare. "And don't say, 'Don't ask.'"

He smiled.

Bronwyn had finally figured out what it was about

his smiles that had bothered her, although they seemed genuine enough. Whenever he smiled, she had the feeling he'd had to go a long way to get the smile and hadn't dusted it before he put it on. But this time it was like his smile was one he had made fresh, just for her.

Though he smiled, he also shook his head and shrugged. He managed to make the movement of his broad shoulders innocent, mischievous—and sexy as hell.

Bronwyn couldn't suppress the tendency of her own lips to curl upward. "And I'm just supposed to believe *you* because you're one of the good guys?"

"I am."

She let go of her exasperation with his evasiveness. He wasn't going to tell her anything he didn't want her to know. There were too many questions floating around and no way to know if turning Julia over to the police would increase her danger. Sometimes the only way to make a diagnosis was to do nothing but wait and see if the patient got better or worse.

Aware she was making herself into an obstacle in the path of a man who saw obstacles as challenges, she told him, "It's obvious this child needs protection, but I don't know from whom—you or someone else. If you do have a plan for what happens next, you'd better start modifying it. The only person I'm sure I can trust is myself. Until I know more, I'm not letting her out of my sight."

She was adorable. Gutsy. Having told him what was what, she bent her attention back to the baby. He liked the graceful curve of her neck accentuated by the deep red strands that had slipped from her ponytail. He didn't know what to call hair that color. It wasn't the rusty brown color usually called red. It was more like black with a red glow—like coals with fire smoldering deep within. If he touched it, would it be warm? He smiled inwardly at his fancy. Soon he would touch it. He would move the strands and kiss the tender white space behind her ear.

Even in a grubby T-shirt and set against the kitchen's shabbiness, she glowed the way paintings by the masters glowed. He could imagine just what it would feel like to sink into that glow.

Sun Tzu, author of the millennia-old *Art of War* wrote, "Opportunities multiply as they are seized." The baby had to be stashed somewhere. If Bronwyn would be happier keeping an eye on her, he could let her. If the baby could be here, so could he. He'd only tried to cover his tracks so that anyone looking for her would have to go through him.

Best of all, he didn't have to leave and figure out later how to get back in Bronwyn's good graces.

Bronwyn looked up and caught him watching her. "Why are you smiling?" She demanded suspiciously.

"I'm not smiling."

"Yes, you are. Not your lips. Your eyes or something. Anyway, you shouldn't be. I suspect I've ruined a lot of your plans." She avoided a flailing baby hand that was going for her nose. "Uh-oh. Have I 'stepped into your parlor'?"

"Are you going to ignore the fact that I told you I'd like to kiss you?"

"I think I should, don't you?"

"I'm not going to let you." He went over to her and squatted on his heels before her, resting his hands on the curved wooden arms of the chair. Caging her. "I am going to kiss you."

He watched her face carefully. He was taking shameless advantage of his superior strength and her handicap of having a baby in her arms—and it didn't bother him one bit.

Bronwyn had managed him; she had confronted him; but she hadn't once backed off. And even now, with him absolutely inside her space, she didn't look alarmed. She looked... curious.

He leaned forward, and still her eyes held his. Which was good. He caught the moment when her pupils flared and her gaze flicked to his mouth. *Yes.* She was waiting for him to kiss her.

He'd intended a peck, just enough to put her on notice. If he had seen fear, he would have settled for her cheek. Seeing no resistance, he settled onto his knees. He knew what kneeling before her meant, even if she didn't. Now he found her lips with his, intent upon learning her.

Ignoring frantic hunger for this slow, sweet feeding, nothing touched but their lips. Time hung suspended. Their breath mingled, warm and moist. He stroked her lower lip with his tongue, and she opened, and then he was searching the silken recesses of her mouth.

Arms full of baby and bottle, she could neither push him away nor move closer. Pressed against the chair back, she couldn't even move her head. All she could do was let him kiss her, let him have complete control of the kiss—the timing, the pressure, the rhythms of it.

His lips were soft, softer than they looked, and he touched them to hers in a way that wasn't sexual at all but more like the kind of kiss that seals a bargain.

But when he was done, he didn't draw away. He stayed right there, lips hovering just above hers. If there had been any of civilization's manufactured scents on him, cologne or aftershave, they were long gone. A dank, ditchwater smell rose from his clothes. Its earthiness made the warm masculine essence of his skin a little salty, musky, and dark, all the more primal. Moist puffs of his breath landed on her lips like a different kind of kiss.

The deep secret reaches of her body went liquid; heat bloomed in her breasts and her inner thighs. The muscles of her neck went lax. The clinician's corner of her mind recognized yielding, submission. How odd.

Now he touched her with his lips again, a brushing slide that traced the contours of her mouth and made her inhale, and then his tongue was hot on her lower lip, hot, stroking velvet.

The baby squirmed. A tiny fist tugged at her T-shirt. Bronwyn readjusted the angle of the bottle. And even so, her whole attention never left what he was doing.

—✺—

The dog pushed her shaggy head into the space between their bodies, batting them apart with her wet nose. Bronwyn's body felt heavy, tight, over-full in some places, empty in others. She looked into Garth's eyes. His eyes were deep, ink blue. The golden-oak skin of his high cheekbones gleamed. His lips glistened with moisture. Bronwyn had no idea how to read the intent expression on his face.

"What is it, Mildred?" she asked the dog. "Are you jealous?"

Mildred shook her head and snorted impatiently. She whined and butted Bronwyn again.

"Then what do you want? Do you want to go out?"

Mildred whined again.

"Oh. My cell phone is ringing." Bronwyn couldn't believe it hadn't even registered. "Would you…?"

Garth rose from his knees in one smooth display of strength and grace.

He disconnected the phone from the charger and carried it to Bronwyn. It was JJ.

"I need to warn you," Bronwyn told her friend after they had exchanged greetings. "We might not have but a minute. This phone's battery isn't holding a charge for some reason."

"Then what I called about will keep," JJ responded instantly. "Tell me how the move is going."

"Weird, that's how. Very, very strange. But listen, I'm really glad you called. I need to ask you—what kind of man is Garth Vale?"

"*Garth*?" JJ didn't attempt to hide her surprise. "David's best man? That Garth? Why do you want to know?"

Bronwyn was aware of Garth leaning against a counter and frankly listening to every word. "Please. I just need your opinion."

"I don't really know him… Hey, hon, Bronwyn wants to know about Garth Vale."

"David's there? I'm sorry, I didn't know he was coming home. I wouldn't have called you—" JJ's time with her SEAL husband was rare and precious. "You didn't have to return my call."

"He came in tonight. Let me let you talk to him." Before Bronwyn could protest, she heard the phone being handed off.

"Hey, Medicine Woman." JJ's husband's voice was as dark, velvety, and melting as the best chocolate. Bronwyn hadn't known him before he was wounded, but JJ said now that his scars had faded, he was even better-looking than before. It didn't seem fair that he had such an scrumptious voice, too. Even so, David's voice didn't have the effect on her breathing that Garth's did. "What's this about Garth?" he asked.

Bronwyn jerked herself back to business. "I need to know if I can trust him."

David laughed. "Hell, no. He's a SEAL. Don't believe a word he says. No matter what he's told you, he's only interested in one thing."

David's sunny insouciance always made Bronwyn laugh. She also felt herself blushing. "I didn't mean that kind of trust."

"Then what are you talking about?"

"I mean, if a situation was serious…"

"Are you in trouble?"

"Not yet. I need to get my eyes wide open, or I might be. But it's not my safety that's at stake. It's a baby's."

"A baby's." David waited for her to elaborate. When she didn't, he chided, "You're not giving me much to work with."

"I can't tell you more. It might make you and JJ accomplices."

"You're committing a crime?"

"Sort of."

"With Garth?"

"Yes."

"And a baby's safety is at stake. Is, or was, the baby on a plane?"

"Yes. How did you—?"

"Nevermind. He doesn't drink to excess. He doesn't gamble. He doesn't hang out in low dives. He doesn't even cuss much. He's a straight arrow. He's a solid officer, a better operator. He'll never sell you out. When he takes men down range, they get the job done, and they all come back. I would trust him with my life. More important: I would trust him with JJ's life."

"Give me the phone back," JJ, in the distance, demanded. "What's going on?" she asked when she had taken possession. "What kind of trouble are you in, and what does a baby have to do with it?"

Bronwyn felt a twinge of unwilling sympathy for Garth. Explaining where a baby came from was hard if you couldn't tell the whole story. "I don't want to get you mixed up in it. With your grandfather sick, you have enough to deal with. Is he worse? Is that why David has come home?"

JJ's elderly grandfather had had a heart condition for years. Episodes of shortness of breath had increased in the past couple of months.

"Granddaddy's about the same. David's home this time because he's teaching a course in battlefield medicine at Lejeune." Camp Lejeune was the marine base close to the beach house JJ rented on Topsail Island. All medics in the Marine Corps were, in fact, navy hospital corpsmen assigned to the marine battalions. Although stationed at Little Creek, Virginia, David took every temporary assignment to Lejeune that he could so that he and JJ could have more time together.

"Now, don't change the subject. And stop trying to protect me," JJ ordered. "It doesn't matter how busy I am, I always have time for you. You suddenly have a baby. All right. Whatever is going on, you're doing the right thing. You don't have to explain anything. All I want to know is how I can help."

Bronwyn warmed clear to her toes. Her friend's reaction was quintessential, practical JJ, letting her know that she respected Bronwyn's right to make her own choices, and regardless, JJ was always, always on her side.

JJ's faith in her was the affirmation Bronwyn needed to go with her gut and trust Garth. Her duty to protect the child superseded her duty to obey the letter of the law. Her unpreparedness suddenly struck her. She huffed a shaky laugh. "Jay, I don't know what I need. I'll be keeping her a couple of days, I guess. Maybe more. Babies need a lot of stuff. I don't even have a place for her to sleep, much less an infant car seat, and—isn't there something called a bassinet? I don't even know what that is. Do you?"

It was JJ's turn to chuckle. "'Fraid not. But the car seat is something I can take care of. Let me give you a loaner. You don't want to buy one if you're keeping her only a couple of days."

"I hate to put you to that trouble."

"No trouble. I'll have someone run it over in the morning."

"What do you mean, 'run it over'? You're in Wilmington."

"Honey, you're used to believing 'all the way across town' is too far to go. Trust me, it won't be long at all until you too will think nothing of driving fifty to a hundred miles just to go out to dinner."

"All right. Thanks. A car seat would be a big help." Bronwyn quickly checked the phone's battery. It seemed to be holding. "Now tell me your news."

"You know the big party to celebrate our wedding that we're planning? David and I have set a date. We held off because we wanted both Garth and you to be here and we figured Garth's schedule might be the hardest to work around—but we can't find him. I can't believe you asked about him."

Bronwyn glanced over at Garth who was leaning against the counter, his dark face inscrutable, making no secret of the fact that he was listening to every word. "Can't find him?"

"I suspect there's more to it than David is saying— you know how many security issues go with being a SEAL—but that's the bottom line. Nobody seems to have heard from him in a while, and no one knows where he's living."

Though he moved not a muscle, she could almost feel Garth willing her to keep silent.

But if his own friends weren't in on what he was doing, how many more layers were there to this story? How many underwater currents that would pull the unsuspecting swimmer this way and that?

If there was one thing she had learned it was that the more secrets one had, the more guarded one became; and the fewer people who were admitted to the center of one's life, the lonelier one became. She had gone down that road with Troy, whose undercover work had forced her to watch every word she said about him.

When there was no telling what stray comment could expose him to danger, it had been easier to say nothing. When everyone else talked about their plans for the weekend, she had kept her mouth shut. A lot of people she had worked with hadn't known she and Troy were serious—she had talked about him so seldom.

JJ had been her lifeline, a center point of clarity, the one person she didn't need to watch what she said to. If there was a soul on the face of this earth she trusted, it was JJ. And if there was one person she refused to be separated from by keeping secrets, it was JJ.

The baby, Julia, was her patient. Not telling JJ details about *her* was one thing. Garth wasn't her patient. She wouldn't keep silent when she had information JJ needed to know. Bronwyn met his ice-colored eyes and took a deep breath. "I know where he is."

Chapter 17

The art of giving orders is not to rectify the minor blunders and not to be swayed by petty doubts.

—Sun Tzu, *The Art of War*

IT WAS A GOOD THING, GARTH DISCOVERED, TO LIKE THE woman he intended to marry. He had never doubted that he would, but he'd always assumed he'd get to know her before he had to make up his mind if he liked her or not. He hadn't realized how much liking would help when she went and did exactly what he didn't want her to.

He hadn't wanted anyone, particularly any old friends in the navy, to know he had come to Bronwyn with a baby in tow. It was too good a story not to repeat.

She had revealed his location, but he had listened to Bronwyn's conversation long enough to learn she skillfully stuck to the truth and yet didn't link his presence to the baby in any way. That would have to be good enough. The trick was to stay focused on the objective and not get hung up on the details. Any plan that kept the baby safe and kept him close to Bronwyn was fine with him.

Julia had slowed down on her bottle. He held out his arms. "Here, let me take her. Talk to your friend."

Julia squirmed and fussed and refused to nestle into the crook of his arm—the way he had carried her earlier.

She felt firmer and stronger than she had before. He brought her to his shoulder and discovered she balanced herself upright very well. Anchoring herself with fist-fuls of his shirt, she studied her surroundings, her wide, slate-blue eyes much clearer.

"You want to have a look around? I agree."

He glanced into darkened rooms on the ground floor as he took the hall to the stairs. He finally found the light switch beside the front door, which was closed and locked as he had left it. Bronwyn probably didn't understand the old-fashioned mechanism. He'd show her how to operate it, but it would be better to replace it with something more secure.

Even with the power on, the two working bulbs in the brass chandelier did little to dispel the gloom of the cavernous space. He'd get replacement bulbs when he went to the hardware store for the lock.

None of the switches seemed to turn on a light at the top of the stairs.

"*Ga-agh*?" Julia loosed her clutch on his shirt to fling an uncoordinated arm toward the dark landing above. Despite her lingering wooziness, she appeared to be focused intently.

"You want to go up there?"

The plump little body undulated like a stadium fan doing a wave.

"All right, a quick look-see."

In a bathroom at the top of the stairs he found a working light. He left it on while he explored the upper floor. Like the downstairs, the rooms were sparsely furnished with old wardrobes and massive beds too heavy and too old-fashioned to be worth the trouble to move.

In the bedroom that looked out at the front of the house, he found clothes in the closet and the bed partially made with green sheets. He flipped the switch by the door but nothing happened. He put it on his mental list of repairs. For now, from one of the other bedrooms, he retrieved a fat little lamp, its base made of knobby white glass. The bed was just what he was looking for. The curved mahogany headboard, almost as tall as he was, and the footboard that came above his waist made it look like a gigantic sleigh. If he shoved it against the wall the mattress would be enclosed on three sides.

"What do you think, Julia? Want to sleep up here?" The baby bounced on his forearm, leaving a trace of warm moisture. "You need a change, young lady."

"She's wet?" Bronwyn asked from the door. The dog stood beside her. "That's a good sign she's not dehydrated anymore. What were you doing up here?"

"Since you don't have a crib, I wanted to figure out some place for the baby to sleep. Here, hold her while I push the bed against the wall."

"Wait. Let me finish making it up first. It will be easier if I can get around it." She smoothed out the top sheet, brought it to the head of the bed, and briskly folded the hem back before moving to the foot.

He liked the smooth, graceful way she performed the homey task. He especially liked the way her shorts pulled tight across her shapely butt when she bent over. Garth balanced the baby on one arm. With the other he lifted the foot of the mattress so she could tuck the sheet under. "Is that what you were doing when I got here? Making up the bed? Did I interrupt you?"

"What?" Bronwyn looked up from mitering a corner. "Oh. No. With the storm coming up, it got too dark to see. When I turned on the overhead light, the bulb flared and then went out with a loud bang. I thought for a second the house had been struck by lightning. Scared the bejesus out of me. Scared Mildred, too. If you factor in the way the floors creak and pop so that it sounds like an invisible person is in the room with you—" She laughed nervously. "Shoot, that's the big reason I wanted to turn on the light in the first place *and* the reason I didn't stay to finish the job after it burned out."

"You think you have ghosts?"

"Of course not. It's just, um… hard not to let my imagination run away with me." The corners of her mouth turned up. "I have to admit coming back into this room was easier since you were in it."

"So, do you believe in ghosts?"

She gave him a pained look. "I knew full well there wasn't anyone in the house. It was foolishness. Do you think a doctor who imagines ghostly presences would have a chance of attracting patients?"

"Okay, Julia, you need fresh underwear," he told the baby, holding her at arm's length and looking her in the face once they were back downstairs. "We're going to see what kind of job I do when I have directions. Will you hold her while I get organized?"

Bronwyn accepted the baby. "You don't want me to diaper her?"

Garth rummaged through the plastic bags. He extracted a large package of diapers. "Do you know how?"

"Um, I'm sure I can."

"That didn't sound like a yes to me."

"I've seen it done," she defended herself.

The almond shape of his eyes became longer and narrower. The intense aqua of his irises took on a teasing glint. "Seen it?"

"All right, its mother or a nurse does the actual diapering."

"In that case, I have more hands-on experience than you. No way am I letting the job I did before be my final grade. Kind of surprised me when I realized I'd never even watched someone change a baby. I need to achieve fundamental competence. I'm going to need to know how, someday. Someday soon, I hope."

Bronwyn's heart thumped, painfully. "You're married?" Why hadn't that possibility occurred to her? Talking with David had reassured her about Garth, but there was a lot more to a man than whether he was a good operator.

Garth pulled more baby supplies from the bags, organizing them on the kitchen's small maple breakfast table. He grinned. "Hope to be."

"Then what were you doing kissing *me*?"

"I was hoping you'd be the one having the baby."

What? Bronwyn backed up and stumbled over a box. For one terrible second she lost her balance and was afraid she would fall and take the baby with her. Then strong arms had her, steadying her.

"You okay?" He peered into her face. "I didn't mean to spring that on you. It just slipped out."

"You can't be serious."

"Well…"

"But it's absurd. You don't even know me."

"Sometimes, when it's right, you just know."

Bronwyn stared. "You really are serious!"

"Hey, don't get upset."

"Don't tell me not to get upset!" Her reaction was out of proportion, and she knew it. It wasn't as if a patient had never propositioned her or jokingly asked her to marry him. She ought to treat the whole thing lightly.

He shrugged. "Okay, but you *are* upset. Hand me the baby. Look, I don't intend to jump off the deep end with you. Why don't we forget it?"

"If I tell you to get lost, to stay away from me, you will?" She asked dubiously as he carried the baby over to table where he'd set up his supplies and laid the baby on it.

"Well… I'd try to change your mind." Keeping one hand on the baby's belly, he flipped over the diaper package to read the instructions. He picked up the diaper he'd already laid out, but he was having trouble opening it with one hand while keeping the other on the squirming baby.

Bronwyn put her hand on Julia to keep her in place.

"Thanks," he told her, still intent on the diagram. "Unfold the diaper like so… plastic side out—well, at least I got that much right… oh, I see where I went wrong. I tried to put it on her backwards. It goes *this* way."

Bronwyn refused to be diverted. "Change my mind? You'll interpret anything I do as meaning I return your feelings."

He was silent while he ripped the duct tape from the baby's diaper and pulled it from beneath her. Bronwyn took it, folded it in on itself, and put it in a garbage bag. She opened the baby wipes and handed him one.

He used it and held out a hand for another. "Do you always foresee this many problems anytime a man acts interested?" he asked.

"Don't make this about me. But just for the record, the fact that you have to ask proves you don't even know me—and I'd say having your baby qualifies as a little more than 'interested.'"

He sighed. "Look. I know you're not in love with me. I don't expect you to be. Yet. I won't push you any faster than you want to go."

"You're already going faster than I want to."

"Okay." Cleansing done, he pulled the diaper between Julia's kicking legs. "I can go slower. Give me a time frame. Are we talking a few days? A week?"

"For what? To fall in love? I might not be in love in a couple of days or a week, either. I probably won't—I mean I won't be."

He pulled the backing from the sticky tab and applied it with surgical accuracy. "Right, but in a week or two you'll know if you like me. You'll know if you ever want to see me again. I'll make you a deal. At the end of thirty days, if you tell me to go away and not bother you again, I will."

"Don't get your hopes up. There's nothing between us, and there's not going to be."

He pulled the backing off the other sticky tab and carefully positioned it to match the first one he'd placed. "Don't lie." His deep voice held a bite. "The attraction is there. You felt it when you kissed me."

"I didn't mean *that*. Look, no offense. I can't see the point of starting anything when there's no chance it will go anywhere."

Julia began to fuss and squirm in earnest, impatient to be let up. Garth lifted her in his arms and straightened to face Bronwyn. He again wore his hard mask, but Bronwyn thought his eyes were a little narrowed. "I'll consider myself warned. But just for clarification, even if I did offer you my heart, I'd be out of the running?"

He seemed to finally be getting the message. Bronwyn sighed. She wished she felt better about it. "Right."

One corner of his mouth quirked cynically. "Are you going to give me the 'It's not you, it's me' speech?"

That did it. She didn't like rejecting people, but obviously he was not going to give up until she made herself abundantly clear. "No. I'll be perfectly honest. It *is* you. From the moment you showed up on my porch, you've lied, you evaded, and you've withheld. You've given me a miniscule amount of data on which to make an informed decision, and if I'm making a mistake about which parts are true, I could lose my license—that means my reputation and my livelihood. I don't *have* anything else."

Bronwyn hated that her voice was shaking. She swallowed a couple of times to get it under control. "This child needs my protection. I will work with you to care for her but don't think my willingness to let you come around means I want any deeper involvement with you. You are forty miles of bad road. There's nothing to do but get past it as fast and as safely as I can and, when I do, not look back."

Chapter 18

The general who wins the battle makes many calculations in the temple before the battle is fought.

—Sun Tzu, *The Art of War*

DRIVING TO BRONWYN'S HOUSE THE NEXT MORNING, Garth felt good. Cheerful. Something he hadn't felt in a long time. A little surprising in the light of the overall challenges he faced.

Yesterday all his assumptions had crumbled. Nothing was as it seemed. Dark possibilities had assailed him, one after the other. Someone hadn't wanted him asking questions or recounting his version of what had happened in Afghanistan. Someone, if MacMurtry could be believed, who was willing to let him and all his men be killed.

Bad as the news was, it was better than the frustration of spinning his wheels. He had a place to start. And since yesterday he had an even bigger problem: If the truth about the baby's origins got out, he could wind up in Leavenworth. To top it all off, showing up with a baby had put him behind with Bronwyn even before he got started.

This morning he'd lifted the adult-sized fingerprints from the bottle and UPS'd them to a contact in San Diego. If the baby had been aboard just any plane, identifying the fingerprints would have been a long shot. She'd been on a spy plane, though, so there was a chance that the person who had put her aboard was in the system.

He'd also poured the few drops left of the bottle's contents into another container and sent it to an independent lab for analysis. When he'd seen how active Julia was once she began waking up, and how noisy, he'd questioned how she could have been quiet for the duration of a flight. Bronwyn thought Julia had been drugged, and he suspected she was right. He wanted to know, not because he wanted the evidence of a crime, but because he needed to know what kind of people he was dealing with.

For now, it was all he could do.

When he'd returned to his trailer last night, he'd pulled up the file he'd made about the qualifications a wife should have. He'd whistled under his breath as he'd run down the list. Bronwyn got a passing grade on fewer than fifty percent. If he didn't have the conviction way too deep to be questioned that she was the woman for him, she would be out of the running. He respected her ambition and dedication, but he had a hard time squaring her present goals with the goals she would need to be his wife. Since it was not possible that she wasn't his mate, her goals would have to change.

Nobody these days said an officer's wife had to jettison her career to support his, but reality trumped ideals of equality every time. Being married to someone in the military was hell on a spouse's career advancement. Instead of being able to strategize each job change as a step forward, frequent relocations forced non-military partners to take whatever was available or even to work outside their fields. While their civilian counterparts moved up in salary and responsibility, military spouses' resumes showed a lack of experience commensurate with their age and a series of entry-level jobs.

Bronwyn couldn't open a new office every time he was transferred. How she would practice medicine as his wife was a bridge they would have to cross when they came to it.

But he was getting ahead of himself. Yesterday, she had been sweeping in her rejection. She didn't want him in her life now and would be happy when he was gone. He had a lot of ground to make up.

This morning he had to start the process of courting Bronwyn.

Bronwyn woke to the sound of a baby laughing and cooing. A cold, wet dog nose snuffled at her neck. Supposedly, interns' excruciating schedules trained them to come awake instantly from a sound sleep. The training hadn't worked for her. She still needed a few minutes to detach the wisps of dreams that clung around her. She knew there was something odd about a baby being in bed with her, but since it seemed no odder or more unlikely than many of her dreams, it didn't bother her.

Mildred blew in her ear. "I'm awake, Mildred," she told the dog. "And you want to go out. Okay, I'll get up." Mildred, hearing the magic word, *okay*, raced to the door. Her heavy paws thundered down the long staircase. There was nothing to do but get up. Mildred would wait at the door for a minute or two, and if Bronwyn didn't come, she would be back.

Bronwyn pushed herself to a sitting position and managed to open her eyes. The uncurtained and far from clean windows let in misty light, making it hard to tell how late it was. The significance of the baby sounds finally occurred to her. Her heart almost stopped. She had a baby to look after. Fortunately the baby was waving her little hands and kicking her feet in apparent delight. She seemed to have come to no harm, but Bronwyn was stabbed hard by guilt that checking the baby hadn't been her first thought.

She patted the round little belly. "Oh, look at you. At least one of us wakes up ready to deal with the day."

Knowing she would be sleepwalking for the first half hour in the morning, Bronwyn depended on inflexible routine to get her through the ordeal of waking up. She laid out her clothes the night before. She set her keys, shoes, and pocketbook in front of the front door. She set the coffee maker to come on automatically and even put a clean cup beside it. She had done none of that last night. She'd insisted Garth leave and had taken herself and the baby straight to bed.

Now, with none of her props in place, she felt like she was swimming through molasses as she picked up the baby and padded barefoot downstairs. In the hall her bare toes encountered a pool of water. Mildred was one of the most trustworthy dogs—holding it no matter what. All the changes going on must have upset her schedule. Bronwyn found a towel that had somehow made its way to the balustrade and wiped up the puddle.

She reached the kitchen. The back door was standing open, a hot bar of yellow sunlight gilding the all-too-apparent dust on the wooden floor. Mildred!

Bronwyn couldn't imagine how she'd gotten the door open. "Mildred," she called, panicked. The yard wasn't fenced, and Mildred was fast.

"I'm watching her." Garth's gravelly voice came from the porch. His masculine shape moved into the light. Bronwyn's breath caught. Her heart skipped several beats.

Elongated by the shadow that flowed across the floor to cover her bare toes, and with his burnished skin edged in gold, he could have been a power figure from a dream, full of portent, the meaning of his message always elusive.

"Come out," he urged. "It's a beautiful morning. Cool."

Her eyes not really open yet, Bronwyn let him draw her outside. The damp chill of the boards under her bare feet made her toes curl. She squinted up at Garth. "Are you supposed to be here?"

"Poor baby." He drew her into his arms. "Morning just isn't your time, is it?"

He threaded his fingers into her hair and massaged her scalp with deep, firm strokes while he ran his other hand up and down her back. She thought he might have pressed kisses to the top of her head. She wasn't sure. She laid her head on his chest and listened to the heavy, slow *da-dum* of his heartbeat and inhaled his wonderful morning man-smell of spicy shaving soap and fresh clothes and masculine musk.

In the cool morning air his heat was comforting. A person might think all the stroking and soothing and warmth would send her back to sleep, but in a minute or two, it was apparent the man knew what he was doing. By degrees she became more alert, more together. Her brain sped up. Her thoughts took on form and order.

With the old brain functioning again, she knew she couldn't continue to stand there, not when her waking-up body wanted to rub itself against his, not when she longed to tip her head back and offer open lips for his kiss. Besides, the baby made a little grunt of impatience, and now that she thought about it, Bronwyn believed that smell indicated the need for a fresh diaper.

She pulled away, and he instantly let her go. Somehow he had transferred the baby to his own arm. "Um, thank you," she mumbled, not sure why she said it, just feeling somehow as if thanks were called for.

"Anytime."

Bronwyn held out her arms. "I'll take her now. She needs changing. And feeding."

"I've got her. Take a minute to have a cup of coffee and get your eyes open." He whistled to the dog, then turned Bronwyn and pushed her gently through the doorway.

Standing at the chipped yellow kitchen counter, Bronwyn sipped her coffee. The coffee was finishing the job of bringing her to full consciousness. As it did, all the things she had planned for today crowded her mind. "What time is it?" she asked in alarm. "A building contractor is supposed to be here at nine."

Garth glanced at a watch with enough dials and functions to land a spacecraft on Mars. "Oh-seven-hundred." He carried Julia over to the breakfast table where changing supplies had been left. "What do you need a contractor for? Are you planning to live here permanently? It will take a lot of work to make this place habitable."

She heard the slight emphasis on the word *here*, the trace of incredulity in his voice. After less than twenty-four hours in the house, she already knew it needed more than a thorough cleaning and a coat of paint. In its present incarnation, the house *wasn't* much to look at; nevertheless, it hurt her feelings to hear it criticized. She stiffened.

"I want to make it not just habitable. I want the make the front part of the house into an office suite. Doctors for hundreds of years had had their offices in their homes. I can, too."

And despite her discomfort with the house's strangeness, seeing Julia all rosy and babbling noisily this morning was the confirmation Bronwyn needed that she would be able to care for patients in this place and see them not just in crisis but all the way through their crisis.

He gave the room another noncommittal once-over. "A medical office, too. That will be a tall order."

The complete transformation she had in mind was a long-term project that could only be undertaken when the grant money came through, but who was he to think he had a right to an opinion about her future? And what was he doing here anyway? She'd made it clear last night that the baby was staying with her—and he wasn't.

"And what, exactly, are you doing here?"

"Right now, I'm diapering a baby," he answered blandly, deliberately misunderstanding the nature of her question. "I got on the Net this morning to research baby care. Picked up several good tips. Observe. I've put a clean diaper under her before taking the dirty one off. I also realized there were a few more supplies you were going to need, so I picked them up."

"How did you get in?"

"Trust me, it wasn't hard. I also stopped at a hardware store. I got new locks for the front and rear doors. I'm going to put a stop to them opening at will."

"Are you saying you broke in?"

"Let's say I let myself in."

"What makes you think entering my house without permission is acceptable—now or ever?"

He turned to look at her, black brows drawn together in surprise. Even so, he kept one hand on the baby, she noted.

"You said she had to stay here, so she does, but the fact that she is still my responsibility is all the permission I need. I'm not going to dump this baby on you and walk away. Sweetheart, you're a whole lot safer with me in this house than out of it. If that offends you, get over it."

As if issuing a fiat was all it took to secure her acceptance, he resumed his conversational tone. "I needed to get here before breakfast. The Internet articles said Julia should be eating solid food in addition to formula, so at the grocery I picked up some jars of baby food, and I wasn't sure what you had to eat, so I bought eggs and bacon, English muffins, and a honeydew melon."

Against her will, Bronwyn felt laughter at his blithe justification bubbling in her chest. "You broke into the house so you could feed us breakfast?"

Garth grinned. "Breakfast is the most important meal of the day."

———

The only one who enjoyed Julia's breakfast was Mildred. Not Julia. Not Bronwyn.

This morning, rehydrated, the aftereffects of sedation out of her system, Julia was a different child. In the light her eyes were neither blue nor gray. They were slate, and sparkling with intelligence and curiosity, they lighted on everything.

Her miniature, long-fingered hands picked up anything within her reach, and whatever she picked up went into her mouth. She had preferences, and she made them known. Her biggest preference was for movement.

As long as she was being carried, she was content to be held, but otherwise, she wanted to move. She squirmed; she rolled; she twisted. She did not want to be held on a lap to be fed. She squealed and made faces and turned her head away from the spoon. She either grabbed for the spoon or batted it away. Grayish blobs of baby cereal and yellowish smears of strained peaches clung unappetizingly to the dandelion fluff of her hair, her fingers, her toes, and everything in between.

As for Bronwyn, her left hand ached from trying to hang on to Julia and keep her oriented toward the business end of the spoon. She didn't look any better than Julia. Her light green T-shirt was smeared; her hands were just as sticky as Julia's; and she could have sworn that she had goo in her hair, too.

Mildred alone was pleased. She had thought snapping at flying gobs of baby food was a great way to start the morning. She sniffed the chipped paint of a cabinet door for any splats she might have missed.

"Let me take her." Garth lifted Julia from Bronwyn's lap. "You go get cleaned up."

"That's right. I almost forgot! I've got a contractor coming."

"About that. I wish you would cancel. A contractor will have workmen coming and going. One guy in droopy jeans and a tool belt looks like any other. There'll be no way to secure the area."

"Secure what area? What do you think they're going to do? The house needs renovation, but I want a contractor to look at the roof, too. I found water on the floor this morning. I need to get as much done as possible before I start back to work."

He dodged a baby hand reaching for his mouth. "It's just a few days. I just don't want you to be letting men you don't know into the house. Tell you what. Let me look at the roof. I can begin on the basic repairs. You won't lose time, and it will probably save you a bundle, too."

He sat Julia in one side of the double sink while he let the water run warm in the other side. While it did, he pulled the blue-and-orange-striped shirt over her head.

"She needs a bath, too."

"I'm giving her one. Okay, kid, off with the diaper." He steadied her with one big, brown hand that spanned her torso while he ripped the tabs. He checked the temperature of the water. He swung the faucet over, letting the stream of water land beside her.

"Alley-oop!" He balanced her on her tummy on his forearm, neatly clasping her legs with his spread fingers. Steadying her with his other hand on her back, he held her bottom under the running water.

"I don't think that's how you bathe a baby."

"It worked last night."

"She's a lot more active today."

Bronwyn wished she would shut up. The size and strength of his hands made his hold secure, if unconventional. There was just something unsettling about those big, strong, brown, long-fingered hands on that little, soft, pink baby. Something that made her lungs clench and fight her attempts to get a really deep breath.

"Julia likes it."

Yes, she seemed to. She was laughing and wiggling. The feeling in Bronwyn's chest tightened. He turned Julia back upright and sat her in the sink. She splashed both tiny hands down in the quarter-inch of water and chortled loudly. Keeping both hands on the baby, he swiveled at the waist to look at Bronwyn. "I've got this. Go get dressed."

Bronwyn looked out the window she was cleaning in the family room to see her friend JJ emerging from a hunter green Land Rover. She hit the off button on her boom box and stopped Chris Young's lament that he wasn't the man he wanted to be in mid-syllable. She ran through the kitchen, remembered Julia, clad in diaper and a shirt that said, "I'm sunshine," scooped her up, and raced down the dark hall.

"JJ!" Bronwyn let the screen door slam behind her.

JJ waved. She wore cream slacks with a jacket woven in bright pinks and oranges. Her black-coffee, shoulder-length hair gleamed in the noon sunlight. She strode to the porch with her signature long-legged, hip-swinging style. "So this is the baby!" JJ stooped down to peer into Julia's face. "Hi, Little One!"

Instead of smiling as she always did when Bronwyn, Garth, and even Mildred came into her line of sight, Julia mewed in protest and hid her face against Bronwyn's shoulder.

The oddest combination of feelings washed over

Bronwyn. A proprietary wish that Julia "showed well" by acting engaging; surprise that Julia suddenly reacted to strangers since she seemed to trust Garth, Bronwyn, and even Mildred without reservation; and the funniest, tenderest clutch in the vicinity of her throat that Julia had turned to her for protection and security.

JJ straightened. "She's a little shy, isn't she?"

"She'll be all right once she gets to know you." Bronwyn hoped she was telling the truth. And, in fact, although Julia still clung, she was already stealing peeks at JJ. "Anyway, *I'm* thrilled to see you. I didn't expect you to bring the car seat yourself!"

JJ laughed. "I wasn't going to send someone else when I wanted to see you myself. Guess who I brought with me?"

Bronwyn didn't have to guess. She could see for herself the medium-height man who had come up behind JJ. A large box with a picture of an infant car seat was balanced on one broad shoulder and packages under the other.

"Her pack mule," David supplied, dropping the packages and lowering the box to the floor. He gave Bronwyn a gentle one-armed hug while cleverly (Bronwyn thought) pretending not to notice Julia. "How are you doing?"

Bronwyn had been prepared to tolerate the husband JJ had married in such a hurry last Thanksgiving, even if she had doubts about the character of a man who would marry her friend for her money. She'd met his younger brothers and sisters at their wedding, though, and had discovered he came from a medical family as she did. They'd been equally unsure of JJ and had thought that by marrying her he was making too large a sacrifice.

Bronwyn no longer doubted that they were deeply in love and that David was good for JJ. She smiled and laughed now in a lighthearted way that she hadn't since they were undergrads. At the same time, there was a new warmth and earthiness about her.

As for David, he appeared to have recovered from his injuries. The scars across his cheek had faded to become part of the landscape of his face. He was the most handsome man Bronwyn had ever seen.

"When he heard Garth was here," JJ informed her, "he decided to ride along."

"Where is he?" David asked.

"On the roof."

"Why the roof?"

"There was water on the hall floor this morning. We couldn't tell where it came from. And after the bad storms last night, he thought he should check it."

"What's all this?" Bronwyn waved at the bags David had unceremoniously deposited on the still-dusty hall floor.

"Oh, a former employee has opened a baby consignment shop," JJ answered airily. "You needed baby things, and she needed customers. It was too good an opportunity to pass up." As head of Carruthers' Cars, JJ supported several charities, but few people knew how generous she really was—how she looked for opportunities to help build other businesses as she had built hers. "I can't wait to try some of these clothes on her. There was the most adorable hat—I had to get it—and wait until you see the purple sneakers."

"You can't turn her into a fashionista!" Bronwyn laughingly protested. "She's not even a year old."

"A girl is never too young to get dressed up." JJ's green eyes looked askance at Bronwyn's less-than-pristine green scrubs top over shorts. "And she's never too grown either, my friend. You have a professional image to project. Scrubs are not going to cut it. You're going to have to buy some decent clothes. And it's my job as your friend to tell you so."

"You want me to bring in the rest of the stuff now?" David interrupted.

Bronwyn seized on the distraction, since JJ had the totally unfair advantage of being right. She turned to JJ. "What 'stuff'? There's more?"

"A crib—high chair—playpen," David answered. "Oh, and a swing. Really cool."

"JJ, you shouldn't have. I don't know how long I'll have her."

"So, when you're done with the things, we take them back to the consignment shop and the owner gets to sell them again. Everybody wins." JJ read the consternation Bronwyn was sure was on her face and sobered. "When I say everyone wins, I include myself. I'm so glad you're here—I need you. I only wish I had thought of a way to bring you to North Carolina myself. I will do anything to smooth your path so that you'll stay. If that includes some baby things… hey, it doesn't get much easier."

"The rest of the stuff?" David reminded them he was waiting for a decision.

Bronwyn swept up the hair that had slipped from her ponytail, undid the rubber band, and re-secured the whole while she thought. "Upstairs, I guess. But I haven't picked out a room for her. And, as you can see, everything is dusty. And there's moving mess everywhere."

David smiled kindly. "Feeling a little overwhelmed, are we?"

"All my plans have been torn up, and I haven't had time to make any new ones."

"We thought you could use some help," JJ told her. "We came bearing brooms and mops in addition to baby things—and we have work clothes to change into. Let David and me help you clean and sort things into some order."

"I didn't expect—"

"If Graziano's here, there's nothing to do but make him work." Garth's deep voice came from the top of the stairs a moment before he appeared. Bronwyn had a feeling he'd been there for some time, listening.

Garth and David did that thumb-grab, handshake-hug, back-thump thing men friends do. Garth kissed JJ chastely on the cheek.

"Spill!" JJ demanded. "The men are off doing manly things but no telling for how long."

Bronwyn checked on Julia before answering. Bronwyn's first act this morning had been to mop the brick-patterned vinyl floor of the addition off the kitchen so she could set Julia down on it. Julia wasn't crawling on all fours yet, but using a sort of commando belly slide, she could travel quite a distance. Mildred, who had lost none of her fascination for the baby, lay on her belly also, watching attentively from the respectful distance Bronwyn had established. "I really can't tell you anymore about Julia than I already have. Just, I think I'm doing the right thing."

"*That's* not what I'm talking about. You, Garth. I want every word, every look, from the moment he got here."

"What do you mean? It's not like that."

JJ gave her an exasperated look. "It's exactly like that. I saw his face when he looked at you. He's smitten."

Bronwyn felt her cheeks get red. "Whatever notions he has, he can get over them. No way am I going there."

JJ turned from the cabinet she was wiping out to send Bronwyn a puzzled look. "I know you were devastated by Troy's death, but I thought you were moving on. Coming here is part of that, letting go of the memories associated with him. You said you were ready for another relationship if the right man came along."

"*Right* man, I said. He isn't."

"No chemistry? Are you sure, because it looked like to me…"

"There's chemistry. It's the kind of man he is."

JJ fisted her hands on the khaki shorts she'd changed into. "What did he do?" she demanded dangerously, ready to spring to Bronwyn's defense.

What had he done? He'd gone out on a limb for a baby when anyone would have said the limits of his responsibility would be to drop her off at a police station or an emergency room. He had been kind and willing to care for others. To get involved. She didn't believe he'd had any part in whatever had separated Julia from her parents, and she did believe he was doing all in his power to restore her to them.

He'd kissed her. He had taken advantage of a moment when her hands were occupied and she couldn't get away from him, which was bad. And it had been the most blatantly carnal, and the most sweetly sensual kiss

she'd ever known, which, let's face it, was also bad—
since her life was complicated enough—but she hoped
he would do it again.

"Nothing," she told JJ. "He reminds me of Troy,
that's all. And not in a good way."

"He doesn't look a bit like him."

Bronwyn made herself consciously remember what
Troy had looked like, something that had become harder.
When the memory had first begun to fade, she'd been
horrified, but after a while she had accepted that he was
receding into her past. She had accepted that a picture
of him no longer evoked *him*, but only memories of the
past. "No. You're right."

"Then what are you talking about?"

Bronwyn didn't know how to put it into words. It was
something she sensed, a restlessness, a hyperawareness,
a feeling that he was always strategizing several steps
ahead. She shrugged.

"Do you want to know what I think?"

Bronwyn and JJ got along because, even though
they were very different, both were confident, assertive
women. Each respected the other's ability to look after
herself and not let herself be overwhelmed by the other's
strength. For both, it was always such a relief to be with
someone they didn't have to hold back with. JJ was a
powerhouse of determination and, once set on course,
not easily deterred. Bronwyn grinned. "No?"

"I'm going to tell you anyway. I think you covered
up and pushed down your feelings for so long, you were
almost as dead as Troy. I think you've become afraid of
feeling anything at all."

Bronwyn heard deep male voices and then the thud

of heavy footfalls on the porch. "They're coming. We'll talk about it later."

"Yes, we will."

———

"It's hot up on the roof." Garth took the ice water pitcher from the fridge. He poured two glasses and handed one to David. "We don't see any shingles missing or any sign that water is coming in through the attic. The water must have come from somewhere besides the roof."

"What does that mean?" Bronwyn wanted to know.

"We'll just have to keep an eye on it. In a building, where you see the water can be a long way from its source. In the meantime, why don't you choose a room for Julia? Once it's cleaned, we'll have a place to put her stuff, which will make the rest of the house easier to square away."

Bronwyn heard a fussy "anh-anh-anh" from the family room and went to retrieve Julia from a tight space between two boxes. She'd crawled in, but she couldn't put things in reverse and crawl out.

"Good thinking." Bronwyn nuzzled the baby's sweet neck, before setting her back down in a clear space. "Once the crib is assembled we'll have a safe place to put *her*—which will also make the rest of the house easier to deal with."

Chapter 19

Go with the flow. Blend in.

—The Moscow Rules

"This is the best choice," JJ, in full executive mode, pronounced when all the upstairs rooms had been looked into. "It's small, and see the shelves? Plenty of storage. It's probably been a baby's room at some time, or maybe a sewing room. That oak tree outside will be fully leafed out in a couple of weeks, so the room will be shaded in the afternoon."

Julia probably wouldn't be here in a couple of weeks. Bronwyn didn't want to think about that. When she was a little girl, she used to dream nightly of going out and finding sick and wounded people and animals and bringing them home to care for them and heal them. The dreams had been part of how she had known she was destined to be a doctor. But wanting to keep Julia and care for her was different. Julia was well. And still Bronwyn wouldn't want to let her go. She pulled her mind from that path.

"I'm not sure. Yesterday, the door was stuck closed," she told them. "What if it stuck with Julia on one side and me on the other?"

David swung the door on its hinges. "It's fine now."

"It's probably warped," Garth added. "If it shows signs of sticking again, I'll plane it down a little."

They were all standing around looking at her, including Julia, who was being carried by Garth, and Mildred, who insisted on being in on the decision.

Bronwyn shook her head. "Even with the door fixed, I won't be comfortable with her so far away. I'm not used to listening for a baby—and I might not know what to listen for. I hear odd things all the time in this house. I'd either be racing up here every few minutes, or I'd be on edge, afraid I was ignoring noises when I shouldn't."

JJ's husband smiled his engaging, teasing smile. "You 'hear things'? What? Don't tell me you have a ghost!"

"No! I am *not* telling you that."

"You're sure?" David glanced around the room with renewed interest. "I think having a ghost might be kind of cool."

She tried a chilling look. "Yes, I'm sure."

Davy, unfortunately, was irrepressible. "Don't tell me you're scared of ghosts," he taunted, full of mischief.

"Of course not. There's no such thing."

Realizing she was not amused, David grew earnest. "I grew up believing in an afterlife. We have lots of stories in my family about people who have passed coming back to communicate. The thought of spirits hanging around a place doesn't seem impossible to me."

"I'd have to see a lot of proof to believe it," Garth put in.

"So would I," Davy acknowledged. "But if there's one thing SEAL training teaches you, it's not to assume you—or the enemy—can't do something just because it's impossible."

"Right." Garth smiled at his friend with gentle affection. "Even coming back from the dead."

The smile changed Garth's face so utterly that Bronwyn was momentarily transfixed. She had already begun to guess that the hard, stiff look he frequently wore was a mask. For a nanosecond, she had a glimpse of who he might be underneath it.

When Garth resumed his customary expression, she felt irritated, out of sorts. "Would you stop with the talk about ghosts?" she snapped. "If you want to know the truth, having a bunch of unexplained phenomena pisses me off. I have all I can do to renovate this place and turn it into a home office with living quarters upstairs. I don't need a great big mystery. I'm looking for a simpler life."

Three pairs of adult eyes stared at her in stupefaction.

JJ put everyone's amazement into words. "You think starting a medical practice where one hasn't succeeded for thirty years (and you're going to have to work another job in an ER to support it) while rehabbing a house that is going to take a lot of work is *simpler*?"

"Okay. Maybe 'simpler' isn't the word. It's that I'm new here. I don't want to begin by having to explain the inexplicable. First impressions matter, and I don't want any suggestion of woo-woo associated with me or this house." She squeezed her eyes closed in exasperation. "I don't even want to joke about it! Do you know how many people will assume I'm incompetent if word gets out that I'm hearing ghosts?"

JJ gave her a look of narrow-eyed assessment. "Would *you* think you were incompetent if you heard ghosts?"

Bronwyn sidestepped. "It just makes me nervous, that's all. Because I don't know what's causing it. I hate wondering if I'm imagining things."

JJ nodded, satisfied for the moment. "Back to problem solving. If you're worried about hearing Julia, how about one of those baby monitors?"

Garth's arctic-blue eyes lit up. "Now that you've given me the idea, JJ, I can do better than that!" He unlatched Julia's hand from his hair and propped her on a hip. "How about a webcam, Bronny? I'll put one where the crib and anything approaching it will be covered. Open your laptop, and you'll be able to see and hear her anywhere you are. Will that give you peace of mind?"

Bronny? No one as diminutive as Bronwyn needed to be called by a diminutive nickname too. It was hard enough for her to be taken seriously. The time to nip the nickname was now… but there was something about a man who wanted to give her *peace of mind*. She nodded slowly. "That will work."

"Then should we bring the crib up here and start setting it up?" David looked to Garth—not to her—for direction, Bronwyn noted.

And Garth answered. "Looks like we have a baby's room."

—◦◦◦—

"Has Bronwyn got tools? The crib's going to need reassembly," Davy told Garth, now that the upstairs baby's room had been selected. "And who knows whether all the hardware is still with it? I didn't check."

"No problem. I brought my tool belt with me this morning, and I should have anything else we need in the utility box in my truck."

"Tool belt, huh?" Davy grinned and cocked an eyebrow.

The brow didn't go up the same as it used to, but Garth had to admit that even with the scars, Davy was still one good-looking dude. He was glad Davy was taken. Garth punched Davy's biceps. "Shut up."

—∿∿—

"Do you know a guy named Renfro?" Garth asked after he and Davy had spent a few minutes catching up and Garth had related the whole story of how he found the baby. He didn't think Renfro knew any more about the baby than anyone else had—MacMurtry, who had been there to pick him up, hadn't been aware. But Renfro was the only missing piece.

Filling Davy in was a field-command decision that Garth was comfortable with. Though Davy wasn't officially "read in" on all Coastal Air did, he had a high security clearance. Garth needed input, and for sure, he trusted Davy more than anyone he currently worked with. Davy, at least, wasn't one of the perpetrators. Typical of Davy, he hadn't asked if Garth knew what he was doing. Garth had missed Davy, and he hadn't known how much until he saw him.

He hadn't known Davy that long before the injuries that had sidelined them both. Davy had joined Garth's platoon in Afghanistan halfway through their deployment, replacing their former hospital corpsman. The mix that makes a SEAL platoon gel is as hard to quantify as an alchemist's formula, but everyone recognized that when Davy came, some magical ingredient had been added. The little band of sixteen men that Garth commanded went from very good to extraordinary.

Davy had something—in addition to sheer

masculine beauty that made women flutter and even heterosexual men's heads turn. He had a joie de vivre, a shining élan that the dirt and darkness of battle didn't cling to.

"You think Renfro's a SEAL?" Davy broke in on Garth's ruminations.

"Could be." Asking if Davy knew Renfro wasn't quite the shot in the dark it might have seemed. The SEALs were a fairly small group, a tight brotherhood, and reputations preceded them.

"Doesn't ring a bell. Want me to ask around?"

"Better to just keep your eyes and ears open. This is some bad juju. You are better off out of it."

"Okay, but I don't know how much I'll hear. I'm pretty out of touch. These days, I take every TDY to Lejeune I can get. I'm living right or something. I get every one I put in for."

"Do you see any of the guys from the platoon I led in Afghanistan?"

Davy shook his head. "All reassigned."

It was possible that all had shipped off somewhere in the intervening months. He and Davy had been the only ones severely wounded. But coupled with someone's willingness to send Davy off base any time he asked, it fit with what MacMurtry had implied: someone wanted anyone who knew how the ambush had gone down to be far, far away.

"Have you ever remembered any of what happened that day?" Davy would know which day he meant.

"Nah. The docs say that with my kind of head injury, I most likely never will." In other words, Davy wouldn't be able to testify in an investigation—which might explain why he alone was still in Little Creek, even part of the time. "Sometimes I have dreams that seem to be about that day, but you know how dreams are. They don't make a lot of sense. JJ thinks I'm dreaming about a near-death experience."

Every sense Garth had went on high alert, but he kept his tone casual. "Near-death experience? Do you believe in those?"

Davy shrugged. "What's to believe? It happens. You remember 'Do-Lord' Dulaude—you went to his wedding? He's interested in that kind of thing. And speaking of him, you know, you should ask him to keep his ears open for you."

"Do-Lord?" Davy and Do-Lord had served together on Davy's first Afghanistan tour. Garth didn't really know Do-Lord. He'd attended the wedding only because Davy had wanted to go and was still restricted from driving. "I thought he retired."

"Officially, he did. But he's still working for the navy. He sold 'em on letting him research ESP in the Teams."

Garth snorted. "He's not a flake, is he?"

"Nah. He's not sitting in a locked rooms staring into a crystal ball. He's going with teams on operations, observing. Trying to learn if ESP can be taught. Gotta admit, it could save a lot of lives. Word is, his research has support from way high up. I've even heard Admiral Stephenson had a hand in getting him the contract. More likely, though, it was that senator— what's his name?"

"Calhoun."

"Right—Calhoun was at his wedding. Supposedly, it's Do-Lord's wife who is some kind of kin to the

senator, but if you ask me, there's more to that association than meets the eye."

Interesting. But Garth ignored the temptation to gossip. "So how can Do-Lord help me?"

"He goes everywhere. And can talk to anyone, any
rank. If your man Renfro is a SEAL and there's scuttle-
butt to be picked up, Do-Lord can do it. Let me tell him
why you're looking."

"Hold that side of the crib up, will you, while I get this
screw positioned," Garth told Davy. He lifted the cordless screwdriver.

When the screw was in place, Garth sorted through
the pile of hardware for another the same size. "Listen,
there's something else I need to ask you."

"Shoot."

"You had a reputation with the ladies before you married JJ."

"Yeah?"

"I just wondered if you could give me any tips."

"What kind of tips?"

"Like... how to get a girl to like you." God, he
sounded like a teenager. Hell, he *felt* like a teenager.
Fortunately blushes didn't show under the dark tan of
his cheeks.

Over the side of the crib he was holding, Davy gave
Garth a puzzled look. "Tips on how to get laid?—you
don't need those. You do okay."

Garth shook his head, unable to elucidate.

"Someone you're serious about?" Davy hazarded.
"Are we talking about Bronwyn?"

"Yeah."

"Uh-oh. This is not good. Bronwyn's messed up, man."

Garth's self-consciousness vanished. Bronwyn seemed fine to him. "Messed up, how?" he demanded.

"She was engaged to this guy, a cop. He got killed in the line of duty. JJ says she's not over it yet."

"Killed recently?"

"About a year ago, I guess."

Garth relaxed. He positioned the screwdriver and pressed the switch. When he'd set the screw, he brushed away a trace of sawdust with his thumb. "So he's out of the picture. Tough for him. Good for me."

"Oh, boy!" Davy's brown eyes glittered with mischief. "Darth Vader's in love. Planning to show her your light saber, are you? *Wahhm-wahhmm!*" He made light saber noises in time with crudely explicit gyrations.

"Cut the crap."

Davy's brown eyes widened in surprise, although they continued to twinkle. "You're serious. I mean, I saw the tool belt, but you're *serious*."

"What does that mean?" Garth growled dangerously. What was so hard to believe?

"I just never expected to see it." Davy laughed. "Darth Vader head over heels!"

Garth felt his face go tight. "I have a part-titanium thigh bone, but I have still a heart."

Doc came around to Garth's side of the crib and squeezed his shoulder, contrite. "I know you do," he said softly. "Sorry." He knelt beside Garth and started sorting screws. "Okay, you know the part about getting clean, right? Women have a much more discriminating sense of smell than men do."

Garth worked on not being insulted by such elementary instruction. He'd asked for advice. Now he had to listen to it. "Yeah."

Except he'd shown up at her house yesterday in clothes dirty and sweaty from a day of working on planes in the heat. And if that weren't enough, he'd come back after a dip in eau de ditch water. No wonder kissing him wasn't an experience she wanted to repeat.

Today he'd shown up showered and shaved but still in work clothes. She was used to dealing with professional men, and he'd let her think he was a maintenance worker at Coastal Air. All right, he couldn't reveal his real job, but he could show her that he cleaned up good.

"And I know the navy sent you to charm school," Davy continued. He referred to the required course in etiquette and manners that was part of officer training. "You know your manners. You want to use 'em. Treat her like a lady."

Had he opened a door for her or held a chair? Had he even said "please" or "thank you"? No, he'd let her think she was so negligible that he didn't even remember meeting her before. And instead of bringing her flowers this morning, he'd brought her a doorknob. All right, he would fix that, too.

"Manners. Check. But can't you give me a little more? You had the reputation as the biggest lady-killer in the Special Operations Command. Tell me what you used to do."

Davy stared at the ceiling for a minute, deep in thought. "Well, once you have the basics, it's mostly about making her feel good. If she accepts feeling good from you, you've probably got a chance."

"A chance?" She'd let him rub her back for a minute this morning. She hadn't stiffened up or pulled away.

"To make it with her. Some girls are impervious. Even yours truly didn't score every time. You might as well find out in the beginning if this girl will let you make her feel good. Back in the day, I always made eye contact and smiled. You know, let her know she was attractive. A lot of it is in the smile. Smile for me."

Garth spread his lips. He didn't have an attractive social smile, and he knew it. Until now, he hadn't felt its lack.

Davy recoiled. "Okay. That's not good. We need to try something else. How about being her knight?"

"You mean like rescuing her from something? She thinks she's rescuing me." He rubbed the back of his neck to ease the ache. "She *is* rescuing me. Well, not me. She's rescuing Julia, but it's my fault. She hasn't complained once about the extra work and time the baby is taking, even though a child to care for is the last thing she needs right now. Me? She thinks I'm more trouble than I'm worth."

"She told you that?"

"Yeah."

Davy clapped him on the shoulder then squeezed it in wordless sympathy. He went back to sorting screws. After a while he said, "You don't make her nervous, do you? They might enjoy looking at hunks, but some women are leery of big, muscular men up close and personal. And you don't come across as the Jolly Green Giant, you know. They don't call you Darth Vader for nothing."

Garth knew what Doc was talking about. His effect on women—except for those who liked his "dark aura" (and they came on to *him*)—was the reason he had so little experience with actual courtship.

"She seems okay with it." That was one of the best things. Even when he'd inadvertently startled her, her response had been, "I've had it with hulking figures!" He smiled into the distance at the memory.

When his eyes came back to Davy's, he was startled at the equal parts sympathetic and surprised grin on his friend's face. "What?"

Davy's chest shook with silent laughter. "Nothing. Changing the subject, I'm glad you finally surfaced. There's something else I want to talk to you about."

"Shoot."

"JJ wants us to have another wedding ceremony. This time with lots of lead time and everyone we know invited. She's worked on it for months, and we've sent out the invitations. I wanted to ask you to be my best man again, but now I don't know if I should—what with the virus that's going around and all. Your resistance is way low."

Garth distrusted the twinkle in Davy's eyes. "What virus?"

"The guys say there's a virus in the NC water that makes a man susceptible to marriage. It gets spread at SEAL weddings. Attend a SEAL wedding in NC, and you're likely to find yourself married within a year."

Garth's belly laugh rang loudly in the sparsely furnished room. He surprised himself—but, damn, it felt good to find something laugh-out-loud funny. "You mean that—what would you call it?—that *urban legend* is really making the rounds? MacMurtry tried to give me some song and dance about it, but I didn't believe him. I thought he was just trying to chap my ass."

"I don't know what MacMurtry was up to, but the story's true. Some guys say no way are they going to any weddings."

SEALs believed in luck, mostly bad, and had a thousand sayings about the predictability of *un*predictability and the necessity to guard against it. They trusted nothing to luck, and yet there was no denying that in the chaos of battle, sheer dumb luck was sometimes why one man survived and another man died.

It was only human to seek ways to assert control over a force so important and so whimsical. SEALs carefully noted coincidences, no matter how farfetched any causal relationship might seem. As a result, most SEALs had a pair of lucky socks or a little ritual they performed at the start of an operation. They habitually sought out some things and avoided others. No matter how irrational their quirkiness was, in the end, the sliver of confidence that the superstition gave them could make all the difference.

"Look at it this way," Davy went on. "I was at Jax Graham's wedding, and Do-Lord's. Based on *my* experience," he warned, "if you're disinclined to marry, weddings might be something to be wary of." His eyes still twinkled, but Garth could tell that even if Davy didn't believe the superstitious nonsense, he didn't completely discount it.

"Are all wedding guests susceptible," Garth asked, thinking he knew someone else who had been a guest at SEAL nuptials, "or just SEALs?"

"The theory is, something about Jax's wedding caused a mutation and now it attacks primarily SEALs. But come to think of it, it could be hitting women as hard as men. JJ went to two SEAL weddings, too. The first exposure didn't take. But the second time? That did it. Her fate was *SEALed*."

Garth grinned in acknowledgment of Davy's pun while he pursued the implications. "Bronwyn has already been to one SEAL wedding."

"True—which might double the odds against you."

"Or it might double them in my favor. If there is a virus, I've already caught it. All I can do now is expose Bronwyn as many times as necessary."

"Yep. You've got it bad all right." Davy punched Garth on the arm. "Welcome to the club."

Chapter 20

AROUND NOON, THE BABY WOKE UP FROM HER NAP IN her new, gently used crib, and the adults stopped for a lunch. While the men went into town for take-out plates of barbecue, hush puppies, and coleslaw, Bronwyn popped Julia into her high chair. From JJ's stash of baby clothes she selected a large bib for Julia and armed herself with a wet washcloth and a roll of paper towels.

"All right, Julia," Bronwyn told the baby, wiping drool from the little chin. "We have orange stuff—pumpkin, green stuff—that would be peas, and something that claims to be chicken and dumplings. Do you believe anyone really made chicken and dumplings, then ground it up and poured it in a jar?"

Julia screwed up her face and rubbed her dandelion-fluff hair.

"No? Neither do I. Julia hated what I fed her for breakfast," Bronwyn told JJ. "But I think she hated being held still more."

"Didn't go well, huh?"

"We both needed a bath afterward. What does that tell you?"

"Well, while you have another go at it, I think I'll make iced tea." JJ whipped some supersized tea bags from her tote and went to the sink to fill the kettle she had unearthed from a packing box earlier. "I brought tea because I knew you wouldn't have the right kind. Where's the sugar?"

Bronwyn twisted the cap from the jar of baby food. Julia opened her mouth in a four-toothed smile and happily slapped the high chair's plastic tray. "You know what this is, don't you?"

"Sugar," JJ prompted, opening cabinets.

"*You* unpacked it." Bronwyn dipped the spoon a quarter inch into the pumpkin. She'd learned this morning not to fill the spoon. Julia crowed and opened wide when she saw the spoon come toward her.

"The sugar's not where I put it." JJ opened a lower cabinet. "There it is, inside a pot. How did it get there?"

"Can I try feeding her?" JJ asked after she'd measured sugar into a pitcher and put the kettle on to boil. "I, um, might need the practice. David and I have decided to try to get pregnant."

"I thought you wanted to wait awhile."

"Who knows how long it will take? I know I want a child. I've decided I should get started."

Neither she nor Bronwyn had ever been particularly focused on a desire for babies, which made Bronwyn ask, "Does the timing have something to do with your grandfather's heart condition?"

"I wouldn't do it if I didn't really want a child, but yes, Lucas would be so happy to see a great-grandchild… he wants to know the family is continuing on."

"Are you afraid if you wait, he might not live to see it? Last night, you said he was about the same. Have you noticed a change?"

"No. It's just a feeling I have."

Bronwyn dipped the spoon in the mushed-up peas

and scraped it carefully on the rim of the jar before carrying it to Julia's mouth—another bit of baby technique she'd picked up. "When a patient's family tells me they 'have a feeling,'" she acknowledged thoughtfully, "I always listen. I'm glad you're not ignoring it." She looked up to see JJ's emerald eyes darken. "What?"

"What about *your* feelings?"

"JJ." Bronwyn rolled her eyes. "Are we back on Troy again? I'm not ignor—"

"I'm not talking about that. I'm talking about how you've tried to ignore who you are. You're a healer. When I saw you in that green dress Mary Cole put you in for my wedding, I realized you hadn't lost your talent. When you decided to come here, well, I thought you were going to let that part of you come out now."

"You mean that twaddle I used to spout when we were in college?" Bronwyn had never told anyone but JJ how and why she believed she had to be a doctor at such a young age—or why her parents had been aghast. "JJ, I was a kid, full of transcendental idealism, seeing things that weren't there."

"I liked that about you."

JJ's wistful, almost shy admission deeply surprised Bronwyn. Practical, forceful, worldly JJ had *admired* qualities most people considered airy-fairy at best—at worst, deluded? Good Lord. The spoonful of chicken and dumpling she was transporting halted. "I got over it. I'm a doctor now."

"You're the same person you were."

"Yes, but I see things differently now. I just have a heightened ability to see patterns and to form a gestalt, that's all. I can make a total picture out of a thousand details which most people would think were unrelated. Since I do it without conscious thought, I'm not always able to put what I perceive into words—so I call it a feeling, an intuition. But it's normal, JJ. Everybody has some degree of it. It's no big deal."

The teakettle whistled. JJ turned away to take it off the heat. She twisted the burner knob to off with an impatient click. "Okay. I'll drop the subject for now. But just for the record, I think you're completely normal—you always were. And I don't think denying and minimizing your gift serves you well. Willfully ignoring the truth about yourself will come back to bite you."

"Let's go out on the screened porch to eat," Bronwyn suggested when Garth and Davy returned with white takeout bags redolent of vinegar and smoky roast pork.

They spread out a quilt for Julia, piled toys around her, and then arranged themselves in a circle on the boards of the porch floor. It had once been painted gray, but now, the only paint to be seen was a strip extending a couple of feet from the house walls where sun and rain never reached. Bare wood showed through on most of the planks.

He ought to point out the need for paint, Garth thought. Under the guise of helpfulness, he'd been calling attention to the house's deficiencies all morning. The more trouble Bronwyn saw with this house, the more attractive any alternative he offered would appear.

But he didn't.

For now, it felt like he and Bronwyn were a couple, united in making the best of things and succeeding.

The shabbiness of the house demanded informality and contributed to lighthearted spontaneity. This simple ease was what he had longed for—only now did he realize how much. He wouldn't suggest that anything about their little picnic was less than perfect. Anyway, the porch would still be here tomorrow.

Garth passed around the grease-dotted bag containing the long, super crunchy cylinders of baked-then-fried corn bread called corn sticks. Next, he pulled out a white plastic quart container. Far more casually than he felt, he said, "Try these, everybody."

Bronwyn removed the container top and looked at the dark, gray-green leaves. The pungent smell knocked her head back, but then her eyes lit up. "Collards? Oh, yes!" She spooned some of the limp, gelatinous-looking mess onto her plate.

Garth's diaphragm relaxed. Bringing collard greens had been a calculated risk, but it had paid off. Davy had been against Garth's addition to the meal. On the inside, Garth's heart warmed with pride. He not only had provided food for his love, but he had guessed right and given her a treat.

Coming back with the forgotten forks, JJ exclaimed, "Are those collards I smell? Yum! Pass them here."

"The barbecue is good, but I chose this barbecue stand because they serve collards in addition to coleslaw." Feeling like a good host indeed, Garth waxed expansive. "I couldn't believe how good collards were the first time I tried them."

JJ stopped piling the greens on her paper plate to look at him. "You'd *never* had collards before you came here?"

"I'd never heard of them. I'm from Colorado. But I'm a convert now."

Davy snorted.

"I keep telling you, David, you've never tasted any that were cooked right." JJ's wifely tone amused Garth. "Collards prepared 'healthy' aren't fit to eat. They need to be cooked with seasoning meat, and cooked until they are limp and lose their color. They might not be as nutritious this way, but I've always been of the opinion that food you won't eat has no nutrition at all."

Bronwyn forked up a bite. "Oh, you're right, Garth! *These* are delicious! But," she added kindly, "it is an acquired taste, Davy."

"When did you acquire it?" Garth wanted to know. "You're not from the South."

"No, I'm from Pennsylvania, but I went to college here. University of North Carolina at Chapel Hill. JJ and I were roommates. JJ taught me to eat collards and other Southern food."

Garth stared at Bronwyn in surprise. "Roommates? You two don't look—"

Bronwyn held up a staying hand. "Do. Not. Say. It."

Impossible. Bronwyn must have started college when she was nine! "But you look too—"

Bronwyn waved a chiding finger. "I'm warning you. Anything you say will insult somebody. JJ and I are the same age."

"Do you still get a lot of grief about looking so young?" JJ grinned, apparently unconcerned by the implication that she looked a lot older than Bronwyn. "In fact," JJ told the men, "she's three months older than I am, but I used to have to buy all the liquor while she hid in the car. Otherwise, there was just too much explaining to do."

Bronwyn bit off the end of a golden corn stick and chewed contemplatively. "It's not as bad as it used to be. No one has refused me entrance to a lab or a postmortem in quite a while. But I still can't order a drink without having my license handy." She sighed dramatically and rolled her eyes. "And even with my hospital badge, I have to keep my license on me to prove to patients I am who I say I am and not a kid pulling a practical joke."

Despite Bronwyn's humorous acceptance, Garth thought it must bug her that other doctors didn't have to do anything—they got respect the instant they walked into a room—while she met with suspicion as soon as she introduced herself. No wonder she was upset by the questions that living in a haunted house would engender.

"And now I have to start all over again," Bronwyn continued. "I'm just hoping at smaller hospitals, word will get around quicker."

"So when do you start your locum tenens work?" JJ asked.

"What's 'locum tenens'?" Garth wanted to know.

"Essentially, it's work for a medical staffing agency, rather than a hospital. You go where they send you. Obviously, they're going to send you places that have a hard time getting or keeping doctors. They'll be sending me to several local hospitals—a shift here, a shift there. The good news is that if you go where doctors are in short supply, the pay is much better."

"I thought you said you were opening an office in this house."

"I intend to. It will be a while before the practice is built up to a level that will support me, though. In the meantime, I have med-school debt to pay off."

Garth saw just the chance he needed to drive a wedge between Bronwyn and her plans to live here permanently. "But if you're going to have to rehab a house before you can open and, once you're up and running, still have to work another job, wouldn't a job in a city hospital make more sense than coming to the backside of nowhere? At least in a city, you can have a life. Here, you have to drive thirty miles to get to a supermarket. The barbecue is great, but Sessoms' Corner doesn't have a lot else going for it, unless you're into hunting and fishing, and I'm betting you're not."

JJ glared at him. He probably hadn't been subtle enough, but he was honestly appalled that Bronwyn had taken on so much hardship to achieve so little. "Do you remember meeting Mary Cole Sessoms at my wedding?" JJ asked.

He did. She had been the sixtyish wedding coordinator, feminine and stylish but possessing the soul of a general.

At Garth's nod, JJ continued. "Well, in addition to being a good friend, she's a brilliant businessperson. Neither Mary Cole nor I would have allowed Bronwyn to sign a contract against her best interests. In exchange for her moving to Sessoms' Corner to open a practice, she gets a house, rent free, large enough to house a medical practice downstairs and living quarters upstairs.

"The house needs work, but it's structurally sound. If she stays five years, she will be deeded the house, free and clear. It will have to be up-fitted to medical office specs, but the community has gotten a federal grant which will pay for the clinical setup."

"So you're going to turn back the clock, be a country doctor, and live above your office? And this seems like a good idea to you?" Garth couldn't keep the harsh tone out of his voice. Her plan was much more complete— and more complex—than he had thought. It meant she met even less than fifty percent of the criteria for success as a naval officer's wife.

Bronwyn's straight posture didn't give an inch, but she got a sad, dignified look in her clear, russet eyes that made her look her real age. "Until Mary Cole showed me how to put together this whole plan, I was close to quitting medicine. All I could see was more years on the medical treadmill."

If she was willing to quit medicine, maybe that was the answer. For sure, it would be easier than trying to meld two careers. "What's 'the medical treadmill'?"

"With all the high-tech advances, a medical practice is expensive to set up and run. Doctors have to see more and more patients just to keep up with overhead, which means they have less time to spend with each. These days, a doctor spends an average of eight minutes with a patient."

"Eight minutes?" Garth couldn't believe it.

"I'm trained in battlefield medicine, where it isn't hard to tell what's causing the bleeding," Davy chuckled grimly, "but I can tell you that's not long enough to spot a problem with nonspecific symptoms."

"Right." Bronwyn shook her head. "But when doctors take longer, they lose money. You want to know the real irony? Part of the overhead they are running so hard to keep up with is malpractice insurance premiums, which can cost hundreds of thousands annually. But studies have shown that the best way to avoid being sued is to take time to build relationships with patients. How's that for a catch-22?"

Bronwyn pushed impatiently at a strand of hair that had worked its way from her ponytail. "It's a treadmill, and doctors can't get off. Expensive, unnecessary tests are substituted for sitting down and listening to patients. And passing out scrips for the drug du jour takes the place of counseling people about their conditions and how changes in lifestyle will make them better."

He recalled what JJ had said earlier about no practice thriving in Sessoms' Corner for thirty years. Out of the corner of his eye, Garth saw Davy frown and shake his head at him. He felt like a slug to be stepping on her dream, but reality *was* harsh. Nobody knew that better than him.

"Do you really think you can make it work where no one else has?"

"It isn't true that no one else has succeeded," Bronwyn objected. "Doctors all over the country are looking at ways to shift the paradigm. As for me…" Her lips moved in a crooked smile. She blew out a breath. "I can try."

JJ covered her friend's hand and offered her a reassuring smile. "High overhead is what drives the assembly-line model, so the first step is to lower overhead. Seeing patients downstairs, living upstairs makes sense. In the era in which this house was built, it was the way many doctors lived."

Bronwyn leveled a determined look at Garth. "Back in those days, practicing medicine wasn't considered a way to get rich, and what I'm proposing won't make me rich, either. But I'll be doing the kind of medicine I believe in."

Now he had the ammunition he needed. The reason men dropped out of SEAL training wasn't that it was exhausting and painful. Their reason always boiled down to one thing: they didn't think it was worth it. Bronwyn had already decided that what she called "the treadmill" wasn't worth it. All he had to do was what he had seen trainers do a thousand times: keep her thinking about why running a practice out of this house wasn't worth it, either.

"But all your plans center on *this* house," he told her. "Do you realize how much money it will take to bring it up to code? You'll spend more than the house is worth." Garth shook his head and looked more at JJ and Davy than at Bronwyn. "I hate to be the naysayer, but from what I've seen of the house, it's one gift horse she should have looked in the mouth. In fact, rather than a horse, I suspect it was an elephant, a white one. Someone has taken a healthy tax write-off for a property there was no way they'd ever sell."

Chapter 21

Hence, to fight and conquer in all your battles is not supreme excellence; supreme excellence consists in breaking the enemy's resistance without fighting.

—Sun Tzu, *The Art of War*

"I'VE DECIDED TO CATCH YOUR GHOST," GARTH TOLD Bronwyn when she opened the screen door wider to let him into the kitchen. JJ and Doc had left after the lunch of takeout barbecue.

Since then, Bronwyn had showered, and as Garth entered, he made brushing by her into an opportunity to inhale the spicy, floral, feminine smell of her hair. It hung in a straight deep-red curtain to her shoulders. She'd changed into a short skirt the color of ripe apricots that showed off her smooth legs and a white, sleeveless girly thing that tied with a ribbon just under her darling little breasts.

After raiding a back room at the airstrip for the equipment he was going to need, Garth had showered, too. And figured shaving again couldn't hurt. And he'd changed into chinos and a crayon-red, crisp, polished-cotton shirt.

Bronwyn rolled her eyes. "Don't start with the ghost again."

"Kidding. I'm talking about finding a rational

explanation. If you knew what was causing it, you'd feel better, right?"

Garth had wrestled with himself. Davy had told him to rescue her. This was the best idea he could come up with. But if he had any sense, he'd do what he could to make the ghostly presence worse. After all, it was in his best interest for her to be uncomfortable in the house. When he returned to operating as a SEAL, she would have to move sooner or later to wherever he was stationed.

He thanked his lucky socks he'd found her the very day she moved in, before anything was set in stone. If she'd been here several years, spent thousands renovating the house, and had a thriving practice and lots of friendships, persuading her to relocate would have been more difficult, maybe even impossible. He didn't want her decision to join her life to his to be painful, so it only made sense to keep her from getting in too deep.

Still, he wanted to eradicate the strained expression that darkened her eyes every time the subject of a ghost came up—and somehow, making her feel better mattered more.

She shrugged, then smiled. Unconvincingly. "I guess. I really just want it to go away, but my next choice would be finding an explanation."

"The webcam for the baby's room gave me the idea. We can do like the TV show *Ghost Hunters*. I can mount closed-circuit cameras around the house."

She emitted something between a groan and a chuckle. "First, because of you, I was in a spy thriller. Now, you want to make my life imitate reality TV. If that isn't proof this is bizarre, nothing can be."

Garth tried not to let that hurt, but it did. Still, he looked for another means of persuading her. "Where's Julia?"

"Upstairs napping in her new crib. She'll be waking up soon."

"And you're keeping an eye on her with the webcam?"

Bronwyn pointed to the open laptop. "Even as we speak."

"That proves my point. Surveillance gives you freedom and peace of mind. Look, I hate to see you on edge. I want to get to the bottom of what's happening. I want you to feel better."

Bronwyn tilted her head, an arrested look in her eyes. After an agonizing pause, she said, "That's sweet." She indicated the box of equipment he had set on the table. "What have you got?"

"I also brought a FLIR—an infrared camera. Basically it's a camera that sees heat."

"I'm familiar with them. They're used to make medical diagnoses." She grinned. "Do you honestly think ghosts have a heat signature?"

He felt the smile on his face widen. Damn. He did like a smart woman. And thinking that he might be helping her relax a little and see the humor in the whole situation put a smile in his heart too. "That remains to be seen, but I'm pretty sure rats or other varmints do."

"Rats?"

"Rats, raccoons, squirrels, bats, birds. They could be living in the walls."

"Oh. All those could be in the house? Maybe I'd rather have a ghost."

"Don't worry. If I find them, I'll get them out."

Again the head tilt. "Okay. You really think something is going on?"

"Something is. You're not imagining it. I also have a Trifield gauss meter for measuring electromagnetic energy."

She nodded. "Good idea. There's so much to do, I hadn't thought of checking the house for electronic pollution—but I should. High EMFs can cause illness. They've been implicated in leukemia in children. But what does it have to do…?"

"A high EMF can also cause creepy feelings, feelings of paranoia—like you're being watched. It can make you jumpy, so that an ordinary noise like a window rattling seems ominous."

"That would explain feeling like something is going on when it really isn't."

"But some paranormal investigators theorize a correlation between the presence of EMF fields and paranormal activity."

Bronwyn's eyes danced. "So a high EMF could make me just *think* I had a ghost, *and* it could also make a ghost more likely to manifest? Talk about circular logic."

"I'm not making up these theories. I'm just reporting them." Smiling into her eyes, he tucked a wisp of dark red hair behind her ear. She let him. It wasn't hot monkey sex, but it was progress.

A little breathless, Bronwyn pointed to another device. "What's that?"

"RF—radio frequency—detector. Might as well cover all the bases."

The RF detector was also useful in locating bugs of the electronic kind, but he didn't tell her that. Whoever had put Julia on that plane had an insider's knowledge of spy craft. It might be too soon for someone to come looking for Julia, but he wanted to be prepared if, sooner or later, someone did. If Bronwyn's house was under electronic surveillance, he wanted to know about it.

Chapter 22

Be extremely subtle, even to the point of formlessness. Be extremely mysterious, even to the point of soundlessness. Thereby you can be the director of the opponent's fate.

—Sun Tzu, *The Art of War*

"Come along, Mildred. The baby's down for the night." Bronwyn called the dog from the door of the baby's room.

Mildred cocked one ear and looked from Bronwyn to the crib.

"Yes, you have to." Mildred's fascination with the baby hadn't eased at all through the day. Bronwyn trusted Mildred, but she couldn't let Mildred get the idea that Julia was her baby.

Mildred sighed and got to her feet, her toenails clicking on the bare floorboards.

"Good dog. Let's go downstairs. We'll find Garth."

Dusk had deepened while they were putting Julia to bed. The bottom stairs disappeared into a pool of darkness. Having friends around today—filling the old place with bustle and laughter, R&B music on the radio, deep male voices, and hammering—had lightened the atmosphere and made it feel more normal, more like any old house in need of some updating. She also was reassured by the glowing red eye of the closed-circuit camera

Garth had mounted in the hall ceiling this afternoon so that any noises on the staircase or at the front door could be studied.

Cameras had also been set up in her bedroom and other places that seemed to be what Garth called *active*. He had been right that she would feel more secure once the cameras were installed. But what helped the most, she had to admit, was that he was here.

When she reached the lower hall, she could see him through the open front door, perched on the porch railing. Despite the easy way he sat, one arm over a drawn-up knee, face blank as if he thought of nothing at all—just a man sitting on the porch railing in the twilight—she wasn't fooled.

He was doing what she had seen Troy do. Behind his mask, his consciousness was sweeping the area as automatically and as relentlessly as a beam from a light-house. He was like a lion whose laziness would disappear in a burst of powerful movement when prey came into range.

Yes, she realized, use of a mask was what was the same about the two men. And also what was different. Troy had been better at it—at animating the mask—which had made it not so obvious. In outward personality, Troy had resembled David more than Garth. He had showed the world a face of good-humored ease.

Garth presented the world a mask of frozen fierceness that hid his sensitivity to the needs of those around him. Anyone who only watched Garth's face wouldn't know how responsible he felt for everyone. In that regard, he really reminded her more of JJ than of Troy. The insight surprised her so much, her heart skipped a beat.

In deciding to make the move to North Carolina, she had accepted that if Troy hadn't died, her relationship with him would have ended. His undercover police work had been his life, and she was fundamentally an afterthought to be squeezed in when there was time. She wouldn't have wanted that long term. She had stayed in the relationship as long as she did because it distracted her from how unhappy she was at the hospital.

Her friendship with JJ had already stood the test of time and of separations, and she knew she would love JJ as long as she lived.

She detoured to the kitchen to pick up her laptop. Somewhere upstairs, in one of the bedrooms she had just left, it sounded like something heavy hit the floor and rolled.

Mildred looked at her, shaggy eyebrows lifted.

Bronwyn opened the laptop. In her crib, Julia slept undisturbed, her hands in loose fists beside her dandelion-fluff head. As Bronwyn watched, Julia brought one fist to her mouth and sucked on her thumb for a second or two. Then the thumb slowly slid away as her mouth went slack again.

"I haven't heard anything else, have you?" Bronwyn asked the dog. "No? In that case, since the baby is okay, I don't think we will dash up there to investigate. We'll just wait and see if the camera caught anything."

Mildred seemed okay with that. She bumped the screen open with her nose and went outside.

Bronwyn paused with her hand on the slat of the old wooden door, thinking about the man she was going outside to confront. Another thing that was different was that Troy had always kept her separate from his undercover operations. He rarely talked about them even after the fact. When they were going on, she might not even see him for a week or two. Whatever was going on *here*, she was as much in the middle of it as Garth was.

Outside, she set the open laptop on a built-in ledge where they could both watch Julia on the screen. Then she leaned her shoulder against a pillar that, like everything else, needed painting but seemed sturdy enough.

"We need to talk," she said. "While Julia napped this afternoon, I researched North Carolina law about child abandonment. We can't play finders, keepers with a child."

His expression didn't change at all. "What does the law say?"

"Essentially, if you find a child, your first duty is to see to its safety, and second, to report it to authorities. But you can't just keep her. That's concealment and conspiracy to further a kidnapping. A felony. We're no longer talking about failure to report neglect—which in North Carolina doesn't even have a penalty. This is a felony.

"At the very least, my medical license is on the line. I *could* go to jail for a long, long time. I only have your word that she won't be safe with the police and that what we're doing is necessary to her well-being. Tell me the truth about how and where you found the baby, and why you think she's in danger."

His blue gaze didn't waver. "There's a lot I can't tell you. It really comes down to do you trust me."

"No. It comes down to, do you trust *me*. You have to give me something that makes your actions comprehensible, or I'll have to act on my own."

"There's not much I can say."

"I'm willing to believe that you're trying to protect Julia. I'm not asking you to breach national security. I've kind of figured out some hush-hush things are going on out at the airstrip, but you told me you're not a SEAL anymore, right? Just tell me as much as you can."

Chapter 23

In the practical art of war, the best thing of all is to take the enemy's country whole and intact; to shatter and destroy it is not so good. Kill one, terrify a thousand.

—Sun Tzu, *The Art of War*

TALKING TO PEOPLE WHO WEREN'T READ IN TO AN operation was bad, but permissible under certain circumstances, as long as these people had a high enough security clearance—which both Davy and his ex-SEAL friend Clay did. Most SEALs might think Garth was behaving stupidly, but they would not be revolted by his actions so far. However, what no SEAL could condone, no matter the circumstances, was a security breach.

Bronwyn had no clearance at all. Breaching security was something Garth had never done—had never even thought of doing.

And yet he was thinking of it. He allowed no tension to creep into the relaxed composure with which he leaned against the pillar. He let no flicker of self-doubt show in his face. But the older, emotional parts of the brain were not so easily controlled. His heart pounded. His thigh, where his palm rested so easy looking, was wet with sweat from his hand.

In taking Julia, no way could he claim he was acting on orders or even that he was independently pursuing an operation's objectives. He was already off the reservation. Nevertheless, until this moment, he had continued to live within the code of silence. He could rationalize what he was doing, or he could admit the truth: he wanted to tell her. Bronwyn stood to lose her license, but she was willing to risk it to protect a child. He owed her some explanations. He was going rogue.

He picked up the laptop. "Let's go down and sit on the dock, okay?" He'd swept the house for bugs, but just in case there was a directional mic trained on them, the twenty-foot drop to the river would make it hard for anyone to listen in without being visible themselves. "Get a sweater. It'll be cooler by the water."

A lane had been cut through the sandy bank to get boat trailers down to the water. It was deeply gullied in places and choked with saplings but still imprinted with car tracks. Mildred raced ahead of them and dashed back, delighted to have company on a ramble.

At the bottom of the bluff, the trees gave way to a narrow beach of grayish sand. After the dark of the woods, it seemed almost bright down there. Near the horizon, the sky was a lemony color.

The short wooden dock had been there a long time. Here and there, gray tatters of rope looped the pilings. Some of the boards were spongy, a few missing. The dock would hold them, though. Garth set the laptop on a fish-cleaning platform.

Bronwyn kicked off her flip-flops. "This is the first time I've come down to the river since I got here. There's always something else to do, isn't there?" She sat down on the end of the dock and let her legs dangle over the water. "It's so quiet, I almost feel like I ought to whisper."

He let himself down beside her. She looked at him expectantly.

"Okay. I'm going to tell you as much as I can, but I can't tell you where the plane came from. And I can't tell you who was on the plane—or why."

"But the outfit you work for—is it legal? I mean, they're not bringing drugs or some contraband into the country?"

"No drugs. It's legal." Mostly. And for the parts that weren't strictly legal, such as avoiding customs, at least it had the blessing of persons high in the government.

"All right. I won't ask any more. Here's my real question. You said you think someone put Julia on the plane to try to save her. I don't understand. If they wanted to save her, why would they put her in such danger? She's a baby. She couldn't take care of herself. I want to believe you, but it doesn't make any sense."

Putting in all the details he had previously glossed over, he described the flight that had been delayed and had almost cut it too close to a thunderstorm, and how he'd found the box containing the baby after the pilot and passengers had left. He had to conclude that someone with a desperate need to get their child out of the country had put the baby aboard the plane.

Bronwyn's clear, russet eyes had lost all their sparkle as he spoke. "Why would someone be so desperate?" she asked.

"In the annals of terrorism, there is a long history of adults who disagreed with a regime being 'disappeared' in the dark of night and their children, now orphans, taken. The children are then sold in black-market adoptions. An adoptable baby is worth a lot of money. The army of El Salvador paid its own way with black-market trade in children."

"*Paid for* itself? But that would mean…"

"Right. Thousands of children were stolen. The military regime of El Salvador was supported by the U.S. government. There's no way the CIA didn't know what was happening. These days, a healthy white infant, pretty, would go for fifty thousand, easy."

"But you don't think Julia was stolen?"

"There would be easier, surer ways to bring a baby into the country if the motive was purely profit. But her parents might have been afraid that they, and anyone who tried to help them, were in imminent danger. The fear that Julia would be killed, too, may have been the reason she was hidden on the plane."

"But to just put her on a plane? Telling no one? Leaving her fate to chance? Someone would do that?"

"Bronny, the thing you have to understand about terrorism—its purpose isn't to destroy enemies. It is to demoralize and control people through fear. Often, terrorists need the people they are preying upon to continue to be productive."

Bronwyn nodded thoughtfully. "And the best way to control a parent is to threaten their children."

"Right. For the last ten years, I've been in failed-state countries where there is no law and no sanctuary. There is only unending strife, motivated by greed, between power factions. People in those places teeter at the tipping point of panic all the time. Jack up the fear suddenly, and they will do things—thoughtless, screwball, sometimes atrocious things—they would ordinarily never do."

"The parents in this case must have believed the danger to Julia wasn't just a threat, it was a sure thing."

"Probably. And for some reason, they couldn't take her and run themselves."

Bronwyn peeled a long, dry splinter from a piling. She broke it into smaller pieces and flung them into the water before turning to him. "So it's a Baby Moses story."

"Baby Moses?" Sounded off topic to Garth, but God knew, he didn't want to dwell on all the things he'd seen happen to children. He was happy to let her talk about anything she wanted to, while he mentally traced the sweet purity of her profile and drew her soft, illusive scent deep into his lungs.

"It's in the Old Testament," she reminded him. Unnecessarily. "Pharaoh's soldiers were going from house to house killing all the baby boy-children of the Jewish slaves. To save Moses even at the cost of losing him, Moses's mother made him a tiny boat of woven reeds and put him in it and floated it where it would be hidden among the bulrushes in the Nile. What's implied is that she hid him in a place no one would think to look for a baby."

"Substitute a banana box for a homemade boat, and that would be about right."

"Suppose there's more to the story? Suppose putting Julia on the plane *was* an act of desperation, but not a crazy one?"

"Meaning what?"

Bronwyn tilted her head. Her hair swung like a curtain—which Garth thought entrancing. He'd like to feel the silken length swing against his hand or against his face as she bent over to kiss him or maybe against his belly when she—

His hands tightened on the dry, crumbling wood of the dock edge. He forced his mind back on the subject.

"Read at face value," Bronwyn continued, unaware of the direction of his thoughts, "Moses was either very lucky or had divine intervention. However, read the story carefully, and you can see a suspicious number of coincidences. I think Moses's mother was as audacious as she was desperate. Saving him by hiding him in the Nile was not as chancy as it sounds.

"First of all," she held up a slender finger, "he wasn't abandoned to his fate. Moses's sister was also sent to keep watch." She raised a second finger. "Second, Moses was put in the river at a spot Pharaoh's daughter was known to visit. Third, Moses was found not by a nobody but by *Pharaoh's daughter*—possibly the only person in the kingdom with the power to keep him alive, despite the Pharaoh's decree.

"Fourth, when Pharaoh's daughter decided to keep him, Moses's sister ran up to her and announced, 'I just happen to know a wet nurse!'" Bronwyn tossed her hand dismissively. "I ask you, was she thinking fast when she offered her mother's services as a wet nurse, or had Moses's mother planned every step?"

He locked onto what she was saying. "You believe someone was supposed to be on the plane to make sure the box was put into the right hands."

"Well, yes. Because the question isn't only where was she coming from and why. We have to ask: who was she going to?"

He'd been so focused on the fact that he was smack-dab in the middle of the kind of dirty mess that would make his efforts to restart his naval career academic (and end the career of anyone he asked to help him), and so appalled to find yet another total innocent set adrift, that after he'd dismissed the possibility that someone intended to sell her, he hadn't pursued the question further.

Had someone planned a drop, the oldest spy trick in the world? Was Renfro supposed to board the plane carrying a box of bananas and disembark at the other end carrying an identical box?

What could be easier than getting off a plane carrying a box of bananas—especially where there would be no customs check to go through after disembarking.

"There was someone who was supposed to be on the plane but wasn't." Renfro. MacMurtry had been there to meet him, but he hadn't been aboard. "I've got some people seeing if they can get a lead on him," Garth continued.

"Do you think he is the baby's father?"

"Don't know. One thing is for sure. If there was someone she was supposed to go to, then that person wants there to be no evidence of any kind of Julia's existence in this country. Someone was using the… company I work for. Someone powerful, with connections to the navy, if they could send a lieutenant to pick up the plane's missing passenger."

"You don't think Julia was expected by anyone in your company?"

"I'd have heard from them by now." And there went any hope, however faint, that his bosses would think he'd done the right thing by acting on his own and reward him. He sneered inwardly at himself. Once a Boy Scout, always a Boy Scout. He'd known he was most likely getting on the good side of nobody. What made him keep hoping for the happy ending?

"Then what are we going to do?"

"Wait. If I can find... the man who was supposed to be aboard, maybe he can tell us more. But I think you need to prepare yourself. It's possible that no one is looking for Julia. If someone wanted her to disappear without a trace, they did a good job."

Bronwyn fisted her hands on her hips. "Then I'm back to where I started. Shouldn't we just go to the police or the FBI? Can't we just tell them the truth? If there's any way to find Julia's family, surely they're more likely to succeed than we are."

He started to tell her he could kiss everything he had worked toward for ten years good-bye if he let the baby's existence and her means of entry into the country become public. But if his only concern had been to cover his own ass, he would have done as he was advised and would have dropped her off at some emergency room.

He'd gone soft. He'd let himself put his own feelings and judgment ahead of the requirements of the job he had to do. Now he had involved Bronwyn. She was pure and sweet and clean, and he'd never wanted anyone more in his life.

She had no idea how ruthless the people were whose way she would be stepping into. She worried about the damage being associated with a ghost would do her reputation? These were people who would think nothing of discrediting her until no one would trust her to mow grass.

They would think nothing of framing her and making sure she took the fall, think nothing of eliminating her altogether. Maintaining security was their job. They would not let the livelihood or life of one innocent woman or baby imperil their mission.

"No."

Bronwyn studied him long and slowly, a little pleat between her dark reddish eyebrows. "Because of those 'national security' issues?"

"Yes."

She was quiet a long time. Far out on the river, a fishing boat's trolling motor hummed, just inside the threshold of audibility. Overhead, a flock of starlings chittered and angled their aggregate being toward a stand of hardwoods on the opposite shore to roost for the night. Closer, in the trees behind them, quail sent a few sleepy *Bob? Bob White?* calls and fell silent.

The water looked smooth and still as glass, but underneath the dock, the river licked and sucked softly at the pilings like the living, moving thing it was.

"I don't have any control in this situation at all, do I?" Bronwyn asked, more contemplative than complaining. "I can't even quit—and live with myself afterward."

"Bronny, I'm sorry. I got you into this. It's all my fault."

"Partly your fault, yes. *All* your fault? I don't think so. You tried to leave and take Julia with you. I wouldn't let you. I was so sure, if there was a choice between us, Julia was better off with me."

"No. It's all my fault. I knew the score. And I knew who you were as soon as you stepped on the porch."

Chapter 24

*We want to be in a situation under maximum pressure,
maximum intensity, and maximum danger. When it is
shared with others, it provides a bond which is stronger
than any tie that can exist.*

—SEAL Team Six Officer

BRONWYN LOOKED AT THE MAN BESIDE HER ON THE DOCK,
his tan face ruddy in the gloaming. The blood red of
his shirt scintillated. His golden-oak skin gleamed over
muscles sleek as a leopard's. He sat, as always, head
balanced, broad shoulders straight, relaxed, utterly still.
He pulsed with the elemental power of a totem. He was
the thunderbird, the falcon-headed sun god, the Aztec's
golden jaguar.

He never made any of the purposeless, unconscious
movements other people do. He didn't rub his nose,
touch his tie, tug his belt, or like some men, check his
fly. Little movements so individual that a friend could
be recognized even if his face couldn't be seen. Not
Garth. He could seem blank. Molded of amber, solid
to the core. Except for the occasional smile, he gave
away nothing.

Now that she knew to look for it, his distinguishing
feature was that he was so *there*. It made his smallest
utterance seem profound, portentous. She struggled for

comprehension. "You knew it was me—we had met be-fore—even before I reminded you?"

"Yeah."

She opened her mouth to speak… and couldn't think of anything to say. Worlds seemed to have passed be-tween this evening and just twenty-four hours ago. She searched for the link between who she was then and who she was now. Couldn't find it. She shook with an empty little laugh of mystified acquiescence. She said the only thing that came to mind. "Was that… only last night?"

He wet his lips and ducked his head a fraction. "Yeah."

Two telltales in a row! Three, if she counted the smile he was trying to hide right now—and really, she thought she should.

She *should* take him to task for playing such a trick. Demand an explanation. Stomp off in a huff, though that wasn't her style. She definitely should call him on deliberately misleading her.

But she was so damned glad to know he *hadn't* for-gotten her. Because she hadn't forgotten him. She hadn't forgotten that instant of unbearable recognition when she had realized he had many of the same qualities Troy did—and yet she felt the attraction.

Like a fresh stab into an open wound, it told her the same forces in her character that had led to the first wound were still active. She apparently hadn't learned a thing. Every cell in her body could cry out to bring him closer. Believing he had forgotten that meeting utterly had made it possible to push aside her visceral response to his nearness. "Why didn't you say something?"

"Because I should have gotten out of there the second I recognized you." His dark voice was gruff. "I knew I was up to my neck in it, and anyone who touched me would get covered in it, too. Instead, I gave myself a dozen stupid reasons why I didn't have to leave. But the real reason I stayed was because I wanted you."

Julia cried out in her sleep. Bronwyn got up and went to the laptop. She tapped a key to make the screen light up. Julia wriggled and stretched. Her sweet little lips made sucking movements before she fell back into a deep sleep.

"How's the battery holding up?" Garth asked.

"It's okay. I had just charged it."

He held out a long-fingered hand. "Come sit back down."

His warm, hard hand steadied her as she lowered herself. When her legs again dangled over the river, he urged her to stretch out. With one long arm he cradled her all the way down.

"This okay?" He pulled his arm from beneath her. The weathered planks were rough, a little gritty. Though the air was cooling rapidly, the boards still held the heat of the day. With her legs dangling, there was a not-unpleasant stretch through her thighs and abdomen, but the position put strain on her lower back.

"Widen your knees. You'll be more comfortable."

She tried it. The pressure on her lower spine eased. She relaxed. The posture created more room for her diaphragm to move. She drew the wet smell of the river, rich with elements of earth, pines, and cypress, deep into her lungs.

"It has a whole smell of its own, doesn't it? The river," she added. She wanted to talk about something else while she absorbed the implications of his revelations. "You know it's a water world. The smell is little fishy like the ocean, but it's not marine."

"Riverine."

"That's a word?"

"The word for the environment created by the river."

"Do SEALs go on rivers?"

"SEALs go anywhere, but water is where we have the tactical edge. There's a saying, 'When SEALs are in trouble, they always go to water.' The coast offers admission to a country, but the river will carry you into its heart."

———

He rolled on his side and propped his head in his hand. The last traces of sunset had disappeared behind the dark smudge of pines on the opposite shore. Intense blue vibrated on the air. Her white skin glowed like alabaster.

"You're so pretty." He was supposed to have said that earlier, he remembered. He smoothed a deep-red tendril from her forehead.

He stroked down the side of her face across her temple, over the elegant rise of her cheekbone, the soft, soft plane of her cheek. The silken skin of her neck. Touching her was a joy in itself. When his skin met her skin, it was like setting his hand on the hood of a quiet and very powerful engine. Insistent heat and fine vibration raced into him. He couldn't wait to plunge into it, to feel surrounded by it. His breath quickened; his body tightened; his cheeks grew hot as the desire he always felt for this woman surged.

She turned her head to look him full in the face. "I'm not... ready."

"Okay." He didn't pretend not to understand. He had known it was too soon. Even so, he had to swallow a lump of disappointment. "Okay." On the upside, she hadn't said no, only not yet. "Let me make you feel good."

"I said—"

"I know. I'm not going to jump you. I'm not going to push you faster than you want to go. Just let me touch you. When something feels good, tell me. I'll do it again."

"But..."

"Bronny, just for a few minutes." He rested his palm on her stomach, rubbing lightly in soft, slow circles. With each upward circuit, his thumb grazed the lower slopes of her breasts. On the down swing, his little finger drifted across her mound. "Just for a few minutes, lie back and let someone take care of you."

Under his hand the rhythmic swell and ebb of her breath deepened into a sigh, releasing tension in her whole body. Her thighs opened. Her eyelids drifted down.

Triumph expanded in his chest at the same time that tenderness punched his stomach like a blow from the inside. He was instantly hard. She was his. His mate. She would receive him into her body, into that hot core of feminine power. Completing him as he completed her, making of their separate contributions a new, richer whole.

She was so beautiful. The fading light made her white skin look more ethereal, his tan, darker, more solid. He watched his hand move over her, keeping his touch light and accidental. A small exultant smile touched his lips when he saw telltale movements that told him, whether she meant to or not, that she was now expecting, reaching for his touch.

Now he stroked his hand over one of those darling breasts, finding the nipple beneath the soft cotton of her top, but still he kept the pressure light, barely skimming. He slid his hand up her thigh, the short skirt no impediment to his questing hand.

By degrees, Bronwyn's mood of receptive curiosity changed to something more demanding. *There*. She needed for him to touch her there. The casual competence of his touches made it clear he understood every landmark of her body. But that warm, hard, long-fingered hand skated nearer and nearer without ever quite… She opened her thighs a bit more in invitation. He took full advantage and stroked gentle, skating glides over the silken skin on her legs' inner faces. Closer… Closer…

Ready to protest his teasing, she opened her eyes and turned her head to look at him.

Deep blue, lazy-lidded eyes appraised her reaction with equal parts calculation and soft-focused humor. He smiled. A smile that was a barely discernible widening of the bow of his lip and yet melting-full, replete with tenderness.

Her throat squeezed painfully around a fist-sized lump. *He really might be in love with me.* The wonder and the terror of the thought flipped her stomach into a free fall. She had dismissed his out-of-the-blue declaration, hoping he'd regret his impulsiveness and let it go.

But what if…

What if it were…

What if it were… real?

Her eyes filled. Her heart chugged into a harsh, bumpy rhythm.

He slipped his arm under her shoulders until her head and neck were cradled in the crook of his elbow. He smelled of hot wind. Of sandalwood and some dark spice like clove. An intensely masculine smell that simultaneously satisfied and made her hungry. He was the best-smelling man she'd ever met. And the best-feeling one.

He smiled deep into her eyes and lowered his head. Slow, soft, thorough, he took her lips in a kiss. Inexorably gentle, licking and biting at her mouth until she opened to the penetration of his tongue and the hot, brave taste of him.

She insinuated her hand between them, intending to ask for distance, and wound up spreading her fingers over the raised definition of pecs that she could no longer resist the temptation of digging her fingertips into. Reluctantly aware of how far out of hand she'd let things get, she pressed at the hard muscles that curved over the joint of his shoulder. He lifted his head but did not release her. Instead, with his free hand, he continued to press firm strokes deep into the flesh of her hip.

She inhaled sharply when the warm, hard hand wandered to her thigh and, with casual strength, lifted it and moved it further from the other thigh. "You said," she reminded him, "you were just going to touch."

His smile was unrepentant. "Yeah. But you knew I'd go as far as you'd let me."

Do not smile, she told the unruly corners of her mouth. *Do not.* "You're going faster than I want to go."

"Your head is talking, Bronny. Not your body. Your

body says something else." He brought his hand back up to slip it under her top.

He palmed her breast with his hard, warm hand, then squeezed with firm, insistent pressure. "These for instance. You know *you* want me to draw them in my mouth and tug on them, just as much as I want to. I want to feel you arch against me when I hit the combination that does it for you."

How did he know? Her eyes went hot with longing. She could have denied a lot of things but not that. She wasn't the kind of woman who easily put sex on the back burner. She hadn't entered into a lot of relationships because few men wanted to compete with the demands of medical school, and even men she found physically attractive didn't feel *good*. She had a collection of sex toys, but nothing remotely simulated the feel of a man's mouth or satisfied the hunger for that stimulation.

She reached to pull his head down at the same time he pushed her top up to uncover her breasts.

The baby made a fussy, whiny sound. They both pulled away and listened. When, after a second or two, Julia quieted, he took a moment to frankly look at Bronwyn's breasts. In a tone of husky reverence he said, "These are about the prettiest things I've ever seen in my life."

With infinite care he took her into his mouth, tasting, testing, questing. Hot, wet twirling tongue, scraping teeth, and then, and then, he trapped the nipple hard against the roof of his mouth and suckled in deep tugging pulls. It was as if he pulled at her whole body. She felt the tug in her womb, and the junction of her thighs throbbed in time.

Bronwyn moaned and fisted her hand in his hair to

hold him to her. As he had predicted, her body arched as she crested the first peak.

He lifted his head to look into her eyes. "You could get off on this alone, couldn't you?"

The baby made another fussy sound, this one more imperative. He went back to kissing her breast, but the mood was gone. Reluctantly, Bronwyn pushed him away. "She's waking up. I have to go in."

Mildred stood up and shook all over. That clenched it as far as Bronwyn was concerned. "Mildred says we have to go in, too."

He straightened her top and helped her sit up. Then, with the fluid grace so characteristic of him, he rose to his feet and lifted her to hers. "If 'Mildred says,' who am I to argue?"

Chapter 25

Pick the time and place for action.

—The Moscow Rules

BACK IN THE HOUSE AND UPSTAIRS, THEY FOUND JULIA had rolled over. She lay on her stomach, propped up on her elbows. Her cheeks were flushed. She looked at them accusingly.

She quieted when Garth picked her up. Her diaper was dry. He murmured the patter that seemed soothing to her, but as soon as he put her back in the crib, she rolled over, sat up, and began fussing again.

While Garth held her in his arms, Bronwyn took her temperature.

"Has she got a fever?"

Bronwyn read the digital display. "Point eight over normal, but I don't think that's significant by itself."

Julia chewed on her fist. It glistened with a coating of thick drool, as did her chin.

Bronwyn fluffed the baby's hair, thinking. "She's been acting like this off and on all day. She may be teething. Let me see your gums, sweetie." Bronwyn pushed back the baby's soft-firm lip and ran a fingertip over Julie's gum. "Yep. There it is. See that little red swelling? She has an upper lateral incisor coming in."

"What do we do?"

"There's not much to do. It's perfectly normal."

Garth tried laying Julia down again, but she howled and lifted her arms as if to say, "Don't leave me like this." The sound clutched at his heart.

"Pain is always worse at night, isn't it?" he told the baby sympathetically as he took her in his arms again. He frowned at Bronwyn over Julia's head. "We can't just let her cry. We have to do something. There must be something that will help."

She colored slightly and shrugged. "It's been a million years since I did a peeds rotation. Babies don't present in an ER with teething pain." She went to the bureau where she had placed her laptop. "I'll see what I can find on the Internet."

"I'm not going to let her just cry." If Bronwyn didn't know what to do, he was on his own. An idea came to him. He shifted Julia to his other arm. "Hang on. I'm calling Dr. Mom."

Surprised at the sudden change in his tone, Bronwyn looked up.

"Mom?" He put the phone to his ear, while Bronwyn listened with surprised interest. After a few greetings, she heard him say, "I have a question. What do you do for a baby that's teething?… Oh, a friend and I are baby-sitting a friend's kid for a couple of days… Bronwyn. You're going to love her, Mom."

He chuckled at something that was said. "Okay. Frozen bagel. What else?" He listened for a minute, then held the phone against his chest to report, "Mom says there is homeopathic teething gel that helps." He returned the phone to his ear.

"Chamomile tea? All right. How long is teething

going to take? A day or two? *Or three*?… Okay. Thanks Mom… Yes I will. Soon… Love you, too." He closed the phone. "You heard."

"Do you just pick up the phone and call your mom whenever you need to know something?" Bronwyn wondered what that would feel like.

"When I need to know mom-stuff, yeah." His shoulders moved in a wry shrug. "Not so much when I need operating info." With his eyes fixed in the middle distance, he looked thoughtful. "But I haven't called her like that in a long time."

He looked thoughtful! Bronwyn gasped, fascinated by the change she saw in him. Suddenly, she had no trouble reading and interpreting his expression. The mask was gone.

"It was kind of good, you know?" he asked, oblivious to her surprise at the change in him. "Why do you ask? Don't you call your mom? Didn't you say she was a doctor? With her, you could double-dip."

Bronwyn shook her head, unable to explain why a quick tapping into her mother's store of knowledge would never have occurred to her. Nor could she explain that she'd asked only because when he'd heard his mother's voice, the blue of his eyes had warmed and the hard line of his lips had softened. He was himself, and yet she had glimpsed another man—or a man from another time.

Bronwyn returned to the purpose of the call. "Did she say chamomile tea was a remedy for teething babies?"

"Yes. Give her a couple of teaspoons from a medicine dropper, or soak a washcloth in it and freeze it."

"I have chamomile. I'll go put the kettle on right now. Today she was happy as long as she was being carried."

"Okay, I'll walk her."

———∿∿∿———

Downstairs, while Garth walked Julia back and forth, Bronwyn filled the kettle and put it on the stove, then dragged the step stool over to the counter. The cabinets in this house must have been built for a giant. She looked forward to renovating so that the cabinets would be lowered as much as she looked forward to new appliances.

"Now, let's see if I can find the box of tea in this disorganized cabinet. No matter how hard I try to put something back exactly where I got it from, when I look for it again, it isn't there. When we were fixing tea for lunch, JJ found the sugar inside a pot. Can you believe it?"

Garth smiled and nodded to show he understood while he continued to stroll through the kitchen, through the family room and back, murmuring to the baby in a soft, rumbly undertone.

She tuned into what he was saying while she poured boiling water over the tea bag in a glass measuring cup, and set it on the counter to steep.

"Do you like history?" she heard him ask the baby. "Then when you are in Germany, you should take the rattling, clattering two-car train to Limburg. It's a town straight out of the thirteenth century. Lots of old, half-timbered houses leaning over narrow, cobbled streets, like an illustration from a fairy tale."

He shifted Julia to his other shoulder and continued. "You're too young to drink the beer, and you should think twice about the cheese—but the really bad stuff comes from the other Limburg. You should try the pretzels. If you like cathedrals, and I'm not saying I do, the one there is kind of pretty."

"You've been to Limburg?" Bronwyn asked. "I loved the cathedral there. It was great to see a cathedral painted in rich colors the way they looked originally."

He rocked Julia side to side. "When were you there?"

"JJ and I did a junior year abroad. How about you?"

"I don't come from people who 'do' junior years abroad." He grinned. "When we want to see the world, we join the navy. I went to college on an NROTC scholarship. Were your parents rich?"

"Not in JJ's class, but… I guess most people—except for the *really* rich—" she grinned, "would say we were. They could afford a junior year abroad for me."

"I don't get it. You told us at lunch that you have huge med school debts. Are you saying your parents paid for a junior year abroad, but not medical school?"

Bronwyn's face felt tight. "They would pay for anything that looked like it would distract me from medicine."

"They weren't proud of you?"

Bronwyn wouldn't mind telling him, but her old, well-worn feelings of hurt mystification were like dusty curtains obscuring the windows into the past. She didn't see through them well enough herself to explain her family's dynamics to anyone else. She shrugged. "It's complex."

He made another circuit of the room. If Bronwyn heard right, he was describing how to build something called a "hide" for the purpose of "laying up" during the day. His red shirt now had a darker red wet spot on the shoulder where Julia's head rested.

The tea had steeped five minutes. She removed the

bag and poured the brew from cup to cup to cool it. When she judged it to be room temperature, she filled a five milliliter dropper with the pale brown liquid.

"I'm ready to start Operation Chamomile," she called.

With Garth holding her, Julia readily took the tea a few drops at a time.

"Is that it?" he asked.

"That's it. One dropper full is one teaspoon. I gave her two per 'Dr. Mom's' instructions. I guess we wait and see what happens." The baby was quieter now, whether from the travelogues and training lectures or exhaustion, it would be hard to say. "Why don't you try rocking her in the rocking chair? Or if you like, I'll take her."

"I've got her."

Bronwyn relished the strength and control with which the tall man lowered himself into the low rocker while holding the baby to his broad chest. The chair squeaked slightly as he set it in motion, in this case a pleasantly creaky sound. Mildred lay down on the floor beside him. In a few minutes, the down-covered globe of Julia's head nestled deeper into the brown curve of his neck.

Chapter 26

Vary your pattern and stay within your cover.

—The Moscow Rules

GARTH KEPT JULIA BALANCED WHILE SHE SQUIRMED HER WAY into a new position on his chest. He'd never thought holding a baby would be such a comfortable, satisfying thing to do. She seemed to find the alignment she was looking for and went lax again. He smoothed her little shirt across her narrow back.

Bronwyn had retreated to the kitchen where she was rinsing the tea things and setting them in the yellow plastic dish drainer. Her back was to him. The light above the sink brought out the deep red of her hair. He liked the clean efficiency of her movements. He didn't like the shadowy look that had come into her eyes when she talked about her parents.

The more he saw of her, the more he knew she was his. Just being with her made joy and lightness expand deep within his chest. And the way she responded to him—God, he wanted her—and it was going to be so good.

But the more he saw of her, the more he realized something held her back. Something dimmed her. He wanted to know what it was. If it was pain, then he wanted to comfort her, and if it was just part of how she was, he wanted to add it into all the other things he loved about her.

"Bronny, when people give 'It's complicated' as an answer, they mean they don't like the looks of the truth, so they're trying to chip enough pieces off it to make it look like something else." The corner of his mouth quirked. "Like a bust of Elvis they're trying to tell themselves is a bust of Lincoln. Chip off as much as they want to. It still doesn't look like Lincoln. It just looks like an uglier and uglier Elvis."

She stopped wiping the counter to look up at him.

"So I'm going to ask you again. Why wouldn't your parents be happy to see you become a doctor? They should have been proud of you for wanting to carry on the family tradition."

She rinsed the sponge and set it on the sink rim. "They didn't need me for tradition. They had Landreth."

"Your brother," Garth clarified. "Because he was male?"

She dried her hands on a paper towel and crossed them over her waist. Despite the casual way she leaned against the counter, he noticed the protective gesture. "I can't accuse them of chauvinism. No, it had nothing to do with gender. They just didn't think I had what it took. They thought a medical education would be a waste since I wouldn't last through my first year in med school."

"Why? You're obviously smart enough."

Her slender shoulders twitched in the suggestion of a shrug. "I'm going to have a glass of wine." She took a bottle of merlot from the refrigerator. "Can I bring you one?"

"Thanks." He waited while she poured two glasses and brought him one. "Sit down," he said, and returned to his questions. "Why, Bronny?"

She curled into the big, fake-leather easy chair and ran her fingers across the duct tape patch on the arm. "They thought I was too imaginative and too emotional to succeed. But I never wanted to be anything but a doctor, so it put us on a collision path."

"I've only known you a couple of days, but I can see what being a doctor means to you. How could they fail to understand?"

Bronwyn's shoulders moved. She took a sip of wine and looked into the distance. "Even before I could read, I liked to study the pictures in my parents' medical texts. They let me because I could be trusted not to destroy them and it kept me amused. I think they thought it was kind of cute to see a tot poring over a big, thick book."

He could just see her in a big chair with her legs sticking straight out and a book bigger than she was in her lap. He couldn't help but smile. "Did you have bright red hair?"

She touched her hair self-consciously. "It was always dark. It hasn't changed much."

"I threw you off-topic. When did you become a problem child?"

"I wasn't one at all. My parents' guests often remarked what a quiet, well-behaved child I was because I was playing quietly on the floor, entertaining myself with a toy." She added an ironic lift to her lips. "I seemed good because I was *happy* listening to my parents and their friends discuss cases and medical procedures."

"How old were you?"

"Four? Five?" Again the tiny shrug. "I didn't tell anyone I wanted to be a doctor—I didn't know I needed to. Everybody knew Landreth would be a doctor. They were proud of him. I assumed they knew the same thing about me."

Julia was beginning to list badly, threatening to slide off Garth's shoulder as she became boneless with sleep. Bronwyn followed him with her eyes as he rose and tenderly transferred her to her infant carrier, making maximal use of his big hands to keep her supported so that she hardly felt the motion. He moved the carrier to a corner further away where the light wouldn't be in her eyes. She squirmed a little to resettle herself, smacked her rosy lips a couple of times, and slipped back to sleep.

"And when you found out they didn't 'know' it?" he prodded.

"I couldn't believe it." Bronwyn struggled to convey how absolutely befuddled she had felt. "Literally couldn't believe it. I just *knew* if I studied hard enough and demonstrated my interest in all forms of healing, they'd get it."

Bronwyn's look of pained incomprehension triggered Garth's instincts to comfort and to shelter. He walked over to where she sat. "This chair's too big for you, and that one is a little low for me."

"You're right." She had to scoot to the edge just so she could put her feet down. "Did you want to change?"

"Got a better idea." Better for him anyway. He scooped her into his arms and sat with her in his lap. He stroked the silky skin of her arm until she nestled against his chest, her head tucked underneath his chin. The fit was perfect. Holding a baby was good; holding a sweet-smelling woman was better.

And there was something about her. A fizz, a vibration just at the edge of awareness like suddenly he was getting more juice. He felt himself brighten, lift, as if gravity had lost a little bit of its pull.

"But studying and proving how smart you were didn't work?"

She laughed painfully. "No. I was only five. When I prattled my child's understanding of all I was absorbing, they laughed or looked embarrassed or told me not to be silly."

"For instance…"

"Okay—like the time the adults were discussing the talents and personality characteristics required by various specialties. I asked what the specialty was for doctors who could see bones and muscles and things under the skin. I thought that was the kind I would be."

He could just see her as a little girl—tiny for her age, with huge spice-colored eyes and that look of intense focus she sometimes had—being laughed at because she saw things her own way and asked questions adults couldn't understand. An amazingly tender awareness of just how special she was filled his chest. He dropped a kiss on her hair.

"And of course, they told you there were no doctors like that," he finished for her.

"Right. Only machines could see inside people." She shrugged, dismissing something before she said it.

He was getting a little tired of those shrugs. He wanted to know what she was leaving out. Unlikely as the answer seemed, he asked the question that came to mind. "*Can* you? See structures under the skin?"

"Actually, most doctors are good at visualizing

anatomy. Some are very good. It really is like they can see inside the body."

He noticed she hadn't quite answered his question. "How about you?"

Her smile was self-deprecating. "I think all those anatomy books I studied at such a young age warped me. I just developed the skill earlier, and it was almost like I didn't have to learn anatomy. And I have to admit I do have a great imagination, so it's not surprising if sometimes… it's just a great imagination, that's all."

She fell silent for a minute. If he hadn't been holding her, he wouldn't have registered the tiny movement of her shoulders. "So you see, my parents were not completely wrong in their assessment. They assumed I would change my mind, and when I didn't, they tried to help me change it."

Good luck with that. He'd already seen that once she set her mind to something, Bronwyn was immovable. "But to take it as far as refusing to help you through medical school?"

She shrugged. He thought she was leaving unsaid how much their lack of faith had wounded her. "They're not bad people. In their own way they were trying to keep me from being hurt. They knew more about what I would face in medical school than I did."

He stroked her silken hair. It was cool on top, but he could feel the warmth of *her* coming through it. "What did you learn in medical school—the hard way?"

"Medical students aren't treated like human beings— any more than SEALs are, but medical students aren't being toughened up so they can be sent to war. The schools use intimidation and relentless competition to turn the students into nervous wrecks who won't question why they are being taught as they are."

"Huh. I'll bet that didn't work on you. What did *you* question?" The thought of his tiny troublemaker standing up to the bigwigs brought a tender smile to his face.

"I asked why the school's curriculum still required vivisection in dogs. Most medical schools had phased out dissection of living animals. With computer simulations, the same lessons could be taught in humane ways."

He went cold inside as he thought about the extraordinary communication and trust between her and Mildred. This woman couldn't treat an animal like a thing. "Did you still have to…?"

"I protested. I even started petitions. Finally, to get me out of their hair, the administration made me exempt from the vivisection labs." She was silent for a moment. "In medical school, they teach you to be distant and professional. They try to make you this objective, emotionless scientist. My parents knew how unsuited I was. It was only later that I realized why the arguments about teaching anatomy through vivisection sounded so specious to me."

"Why was that?"

"It was because the real lesson was: If they wanted to be doctors, the students had to make their interest in science primary, and shelve their capacity to care about a living creature."

"But you rejected that."

"I did, and I do. But you can see why my parents thought I wasn't cut out for medicine and believed, if I went to medical school, I would only fail and quite likely embarrass them in the process."

He didn't know if he did see. Bronwyn's clinical competence was so obvious to him that her parents' attitude seemed over the top. If he pressed her further right now, though, she'd likely shut down, and he didn't want her to. God, he didn't want her to.

She sighed and then rubbed her cheek against his shirt. "What's going to happen to her?"

"Julia, you mean?" It was his turn to sigh. "One step at a time. First we do have to figure out, if we can, how she came—"

"I know that. I was just thinking. I've been sitting here trying to explain to you how *I* came *here*. I might feel lost as all get out, looking for where I belong, but I do *have* two living parents, a living grandmother, a brother… what will Julia feel if she has to grow up never knowing where she came from?… How about you? Where's your family?"

"My mom and dad are in Durango. My married sister, her husband, and two kids live in Golden. My one living grandfather has a small horse ranch in the high meadows of the Rockies, near Steamboat Springs."

"You obviously love them a lot. I can hear it in your voice. Do you see them much?"

"I love them. But it's hard for a SEAL to stay close."

"But you're not a SEAL anymore."

He hadn't told her his civilian status was a cover. He had lied to her and not corrected the lie. And hell, after MacMurtry's revelations yesterday, maybe he hadn't lied. Maybe he wasn't a SEAL. His reasoning was fallacious, and he knew it. It was another problem they'd have to solve when they came to it. "What I am right this minute is a man—who wants you, very much."

Bronwyn leaned back against his supporting arm in order to see his face. "You've got to promise me you won't push me to get serious."

"Why? You know this is right. You know this is good between us."

"It isn't good. I have too much to do to get myself established here. I don't need the distraction."

"I'm a distraction?" That sounded good to him.

"Yes." There it was again. That don't-mess-with-me look.

"Look, I know I sprang the marriage thing on you, but this is how the men in my family are. My dad has told the story a million times—how he saw my mother in a Laundromat on the edge of the UC campus and knew, right then, he was going to marry her."

"Did she fall in love with *him* at first sight?"

"Huh. I never thought to ask her that."

She gave him a dry look. "I'll bet your sister did."

He thought of his mother and sister. Sometimes what they laughed and talked about was incomprehensible to him—like the words were English but had been arranged into a different language. He chuckled. "Yeah, she probably did."

He had to grin at the told-you-so expression Bronwyn aimed at him through her sparkling eyes. "You are so beautiful," he said.

He liked everything about her: her large, wide eyes that he literally thought he could drink from, her ardor for medicine, her willingness to risk everything for the benefit of a child. He made up his mind right then that no matter what it took, he would not let her offering shelter to Julia cause her to lose anything. He liked her short little nose and her smooth legs, and he loved those darling, dainty, cupcake breasts. Even her bare toes (she went barefoot most of the time) were adorable.

He captured her hand. Against his own deep tan, its whiteness made his heart shake at the thought of its fragility. Despite the slender bones, he felt the tempered strength living deep within, the focused intelligence and precision. That *thing* about her that lightened him suddenly intensified and fed some deep hunger within him.

Holding her gaze with his, he lifted her hand to his cheek and held it there, then moved it across his lips, relishing out the slick hardness of the nails, the softness of the finger pads. He folded her fingers and ran his lips over the knuckles. She didn't want to hear how he felt, and he wasn't sure he had the words anyway— but he would show her, as much and as often as she would let him.

He turned her palm over to give it the same loving attention. "Let me stay."

Bronwyn felt detached, almost voyeuristic, observing her hand being made love to as if that were an end in itself. He held her palm to his nose and frankly inhaled, drawing deep the pleasure of her scent, and then bathed the palm in the warm moisture of his breath, heated by the vital fire within him.

He licked his tongue in tantalizing passes over the webbing between her ring finger and pinkie and between her ring finger and middle finger.

The sensation was exquisite.

She was surrounded by his heat, by the wonderful, hard resilience of the muscles of his arms cradling her, by the smell of cloves and hot flesh.

Suddenly, she discovered that the arousal she thought had gone away hadn't. It had simply hit a plateau. It burst into life again, hot, pulsing, needing— stealing her breath.

"They used to say that there was a special vein that ran from the ring finger straight to the heart," he told her. "Can I find the way to your heart by doing this?"

"You can find your way into my bed, that's for sure." She lifted her arms to his neck, turning her face up to his.

"That's a start."

They kissed a long time, stoking the fire of their mutual desires. She moved onto her knees, straddling him to bring their mouths into better alignment. For a few minutes he let her have control of the kiss. He relaxed against the chair's headrest while she covered his cheeks and forehead with kisses. She kissed his eyelids and ran her tongue across the silken bristle of his lashes. She went back to his mouth and reveled in his hot, dark taste while she dug her fingers into the thick ropy muscles that shaped his neck.

His big hands slipped under her white cotton top. He pushed it up until he could pull it over her head. Lifting her easily to hold her in place, he slid down the chair until his mouth was level with her breasts. "Been wanting to do this again, ever since I stopped out on the dock."

He tongued one nipple in lazy swirls and then lifted her away to admire the puckered and hardened tip, gleaming rosy and wet. He ministered to the other breast and again assessed his handiwork with a hot, blue, possessive gaze. As he looked, her nipples puckered more. He smiled.

He opened his mouth over the first breast and added the stronger strokes she craved. He suckled in deep pulls that plucked at the hidden seat of pleasure at the junction of her thighs. Heat and pressure built there with every hot tug of his mouth.

"Brace your arms on the chair back. Need my hands for other things."

His hard hands kneaded the globes of her bottom and then pushed her skirt up to her waist. The high cut of her bikini panties admitted his fingers easily. He stroked the silky curls he found there. He pushed the panty further out of his way. With a fingertip he traced the seams of the soft folds. With her legs spread as they were, the panty crotch kept trying to snap back into place, and there wasn't room for his whole hand.

After a few minutes he growled in frustration. "The panties have got to go, Bron."

Eager to divest herself of any barrier to his touch, Bronwyn sat back on her heels—at least she meant to, but both she and Garth had worked closer to the chair's edge than she realized. She began to tip over backwards and to fall between his legs. She grabbed his forearms at the same moment he steadied her with his hands at her waist and brought his knees together. In the nick of time, her bottom rested on his rocklike thighs.

His cheeks had extra color underneath his tan; his nostrils were flared; his features had the taut look of arousal. He looked up at her, his blue eyes lifting at the corners. In a dark voice flat with understated humor, he said, "I'm afraid the chair is not rated for this activity. We've pushed it beyond its design limits."

Her chest was heaving; her whole body thrummed;

her brain was cloudy with arousal. *He* was just as turned on, judging from the bulge under his fly.

And he could make a joke.

It surprised her. It shocked her. It forced a readjustment of all her expectations about him. He was so controlled, so intensely focused on his objectives and so unyielding in the standards he set that she hadn't guessed he could laugh at his or her clumsiness. The fact that he *could* laugh let light into a place that had been dark and airless for a long time. It was like a door had opened to another dimension, like the walls had disappeared and suddenly she was in a far larger place.

With a knowing far deeper than any rational thought, which she was incapable of right that minute anyway, she knew he was a man she might love. In fact, with the first tenuous threads of feeling, she already did.

Still steadying her, he sat up with the ease of a man who could do a hundred crunches without breaking a sweat. "Put your arms around my neck," he told her. When she complied, he kissed her long and slow. Then, with one arm cradling her bottom, one arm around her back, he lifted her and stood. Slowly he let her down until she could stand on tiptoes.

"What is it?" he asked, sensing something had changed.

"You *are* in love with me. I mean, you didn't get all testy and short a minute ago, the way men do when a seduction scene goes south. You really do have something in mind other than a roll in the hay."

"Right. If I'd had any sense at all, I wouldn't have started things in a chair when there's a perfectly good bed upstairs."

"What does that mean?"

"It means I'm not looking for a quickie—not that I would turn one down. I'm not looking for a one-night stand. I'm looking for *real*—and forever and forever."

Chapter 27

"WELL, IF WE'RE GOING UPSTAIRS TO BED, DO YOU WANT TO take Julia up to her crib and let me go out with Mildred for her last potty stop, or do you—"

He stopped her question with a kiss. "You go on up with the baby. I'll supervise Mildred. I want to make sure that the new locks are set and working properly. I'll be up in a minute. What?" he asked at her sudden chuckle.

"It feels so, I don't know, so domestic."

He winked at her. "That's the plan. Come on, Mildred. Let's check the perimeter."

"I like this." Garth said a few minutes later as he took his wallet from his hip pocket and laid it on the dresser. "It feels like a wedding night." He unbuttoned his shirt while he kicked off his shoes. The open shirt revealed a swath of smooth, brown skin. He shrugged off the shirt and opened his pants all in one coordinated movement, and there he stood.

Bronwyn's breath failed her. Her heart shook in deep thuds.

And she smiled too. He was not unaware of his masculine beauty and not averse to showing it off to impress her. She could name every muscle and every bone in his body, but she had no word for the sleek, all-encompassing male perfection he embodied. His penis jutted full and proud, dark with arousal.

With the masculine grace that characterized him, he

walked over to the bed and rested one knee on the sheet. He looked down at her, a smile playing around his lips.

"Do we need to have the protection talk?" he asked. "I've been thoroughly checked out, and I'm good. And as of this moment, I'm in a committed, monogamous relationship. But I have protection with me."

"I went off the pill after…"

"Fine." He picked up his pants and drew several packets from the pocket and set them on the bedside table. "Light on or off?"

"On, please."

He got between the sheets and folded her carefully into his arms, surrounding her in his warmth and smooth skin and the scents of citrus and clove and aroused male.

"I want to go slow, Bronny. I want to make it last and last. And I want to please you. But, God, I want you so much." He stroked her hair with fingers that trembled slightly. "See, I'm shaking like a kid. Like this is my first time."

Her heart went soft at his admission of vulnerability. Funny, how she could actually feel a warm, melty feeling just under her sternum. She reached up to touch his hair, relishing the thick pelt and the velvety prickle at his nape. "Go slow next time."

He raised up over her and stroked her whole body with his while she spread her hand on the skin of his back. Stretching, she cupped his buttocks, trying to pull him into closer contact.

He began dropping kisses with every pass. Her nose, her forehead, her cheeks, her chest. Marauding playfully, never letting her guess where he would strike next until she was giggling and breathless. And opening her legs, he lifted her hips, trying to bring her body into contact with his penis.

Abruptly he was serious. He took her face in his hands as he let himself settle into the cradle of her thighs. "Oh, Bronny, Bronny. I've waited forever for this," he whispered. "You feel so absolutely right."

He kissed her deeply, melding their mouths for long minutes, with intermittent forays to her ears, her throat, her breasts until she was twisting and surprising little moans came from her throat.

His fingers found the place between her thighs. "You're wet," he said. "So hot, and silky. I'm going to make you mine now. Mine. Do you understand?"

She shivered. She didn't know if she nodded in agreement or in dissent. She was past anything but wanting his hardness filling her now. He positioned himself at the entrance to her body and pushed slowly within.

Despite his assertion that he couldn't do *slow*, he did. He thrust slowly and tirelessly as sensation piled on sensation.

"Harder," she cried, but the steady relentless rhythm demanded that she accept his loving.

They were both slick with sweat. She could feel his heart pounding against hers, his breath rasping loud in her ears. The room filled with the heavy, earthy scent of sex, mingling with the spiciness of him.

And then it was there, cascades of shuddering, shaking release as they fell together.

Garth rolled off Bronwyn. He stared at the ceiling, waiting for his breathing to return to normal. That had been... intense. Even though his body was cooling, he could still feel a warmth deep within—he didn't know—his cells or something. His bones, his whole body hummed as if it resonated with some super-powerful, perfectly tuned engine. He felt for Bronwyn's hand, folded it within his own.

When he could speak, not knowing if he was talking to her or himself, not sure if there was any difference, he said, "Bronny, it's never been like that before. I've heard it's different when you love someone, but I didn't guess it would be that different. It was... I think that was making love."

He rolled onto his side and propped his head in his hand. He lifted a strand of her silken hair and arranged it to lie straight and smooth against the pillow. "I love you. Are you in love with me yet—at least a little?"

She turned her head to look at him. "Maybe." She smiled, slow and soft. "A little, anyway. Don't make too much of it. I'm not ready for the big commitment."

"How much, would you say? Fifty percent?"

"I just told you not to make too much of it."

"I'm trying *not* to—see, that's why I need an estimate. Is fifty percent too much? Come on. It doesn't have to be precise."

She laughed a little, helplessly. "You're not going to give up, are you?"

"Work with me. I'm just trying to get a feel for the trend."

"Forget it." She pushed at his shoulder, and he obligingly went over on his back. Cool silken tips of her hair brushed his face as she brought her mouth to his. "You're just going to have to go with the flow."

Her tiny, strong, *intelligent* hands drifted over his chest to flick the copper disks of his nipples. When he sucked in his breath at the sensation, she looked very satisfied. She *liked* turning him on, and the knowledge itself was a potent aphrodisiac. Against all odds, this soon after the most fantastic orgasm of his life, he was already getting hard.

He quickly opened another condom packet. "Is this what you call going with the flow?"

"It is."

He crammed a couple of pillows under his shoulders, and then he lifted her by her hips to help her straddle him. "I like to see all the action," he told her. He found the plump, delicate folds between her legs. "Put my fingers where you want them," he urged, his voice rough with arousal. "Show me what you want."

Warm, soft wonder filled Bronwyn's chest. Her clitoris was super-sensitive, and until she was very aroused, she couldn't take direct pressure on it. He was arrogant, overbearing, and occasionally clueless but so willing to learn—not just now, but in everything. This was what she was falling in love with. Bronwyn took his hard, warm fingers in hers and used them to stroke herself.

He was watching his hand stroke her, his lips slightly parted, his expression intent, as he played and sought every nuance of pressure and direction. Excitement spiraled, wound tighter.

She took him in her hands and positioned him at her entrance. She sank down until he filled her to exquisite fullness.

Thought fled. There was only the sensation where they were joined, the gathering spirals of energy deep in the most central part of her. She moved on him. He reached up and kneaded her breasts, thumbing the nipples. The pressure burst, and suddenly she was coming in shuddering waves that had her laughing and crying. Seconds later, he was holding her hips as he drove into her seeking his own completion.

Bronwyn collapsed panting on his hard chest. He rubbed her back and buttocks with long, firm passes as she recovered her breath.

He kissed her shoulder. "This is so good."

"Why didn't we see each other when we met? We've wasted a lot of time." Garth tenderly stroked Bronwyn's cheek as they lay nestled together, her head on his chest.

"I can't speak for you, but I know my part. I was still blinded by grief. That expression is literally true, you know. You feel like you're in a pitch-black room looking at the world through a tiny peephole. You can only see what's directly in front of you. When what little you can see moves, when it isn't in the peephole, it's... gone. Out of sight, out of mind."

As she spoke, Bronwyn idly explored the contours of his chest, measuring, learning him by touch. He liked it. "But there was more to it." Bronwyn began speaking again. "Anytime I was near you, I had some sort of posttraumatic stress flashback, or something. I shook all the way through the ceremony and got away as fast as I could afterward. By the time I came back, you had left to catch your plane."

Garth hadn't really meant anything by the question. In his opinion, it wasn't the kind of question that had an answer. It had been more a comment on their inefficiency, okay, mostly his, because she apparently could name her reasons. He didn't know why—since he was looking for a wife, and he was at a wedding, for Chrissake—he hadn't even considered her candidacy.

But she'd had a flashback. "Davy told me there was some guy who died. Do I look like him?"

"No. But I think I looked at you, and my unconscious warned me that what had happened to him would happen to you."

"Almost had happened to me. They tell me I almost bled to death. I didn't have a pulse for about five minutes."

"I'm glad they got you back."

"Have you ever had a patient who had a near-death experience?"

"You mean, where people see the bright light and think they go to heaven and talk to Jesus? No, but I've heard of them. Who hasn't? Why? Did you have one when you were without a pulse?"

He chilled at her not unkind but slightly amused and indulgent tone. He had never attempted to discuss the experience with anyone, because that was exactly the response he'd thought he would get—but he hadn't thought he would get it from her.

He made himself say lightly, "I'm not sure I went to heaven—it looked more like Colorado—and I *know* I didn't talk to Jesus." He chuckled. "Actually, I talked to Davy. But I didn't have a pulse. If I wasn't dead, I was the next thing to it."

"Every cell in the body doesn't die at once. The brain releases all sorts of chemicals, endorphins that can make you feel wonderful, peaceful. Seizure activity in the parietal-temporal lobe makes people see bright lights and stimulates oceanic, religious feelings. Add to that the drugs the patient has been pumped full of… It's no wonder people whose bodies were on the verge of death report bizarre experiences, but there's no reason to think they visited an 'afterlife' and came back. People who have been nowhere near clinical death have had similar experiences."

With all her talk today about finding the human side of medicine, he hadn't expected her to have a hard-science reaction. More importantly, he hadn't expected so little understanding of what he wanted to talk about from the love of his life. He hadn't thought they had to mirror each other in every detail, but he had thought they would meet at the really important places.

"I read those 'scientific' explanations. The only people they would satisfy would be people who never had the experience. I don't know what it was, and I don't know what it meant, but it was real."

She felt his withdrawal. "I'm sorry if I don't seem to take you seriously. I'm not suggesting it didn't really happen in your experience. I'm sure it did. But you have no idea the things people can say under drugs."

Chapter 28

Don't look back; you are never completely alone.

—The Moscow Rules

THE NEXT MORNING, GARTH RETURNED TO THE AIRSTRIP, carrying the recordings the video cameras had made. However undemanding, he did have a job and needed to report in, and at the airstrip he also had access to computer programs that would make reviewing the data easier.

When he drove into the garage, his eye fell on the red canoe. Although God knew there was no lack of electronic toys and gizmos available to him here, his need to get outside and to move fast on the river that was over a mile wide in places had made him buy a speedy seventeen-foot bass boat, now loaded on its trailer. But to experience the peace of the slow-moving blackwater river, he had needed a canoe for excursions of relaxed exploration. He'd spent a lot of time with both.

He ought to tie them up at Bronwyn's landing. He'd have to get a baby-sized life jacket for Julia, and one for Bronwyn, but it would be fun to take them out whenever he felt like it.

He had never made any attempt to disguise how few hours he really logged on the job. When he'd pointed it out, he'd been told not to worry; he'd get busier soon.

He now recognized as literal truth what he had suspected. There was no need for him to be assigned to the air strip at all. Someone coming in a couple of days a month could easily keep up with all there was to do. In fact, given the paucity of traffic, he wondered if the strip itself was even needed. Sure, its combination of isolation and accessibility made it ideal, but it hardly paid for itself.

After checking the encrypted messages and noting on his calendar a package retrieval requiring diving gear, he called Clay. Clay would man the boat that they would take into international waters.

His work dealt with, Garth settled himself at his desk to hunt through last night's DVRs for whatever had caused the noise Bronwyn said she had heard. Watching empty rooms hardly made for an action-packed, thrills-a-minute cinematic experience. However, watching and waiting without letting his mind wander was an essential skill for a SEAL. Simple patience was a rare commodity and gave anyone who had it an enormous tactical advantage.

On the screen he watched himself and Bronwyn, led by Mildred, walk into the baby's room. Realizing he was past the time of the incident, he ejected the disc and inserted the one from the camera covering the hall and staircase. If he could establish the exact time of the incident, he could narrow down his search.

He cued it up to the approximate time and watched Bronwyn and Mildred descend the stairs, Mildred's thick, black nails clacking loudly on the bare treads. Bronwyn's flip-flops, decorated with huge, sparkly flowers, made soft slapping noises.

Bronwyn looked adorable and absurdly young in her little skirt and the sleeveless cotton top he now knew for a fact she went braless under. He tried to imagine her in clothes that made her look closer to her real age. It couldn't be done. He was in for a lifetime of jokes about cradle-robbing. Not that he cared.

On the screen, while still standing in the spill of light from the upstairs, Bronwyn stopped to peer into the dark down the stairs, an apprehensive look on her face. He could see her push her shoulders back, her face tight and determined, and start down. Instead of racing to the bottom as she usually did, Mildred paced her step for step.

About halfway down, they became indistinct. The camera wasn't sensitive enough for the low light conditions. The picture became snowy with what looked like microwave interference for a half-second. Woman and dog stopped and looked around as if they had heard something. Unfortunately, the sound, if there had been one, wasn't picked up by the microphone on the camera.

That was interesting. Electronic interference at the precise instant was probably a coincidence but worth noting in his log.

He highlighted the section and set it to loop. Instead of allowing his eyes to dart randomly around the image, he scanned in an organized pattern, starting with the space closest to Bronwyn and working outward in successive passes—a sniper technique.

Again he noticed the movement of her shoulders. He froze the action. A lot of people believed that by watching a person's eyes, they could read that person's intentions. Bronwyn's eyes were always clear and guileless.

He could look into them all day, happily, but they gave little clue to how she felt or what she was covering up. He'd noticed last night how frequently she shrugged when talking about something personal. Ah. *Bronwyn's* giveaway was her shoulders.

He smiled a little at the discovery. Finding his forever love was turning out to be a richer, more fulfilling experience than he had ever anticipated. The tiny bracing of her shoulders told him she was steeling herself to descend the stairs.

Who knew that with every tidbit he learned about her, he'd feel as if he had uncovered priceless treasure? And who would have guessed he would become vulnerable whenever she was vulnerable? She shouldn't have to feel apprehensive about a problem so easily dealt with.

He'd noticed the lack of a two-way switch for the hall light. Rewiring had to wait for the major renovations, which if he had his way would never happen, but he could rig some kind of switch—a photoelectric cell, a motion sensor, something. He jotted a reminder to swing by the home improvement store to study his choices.

He hit "Start" again. Once Bronwyn and Mildred were in the shadowy area, it was hard to make out, but he had the impression Mildred was looking at Bronwyn. The figures were too indistinct to be sure. And since the camera's mic hadn't picked up the sound, he'd probably learned all he was going to.

His cell phone beeped. The caller ID window read, "Restricted."

"I got a hit on Renfro, already—if you can believe it," Davy told him in his husky baritone. "JJ has given me a list like you wouldn't believe of jobs I have to check off for our big wedding bash. I had to call Lon Swales—you know him, don't you?"

"Sure." Lon was a senior chief petty officer, a burly man in his forties known for being a great instructor and for his dedication to the well-being of the men under him. Men like him really ran the navy, and everyone knew it.

"I asked Lon if he knew a SEAL named Renfro. Turns out Renfro was one of Lon's B/UDS trainees."

"Any idea where Renfro is?"

"Renfro got out as soon as he finished his first hitch, according to Lon. Went with Blackwater for a while, but he likes to operate solo."

"Did Lon say what kind of gigs?" With their antiterrorism training, SEALs had many saleable skills in the post 9-11 world. There had always been a shady market for hired guns and men who would fight for whoever paid them. These days, legitimate businesses all over the world required protection. In the private security field, a man with language skills and leadership experience could pull down a quarter- to a half-million dollars a year. But companies like Blackwater weren't an ex-SEAL's only choices. These days, the CIA and other intelligence agencies outsourced espionage and interrogation work to private providers. Intelligence was big business.

"Bodyguard." Davy told him. "Armed escort. Lon suspects some bounty work. Got a reputation for being discreet." That probably meant Renfro was willing to look the other way, or maybe deliver whatever his high-profile clients asked for—including people who didn't exactly want to come.

"That it?"

"That's it. He's pretty shadowy. Like I said, he likes to operate unaccompanied. Unless we ask exactly the right person—or get our hands on his dossier—we likely won't learn more. Though there's never any telling what Dulaude knows."

Like their animal counterparts, SEALs were, by and large, gregarious creatures. A SEAL who really liked to work alone was relatively rare. Garth had been warned when he took the assignment with the unnamed agency not to stay in contact with old acquaintances. Since he'd foreseen a stint of only a couple of months, it hadn't seemed like a problem. Now he realized how the prohibition had cut him off.

The last several months had taught Garth he didn't want to operate alone. Much as he disliked this mess he was in, an upside was that it had put him back in touch other SEALs. It was time he began to make full use of the resources they offered.

"Are you in regular contact," he asked Davy now, "with Dulaude? Could you ask him to meet with us—using a cover? There might be no connection between Renfro and Julia, but finding Renfro is the next step, and I'd like Dulaude's input."

"No problem. I'll get back to you on an ETA. How about Lon? If I mention the meeting to him, he's going to want in. He says you are one of the most solid officers he ever trained."

In the SEALs, officers were trained by enlisted, which meant enlisted men had power over which officers made it through. Knowing that one day their lives might depend on an officer, they made no secret of the fact that officers were held to a higher standard.

Lon's praise, particularly now, warmed Garth's heart. "Sure. Bring him along. A senior chief will have a lot of experience—and a lot of wiliness—to bring to the table."

Work done for the day, Garth reset all the alarms and also placed one of Mildred's hairs between the door and the jamb. The people he was concerned about undoubtedly knew as much as he did about how to defeat electronic security and cover their tracks. The hair wouldn't keep anyone out, but he would know if the door had been opened in his absence.

So far he hadn't detected signs that he was under surveillance. No sign that anyone was even aware a baby had been aboard the plane. MacMurtry had had no interest in the plane at all, once he learned Renfro wasn't aboard.

The preponderance of evidence suggested Garth's theory was correct—someone had stashed Julia on the plane, and any plane going to the States would have done. Some part of him wanted Bronwyn to be right, though. He wanted to believe Julia had been sent to someone, someone prepared to receive her and keep her safe.

He tabled the thought. Julia was safe with him and Bronwyn. And he needed to pick up more things at the home improvement store.

Business was light at the big store. Acres of asphalt soaked up every bit of the sun's heat, making the parking lot into a burning black blanket to be crossed. The cooler weather of yesterday was clearly over. The humidity was rising. Solid-looking white towers of cumulus clouds piled together on the horizon.

In the lighting section, Garth determined that lights

activated by motion detectors were the best solution to the dark stairs. He selected two, decided the front and back porch lights should be similarly equipped, and tossed two more into the cart.

When he saw packages of outlet covers, he realized they were just what he needed. Julia wasn't quite crawling on all fours yet, but her commando-style locomotion took her where she wanted to go.

Next he thought he ought to look at fencing—just to see what was available. It would be nice to be able to send Mildred out to pee on her own.

He moved on to the power tools—having the tool you needed made all the difference. He picked up a cordless drill. It was sort of shame Bronny wouldn't be staying. He could think of lots of projects he'd need a drill for.

"Well, hello there!" A large man in a work shirt with an air-conditioner manufacturer's logo and *Doug* embroidered over the breast pocket rounded a display of circular saws. Garth recognized the volunteer EMT.

Garth returned his greeting. "How are you doing?"

"Great," Doug answered. "Watcha buyin'?"

"Don't know yet. Wondering if I need a cordless drill. You got any experience with this brand?"

They discussed the relative merits of drills for a few minutes until Doug said, "You handled yourself pretty good the other night getting that woman and her little boy out of that car."

"They all right?"

"Yeah, but they wouldn't have been if you hadn't gone in after them. She shouldn't have been going that fast."

"She would have been smarter to go slower, but she wasn't going all that fast. Only about forty-five. I was right behind her. People just don't realize how little water it takes to hydroplane."

They moved to the checkout. While they waited in the short line, Doug said, "You ought to think about joining the squad. We have a good time when we get together, but the real reason to join is that we look after our neighbors and our families."

A group of men and women banded together to help people in their community handle emergencies—it sounded like something he'd like to be part of, but Garth shook his head. "I don't know how long I'll be here. I'm likely going to be changing jobs."

"Well, come on by anyway."

"Uh, listen." Garth, conscious of his pleasure in having a guy-buddy, said as the line inched forward. "If you wanted to take a girl to a nice place without going into Wilmington, where would you go?"

"What do you want to eat?"

"Not barbecue. Something special." Every town had a barbecue stand, a hole in the wall from which takeout barbecue was sold. Most also had a sit-down, eat-in barbecue restaurant, decorated in a pig motif, brightly lit, and shouting family atmosphere. "Something with ambience, you know? Romantic. But not just like every other nice restaurant you ever went to. Memorable."

"How about an oyster bar?"

"An oyster bar?"

"Best oysters you ever had, and it's an experience. Folks come from all over to go there. From Raleigh, from Virginia—I've heard of rich people in New York chartering a plane. My wife loves it. I take her there every year for our anniversary. It's further away than Wilmington, though."

"All right. I'll put that on the list. You wouldn't happen to know where I can find a good baby-sitter, would you? My girlfriend has a baby."

"Sure do. My wife runs a day care. Several of her helpers also do sitting." He pulled a wallet from his hip pocket and took a business card out. "Give her a call. She'll put you in touch with somebody you can trust."

The exit doors whooshed open, and they were hit by a blast of steamy air that instantly penetrated their clothes. "Whew!" Doug pantomimed wiping his brow. "Hot already. Course, that's good news for the air-conditioning man." The big man grinned. "A few days of this, and folks'll be calling right and left—and none too happy to learn I can't be in two places at once."

"Let me ask you about a problem with an air-conditioner."

Doug listened to the description of Bronwyn's unit and said, "You can probably replace some parts and get another year out of it, but you're not going to fix the real problem, which is, it's old and inefficient." He produced another business card, this time from his breast pocket. "Let me come look at it. I'll quote you a good price."

"Let me think about it. I'll give you a call."

Garth tucked the card into his pocket, doubting if he'd ever use it. The object was to make Bronwyn less comfortable. In his plan to detach Bronwyn from her house, he hadn't been able to utilize the ghost, but a lack of air-conditioning would make staying in the house equally uncomfortable.

Chapter 29

BRONWYN TIPPED THE BOTTLE OF FORMULA TO LET THE LAST couple of ounces fill the nipple. Julia's sucking had slowed. A couple of times her long, pale lashes had come down, but when Bronwyn attempted to slip the bottle from her lips, Julia's eyes had opened again. And so the desultory feeding continued.

Bronwyn took a deep breath and blocked from her mind the thousand chores she needed to return to as soon as Julia finished. If there was one thing Bronwyn had learned since acquiring a baby, it was that there was clock time, and then there was baby time. Baby time won. It took exactly as long to give her a bottle as it took. When they were busy, some parents of children this age put the child in the crib with the bottle propped in a holder. In other situations, Bronwyn might have done that, too, but not with Julia, not now.

Julia had been a little fussy all morning, but not like yesterday, when she'd cried unless she was being carried or rocked. Today Julia seemed fragile, easily overset by life's vicissitudes—which for a baby were a toy out of reach, a bottle slow to come, the need of a fresh diaper.

Bronwyn blinked away the soggy, yearning guilt that threatened to submerge her. What was really wrong, she suspected, was that she wasn't doing a good enough job. She didn't always anticipate Julia's needs. She wasn't skillful with diapers or meals. She didn't know the right songs to sing or the form of stroking that soothed.

Julia could tell Bronwyn was not her mother.

Julia had been ripped from the comfort of every familiar smell, sound, and sensation. She wouldn't understand if Bronwyn used words to promise security, and so Bronwyn held the baby while she took her bottle. Just so that Julia would know that incomprehensible to a baby as her life had become, she was not alone.

The silicone nipple slipped from Julia's lips. With a corner of the baby's bib, Bronwyn carefully blotted the milky smear in the corner of her mouth. Then she noted the amount of formula Julia had taken on her chart.

After she had laid the sleeping infant in her crib, Bronwyn drew the pink blanket over her and set the little cloth doll near her head. Whether Julia recognized them as the bits she had retained of her old life, Bronwyn couldn't tell. She hoped they helped.

She raised the crib's side and stood, her forearms resting on it, watching Julia sleep for several minutes. Julia wasn't hers. Bronwyn wiped at the trickle of wetness on her cheeks and swallowed the fist-sized lump in her throat. Not even the shadow of the *temptation* to dream of keeping Julia could be allowed to cross the threshold of her consciousness. But as inadequate and unskilled as she repeatedly felt, sometime in the past twenty-four hours she had fallen completely in love with this child.

~~~

Mary Cole Sessoms was on the phone. "Glad I caught you." Mary Cole had a much more Southern-sounding accent than JJ did, but she was no less commanding. "A friend just called me, and I told her to call you."

Bronwyn's heart skipped a beat. The house... my God, the house would have to improve to earn a grade of D-minus. With JJ's and David's help yesterday, they'd gotten it dusted and swept, the bathroom cleaned and disinfected, but that wasn't even a start on what the house needed to be livable, much less presentable.

And there was a puddle on the hall floor, again.

Bronwyn dashed to the dirty-clothes basket in the kitchen for a towel to mop it up with. "I'm not ready to see patients."

"I told her that. She's a contractor, very exclusive, very top-of-the-line work."

On her hands and knees, Bronwyn swabbed the dull oak boards that retained only a trace of their finish. "Oh, no! Then she really can't see the place the way it looks."

"She's exactly the kind of influential person you want on board with you. She's not only a successful business-woman, she sits on committees of several statewide non-profit organizations."

"I'm sure she's a lovely person, but—" At a loss for words, Bronwyn stopped speaking. If Mary Cole, con-summate businesswoman, didn't see that Bronwyn had nothing resembling an office, Bronwyn couldn't think of what to tell her.

"Bronwyn. This is not the moment to go all shy and self-effacing. The woman I'm talking about could pick up the phone and talk to anybody in this state—and she wants to talk to you."

"Because *you* told her to."

"I suggested it," Mary Cole acknowledged with

wounded dignity. "One person tells another. That's the way it works."

"All right. But my first impression won't be very impressive." Bronwyn was afraid she sounded as petulant as Julia. "The air-conditioner barely functions."

"Oh, don't worry about a thing." Mary Cole was suddenly all breezy cheer. She knew she had won. The woman was a magnolia-scented steamroller! "Trust me on this. She's going to love you."

~~~

Seconds after the call ended, the cell phone buzzed again. A woman named Carole Blankenship introduced herself. "Mary Cole Sessoms suggested I talk to you."

"Mary Cole is one of my biggest boosters, but I'm afraid she may have misrepresented me. I'm not seeing patients. My office isn't open yet."

"She said you might say that." Carole dismissed the objection. "But she also said you're the one she would talk to if she were in my position. Mary Cole swears she'll never let another doctor tell her not to worry when she *is* worried. I know you're not seeing patients."

Bronwyn looked around the kitchen. She tried to see all that had been done, instead of all there was to do. Four adults working together had been able to accomplish a lot. The rooms had been dusted, the boxes unpacked and stored away, the floors swept, the downstairs windows washed, and several layers of grime removed from the kitchen. Still, while habitable, the house was a long way from impressive. "Um—"

"I'm in my car on the way back from Durham. I can be there in twenty minutes."

"You don't understand. My furniture hasn't come. I not only don't have an office, I don't even have a living room. Plus, I'm—um—baby-sitting the daughter of a friend. She's down for a nap, but she might wake up."

"Oh, I love babies. Don't worry. Mary Cole told me you're planning extensive remodeling, which the house is in desperate need of. My business is renovating and repurposing old structures. I understand a work in progress. I've seen houses in every state of debilitation and rehabilitation there is, and I've done many a consultation sitting on the porch steps."

Bronwyn had just had time to change into brown slacks and a tailored, pale peach cotton blouse when she heard a car in the drive. She slipped her narrow feet into plastic jewel-studded turquoise sandals.

At the door she met a woman in her middle years and completely comfortable with it. Her wavy black hair had been allowed to gray. Dramatic silver wings framed sparkling, cobalt blue eyes. Only a little taller than Bronwyn, the woman's round figure was perfectly complemented by a simple black cotton dress and lipstick-red patent spike heels.

"Thank you for seeing me." She held out her hand. "I'm worried to death and I had to talk to someone, but I promise I won't take up a lot of your time. My husband, Spud, had a lump in his groin."

Spud? This elegant woman with the same cultured Southern accent as Mary Cole had a husband named *Spud*? Bronwyn hoped she kept her expression neutral. She might not have succeeded because Carole went on, "Well, his name is Thaddeus, but his daddy was Thad, and everybody has always called him Spud."

"Let's go out on the side porch," Bronwyn told her. "The breeze is nice, and I'm afraid my air-conditioner is on its last legs. I've carried some kitchen chairs out there—we won't have to sit on the steps."

When they were seated, and after a quick glance at the laptop showed Julia sleeping soundly, Bronwyn asked, "What does your husband do?"

"He's a farmer. He has three farms and rents three more. Over five thousand acres. The doctors at Lords wanted to know that, too. Spud says he's probably been exposed to every pesticide, every weed-killer, and every defoliant there is. He's walked in fields that have been sprayed and come out with his pants saturated, wet from the waist down."

Nobody thought of farmers, famous for their conservatism, as daredevils, but farming was one of the most hazardous ways to make a living. Farmers had to work around cows, horses, and pigs big enough to crush a man, and operate monster-sized machinery. But even if they didn't raise animals or crops that needed mechanical harvesting, the danger that really couldn't be avoided, only minimized, was exposure to a huge array of dangerous chemicals.

"The lump was in his groin area, you say? Did you see it before it was removed? What did it look like?"

"The skin was red over it, and you could feel it just under the skin. He hates doctors, and it was the size of a walnut before I could get him to have it checked out. They did a biopsy and said it was cancer, so we went to Lords and had it removed."

Bronwyn nodded for her to continue.

"The doctors came in to talk to us today. Here." She

handed over a piece of paper. "This is the official diagnosis. Now they want to do aggressive radiation. They want to radiate from his neck down—his entire torso."

"That's a lot of radiation." Bronwyn said mildly, hiding her shock.

"Spud says he's not going to do it. He says if the cancer is going to kill him, so be it, because the radiation will kill him, too."

Carole swallowed hard. Her eyes filled, but she didn't let tears fall. She took a deep breath and sat a little straighter. "If his time is up, I will face it. But I'm *not* going to let him die of something he could be treated for—just because he hates doctors. If I have to, I will *make* him take the treatment." She reached for Bronwyn's hand. "But here's my problem. What they're saying doesn't make sense to me."

It didn't make sense to Bronwyn, either. That much radiation, particularly of the abdomen, would make Spud terribly sick. "What did they tell you?"

Gradually, with many digressions, Carole's primary concern emerged. "When I tried to get them to explain it, they said the problem is that they are sure the tumor they removed is a metastasis, spread from somewhere else. But they don't know where the primary site is. They can't find it."

"That's not that uncommon. About forty percent of the time, the primary site can't be established."

"But they don't know where *any* other metastases are. They x-rayed, they scanned, they biopsied. This is the only tumor they know of. And they can't really tell what organs the tumor may have started from. It's cancer, but they don't know what it is." Carole looked into the distance. "I just don't know what to do. They say radiation is his only chance. If we wait, the cancer will spread and then it will be too late."

"But you don't sound convinced. Have you asked for a second opinion?"

"When I asked whether we needed a second opinion, the doctor said we could go anywhere we want to but they'll just tell us the same thing." Carole's eyes filled with tears again. "Spud's a strong man, Bronwyn. A vigorous man. He farms over five thousand acres and has men working for him, but he's not sitting in an office in a suit. He's out there in the fields with them working every day. It's his joy."

Carole was beginning to repeat herself, a sign that her concern hadn't really been addressed. "What would make you feel better?" Bronwyn asked.

"Me? I'm not worried about me."

"I know. Your husband is the patient. But you're the one *here*. You're the person I can help right now. You say you're worried, and I'd say with good reason. What would reassure you?"

Carole was silent for a long moment. She played with her wedding ring. The anxiety in her cobalt eyes changed to decisiveness. "If I just *knew*. They say radiation is his only chance, but they don't seem to have a target—that's why they want to radiate such a wide area. But Spud says it will kill him."

"So you don't feel sure of the diagnosis. What happened when you mentioned a second opinion?"

"Oh, the doctor got angry. You should have heard him—all huffy and arrogant. He told me that by even *talking* about any delay in starting treatment, I was risking my husband's life. What do you think? What should I do?"

"If you want a second opinion, you should have one. The doctors at Lords might be right that radiation is his best chance, but having faith in a treatment is also important. It sounds to me like you're not sure about the treatment because you don't think they have enough information on which to base a treatment plan."

"That's right! That's *it*! I tried to explain that we're not trying to deny that Spud has cancer, and we're not looking for the magic bullet that will guarantee a cure. If Spud has a terminal illness, we will deal with it. But every time I tried to question the doctor's reasoning, he just got huffier and more condescending, and I felt foolish—like I was too stupid to understand."

"Trust yourself. They might be satisfied with what they've found out, but you're not. If they're wrong, *you're* the one with the most to lose. Don't ask. Tell them you want a referral."

"I can do that?"

"Yes, you can. And by law, they have to. The doctor at Lords was way out of line."

"Where?" Carole's deep blue eyes were no longer shadowed with anxiety or weakened by indecision. Suddenly Bronwyn could see the self-assurance of a woman who had created a successful business in a male-dominated trade. "Everybody says Lords is the best in the South."

"Sloan-Kettering." The answer popped instantly from Bronwyn's mouth.

"Where is Sloan-Kettering?"

"New York City."

"Why there?" Carole snapped the demand for more information out crisply.

Bronwyn hid a smile. She could just imagine how offended those doctors with delusions of godhood had been if Carole had used that tone when she questioned them.

The truth was Bronwyn didn't know exactly why she had said Sloan-Kettering, since there were other good cancer centers. She only knew she had been absolutely sure. But the last thing Carole needed was another doctor saying, *Do it because I said so*. "That's a good question. You could ask for referral to Duke, but I think it's important to look at treatment options in different area of the country. Medicine isn't practiced exactly the same everywhere. You will see doctors who have trained in other places and, therefore, might have had good experience with a different approach to treatment. And of course, Sloan-Kettering is an entire hospital dedicated to cancer treatment. They see a huge variety of cancers. If they concur with the doctors at Lords—okay. Well, then you'll know."

~~~

"I saw my first patient today—well, the second one, if you count the munchkin—but my first official patient. Mary Cole sent her."

"Um-hmm." Garth murmured, to let her know he was listening. He liked these times when they lay in the dark after making love and talked.

"Here's the thing: she's wealthy, educated, used to feeling powerful. But dealing with grave illness strips people. They have too much at stake. They don't know what questions to ask. With her connections she could have talked to anyone in this state. But she had to come to me to find out she could and should get a second opinion."

"I detect a note of wonder or disbelief in your voice."

"Yes, you do. And I'm feeling both. For a woman with her resources to be unable to find a doctor who would simply listen to her… it's mind-boggling. But it is the state of the art. Anyway, seeing a patient felt good. What I did made a difference."

"And all you did was listen?"

"Yes. Sounds unlikely, doesn't it? I imagine other people she had talked to thought the issue was that her husband was opposed to radiation therapy, but what really had to be addressed was her fear that the doctors had insufficient data to make a good treatment plan. I had to listen for a while before I understood that was the problem. The arrogant SOBs at Lords had browbeaten her for daring to question them. In spite of her confidence and intelligence, she had been no match for them."

"How long did you listen?"

"I'm not sure. More than eight minutes, I can tell you that."

Bronwyn turned on her side and put her head on Garth's chest. "People are so vulnerable to the power games doctors play," she mused aloud. "In managing her business, Carole would never have let anyone get away with the emotional coercion that doctor was using."

For the first time, Garth felt real doubt that Bronwyn would be able to handle the moves that being married to him would entail. While it was true that as an ER physician she could likely get a job anywhere, asking her to do so would be asking her to be less than she was. He would have a hard time doing that.

Chapter 30

*Now the reason the enlightened prince and the wise
general conquer the enemy whenever they move and
their achievements surpass those of ordinary men
is foreknowledge.*

—Sun Tzu, *The Art of War*

"DID YOU MAKE AN APPOINTMENT WITH A CONTRACTOR TO
come this morning?" Bronwyn asked Garth a couple of
days later as she adjusted the yellowed but functional
blinds to keep out the hot morning sun. She worked
as hard to regulate the temperature of the house's interior as the air-conditioner did. Garth hoped she was
wearing down. He hated the necessity of letting the air-
conditioning go unfixed, but it was for her own good.

"I heard from Davy an hour ago that he, Do-Lord,
and Lon were on their way, but I don't know anything
about a contractor. Why?"

She gave him a worldly-wise look. "Something that
looks like a contractor's van just pulled up."

"Stay here."

It was indeed a commercial van, complete with lad-
ders mounted on racks on its sides. Garth laughed when
the "contractors" piled out. They were Davy, Do-Lord,
and Lon, all wearing bill caps and blue coveralls with a
building contractor's logo emblazoned on the back.

"Glad you could come," he called, meaning it. He waved them inside. The pleasure he felt was out of proportion, given that he wasn't closely acquainted with either Do-Lord or Lon. But damn it felt good.

His job with Coastal Air had isolated him and had put him into solitary confinement, and he hadn't even noticed it. What did that say about where his head had been? Things were clearing up now. He couldn't wait to get back to being who he should be: a SEAL. He hoped these trusted friends would be able to tell him whether MacMurtry's story was in any part true.

Lon looked at the entry and staircase curiously when greetings were over. Lon had aged since he was Garth's lead B/UDS instructor. He must be close to fifty now, and his once sandy-red hair was heavily streaked with silver. Even so, his burly build showed no hint of softening. "How much surveillance do you think you're under?"

"So far? None that I can detect—which, given the situation, is weird."

Lon nodded. "Then what's with the cameras?"

Garth explained about the "ghost." Lon accepted the story without comment, but the eyes in Do-Lord's bony, homely yet handsome face lit with interest. Anything having to do with the paranormal was right up his alley. In addition, he was known to be an information sponge, always curious, always eager to explore new territory.

"Come on," Garth told them. "I'll introduce you to Bronwyn."

"Everybody, this is Bronwyn," he told them when they had joined her in the family room at the back of the house. "And Bronwyn, this is Caleb Dulaude, aka Do-Lord."

"Yes. I've heard about you from Mrs. Lilly Hale Sessoms." Bronwyn offered her hand to him. "She includes you among her grandsons—but I gather you're not related?"

"I've been fortunate enough to be unofficially adopted by her," Do-Lord acknowledged with a way-too-charming smile. "She's a special lady."

Garth touched Bronny's arm. Okay, so he was marking his territory. So sue him. "And this is Senior Chief Lon Swales."

"Nice to meet you." Bronwyn pointed from the senior chief to Do-Lord. "Are you two related?"

"No, ma'am, though we've been asked that before." Lon gave Do-Lord a derogatory look. "I don't see the resemblance myself."

"Me either," averred Do-Lord. "I'm so much better looking, there's no comparison."

Lon turned back to Bronwyn. "Doc here tells me you've got a big renovation project. I thought I'd better see it for myself. I used to flip houses as a sideline before the market went south."

Bronwyn looked around, puzzled. "Who is 'Doc'?"

"Davy," Garth told her. "SEALs usually call hospital corpsmen 'Doc.'"

"Oh, yes, of course. I wasn't thinking. JJ always calls him David."

"Are you used to thinking of yourself as 'the doctor'?" Lon asked with an impressive degree of insight, Garth thought. "Would you prefer for us to call you Dr. Whitescarver?"

"Not at all. I'd like for you to call me Bronwyn. I meet few enough people who see me as, first of all, a person. And yes, I'll be delighted if you will share your renovation expertise. My plan was to work on the house a bit at the time, but I'm afraid I was naive and didn't understand what was entailed. I'm not going to give up, but the prospect seems overwhelming. I've had one general contractor come from one of the larger towns, and his bids were scary-huge."

Lon looked to Garth, "Where do you want to start?"

"There's water coming in somewhere. Doc and I checked the roof. Maybe you can figure it out."

A half-hour or so later, the outside door opened and the four men trooped into the family room with Davy limping and being supported on either side by Garth and Do-Lord.

"You guys are trying to make me look like a cripple," Davy groused. "I don't need this much help."

Bronwyn quickly shoved the battered coffee table in front of the big brown chair. "Sit him here. Put his foot on the table." She rested her hand on his foot. "What happened?"

"Stupid. I stepped off the ladder wrong. Really. I'm not hurt."

"Let the doctor tell us that," Lon told him. "He didn't want to come in at all."

Garth gently swatted the top of David's head. "I thought I was going to have to threaten to carry you. Again." Bronwyn was stunned at the amount of tender affection she saw in Garth's face and equally stunned that the other men didn't seem to perceive it.

"What do you mean, again?" David asked.

Garth grinned. "Don't you remember?"

"Sorry. No. *Wait*..." David looked puzzled. "Actually, I do. But... where were we?"

"Afghanistan. When you were injured."

David shook his head. "That can't be it. I don't remember being hit in Afghanistan. The docs say I probably never will."

"But you do remember I threatened to carry you?"

"Yeah, I have dreams about arguing with you about whether I'm dead or not," Davy laughed at the absurdity. "But in the dream we're not in Afghanistan—we're in Colorado."

"What are you two talking about?" Do-Lord interjected.

Garth answered. "I had a near-death experience when I was wounded. Davy was there. He was part of it. It was so real. Beyond real. Something about this," he indicated the group, "reminded me. I think Davy remembers it, too."

"Wait," Do-Lord held up a hand. "Don't say any more. You need to write everything down independently before you compare stories."

"In a minute," Garth said. "First let Bronwyn look at Davy's ankle."

Bronwyn visualized the bones and the complicated arrangements of ligaments and tendons on the inside as she ran her fingers over the skin of the ankle. She detected swelling and a small degree of darkening of the skin. "Nothing too serious, I think."

"I told you guys. It's already stopped hurting. And the swelling is going down, too."

Lon frowned. "Are you looking at the right ankle?" he questioned Bronwyn. "That's not how it looked a few minutes ago."

Bronwyn looked to David for confirmation that she had examined the right ankle. "Garth told me how fast you men heal."

Lon's bushy, sun-bleached eyebrows slammed together. "Not *that* fast."

Bronwyn shrugged. "Well, anyway, it will be all right, I think. It may take a little while longer for the bruising to disappear, but it should go away soon, too."

"Here." Do-Lord handed David and Garth pencils and paper when they had moved out to the porch, hoping to find a cooler spot. "Write down what you remember. Add sketches if you need to. Include as much detail as you can. Try not to censor. Don't worry if it doesn't make any sense."

While Garth and David wrote, the porch's silence was broken only by the soft clatter of the magnolia's leathery leaves when the wind picked up.

Julia woke. Bronwyn changed her and brought her downstairs. She fixed the baby a bottle of juice. Julia's usual dandelion fluff of hair had been matted with sweat. For their size, babies needed a huge volume of fluids.

"Let me have her," Lon said when Bronwyn returned to the porch. "I can give a baby a bottle."

Bronwyn passed the baby over, prepared to take her back if Julia didn't react well to a stranger. But Lon tucked the baby into the crook of one brawny arm with sure competence. Julia relaxed in his hold and in a second or two appeared interested only in her bottle.

Left with nothing to do except observe, Bronwyn tried to keep her expression neutral. She had a hard time believing how seriously these tough, practical, earthy men were taking this exercise. And they were actively engaged even though they teased Do-Lord about making them into guinea pigs for his research.

Joking and teasing was how a group of dominant, aggressive men related—when fighting was out of the question and competition would be nonproductive. Bronwyn knew. She'd seen, and taken, plenty of it in the medical world.

Among these SEALs, the teasing was rougher, but also, she thought, better-natured. It didn't disguise the obvious respect they had for Do-Lord and the formidable intelligence he hid under a good ole boy persona.

A typical group of doctors would have been scathing in their derision, and probably refused to participate as well.

"I'm done." Garth handed his writing tablet to Do-Lord.

After glancing over what he had written, Davy followed suit. "Me too."

"Now we're going to score both accounts just as we do for remote viewing experiments." Do-Lord opened his coverall and extracted a pair of wire-rimmed glasses and a highlighter from his shirt pocket.

Bronwyn smiled on the inside. She had already guessed Do-Lord was a nerd in SEAL's clothing. With the gold glasses perched on his nose, she knew it.

Swiftly he went through both accounts marking words and phrases in yellow. He turned to Bronwyn. "Have you heard this story before?"

"No."

"Do you believe in the paranormal?"

She didn't want to offend Do-Lord who was clearly serious about his hobby. Bronwyn sought for a tactful way to say she didn't. "I think most of what people call ESP is the mind's ability to draw conclusions from a lot of minimal cues. The brain takes in thousands of times more information than we are consciously aware of. It's a wonderful ability that too few appreciate, but there's nothing 'extra' about it."

"Good answer!" Over the rim of his glasses Do-Lord sent her the prideful smile a true academic gives a promising student. "Your skepticism will be useful. I'll let you be the other independent judge of whether their stories match." He addressed the rest of the group. "Ideally, we'd make sure both judges were completely blind, of course—unaware of who wrote the accounts and of each other. But we're not looking for scientific rigor in this case; just enough validation, or not, to establish a hypothesis."

Julia had finished her bottle and Lon had propped her on his broad lap while he listened to Do-Lord. Keeping an arm as solid as a tree branch around her, he aimed a pointer-finger pistol at Do-Lord. "Step away from the chalkboard, Professor. You've gone into lecture mode."

David leaned confidentially toward Garth. His whispered aside was clearly audible. "He didn't used to be this bad. Comes from being married to a PhD in biology."

"Cut the clowning, guys. You doan thenk"—Do-Lord's accent suddenly thickened—"they gonna pay me the big bucks, if I talk iggorant—which I am."

Do-Lord grinned at the guys' loud hoots and catcalls "Show a little respect." He produced another highlighter—green this time—and handed it to Bronwyn.

"Try to avoid getting caught up in the story line. Instead, highlight words or phrases that are the same—or that mean the same thing."

"So what conclusions do you draw?" he asked Bronwyn when she had finished.

Bronwyn studied the papers dotted with green where the words had matched. She tried to ignore the cold flutter under her breastbone. She had been certain she would find the internal correspondences to be flukes. Instead, she had found more unanimity in the two accounts than Do-Lord did.

She had been prepared to be gracious in disagreement. Now she could only be honest."Um... I would say that even though Garth claims to remember an event, and David says he's only recounting dreams, both are telling essentially the same story." She shook her head hoping to dispel the sense of unreality. "But I don't know how to explain it. I can't believe they both left their bodies while they were near death."

Do-Lord tilted his head. Behind the glasses, his keenly perceptive gaze turned kindly. "Many impossible things turn out to be possible when the exact circumstances under which they occur is finally understood," he replied in a soft voice.

"True. But... But thinking people don't take this woo-woo stuff seriously! Frankly, I can't believe that you, a SEAL, are spending even a minute looking into it."

"I'm a private consultant these days."

"Yeah, he's the only one of us," Davy pointed out, laughing, "who really *is* a contractor."

Lon grinned. "Yet another piece of the war machine.

Another opportunist feeding at the public trough, making three times what he could have if he were still in the navy."

"Cut it out, guys," Garth ordered. "In Do-lord's case, that's not a fair assessment. Do-Lord is working for his country. He's probably more useful out of the navy than in it." Speaking to Bronwyn, he explained, "Do-Lord is researching ESP in battle situations. He hopes to be able to teach officers to make better use of it." Garth's blue eyes lit with humor. "On a line-item budget will be called leadership training, but if he were still in the navy the course content would never be allowed."

Bronwyn could feel her eyebrows climbing up her forehead. "You *teach* this woo-woo stuff?"

"Um, Bronny," Garth grinned, "I don't think I mentioned that Do-Lord has a PhD in psychology and that since he got out of the navy, when he's not doing field research, he teaches courses in maximizing intuition's helpfulness. Maybe you shouldn't call what he does 'woo-woo.'"

Bronwyn bit her lip at her own gaucheness. "I didn't mean to insult you. I was surprised, that's all—because you are so obviously rational. You're intelligent and well educated. According to David, you're married to a scientist. Surely you know there is no credible scientific evidence for anything paranormal."

Do-Lord tilted his head—this time as if he suddenly found her to be an odd specimen. "What do you call credible—or scientific? Only people who have never looked at the research would say that. Seventy or eighty years of rigorously controlled experiments, including experiments conducted by the military, have proved that ESP exists." His hazel eyes turned hard. "But some people, if they can't question the methodology of an experiment, will still call it unbelievable and attack the credibility of the researcher."

Bronwyn looked down at her hands which had somehow become tightly clasped together. She carefully relaxed them and looked up. "I *have* insulted you. I'm sorry." How had she become the one in the wrong? "But you must admit, any rational person…"

"Maybe you're the irrational one. Somebody told you psychic phenomena were impossible, and now you continue to believe them, instead of believing data you yourself obtained. That's irrational." Do-Lord peered at her intently. "Why would you do that? What are you afraid of? Are you afraid of knowing what you know"— he let the question hang—"or are you afraid you already *know too much*? Are you afraid if you admit that you'll be kicked out of the science club?"

Was she afraid of knowing too much? She had seen the fear on her parent's faces when she knew things they thought she shouldn't. As for being afraid of being kicked out of the "science club"—maybe she was. By their actions, her parents had said she wasn't one of them—meaning if she saw and heard and experienced "impossible" things, she could never be a doctor. Had she absorbed their fear without asking if it was rational?

"Do all of you," Bronwyn asked the other men, "believe in this kind of thing?"

Lon gave her a canny look that made her wonder what conclusions he had come to about her. "Do-Lord here has a theory that a lot of talents and abilities have a psychic component. Me, I don't really care. I like understanding the science behind what SEALs do, but what I *believe* in is what works." He pointed to Garth. "Take the lieutenant here. He's got a reputation for not losing men. He either has precognition or phenomenally good luck. *I don't care.* All I know is he sent Doc away from the team, and because he did, everyone survived."

"All survived *except* Doc," Do-Lord pointed out grinning, "if we believe their independently gathered accounts."

Bronwyn recalled her first sight of David and her instantaneous impression that surviving his injuries had been a miracle. She looked at David. "Do you believe it really happened—you were dead and Garth brought you back?"

He rubbed his chin. "I would have a hard time swearing to the actuality of anything that happens in a dream. I know Garth, though. I served under him. I know what matters to him. If there was any way he could drag me back to the land of the living, he would."

"But do you think there *is* a way?"

David turned on the cocky charm. Bronwyn *felt* him do it. "What can I say? He's a SEAL. Any man who graduates from B/UDS has learned to push past what his mind tells him he can't do."

Bronwyn turned to Garth. "You?"

"I'm with Lon. I don't much care whether it's possible or not. It was the most real thing I ever experienced. And Davy and I *are* alive."

"Do all SEALs believe this way?"

Bronwyn *felt* them elect Do-Lord to answer her. "Most will agree that an extraordinary degree of intuition is not unusual in SEALs. Whether they 'believe' in psychic phenomena or not, none would doubt the reality of gut feelings. I think it's a by-product of our training."

"By-product of what training, exactly?"

"SEALs learn to pay attention. The better observer you are, the more you see not what you *think* is there, and not what you *wish* were there, but what is right in front of your eyes. You learn how often the mind is acting as a barrier between you and reality, rather than a window on reality. You will become disillusioned." He smiled at his little pun. "Of course, most people have no need to be disillusioned. They are perfectly comfortable with their niche and are successful in it."

"Are you saying that people become disillusioned because they need to be?" Bronwyn's slow disillusionment with medicine had been exquisitely painful. Did that mean that losing her false notions had been a necessary shedding of old skin?

Do-Lord's hazel eyes softened. His slow nod held compassion. "A lot of the time, the first stage of wisdom is disillusionment. Sometimes we can just discard old ideas. Sometimes they are ripped from us, taking a lot of skin," he added in an odd echo of what she had just been thinking, "and we walk around raw and shocked, every nerve ending exposed, and even when the skin grows back, we are not the same as we were."

"There he goes with the philosophical bullshit again." David lobbed a balled-up piece of paper at Do-Lord's face.

Bronwyn whipped around, shocked at his insensitivity. Where was that vaunted SEAL intuition now? Didn't

David know Do-Lord was talking about a disillusion-ment that had happened to him? That had caused him great pain?

"That's not *philosophy*, Davy. You idiot, didn't I teach you anything?" The senior chief stopped bounc-ing Julia on his knee and raised his eyes heavenward. "I tried, Lord. I tried to raise 'em right, but Graziano's too stupid to find his dick in the dark—no offense, little girl—and Lord, Dulaude has gone all touchy-feely."

The "no offense, little girl" tipped Bronwyn off. She doubted if the senior chief ever said anything he didn't mean to. They *did* know deep emotion lay be-hind Do-Lord's words and were giving him a chance to recover.

She decided to go along with the lightened mood. She aimed a wry smile at Garth. "Okay. In the name of letting go of preconceived notions, I'm trying to get my mind around it. Let me see if I've got the basics. You're telling me you were a ghost. And David was a ghost. And you met in heaven."

"I don't think it was heaven," Garth deadpanned to Davy. "Do you think it was heaven?"

"No. I think it's what my mother called the border-land—even if it looked like Colorado."

"And although I might have been clinically dead—ergo, ghost-enabled—for a few minutes," Garth ex-panded, "Davy was alive when he was found. The only evidence that we were both dead is that we each inde-pendently remember Davy saying he was dead and me talking him out of it."

Davy sent Garth a smile of such unalloyed tenderness that Bronwyn's eyes went hot with unshed tears. "You wouldn't leave me behind," he said. "You went to the borderland to get me."

Lon handed Julia to Bronwyn. He slapped his knees and stood. "Well, now that we've got that settled, I have a procedural question." He turned to Garth. The kindly baby-holder disappeared, and suddenly Bronwyn could see the instructor who believed in dealing out pain as a learning aid.

"When the hell," Lon growled, "are you going to get to work on the air-conditioner—*sir*? I seem to re-member you're not a complete idiot about machinery. Remarkable, you being an officer, *which* are not noted for their brains or their propensity to do actual work… Sir."

Bronwyn set the baby on her knee. Her jaw dropped. "It can be *fixed*?"

The harshness of the older man's expression abated slightly. "You still need a new system, but it can work better than it does. It'll do until you're ready to start major renovations. If Lieutenant Vale didn't have *shit for brains*—no offense, ma'am—he'd already have it taken care of."

Garth took the insult to his intelligence and work ethic philosophically, though Bronwyn detected a tight-ening of the corners of his mouth. "Well, me being a poor benighted officer and all, I guess I was waiting for the guidance of a senior chief, *which* are known for their understanding of how things run. I only hope you are right." He stood. "Men, let us commence Operation Cool Air."

Chapter 31

BEFORE SHE WENT TO HER ROOM THAT NIGHT, BRONWYN peeped in on the sleeping Julia. In the dim glow of the night light, she had the impression the baby was sleeping better in the cooler house.

Bronwyn was standing in front of the tiny dresser mirror trying to see what her hair looked like—not that she could tell much between the cloudy mirror and the light from the bedside lamp behind her. Oh for the day when she had had a master bath with large, well-lit mirrors! Garth appeared in the mirror behind her.

Bronwyn finger-combed her hair. "I have a question," she said to his reflection. "Did you have a premonition? Is that why you sent David to the next village?"

He set large, warm hands on her hips and slipped them slowly up her rib cage, brushing the sides of her breasts. "No. If I had, I would never have sent him. And we wouldn't have gone into that ambush, either. I would have aborted then and there."

"Oh. I didn't think of that."

"Right." He lifted her hair and trailed kisses down the side of her neck, occasionally letting her feel his teeth. "And I'd still be in a regular outfit, being sent all over the world, and you and I would most likely have never met, which would be a damn shame."

He gave a definitive nip to her shoulder tendon. Bronwyn's whole body shuddered. Her breasts peaked.

On the inside she went all hot and liquid. She leaned her head further to give him better access. "So, are you saying, if none of this had happened, you would still be a SEAL?"

Knowing what she wanted, he licked at the little spot just behind her ear. He fiddled with the large white buttons on the shoulders of her bateau-necked cotton sweater. "How do these things work?"

"They don't. They're just decoration." In the cooler house, it had been worthwhile to get a little more dressed up. She turned around and laced her fingers around his neck. "You know you asked me one time why we didn't get together the first time we met?"

"Yeah?"

His wary tone made her smile. "Don't be scared. I'm not trying to lure you into a conversation about feelings. I just realized I need to apologize to you, that's all."

"For what?"

"The first time I saw you, I thought you were the kind of person that other people aren't real to. People are like moving pieces of the landscape that have to be kept up with, but they don't really register—you know?"

He went very still. "Like Darth Vader?"

Bronwyn was surprised at the comparison. "Well, he is like that, I suppose. But I wasn't thinking of him. You're much too hot to be a Darth Vader. And Darth Vader would never try to snatch one of his troops from the brink of death."

"You think I'm hot?" Manlike, he seized on only one part of what she had said.

"Yes, but don't throw me off the subject."

"The subject isn't sex?"

"You didn't answer my question."

"What question?"

"Do you wish you were still in the navy?"

"That's not what you asked."

"If you didn't forget the question, why didn't you answer?"

He smiled a smile of practiced friendliness that seemed oddly genuine. "Work with me, Bronny. I'm trying to seduce you."

"I'm in favor of that, but I can still multitask."

"No you can't."

"Yes, I can."

His eyes gleamed hotter blue with competitive zeal. "Want me to prove it?"

She had a competitive nature herself. Came with the territory. "Go for it. It'll be the perfect win-win."

"Glad you see it that way."

"Not for you. I meant a win-win for me. If I lose, I win, and if I win, I win."

"Okay. You asked for it." With casual strength, one arm around her legs, one around her hips, he swept her up and tossed her over his shoulder.

"What are you doing?"

"Taking you downstairs."

"What for?"

"I want a midnight snack.

Laughing wasn't all that comfortable with her diaphragm crunched against a hard shoulder. Bronwyn did anyway. She loved this playful side of him. She thought she should challenge him more often.

He started down the stairs, with her giggling all the way. At the foot, he smacked her on her bottom. "Show some respect." It wasn't painful—more a tingle of nerves jolted awake. *All* the nerves in that area. It was surprisingly erotic. Her breath caught. She wiggled a little—not to get away, to get closer.

"Liked that, huh?" His big hand kneaded her bottom with firm, knowledgeable strokes. He felt for the waistband of her panties and dragged them down. They dangled around her ankles. "Bare skinned, it will feel even better."

She tensed but relaxed as he continued to knead. "You're wet," he said as his fingers dipped deeper. Suddenly the flat of his hand smacked her again.

A hot wave of sensation traveled the whole area. Tissues swelled. Bronwyn had never felt so undignified and so turned on in her life. But a protest seemed called for. "That's not fair."

"SEALs never fight fair. Anyway," his hand landed again, "it's better if you don't know when it's coming."

Arrived in the kitchen, he flicked on the small Tiffany-shaded light over the breakfast table and, without ceremony (but making sure she didn't bump her head), dumped Bronwyn on it. The salt and pepper shakers rolled unheeded to the floor.

He leaned over her, his arms braced on either side of her head. "Are you ready to concede yet?"

"What?" Why had she thought his eyes were the color of icebergs? Right now they were the hot blue of flame.

He grinned triumphantly.

"You think you can win *that* easy? No way." She bit her lip to keep from laughing. "And anyway I didn't know we were on," she accused. "You said you were coming to get a snack."

The smile that illuminated his dark face now reminded her that the human gesture of smiling had probably evolved from snarls of aggression.

"I am here for a snack." He sat down in a kitchen chair and hitched it closer to the table. He grasped her hips and slid her forward until her hips were just on the edge. "You're it."

He draped her legs over his shoulders and carefully, competently opened her to his gaze. "Oh, yeah," he breathed. "Just what I had a taste for."

He took his time looking her over. He ran his fingers along the place her buttocks curved into the backs of her thighs. He stroked the silky skin of their inner faces. And never stopped looking. "The skin is a little pink here." He scraped lightly. Heat flooded her entire body. "I didn't hurt you, did I?"

"No, but maybe you should do it a few more times just to make sure."

"Another time, maybe. Right now, I gotta do this." His mouth closed over her. His hot, wet tongue delved deep. In a long, slow swoop he reached the clitoris and flicked it.

He twirled around here and there, voluptuous sensation piling on sensation, and then from the long, slow build-up, with the tip of his tongue, he flicked it again.

Lightning zinged from that one place, punched her heart into another gear, and she would swear, heated her eyes. Her legs tightened. She tried to lift her pelvis to bring herself closer, but the position she was in gave her little leverage.

He patted her belly. "Patience, my sweet. You're supposed to be asking me questions, you know. Multitasking."

"Don't gloat."

"How can I gloat? You said you win either way. I'm just trying to make sure you win big."

At his self-righteous taunt, laughter shook Bronwyn's belly, and just like that, without him doing anything at all, she crested another peak.

He applied his mouth again, odd forays stringing heat to heat, and when he flicked again from the underside, she screamed a little. He did it again and again, by tiny increments bringing the flicks closer and closer together until she had to bite down on her fist to keep from crying out continuously, while the pleasure crested from peak to peak like a flashing strobe light. Every nerve vibrated.

And then there it was. Every muscle clenched. The pressure exploded in shuddering bursts. She undulated, wracked with climax after climax.

And then he rose up, gripped her hips, and plunged himself into her. Stretching her, sending her into more spasms, more release as he pumped once, twice, three times, went rigid, and with a shout came.

He collapsed over her, gulping for air and keeping his weight on his forearms so that she could breathe, too.

"No more," he gasped, his dark voice raspy and harsh. "No more contests. I thought I was going to die."

———

Later, when they had showered, Bronwyn came into the bedroom. Garth looked out the window, a white towel wrapped loosely around his hips. His legs were a lighter shade of oak than his torso. Garth turned when he heard her. He smiled. His eyelids drooped in lazy satiation.

She went to the bureau and extracted one of the gauzy cotton gowns. Knowing he was watching, she dropped her towel, shook out the gown, and slipped it over her head. Never had any man made her feel so sexy and desirable.

She thrilled to know she had the power to bring that look of sexy contentment to his face. She kicked her towel out of the way and went to him. She laced her hands on the back of his neck. "I have another question. Something I thought about all day. If you hadn't come across David, in what he called the borderland, would you have come back yourself?"

"I don't know." Garth detached her hands from his neck. He went to look out the dark window.

Bronwyn regretted the loss of physical contact, but so many subjects were closed between them. She saw a chance to get to know him better and wasn't willing to let it slide. "Can I touch your back?"

"Yeah."

Bronwyn stroked the deep groove of his spine, hoping to let him know he wasn't alone. "He thinks you went to get him. Did you?"

"I was bothered that he was somewhere wounded, alone. We train to have each other's back at all times. It gives you something, an extra bit of morale, to know you always have at your side a man who would give his life to save yours. Every SEAL is prepared to die, but the worst thing for all those who are left alive is when a SEAL dies alone."

"But once you were with him, he wasn't alone."

"Yeah. But then it felt wrong, period."

"Wrong? Okay, I get it that SEALs don't consider *just* dying to be wrong enough. But you're saying you decided to come back because he…"

"Right." In profile she watched his lips quirk upward, acknowledging her humor. "Someone had to change his mind." She felt his back tense. The muscles of his shoulders bunched. "It was morally wrong. Cosmically wrong. He didn't deserve to die. It was a miscarriage of justice of monstrous proportions."

"Why?"

He turned and looked at her in surprise—as if his reasons were self-evident. "You've seen Davy. *He's*... *good*—you know—a *good* man."

Bronwyn shook her head, denying what he implied. "*You're* a good man."

His face was the most expressionless it had been in days. And still she saw something like hope or wonder fill his eyes until they glittered. "You think so?"

"That's what I was trying to tell you before. I didn't think so at first, but now I do."

Chapter 32

ON ONE OF THE FEW OCCASIONS IN HER LIFE, BRONWYN woke the next morning as dawn was breaking. She pulled on yesterday's clothes and stole from the house.

Sometimes you find out things about yourself you didn't really want to know. Bronwyn had yesterday, when she compared her attitude about paranormal events to the attitude of the men. Somewhere along the line, she had become as hidebound and as unwilling to look at data that disagreed with her beliefs as the most rigid of her professors. It wasn't how she thought of herself; it wasn't how she wanted to be.

Scrubby pines had been allowed to encroach on the house during the years of its neglect. As she cut across what should be lawn, her feet slid on pine needles. She inhaled the wet resiny smell of the pines and felt the sticky prickle of their needles on her arms as she brushed by three- and four-foot pines that were bright yellowish-green. Funny, the scrub pines were soft, almost fluffy-looking from a distance.

Finally she found the overgrown path to the river. The sandy soil was soft underfoot. Overhead, a woodpecker's hollow hammering bounced from tree to tree.

The barely discernible path abruptly slanted down. Through the trees she caught glimpses of shining silver, and then she was out of the trees and on a narrow strip of sand, and there was the river.

In the breathless stillness of dawn, in the east where the sun was just clearing the distant pines of the opposite shore far down river, the water had a silken look. Around her was an all-encompassing stillness—as if she had penetrated to the absolute center point of creation about which all else moved and turned.

This was the peace like a river.

Pink was a meaningless name for the liquid luminescence suffusing the air. It was the color of hope, the color of thoughts more profound than any human utterance. It was the color of the still point between past and future, the place of forever.

Pilings, like black, upraised fingers, poked through the mirrored surface of the water, cradling the gray, weathered planks of a narrow dock. Here and there between the rough boards were black blanks. So black, so blank—it was as if the dock had been built to bridge a chasm, a hole in the fabric of the universe.

The dock was her very own promontory into limitless space. Promising little safety, it lured, charmed, and tantalized with invitation to "Come in. Come, get as close as you can to walking on water."

The first plank was spongy underfoot, but it took her weight. She moved onto the next and then the next, ignoring her heart's swooping flutter when the dock chose to sway just as she stretched her stride across a three-plank gap. It hadn't seemed so challenging when she had come here with Garth. She made it to the end; that was all that mattered. She rested her hand on the deeply grooved piling, damp from last night's dew, chilled by the morning air.

She had entered medicine because she wanted to tend

the sick and wounded, to ease their suffering and to heal them. For a while the frenetic energy and fast pace of the ER had satisfied her. Her patients were the sick and wounded, and they needed her right now. She wasn't an adrenaline junky—okay, she was, a little—but what had really appealed to her about the ER was that she liked challenges, liked to rise to the occasion.

All this she had thought before. This morning she pushed on mentally. She didn't believe in ghosts, the supernatural, the afterlife, but it wasn't because she believed only in what she could see. It was more because believing that everything either had scientific explanation or it didn't exist, maintained the illusion that if she knew enough, life would be predictable. Such an attitude offered a firm-feeling but very false sense of security—as she should have realized the morning she walked into Trauma Room 3.

A fish plopped, loud and close. The sound jarred her from her reverie. She turned to face the shore. Looking up the long slope, she could see undulations left by the river's slow eons of shaping the land. She could also see bits of her house's roofline and hints of the house through the thick screen of pine and bay magnolia.

Once upon a time, the house had gleamed white and proud. It would be that way again.

She had come here when she recognized that if she continued to squeeze herself into modern medicine's paradigm of caring for patients, she would die. Now she recognized that as long as she continued to suppress her ability to see all that she saw, whether it fit her ideas of how the world worked or not, she would only be half-alive.

Garth met her on the porch when she returned to the house. He handed her a cup of coffee and laid a companionable arm over her shoulder. He gave her a moment or two to drink before he asked, "What were you doing down at the river?"

"Thinking. So many nights after Troy died and my world came crashing down around me, I sat up, hanging on, just hanging on, until the sun's first rays signaled night's end. This morning I woke with that verse from Psalms in my mind, 'Weeping may endure for a night, but joy comes in the morning.'" She squeezed his waist and leaned closer. "This morning I realized I didn't have to wait for dawn. I decided to walk toward the east to meet it."

Chapter 33

"WHAT'S THIS PLACE WE'RE GOING TO?" BRONWYN ASKED as Garth exited off the highway and drove into the small town. They seemed to be going through a warehouse district. The windshield wipers slapped a desultory rhythm, clearing what was more a coalescing of moisture than rain.

"The Sunnyside Oyster Bar."

"And why are we going there?"

"I asked Doug Cruikshank to recommend a special place. I get tired of the restaurants that are really the same. Anyway, he said if we wanted authentic eastern North Carolina without the hush puppies, something you'll never find anywhere else, this is the place."

He turned the big pickup into a gravel parking lot beside a building so small, it didn't look like it could contain anything. He stopped the truck and came around to help Bronwyn out.

For their first official big date, she had put on a short black skirt and the soft-pink, short-sleeved sweater JJ had given her, and her highest heels. The sudden cool spell had dictated a raincoat. Now a damp wet wind brushed her bare legs, found its way under her coat hem, and chilled her thighs.

As soon as she stepped onto the sand and packed gravel underfoot, a wobbly rock threatened to tip her. She extended her arms for balance in a move she knew was something less than graceful. "This is it?" she asked. The restaurant didn't even have a paved parking lot. "This is the special place?"

"Look over there." He pointed to a stretch limo, gleaming and supercilious-looking among pickups and SUVs. "Doug told me this place is a bit of a destination. Guess he was right."

Inside they found themselves in a large, dark room with an ear-damaging noise level punctuated by the steady slapping of the screen door as clumps of people entered and exited.

The big room's one source of heat was the hot air blasted from an overhead industrial heater. The center of the room was hot, the corners and near the door distinctly chilly. Old black Formica-topped pedestal tables were shoved higgledy-piggledy. Around some of them, people in ladder back chairs that had lost most of their varnish crowded two deep, while other tables had no one (and no chairs either). A huge flat-screen TV blared the UNC-Clemson game. The room was mostly lit by neon beer signs.

When the outside door opened, which it did almost constantly, damp chilly air diluted the cigarette smoke inside.

Garth looked as stunned as she felt at this example of fine dining. "Umm, wait here," he told her.

In a minute he returned. He put his lips next to her ear in order to be heard. "The next room is quieter and nonsmoking."

In the next room, white painted, unsanded board walls glared under the long fluorescent tubes in the ceiling. Pinball machines lined one wall. On the other side of the room, two orange vinyl booths offered seat-ing—although there was still no evidence that people ate there.

The sitter had assured Bronwyn when she asked that there would be no babies in infant carriers. In fact, Bronwyn saw no children under the age of ten or eleven. While there were a couple of foursomes, she saw only one other couple on what looked like a date.

Most of the crowd looked like multigenerational fam-ily groups. Well, except for the New York models on long skinny legs, their perfectly made-up faces frozen in bland or bored or maybe stoned expressions. She assumed the limo out in the parking lot was their ride, since she saw no one else remotely sophisticated looking.

Even if you counted the dive near the hospital where college students and interns hung out, Bronwyn had never been anywhere less classy or possessing less fine-dining ambience. And though everything was worn, chipped, scratched, and patched together or mended, the place was spotlessly clean and filled with happy, laid-back people, laughing and shouting at the top of their lungs (except for the New York models), and a fresh, warm ocean-y smell.

"Grab that booth," Garth directed when one emptied. "I don't think we should wait for service. I'll get us some-thing from the bar." He returned shortly with two beers. "It'll be about thirty minutes before we can be seated. They told me fifteen if we didn't mind sitting separately."

Finally they went down two steps into the oyster "bar," a small room, again with board walls painted white, where a U-shaped counter covered with galva-nized tin took up most of the room. Fixed barstools left only enough space for patrons to approach them single file. Coats hung on one wall. Garth took her coat and hung it up.

In seconds, a man with a seamed face the color of eggplant appeared before them. His sinewy arms were bare, his deep amber eyes knowledgeable. "I'm Samuel. This you folkses' first time here? Well, welcome to the Sunnyside."

His knuckles were large and stiff. On the fingertips, his skin was so thickly calloused it was grayish. With deft movements he spread paper place mats before them and, like a magician fanning cards, dealt them each three shallow white crockery bowls and a bread plate. One bowl he filled with cocktail sauce, one with melted butter. "You from the Coast Guard Station at Elizabeth City?" he asked Garth, putting plastic wrapped saltines on the bread plate. "You look like one of those swimmers."

"What swimmers?" Bronwyn asked.

"Swimmers like they train at Elizabeth City. Coast Guard rescue swimmers. World famous. My grandson just graduated from there. The Coast Guard saved over 33,000 lives after Katrina. My grandson was just sixteen, yep. He saw it on the TV, and he said, 'Granddaddy, thas what I goan do.' An' he did it, too."

There was no menu. Samuel told them they could order steamed oysters, steamed shrimp, or steamed scallops. Garth and Bronwyn settled on oysters, which were ordered by the peck. In a few minutes, Samuel brought the oysters in a galvanized bucket and dumped them with a loud clatter into a deep gutter. Briny steam billowed.

The oysters were as delicious as promised. Samuel shucked them with his bare hands so fast and smooth it was hard to see to see how he did it. One gleaming oyster would appear in the tiny bowl, and when Bronwyn ate it, another would appear.

Bronwyn dipped her oysters in butter and listened to Garth draw Sam out in that easy way he had. She supposed it was skill developed by being in the military, meeting so many strangers and needing to get acquainted fast, It was a facility she envied.

Once or twice, Bronwyn found herself missing Julia and hoping she was getting along okay with the sitter. She mentioned it to Garth, and he handed her his cell phone.

"Thirty-three thousand," Garth said, as he started the truck for the drive home. Bronwyn glanced at him sharply, struck by a note of wonder or awe, something she'd never before heard in his voice.

"What?"

"The Coast Guard rescued 33,000 people in the aftermath of Katrina."

"Were you involved in the rescue effort?"

He was silent so long, Bronwyn wondered if she should repeat the question.

At last he shook his head. "Some SEALs were. I was... out of the country."

Bronwyn wanted to ask, *Where were you? What were you doing*? But she'd already learned that when she heard the tiny hesitation, it meant, *Don't ask*. She stifled a sigh of frustration. She wanted to keep the conversational ball rolling. She wanted him to tell her what that odd note in his voice had meant. She took a guess. "Thirty-three thousand. That's a lot. Almost too many to get your mind around. Do you wish you had been part of it?"

"It's more than I ever did, that's for sure."

"What does the number matter? SEALs save people. They do hostage rescues. I'm sure you've helped anytime you could."

He flipped on the windshield wipers. "Yeah."

"And you must have believed when you were operating that you were contributing. That destroying terrorists ultimately saved lives all over the world."

"That's the theory."

This laconic gruffness of Garth's was a mood Bronwyn had never seen. "I'm not helping, am I? Something is bothering you. I wish you'd tell me what."

"Nothing. It's all right. I just wish I'd been there, that's all. They knew they did something good."

He tossed off the comment like it was a careless observation, but the longing just underneath the surface tore at Bronwyn's heart. "Well, I know two people you were there for. Maybe it wasn't as dramatic as plucking someone off a roof, but you saved them from certain death."

"Who?"

"David and Julia, of course. Oh, and the little boy trapped in the car. That's really a lot of people in a short time. I think rescuing people *is* what you do."

"Huh." The sound was noncommittal, but in the light of the dash, Bronwyn thought Garth's face relaxed a little.

She laid her palm on his hard bicep. "You're a good man, Garth."

He was silent. Bronwyn saw him swallow a couple of times. Then he cocked a hopeful eyebrow. "And a great date?"

Not knowing exactly what had happened but relieved

at his lightened mood, Bronwyn laughed and shoved at his arm playfully. "Well, I've never had one like it, so you win the novelty prize."

"But did you like it?"

"You know what? I really did." While the atmosphere had been distinctly not aphrodisiacal, there had been something innocently carnal about eating oysters for the pure enjoyment of them with no pretense of fine dining, no dilution of the experience with refinements.

On the drive home they laughed at their immersion into a North Carolina experience, wondered if the models had eaten anything at all, and told stories of their childhoods.

Chapter 34

*Civilian friends tell you not to do something stupid when
you are drunk.*
*Team guy friends will post 360-degree security so you
don't get caught.*

—SEAL joke

OUTSIDE IN THE SOYBEAN FIELD ADJACENT TO THE RUNWAY,
a behemoth tractor's deep-throated put-put-put shook
the air. The tractor had been out there all morning, and
as the sun climbed to noon, it still labored. In his faux-
wood paneled office, Garth checked his log to make sure
he had done every job scheduled for the day. He had.
Which gave him time, he thought as he put his work
boots up on the desk, to think about what else he could
do to move Julia's situation along.

Seventeen days had passed since Garth had pulled the
baby from the cardboard box. If someone was looking
for Julia, she wouldn't be that hard to find. He hadn't
put her into the hands of the system because he hadn't
wanted her to disappear, but he had left enough of a trail
that anyone who knew she had been on that plane would
be able to find him.

If anyone was keeping him under surveillance, he had
found no trace, either at Bronwyn's house or here. It was
possible that Julia's origins would forever be a loose end.

It might be time to assume that he and Bronwyn would have Julia forever. If they were going to raise her as their own, then she needed papers. A birth certificate, adoption papers. At the very least, and soon, she needed to added to his medical insurance policy.

There was one lead left that he hadn't pursued, figuring his buddy in San Diego would call if the fingerprints Garth had sent could be identified. Garth reached for his cell phone but hesitated. Warned by some instinct, he went to his cache of prepaid cell phones. He chose the one he'd bought in San Diego and entered his friend's number.

"What the hell are you into?" his friend demanded as soon as Garth identified himself.

"Why? You mean you *have* an ID on the prints?" It had been a hell of a long shot, given that the flight didn't originate in the States. You couldn't find all people using prints—only those who had ever been fingerprinted, and that number was miniscule, compared to the population of the world or even the western hemisphere. "That's great!" Garth told him. "Why didn't you call?"

"Can this call be traced?"

So his impulse not to use a number identified with him had been correct. "Not easily. It's a prepaid."

"All right. The prints belong to one Christine Freytag. I *didn't* call, because *you should not have those fingerprints*, and *I should not have searched them*. Someone has blocked access to her file, and even by looking for it, I attracted attention."

"You've gotten flack?"

"Nothing overt. I found keystroke tracker software on my terminal inside six hours. Somebody knows I traced fingerprints I should have no interest in. See, there's a little problem. She's dead."

·The news hit like a blow to the solar plexus. Garth had known there was a possibility, even a likelihood, that whoever had put Julia on the plane was in deep, deep peril, but still... Even though he wanted her to call him daddy—once she learned to talk—Garth didn't want Julia to be an orphan, to never know the people she had come from. Still, a name gave him a place to start. Maybe he could find Julia's relatives. "Christine Freytag. She was American?"

"Without a doubt. Born in Leland, Texas. Died in Islamabad."

Islamabad? That didn't compute. The plane carrying Julia had come from South America. "Died when?"

"Two years ago." Garth's contact spoke with grim emphasis.

But Julia was only eight months old. "That's impossi—"

"No. What's *impossible* is that you ever called me in the first place. I've got a wife and kids to support. If I lose my security clearance, I lose my job. Don't call back."

Chapter 35

"WHAT ARE YOU LISTENING TO?" AT THE SOUND OF GARTH'S voice, Bronwyn looked up to see him standing over her in the living room where she was scrubbing baseboards. Julia, in a yellow romper accessorized with an already-soaked bib that said "Top Baby," sat on a quilt strewn with toys. It was the most natural thing in the world: Bronwyn smiled and lifted her face to him, and he dropped a kiss on her lips, equal parts casual and possessive—just like—just like the relationship was real.

"Puccini arias," she told him, as he straightened and went over to pet Mildred and pick up Julia.

"I thought Puccini was a mushroom." He lifted Julia high over his head, making her kick her legs and squeal with high-pitched baby glee.

Bronwyn loved how the slight gleam of his smooth brown skin highlighted every hill and dip in the muscles of his arms. She loved how his play with Julia was far more vigorous than hers and yet Julia was always secure in his long-fingered brown hands. She loved that he was a strong man who absolutely knew his own strength.

Bronwyn bit back a smile. "*Porcini* are mushrooms; Puccini is a composer—as you very well know."

"I'm just afraid you're messing up her mind. She's too little for all this yelling and screeching. You'll turn her off music for the rest of her life." He brought Julia down and blew a raspberry against her round, little tummy.

"I'll play *The Magic Flute* then. Mozart is good for you. Studies have shown thirty minutes of Mozart to be as effective as Valium."

Garth snorted. "And doesn't that say it all?"

"It also raises children's IQs."

"Yeah, but all this opera? The stories are all tragic, and she hasn't even learned English yet. She needs to be listening to Barbara Mandrell and Wynonna Judd— somebody who sings in American."

They continued their mock argument while Garth played with Julia and Bronwyn finished washing the section of wall. No way was Bronwyn going to admit she had as many Country and Western albums as she did classic rock, reggae, and Irish ballads.

In truth, Bronwyn was so eclectic in her musical taste that she wasn't sure she had any taste at all. She just liked a piece of music if she did. Her classical collection ran more to *Bach's Greatest Hits* than violin concertos. Even the album playing now was a collection of arias, not a complete opera.

The track ended. After a tiny silence, the piercing, blinding simplicity of "O Mio Babbino Caro" filled the room. As always, the aria made Bronwyn's breath catch in her chest, as if she didn't know whether to inhale or exhale.

Garth stopped blowing raspberries on Julia's neck to listen, and Julia ceased giggling and trying to catch his nose. Instead, the baby froze with her little hands in the air, her dark blue-gray eyes wide and fixed, her pink little lips open in a confused smile.

Wordlessly, Bronwyn pointed to her, but Garth had already sensed the change in the baby.

As the short song played, Julia's eyes searched the room ever more frantically, stretching to look over Garth's shoulders, first on one side and then the other, and then twisting in an attempt to see behind herself. She held out her arms, babbling pleas in baby-speak.

The aria ended. Another started. Still Julia searched. At first, her cries were angry and imperious, and then by slow degrees, the little mouth turned down. She lowered her arms. Gulping sobs shook her chest. Garth patted her and murmured to her, but she would not be comforted.

Bronwyn wasn't sure whose distress was harder to take, the baby's or Garth's. She dried her hands and stood. "Give her to me."

She took the sweating, trembling little body. She cupped her hand around Julia's head and pressed it into her neck, holding her tight. "Cry it out, baby. Just cry it out. I know I'm not your mother, and that's who you want. But somebody's got you. I've got you. You have to cry, but you don't have to cry alone."

Later, while Julia sat white and dazed-looking in Bronwyn's lap, Garth wet a washcloth with warm water and gently washed her face. They had moved to the family room so the baby could be rocked.

He tossed the washcloth in the kitchen sink and returned to the family room. "She recognized that song, didn't she?" he said, more thinking aloud than questioning.

"Yes, I think so. It must be someone's favorite. I think she thought…" Bronwyn had to pause to swallow the lump in her throat. "Um… whoever… had at last returned to get her. I knew she must be missing every-thing familiar, but I hadn't really realized how brave, how stoic she's been trying to be. Garth, we have to find her mother."

Garth leaned forward with his forearms resting on his thighs, his hands clasped loosely between his knees. His laser-blue eyes rounded with sorrow. "That might not be possible, Bronny. I finally heard from my contact in San Diego who was running the fingerprints on Julia's bottle. The woman who made those prints was an American but she's been dead for two years."

"I don't know what that means."

"It means whoever left those prints had changed her identity. And since, even though she's been 'dead' two years, her file is still inaccessible, I'm guessing she was an agent employed in highly sensitive operations that are still going on. The kind of setup…" He paused like he wanted to make sure Bronwyn got the point. "The kind it would be smarter to jump out of a plane with a ripped parachute than get involved with."

"Two years…" Bronwyn mused, following her own line of thought. "Are you sure it was two full years?"

Garth's lips twitched in wry humor. "I'm not sure of anything at this point. Why?"

"I was thinking, what if she faked her death because she realized she was pregnant? That would have been seventeen, eighteen months ago."

"She might have also faked her death, with the help of her handlers, so that she could go somewhere else and make being pregnant, a woman with a family, part of her cover."

Bronwyn's heart squeezed. She felt a little sick to her stomach. "Someone would *do* that?"

"Don't you remember the sleeper cell of Russian

spies that were arrested not long ago? They were married, had jobs, had children born here."

"But they weren't doing things..." She broke off and laughed without humor. "I started to say they weren't doing dangerous things, but I guess I don't know *what* they were doing."

"No." His tone was cold and final, his face a grim mask of darkness crafted to hide the darkness he had looked upon. Except, of course, that the very presence of the dark mask revealed how much damage the dark deeds he had seen, and done, had done to *him*. To this good man.

Bronwyn fought the constriction in her chest and in a second or two was able to breathe around it. She stood with Julia in her arms. "I'm going to fix her a bottle."

In the kitchen, Julia on her hip, Bronwyn retrieved a bottle from the refrigerator door, ran a bowl full of hot water, and set the bottle in it to warm. Julia had proved to be not at all fussy about the temperature of her formula, but today Bronwyn thought the infant's little system had had all it needed to cope with. Chilling her stomach with ice-cold formula wouldn't help.

"All right. Back to Julia," she said when she had returned to the platform rocker. She tucked a burp cloth over her chest and nestled Julia to her. Julia took the bottle eagerly as if thirsty.

Garth had risen to pace while Bronwyn was out of the room. "What about her?"

"Julia could be taken away from us at any moment, and right now she doesn't even have an identity. If the fingerprint-woman was her mother, then Julia *is* an American citizen. She has rights and protection under the law. Possibly there are even some Social Security benefits coming to her. Sooner or later, we will have to go to the authorities to make her legal and secure her future."

Bronwyn took the bottle away so that Julia could get a breath without swallowing air in the process. Julia sighed deeply, and Bronwyn felt the tiny, soft body relax.

When Julia was suckling again, not so frantically but more contentedly, Bronwyn looked up at Garth who was roaming the room with his nearly silent tread. "You have theorized that whoever was responsible for her being on the plane wanted her to disappear. They *wanted* her to be untraceable. Do you realize that at this point we are helping them, rather than Julia?"

"We don't have to expose Julia to any official scrutiny. It would be possible to get her every kind of paper she needs."

"Fake? No. I want real for her. She's entitled to real. I want her right to be in this country to be unquestionable. And if she has no legal next of kin, or if they don't want her, I want to adopt her. Legally."

"I've explained—"

"I know. And I've been thinking about that. The way to deal with shadowy, powerful people is to get equally powerful people who aren't shadowy on your side."

Garth smiled cynically. "Do you know any of those?"

"I know people who do. Did you know that Miss Lilly Hale numbers among her acquaintance two former presidents—one of them living? And she's some kind of kin to Senator Teague Calhoun of North Carolina. JJ knows him, too. And I can ask my parents. My father is one of the top cardiologists in the country. He has treated some very important people."

"You haven't been willing to ask your parents for one single thing. You would go to them for Julia?"

"She's so vulnerable. We've got to get her to people who won't just hide her. They can really protect her."

"Can you wait? I'm still hoping for a lead on… the other passenger—the one who missed the plane."

Bronwyn heard his hesitation. He'd almost said a name and stopped himself. She fought down the pain of knowing that she still wasn't in his confidence. She no longer cared what state secrets he was responsible for keeping. Every time she really started to believe they were in this together, she learned that he believed he was in it by himself. "I'll give you until the wedding. But after that, I'm going to act."

Chapter 36

"YOU NEED A NEW CAR." JJ SQUEEZED HERSELF INTO THE passenger seat of Bronwyn's ten-year-old Mazda. Bronwyn was driving because the baby's carrier was such a pain to transfer to another car.

Bronwyn waited for her to buckle in. "Pray this one holds out another year, at least."

"Why? I was hoping you'd have more cash if you lived in a place that was rent free."

"Theoretically, I do. In practice, there are always so many little things to buy when you move. I start my new job in a couple of weeks, so I'll have money coming in until the office is ready to open. Even then, realistically, it might be several years before it will support me. If ever."

JJ squeezed Bronwyn's shoulder. "I'm so glad you're here—I don't want you to worry about money. We're going to make it work somehow. And you know I can find you a car you can afford."

"No, JJ—" Bronwyn broke off her protest when JJ's phone chimed.

JJ held up a finger to signal Bronwyn to wait and answered it.

"Of course, Senator," Bronwyn heard JJ say, after greeting the caller. "We'll be happy to welcome Admiral Stephenson. If you like, I'll send him an invitation... Fine... And can we expect to see your daughter, too? She was included in the original invitation, and there will be other young people her age… Splendid. I'll look forward to seeing you all." JJ closed the phone and turned to Bronwyn. "You'll never guess who that was."

"Okay, who?"

"Senator Calhoun."

"Himself? Not an aide?" Calhoun sat on the powerful Senate Armed Services Committee.

"Himself. Back when I saw him at Christmas, he told me he wanted to be invited to a wedding celebration if I had one, so I sent him and his wife an invitation. I didn't believe he intended to come. I thought he was just being—you know, political. I expected to get polite regrets and a present. But no. His plans have changed. He and his wife will be at their summer home on the Intracoastal Waterway. They'd like to come, but they have a house guest they'd like included."

"The senator called you himself—to take care of that kind of detail?"

"Yep." JJ dismissed the senator's oddity with a shrug. She quickly accessed her guest file and added a note. "That adds four to the official guest count and brings the total to 514. It's a good thing I decided early on not to try to have the party at Granddaddy's house. I swear, it looks like everybody I invited is coming, and a lot of them, like the senator, are bringing others."

"I imagine everyone is curious about who you married."

JJ's full lips quirked in a cynical smile. "And after the gossip earlier, they want to be seen on the winning side."

JJ directed Bronwyn to make a right turn onto a blacktop that angled off through a dense pine forest. Abruptly, the forest left off and Bronwyn could see a large stone-and-stucco house painted Tuscan ocher and built to impress. It sat on a high bluff overlooking the Intracoastal Waterway. Bronwyn stopped the car to peer at the mansion through the windshield.

"What do you think?" JJ asked.

What could Bronwyn say? "It's… staggering? Stunning? It looks like an Italian villa—the kind that's owned by an Italian prince."

"It was built by a railroad magnate before World War II, was owned by Abigail Anderson—"

Bronwyn unbuckled her seat belt and faced JJ. "The *movie star*? Movie stars had summer homes here?"

"Still do." JJ pointed. "Kevin Costner's place is that way." JJ made a small face. "Most of the homes along this section of the Intracoastal are owned by people who are rarely here. It has become an enclave of the super-rich." JJ put her hand on the door handle. "Are you ready to see the inside? We're meeting the wedding planner for final approval of everything."

Bronwyn got out and opened the rear door to extract Julia from her infant seat. "You mean everything isn't already set?"

"We-ell, it is. I didn't have to meet with them today," JJ admitted, "but you and I didn't get to do anything together for my first wedding. Not even go dress shopping. Now you're here, and I'm determined to share things with you."

"In that case, share this bundle of joy." Bronwyn released the straps and handed her the baby.

"Gladly. You know, I never thought about babies much, but I'm starting to really want one of my own." She rubbed noses with Julia, making her chortle, and then sobered. "Bronwyn, what are you going to do?"

"About what?" Bronwyn slung the diaper bag over her shoulder.

"Julia. Haven't you gotten attached to her?"

"Yes! I can't believe how much I love her. I would keep her forever, but I remind myself every day, she's not mine. I knew from the outset I would only have her for a season. She is someone else's by rights."

"But what if… what if they are bad people, or if it's a bad situation? I mean, something was wrong, or she wouldn't be with you."

"True. But you know, you can't just take a child and keep it, even if you think you are doing the right thing. On the other hand, if I try to go to the authorities with the truth at this point, I'm screwed, but more importantly, I don't know what would happen to Julia."

Bronwyn took a deep breath. Julia had to be given legal status, but given the complexities of her case, an end run around the system was called for.

"I don't know what to do—" Bronwyn gasped as she realized the answer had been handed to her on a silver platter and she hadn't noticed until this instant. "Since you brought it up, I have a favor to ask."

"Anything."

"Can you introduce me to the senator and make sure I have time to talk to him privately?"

Chapter 37

"I'VE BEEN GOING OVER THE RECORDINGS," GARTH TOLD Bronwyn a few nights later, after Julia was put to bed. "I haven't been able to catch any source for most of the sounds."

Bronwyn finished folding the tiny baby shirt. She added it to the baby items she was sorting onto the sofa seat beside her and reached into the basket at her feet. She had done more loads of clothes since Julia came to her than in her entire life.

"So there's nothing? Oh, well. I appreciate the effort, and I'm not disappointed. Whatever it was seems to have died down. It was probably just my imagination." She grinned at a sudden thought. "Or maybe ghosts are camera-shy. All you have to do to get rid of one is train a camera on it."

"I'm glad you're comfortable enough to make jokes about it. Because I didn't say there's nothing on the tapes."

Bronwyn stopped folding a washcloth to look him full in the face. "What *are* you saying?"

"I've put everything on one disc. Come over here." He indicated the big brown chair that he'd pulled the scarred coffee table up to. His open laptop sat on it. "I'd like to show it to you."

"I've done a split screen on every incident," he said when they were where they could both see the screen. "Most of the time, there's nothing to see when the noises happen. In fact, most of the time, the recorders didn't even pick up the noise."

"You mean there wasn't really a noise? I'm hearing things?"

"No. It's real. Remember, I've heard it, too. And, several times, apparently so has Mildred. Most likely, it's just indistinguishable from all the ambient sound. I'm going to show you the two clear incidences that were recorded." He tapped the space bar to wake up the machine and started the disc.

"Here's the first." He pointed to the right side of the screen. "That's the empty bedroom. You'll hear a clearly audible thump, picked up by the mic there, but there's no obvious cause."

"That's me in the split screen. In the kitchen. Looks like I'm opening a jar."

"Watch it again. This time, watch yourself. I'll set it to loop. Watch yourself and watch Mildred."

Bronwyn studied the picture. "I don't see anything. I'm opening a jar. There's some interference. When it clears, I look like I'm listening for something... so does Mildred."

"Okay." He consulted some notes. "Here's the next one. Your bedroom. The sound is picked up by the mic on the camera."

This time the split screen showed Bronwyn reading, Mildred at her feet. The picture was snowy for the blink of an eye, and then Bronwyn looked up as if she'd heard something, and Mildred looked up at her.

"Did you see it?"

Bronwyn shrugged. "See what?"

"You saw the interference—looks like a short burst

of microwave or shortwave radio interference? Did you notice that when Mildred looks up, she looks at you?"

"That doesn't mean anything." Bronwyn chuckled fondly. "She always expects me to deal with 'ghoulies and ghosties and things that go bump in the night.'" She ruffled the dog's raggedy neck. "Don't you, girl?"

"Okay, moving right along. Remember when you told me the leak had started up again? This is recorded by the baby's webcam."

Bronwyn was leaning over Julia's crib. The split screen showed the staircase. Bronwyn appeared to be wiping her cheeks with the flat of her fingers. An instant of snow. Mildred looked at her. In the other scene, there was an instant of snow. When it cleared, a puddle was widening on the landing floor.

"Where did it come from? I mean, I *knew* it wasn't Mildred…"

"Here's another. This time there's no split screen— just you. Watch the table behind you."

Bronwyn watched. The camera had caught her walking past the little breakfast table. The table was empty. It was obscured as Bronwyn walked in front of it. When it was visible again, a book lay on it. The hair stood up on her neck.

"The book. It wasn't there. And then it was!"

"Right. I'm going to slow it down. At first the book appears to be an inch or so above the table. Then it drops. You hear something and look around."

She watched the replay with the same grisly fascination of watching a train wreck. Her insides felt like they had been hit by a blast chiller.

After the day Bronwyn had spent with Garth's SEAL

friends, she had begun to come to terms with the flashes of knowing, of literal insight into what was taking place under the skin. She had tried to adopt Lon's attitude and just not care whether the ability was psychic or not. If it worked, it worked. She didn't have to talk about it, and as long as she didn't, no one would know. But this?

Eyes wide, she watched the book blink into existence and then drop the couple of inches to the tabletop. This wasn't a clever trick her mind had learned to do. This was breaking the laws of physics! No one could say it was normal or natural.

"No. It's impossible!" She struggled for an explanation. "You've messed with the cameras."

Garth blanked the computer screen. "I wouldn't do that. I don't have the skill, and if I did, I don't have the time."

Bronwyn drew deep breaths. "All right. I'm going to stay calm. There's a rational explanation."

Garth smiled apologetically. "I emailed everything I collected to Do-Lord, font of all paranormal wisdom. He says what we have is fairly typical poltergeist phenomena."

Horror scenes flashed in her mind. She felt the blood leave her cheeks. "Like the movie?" Her throat was so tight she could barely croak.

It seemed like the more upset Bronwyn got, the calmer and more almost bored Garth acted. "No, that was Hollywood hype." He dismissed the movie with a casual wave. "But poltergeist stuff, like what has been happening here, really happens, and it's not all that uncommon. The word poltergeist means noisy ghost, but Do-Lord says it's badly named. There's no ghost at all.

The entity doing this is very much alive and embodied. It's you."

As an intern, she, too, had learned that measured, unemotional way of delivering bad news. On the receiving end, she discovered that it matched what she was feeling so poorly that it made her feel crazy. "You're going too fast. Slow down." Bronwyn sprang to her feet and began to pace. "What do you mean, it's me?" She pointed a finger as if accusing the laptop. "I wouldn't begin to know how to fake all this."

"Calm down. I didn't say you're faking it. The technical term is psychokinesis, PK for short."

Her old scorn for pseudo-science began to take hold, steadying her and making her feel rational again. "Assuming there is any such thing as a poltergeist, what makes you think it's me?"

"I can't prove you caused it. But I can show you that it doesn't happen when you are not in the house. Do-Lord says typically the phenomena manifests around one person, and if it's any comfort," Garth's lips curved slightly in a sympathetic smile, "poltergeist phenomena tends to be self-limiting. It happens off and on for a couple of weeks or a month or two and then stops. As you already said, it seems to have stopped already."

"But why?"

"Usually, the person who, shall we say, is the locus of the poltergeist is a teenage girl or young woman, socially isolated, who is experiencing a lot of emotional and physical upheaval. There's been a breakup or death, or a move, and a lot of feelings of anger and grief and upset are going unacknowledged—not dealt with."

Okay, that described her. Ever since Troy's death, she

had been the poster child for life in turmoil, little as she wanted to admit it. "Is there always a—living person?" Good Lord! Was she really *hoping* that a ghost, an actual ghost, was haunting her house?

Garth nodded slowly, his lips twitching as if he'd had the same thought. "Most of the time, yes. According to Do-Lord, everything we've seen is absolutely classic. Strange noises and knocking, items moving around, light bulbs blowing. And by the way, even the puddles of water aren't that unusual. Sometimes the water appears running down walls or even dumps on people."

Bronwyn felt her anxiety rising again. It didn't matter if she believed or not; stuff had happened, stuff that a camera could capture. "Weird."

"What *didn't* happen was for things to break mysteriously. Some poltergeists are really destructive." He smiled tolerantly. "But you're not the type to smash things."

"You seem really convinced it was me. But I'm telling you, it wasn't. I can't levitate books or make water appear."

"Again I have to quote Do-Lord. He thinks the person has psychokinetic talent that isn't under their conscious control. In this case, I would have to agree. After all, what is the ability to heal but that?"

"*Heal?*" Bronwyn snorted in disbelief. "I can't do that, either. Sure, medicine is called the healing profession, but doctors can't heal. I can set a bone, sew up a wound, give medicine, but the body heals itself."

"Don't give me that. I've seen what you do. You healed Julia, you healed my scratch, you healed Davy's ankle."

"*What?* No. Be rational. Getting better was completely natural, totally predictable in every instance."

Garth rose and put his hands on her shoulders, holding her in place. "Is it rational to refuse to see the evidence before your eyes? What's so hard about seeing that you have the ability to heal?"

"Can't you see my shingle? It would read Bronwyn Whitescarver, MD, Psychic Healer. No thank you."

"It's not about what you tell the world. It's about what you know about yourself."

She shook her head. "No. No doctor could believe I heal, and no doctor could respect me."

"Do you see any other doctors here?"

"No, but…"

"Face it, Bronny. The doctors you'll never win the respect of are your parents. You say you stopped listening to them years ago, but you still carry them inside you. When are you going to wake up and face the truth? It isn't their respect that will make a difference to you, but your own."

"But I can't—"

"Listen, your parents might love you, but they are not on your side. The world is a harsh place. Tell all the lies you need to to protect yourself—even from your family. But I'm on your side, so don't lie to me. And don't lie to yourself. Not anymore."

She looked at him long and slow, and Garth watched Bronwyn's face turn—what? sadder? lonelier?—than he had ever seen it. If he had caused that expression, he wished he would have kept his mouth shut.

Chapter 38

GARTH CUT THE LAST STRIP OF GRASS IN BRONWYN'S YARD. He killed the mower's motor and leaned on the handles, looking around. He had cleared a lot of the brush and subdued the blackberry brambles. There was more to be done, but it was beginning to look like a real lawn.

He could have persuaded himself not to bother. As soon as he was gone, the brush would come right back. If he was honest, he hadn't even done it because it would please Bronwyn. He had taken on the task because it was a job that needed doing.

He pushed the lawn mower the few feet to the storage shed. The door was still warped and hard to get open, but once in motion, it swung easily on oiled hinges now.

Mower and yard tools stowed, he stepped out of the musty dimness of the shed into the mellow light of late evening.

Another job needed to be done today. He hadn't put it off—exactly. He'd been carrying around the ring since the oyster bar date. He'd just been waiting for the right time. But time was running out. Tomorrow night was Davy and JJ's big wedding bash. Bronwyn had given him until then to settle Julia's future—or she would—and he believed her. She didn't know how completely he would be screwed, of course, and she didn't understand she'd be shooting down her own future.

The problem was that Bronwyn had never said she

loved him—after that time she'd joked about it. He thought she did, and God knew he loved *her*. He was so damn grateful she had turned to him for comfort the other evening. Holding her had been better, more satisfying than a lot of sex he'd had. And thanks to air-conditioning (and Lon's push), she had stayed in his arms all night long.

She thought he was a good man, and that almost meant more than saying she loved him, but he no longer thought she would make up her own mind in due time to marry him.

Well, he couldn't ask her in sweaty lawn-mowing jeans. He tried not to be relieved to put it off another half hour while he showered and changed. But he was.

The wicker settee Miss Lilly Hale Sessoms had given her didn't allow Bronwyn's feet to touch the floor. She dealt with it as she had all her life; she folded her legs under herself. But the real source of discomfort was what Garth was saying. He looked wonderful in a yellow shirt that brought out the gold in his deep tan. And showered, his jaw gleaming slightly from a fresh shave, he was positively yummy. But his blue eyes were serious.

He took her hand. "And I'm asking you, will you marry me? I know you don't want to leave here, and you shouldn't, this is your place. I've held off because I kept thinking I couldn't ask you to move. Life in the navy will take me all over, and you can't live just any-where. We'll have a long-distance relationship and that isn't ideal, but it's doable."

Life in the navy? She couldn't believe it. "Whatever

secret thing you're doing for Coastal Air isn't enough? You want to go back into the navy? Back to being a SEAL?"

"It's who I am. It's what I've always wanted."

She sighed sadly. "No matter what I think I know about you, there's always another piece, isn't there?"

He went mask-faced. "What do you mean?"

"You knew this was what you wanted, but you didn't tell me until now, and even now, I think I'm only hearing part. I love you, but it doesn't matter because you will never quite let me love you."

"But you love me."

Obviously he'd heard only the part he wanted to hear. "Yes, God help me, I do. And the truth is, living separate from you will be no problem. I can love you as just as much as you're ever going to let me from a distance of several thousand miles. If it was only about love, your idea of a long-distance relationship wouldn't be all that bad.

"But do you think I'm going to put up with a relationship in which you disappear—no warning—and you can't tell me anything, and it's for my good"—her voice was rising, and she didn't care—"and if I don't see or hear from you, it could be because you're dead, or it could be because we've broken up and you don't have the courtesy to tell me!"

He had the nerve to look surprised at her vehemence. "But JJ—*your best friend*—seems to be handling the lifestyle just fine."

"News flash: JJ is a different person—a real different person. Right now she's satisfied that she and David live parallel lives. Right now, in case you haven't noticed,

David comes to *her*. She does not go to him. The first time she *needs* to go to him and he isn't there?" Bronwyn laughed cynically. "It's going to be a different story." She could sit still no longer. She jumped to her feet.

"But I've already done the parallel lives thing once. I wouldn't see him for a week or two, and I was so busy that if he had been around, I probably wouldn't have had time for him. We didn't have a schedule. We had no expectations of each other. He'd be gone, and then he'd show up. And then, there was the time he'd been gone for a while, and suddenly, there he was." Abruptly, Bronwyn sat back down. "On a table. In Trauma Room 3."

"God." Garth's face went ashen under his tan. "You had to see that?"

"Yeah. Half his face was gone."

The room was quiet. Feeling the tension in the atmosphere, Mildred got up and put her face in Bronwyn's lap—whether to get or give comfort, it would be hard to say. Bronwyn massaged behind the dog's velvety ears for a minute. Mildred subsided to lie at Bronwyn's feet.

"That was bad," Garth said, his tone gentle. "But you know, trauma happens to all kinds of people. There is no job, no way of life that will guarantee you won't die suddenly."

Bronwyn's laugh was short, sharp. Ugly. "Don't you think I know that? The problem wasn't just that as a result of his job, he died. It wasn't that the job robbed me of him. It's that the job *had been robbing* me of him all along. After he died, I added up all the hours we had actually spent together in a year of dating. It came to thirty-nine days.

"And the fault wasn't just his job, it also was mine.

When you've been up for thirty-six hours, the choice between sex and sleep is a no-brainer. Sleep wins. Candlelight dinners and long soulful chats? We got along at first because he got my crazy schedule. Our dates went like this: have you had your dinner break yet? How about I come by and take you to the cafeteria?"

The air-conditioner clicked on. Cooler air stirred in the room.

"Now do you see why I won't marry you?" Bronwyn asked, calmer now. "I won't plan a life with you. Been there done that."

"But you admit part of the problem was your work schedule. It wouldn't be that way. You won't have to work in the ER if you marry me. You can have your practice and work sane hours. I'll take care of you, Bronny. I'll take care in every way I can."

Bronwyn wished he weren't such a good man. She wished she didn't know how much his heart was in exactly the right place. With a gentle sigh, she said, "Your integrity is always about the work, the mission, the operation. Look at how often you've already lied to me, and even when you didn't tell a lie, you misled me.

"And then there are all the things you *have to* withhold. Whole huge chunks of your life I can't know about. I'd get maybe half of you. Or would it even be that much? Because part of the time when you were with me, you'd be thinking about things you couldn't share.

"And when you were away, things would happen to you—" Hot tears filled her eyes, but she didn't let them fall. "Things that hurt you or changed you, and you wouldn't be able to give me a heads-up, and I'd be confused and thinking, 'What the heck is going on?'"

"The things that happen—oh God, Bronwyn—there are things I don't *want* you to know."

"Those would keep us apart, too," she acknowledged sadly. "I can't ask you to give it up for me. I won't. It's your life. I don't want you to give up your passion. But I don't think it *is* your passion.

"You are not who you think you are. You're smart enough to rise as high as you want to, and you're a strategic thinker. But it doesn't occur to you to play the game. You're not ruthless enough. You *notice* the collateral damage. You're not going to put the welfare of the navy first. Anytime you do, it's going to hurt you. You'll start looking again like you did when I first met you—like you were carved from a piece of wood."

"Is this because he died? Anybody could die, anytime. Life doesn't come with any guarantees."

"You're not listening to me—you're just trying to win." Bronwyn chuckled sadly.

He smiled a tad sheepishly. "I really, really want to win."

"I know you do. But try to listen to what I'm saying. I'm not afraid that you or someone I love will die. Everyone dies. But because *he* died, I did cross a bridge sooner than I would have. A one-way bridge. I didn't tell him who I really was. I used all *he* hid to hide me from myself. There was never time or space to go deeper. I don't blame him. I know now I had as much in that relationship as I was really looking for."

Bronwyn looked deep into Garth's beautiful eyes, willing him to understand that what he was offering was not enough. "But it's not what I'm looking for now. And it's partly your fault. You kept telling me to dig deep, not accept my limits but push beyond them, not let 'impossible' stop me."

———~~~———

Garth took his coffee onto the porch the next morning and stood looking down at the river shining through the trees in the morning light. With the brush cleared, the river could be seen from the porch now. They had talked about removing a few of the pines.

Bronwyn came out to stand beside him. She didn't offer a kiss. They'd gone to bed last night, even made love, but when it was over, they hadn't talked more. They had each rolled to their own side of the bed, as if living apart had already started.

This morning she wore lightweight slacks and a short-sleeved pink sweater that dipped down really low but was kept decent by a lacy thing underneath that covered her breasts. "You look nice," he told her.

"Look," she said, all business, "JJ wants me to get into Wilmington early so that I can go with her to check the decorations, make sure everything is in place. So I'm going to load up Julia now."

He tried to draw her out. "Check the decorations? Isn't it a little late for that? The wedding is tonight."

"She doesn't really need my input. She wants me to share it with her. It's a girlfriend thing."

He tried again. "I thought the sitter wasn't going to be at JJ's grandfather's house until six."

"She's not. But the housekeeper is there. And we won't be out long."

Was this the way it would be? Giving facts but sharing nothing. He gave in. "Well, I guess I won't see you until the party then. I have a delivery to pick up at the coast."

"You'll be gone all day, too?"

"Probably."

"In that case, I think I'll take Mildred, too."

"Will she be okay there?"

"She and JJ's dog get along well, and there's a fenced-in run. She won't have to stay in the house."

"Okay. Then I'll see you."

"All right. See you."

"Bronwyn?"

"What?" Her face was a study in respectful disinterest.

It's not supposed to be this way, he wanted to say. When you found the one, she was supposed to know *you* were the one. She was not supposed to say, "No way." He would make her change her mind.

But he couldn't refute anything she said. What she said was the way it was. The way it had to be. Since becoming a SEAL, he had drifted further and further into a world that regular people couldn't imagine, much less share. If he hadn't had these few weeks of living almost like other people did, like his parents did, he might not have really understood what she was saying.

He felt like something in his chest was breaking, and now he told himself the real story of what had happened after they had argued to a standstill. They had gone to bed and made slow, sad love. She hadn't been able to come. He had used all his skill, but finally she had said it was all right, and would he just hold her, that would be just as good, so he had. But in a few minutes they had rolled apart.

This morning they were perfectly polite. Quietly

taking care of business. Two people who were going to go on, but not together.

It was not supposed to be this way.

Where had he gone wrong? Why did he keep encountering situations that were not the way they were supposed to be? It had been happening since Afghanistan, and nothing he did seemed to fix it.

Was it the situation that didn't fit, or was it him?

She was looking at him, waiting for him to say something. "Um, nothing. See you."

Chapter 39

Everyone is potentially under opposition control.

—The Moscow Rules

GARTH ACTIVATED THE GARAGE DOOR OPENER CLIPPED TO the visor. He drove into the hot, stuffy shade of the metal building and wondered how he could engineer it to cool passively the way Bronwyn's house did. What made the house stay cool wasn't only that the house was built to breathe. It also had strategically placed trees. Shade trees would be a bad idea at an airport. The temperature gradient between trees and grass could cause turbulence that could crash a small plane. Oh well.

He knew what he was doing. Trying to think about anything so he wouldn't think about why nothing was the way it was supposed to be. Trying not to think about how he'd screwed up so badly that having found the one woman for him, he had picked one who didn't want what he was. Was that screwed up or what?

He unlocked the storage compartment in the pickup's bed and took out his diving gear. He'd washed and dried it as soon as he was finished with it. Now, before putting it in the storage room in the garage, he took the time to examine every fastening, every gasket, every hose and connector. The habit had become so ingrained, no matter how tired he was, that he wouldn't be able to rest if he didn't. *If you take care of your equipment, it will take care of you.* He no longer did it because it was part of being a SEAL. At some point, it had become part of him.

He'd had a lot of thoughts like that in the past couple of days. Imagining what it would be like to be a SEAL, operating again. He'd come to realize that, no matter what he did, he'd be a SEAL the rest of his life.

Equipment checked and properly stored, he turned out the light, turned on the alarm, and left the garage. Outside, the long twilight of late spring turned everything blue, making distance deceptive. In the few minutes he'd been inside the garage, a Tahoe had pulled up to his trailer. The big, glowing taillights of the Tahoe punched red holes in the air.

The timing was too perfect. Garth would be willing to bet the car had been hidden on a logging road nearby until he returned, because the driver didn't want Garth to know someone was waiting for him. Garth shook his head at such sloppiness. If his visitor wanted the element of surprise, he should have given it fifteen minutes more.

A man—five-nine, one-sixty, athletic build, short-sleeved white dress shirt, black slacks—emerged and stood in the open door, letting the light from the car's interior illuminate him. His right hand looked stiff. He rested it on the SUV's top.

He was an operator. He was using his casual stance and absent-minded air to give Garth a long time to see who he was and ascertain that he carried no weapons in his hands.

"Evenin'," Garth called in his best North Carolina drawl. "What brings you out here?"

"I'm Dan Renfro." Garth's visitor offered his left hand, holding the right aloft. "Sorry I can't shake. Hand got busted. It's still healing."

So this was Renfro, the independent contractor who had missed the plane Julia had been on. From the looks of his hand, every finger had been broken. Several red scars crossed his eyebrows and cheeks, and his nose looked swollen. Renfro hadn't just been in a fight; he'd been beaten scientifically and thoroughly.

"Garth Vale," he supplied. "What can I do for you?"

"Wanted to talk to you about a shipment."

"What kind of shipment?"

"Perishables. Bananas."

Renfro was the missing piece, and he had said two of the words on the box. He knew about Julia.

Happy as he was to think he would finally get some answers, Garth was conscious of a deep anger. If Renfro had any part in the debacle that had almost cost Julia her life, then whoever had worked him over had done the world a service, as far as Garth was concerned. The only thing they'd done wrong was that they hadn't finished the job. For the first time in a long time, he could feel that his Darth Vader mask had reappeared. His face was hard, his eyes hard. Garth kept his face impassive, giving nothing away. "Let's go inside."

He unlocked the trailer and gestured for Renfro to enter ahead of him. Garth flipped on the overhead switch, lighting the utilitarian metal desk and filing cabinet.

Renfro glanced at the fake-oak-paneled walls pinned with aviation maps. In the fluorescent glare, more healing cuts and scrapes were visible. The skin around his eyes was yellowish with fading bruises. One eye was badly bloodshot. He swayed slightly. He looked exhausted, shaky.

Garth said nothing, waiting for Renfro to make the next move.

"Look, I'm not going to play spy verse spy games." Renfro's face was the mask of a man who has been struck blind with fear and grief. To Garth's surprise, Renfro's eyes filled. "Please tell me you found the baby on the plane! I've already talked to everyone else on the flight. They couldn't tell me anything. Did you... was there...?" He choked and swallowed.

"She's safe."

Renfro's knees buckled. He blindly felt for the desk.

The man was in a bad way. Thinking he looked about to faint, Garth shoved the straight chair under him. "Sit."

"You found her? Alive?"

"Yes, alive. No thanks to whoever was responsible."

"Thank God... I had to come. I had to know. I was responsible—at least for getting her into the right hands—and I failed. If she hadn't been found in time, then I was looking for a dead child, but I couldn't stop until I knew what became of her."

Garth respected a man who didn't think his responsibility for a mission ended if the mission failed, and he might have compassion for the man's mental suffering, but it wasn't in his nature to comfort a man over a screwup as big as this. "What the *hell* were you thinking?"

"The plan stank from the beginning. I told my client so and told him to let *me* get her out of San Feliz and into the U.S.—my way. He was absolutely adamant that there could be no record of her entering the country." That fit with what Garth had already surmised.

"With a little lead time, I still could have managed it, but no. It had to be right then, that day. I was stuck with someone else's plan." Renfro passed a shaky hand over his forehead. "I could have turned it down, but the money was good, and hey, it would get *me* into the country without a passport stamp, too. It was easy money, and I was doing no harm."

That deserved no comment.

Renfro gave him a knowing look. "*You* know what I mean. You know how it is when you operate—you do what you need to do. As much as possible you try to work for our team, but there's not always a lot of difference between the good guys and the bad guys. It's not that often that your conscience is completely clear, you know?"

Renfro gave a distinctly unmirthful laugh. "I'll say this for the admiral, he knew which buttons to push. It was a half-assed plan with no redundancy built in. I wouldn't have done it just for the money. But they convinced me the baby would die if she wasn't gotten out."

"Why the big rush?"

"The baby's mother—"

"Wait. Was that Christine Freytag?"

"That was the word on the street. I knew her as Sonya. Apparently, in her former life she had operated in Europe and pissed a lot of people off. She got pregnant, so she faked her death—with a lot of help from some highly placed sources, went to San Feliz as Sonya Everhart, and had a baby. She started operating again a few months ago. Said she needed the money, but you know, some people can't quit. They need the rush."

"So she's not dead?"

"Oh, she's dead all right. She died on the way back to her car after putting the package on the plane. I saw it. Execution style. Three shots to the head. Somebody knew exactly where she would be."

"Shit."

"Yeah."

"And you?"

"They knew about me, too. Me, they just beat to a pulp. I woke up a couple of days later in a hospital."

"You said earlier, 'The admiral knew which buttons to push.' What admiral was that?"

"Did I? Shouldn't have said that. It's the pain medication."

"What admiral?" Garth persisted.

Renfro ignored him. His bloodshot eyes pleading, as if he couldn't be sure he'd understood before, he asked again, "The baby? She's really safe? She was okay when she got here? They said the mother knew how much sleeping medication to give her, but the thought of drugging a baby that small scared the hell out of me."

"She's okay."

"I went to see... the party that hired me to get the box off the plane and make sure she was passed into the right hands. I had to know—you know? I had to know if she made it. He said he didn't know where she was."

Renfro covered his eyes. His shoulders shook. Garth waited him out.

After a while Renfro raised a tear-streaked face. "The cold son of a bitch. When he learned Christine, aka Sonya, was dead, he assumed the baby had never been put aboard the plane. I told him I knew she had been... and he told me to forget it. Keep the money and forget it."

"Who were you supposed to take her to?"

Renfro fingered a scar on his forehead. "I didn't have a name. Just a woman who would meet me at the rest stop on I-40 at Clinton."

"Did MacMurtry know what you were bringing into the country?"

"Henry MacMurtry?" Renfro looked puzzled. "What does he have to do with it?"

"He was waiting for the plane. When you didn't get off, he made a call and left."

Renfro looked like he couldn't make sense of anything. "It's all so crazy. He went to all the trouble to get the baby into the country—"

"You mean the man who hired you?" Garth put in.

"Right. But I had the feeling he was *relieved* the operation went south. Does that make any sense to you? It didn't to me. He hadn't even looked for her!"

"You know what the Moscow Rules say, 'Any operation can be aborted. If it feels wrong, it is wrong.'"

Renfro gave a pained snort. "I shoulda remembered that. The whole damn thing felt wrong from the git-go to me. I guess he decided to cut his losses and move on. But, my God, it wasn't a stolen piece of technology. It was a *baby*!"

Garth's Darth Vader mask split right down the middle. Like a hunk of warm chocolate cake dropped on the floor, it scattered into dark crumbs. Renfro had lived for weeks with the awful possibility that Julia might not have been found in time and, if found by the wrong people, would almost certainly have been made to disappear without a trace. He had lived with the fact that he had compromised his values and, instead of saving a child, might have been complicit in her death.

A compassionate, forgiving smile spread over Garth's cheeks, pulling and shaping muscles that being a SEAL hadn't caused him to use in years. "It's okay, man. She's fine."

"Where is she?"

"You know I'm not going to tell you. I don't know you. The hardest part about this whole thing has been not knowing who I could trust—who wanted to keep her safe as much as I did."

"Yeah. It's a hell of a note when you find out *you* want an operation to go off without any hitches more than your bosses do."

"Tell me about it!" Garth got a cup of water from the cooler and handed it to Renfro. "This isn't over, you know. I'm not going to do anything to put the baby in danger, but somebody needs to be held accountable. I had already figured out it was someone with navy connections. Who hired you?"

Renfro's eyes narrowed in a knowing look. "Think about *where* you are."

Garth looked around the unimpressive office. "Coastal Air?"

"And you were recruited by Operation TANGENT—weren't you?"

Whoa! Renfro knew the secret name of the black-ops organization that sold Coastal Air's services to the intelligence community. Garth said nothing, but he was fairly sure his eyes had given away his shock.

"Uh-huh." Renfro nodded wisely. "Now don't give me any details. Just tell me how you happened to be free when TANGENT came calling. Bottom line."

"Bottom line? Bad intel."

Renfro drained his paper cup and tossed it into the trash can. With his scary yet knowing eyes fixed on Garth, he settled back. "Listen carefully. I don't know who owns U.S. Security, but U.S. Security owns Coastal Air. And another division of U.S. Security, Rache-Carlyle, collects intel in Iraq and Afghanistan.

"My friend, there are over four thousand corporately owned intelligence contractors being paid by the U.S. government. Nobody knows how much is being paid to whom, or for what services, because the contracts will never see the light of day. But there's one piece of information everybody knows: On Capitol Hill, an intelligence contractor's best friend is retired Admiral Jonas Stephenson."

Stephenson was very much an éminence grise, a shadowy figure who always seemed to be associated with power. Although retired, he "consulted" with the Pentagon and was understood to have a finger in a lot of pies without having any title himself. In some quarters, it was speculated that he was at the top of a gray-ops outfit. Garth wasn't in any position to know.

Renfro was implying that Stephenson had had a hand in producing the false intel that had almost led to Garth's entire platoon being killed—and also had pulled the strings to get Garth placed where he could talk to no one. And, though Renfro carefully hadn't said so, Stephenson was the one who had hired Renfro.

Out of the blue, as it often did, the memory of Garth's

near-death experience intruded. As always, it was as fresh and as vivid as if it had just happened.

In that space beyond worlds and beyond worldly ambition, he had known that he didn't like his Darth Vader mask and that the mask had been on the verge of becoming his personality.

All SEALs didn't become Darth Vaders. He didn't have the introspective skills to understand why it had been necessary for him, and he didn't think it mattered now, anyway. The important thing was that he had questioned if the SEAL he had become was the SEAL he wanted to be.

What he had not questioned was whether being a SEAL and being a man were the same things. And of course they weren't. Now he asked himself could he ever be the *man* he wanted to be while at the same time being a SEAL.

At every turn, ever since Afghanistan, his life had seemed to go off track, and nothing he did seemed to fix it. Now he saw it had gone off track even earlier. In the near-death experience, he had recognized the truth about himself, but he had not been able to bring the lesson back with him until now.

Bronwyn had made it abundantly clear that though she loved him, the life she could build with a SEAL was not a life she wanted.

Oddly enough, Renfro had offered him the other piece of the equation in his cynical summation: *"You know what I mean. You know how it is when you oper-ate—you do what you need to do. As much as possible you try to work for our team, but there's not always a lot of difference between the good guys and the bad guys.*

It's not that often that your conscience is completely clear, you know?"

When he'd looked at all he'd done the last couple of weeks, ever since he found Julia, he hadn't had any trouble telling if he was one of the good guys or the bad. He had known, even though he'd had very little idea which team he was on, or if he was on any team at all. And deep in his heart or his soul or wherever conscience resided, his was clear.

Bronwyn, on the other hand, had never had a moment of doubt. Whenever she saw the morally right thing, she did it—but not in rote obedience to some moral precept. Instead, she always set her path by her personal moral compass.

The doorway, the possibility of being the man he wanted to be, lay with Bronwyn. She had told him once, "I came here looking for the place I fit. I wanted a place that was mine. I think I've found it. I want to sink my roots deep." He could live and thrive anywhere, therefore wherever she needed to be, there he wanted to be also.

He had thought tonight's wedding-do would be about trying to make the connections that would take him back to being a SEAL.

Now his mission objective changed.

He thought for a minute. He had intuited for a long time that something stalked him just outside his vision, like a cat waiting for the opportunity to strike. Well, he knew where the tiger was, and he would no longer wait for it to choose its moment. He was going to poke it.

He opened his phone and selected MacMurtry's number.

When MacMurtry answered, he said, "I need for you to deliver a message to Admiral Stephenson for me. Tell him, 'The bananas arrived as scheduled, and payment is due.'"

Chapter 40

"I'VE ALREADY TOLD DAVID, HE AND HIS CRONIES CAN'T disappear to some table in a corner." JJ addressed Bronwyn over the drying lights in the nail salon. JJ had decreed she and Bronwyn would have a spa day to get ready for the big event that night. Inevitably her main topic was her plans and preparations for the evening.

"They can talk to each other in a way they can't to anyone else," she explained to Bronwyn. "It's just the way they are. Don't let that make you feel shut out."

Bronwyn couldn't look at JJ or she might cry, and she couldn't use her hands until her nail polish dried. "Oh, I don't anticipate a problem along those lines. We won't be together."

Shocked out of her preoccupation, JJ's brows came together. "What do you mean? I thought you guys had been getting together in every known position and a few that are believed impossible for humans."

Continuing to avoid JJ's eyes, Bronwyn shrugged. "I probably won't turn down sex with him—I'm not an idiot—but I'm not going to try any sort of committed relationship."

"Are you still focusing on Troy? You've got to let him go."

With a safer topic, Bronwyn could, at last, meet JJ's eyes. "I have. He's gone. He was wonderful. I loved him dearly, and a part of me will always love him, but he's gone."

"Then what's the hang-up?"

Bronwyn took a deep breath. "I'm not hanging back because I'm afraid I won't find anyone like him. I'm hanging back because I'm afraid I have."

"You are an idiot. You let go of the love and kept the grief."

Bronwyn hadn't expected an attack. It dried any incipient tears right up. "*What?*"

"You're letting the fact that he died be the defining moment of the relationship."

"I'm really not, JJ. But when he died, I had to face how little relationship there had been. I would have seen it sooner or later. But because he died, I had to look at it sooner. I'm not going down that path again."

"You've come to the wrong conclusion. He was a good man. You could have done a lot worse, but he wasn't right for you."

Bronwyn looked up in surprise. "You never said that."

"What was I going to say? You loved him, and it would probably have been enough. But you would have forever been the one to take care of him. He wouldn't have taken care of you. He didn't really see you. He helped you keep your knowledge of who you are buried."

"What do you mean?" Bronwyn asked, but she was afraid she knew.

"When you touch people, you heal them."

Oh, God. Not again. "No, I don't. I can give you a long list of people I haven't healed, and their address these days is the cemetery."

JJ rolled her luminous green eyes. "I know you're

not Jesus. You don't have uncanny powers or anything. But you do heal them. Granddaddy is always better for a week or two after you see him."

"Lucas has heart failure. There are good days and bad days. Good weeks and bad weeks. JJ, don't start hoping I can—Sooner or later, his heart will give out."

"I don't care if you make him live longer—and neither does he. But you make the life he has better. That's why I wanted you here."

"JJ, I want to be here for you and for him, but you're making up expectations—"

"Oh, for goodness sake!" JJ risked her manicure to throw up her hands. "I know what I see." She smashed her spread fingers flat under the lights and glared at Bronwyn. "I thought you were done with hiding out. With hanging back. You know what the real trouble with Troy was?"

"Yeah. He was an undercover cop, an adrenaline junkie, and it killed him."

"All true, but not what I'm talking about. He wouldn't have brought you a baby to care for. He wouldn't have thought of caring for her. He would have dropped her off at a hospital. He would have said, 'Shit happens,' and forgotten about her. And do you want to know the real reason he would have done that?"

"I don't think I do, but you're going to tell me anyway."

"It would be because a mere baby's concerns aren't part of his game. And neither were yours. He didn't *want* you to be special."

It was the truth. She couldn't see Troy doing any of the things Garth had done. Troy had helped her hide, had given her the distraction she had needed to enable her to stay one more day in the ER.

The problem with Garth was that he *wasn't* like Troy. He didn't want to take her away from herself. He was determined to accept all of her. Including the parts she'd rejected. No one in the world could be less woo-woo, less airy-fairy, speak less New Age babble than he, and yet he had calmly accepted the way she was.

He didn't settle, ever, for what she would give him, what she would show the world. His was a strength she could depend on. With him, she didn't have to watch out, lest she throw him a curve ball. She hadn't had to watch out with Troy; Troy wouldn't have *seen* a curve ball.

And JJ, with a long-term friend's insight, had recognized how deeply the question was mired in whether Bronwyn would acknowledge to herself that she was a healer.

While some doctors acknowledged the validity of forms of healing besides allopathic medicine, most didn't think of themselves as healers. Somehow, healing had become the opposite of science. But healing was another one of those things over which Bronwyn had no control.

She could do much to assist the body, to create the conditions that would support healing, but ultimately, what she had said to Garth was right. Healing was something that took place within the body—outside the doctor's ability to cause it.

She knew she had little or no ability to direct whatever people sensed as "healing," so she had, once again, resisted seeing what she couldn't control. She smiled a little at her own intransigence.

Choosing to have a relationship with Garth would offer her a thousand daily opportunities to see what was beyond her control—even if he left all thoughts of a military or secretive career behind. As JJ had once observed, the trouble with alpha men is that you can't control them. They are controlled internally by what they value.

His calm but not blind acceptance of who she was, if she accepted it herself, would be a bulwark against straying into the irrational, which was ultimately what she feared.

The fear, she recognized, was not really hers. She had inherited it from her parents. All their worshiping of the god of science had not stopped them from seeing in her what "science" couldn't explain and, because they couldn't understand it, fearing it.

SEALs, at least the ones she had gotten to know, didn't fear the unknown. Instead they met the unknown as a challenge, as an opportunity to learn, to grow, and to increase in strength. And when she looked within herself, she found she didn't fear the unknown, either.

She had already set about freeing herself from some of the limitations with which her parents had enclosed her. Now, she loosed this one.

She didn't know whether she could build a relationship with Garth, but she now gratefully accepted all he had already given her.

Chapter 41

"THIS IS QUITE A BASH YOU AND JJ ARE PUTTING ON," Garth remarked to Davy, sitting to his left while he glanced around the huge, elegant ballroom with its ceiling several stories high and elaborate stonework balconies. With one foot, Garth pushed out the empty chair beside him and propped his leg on it. His thigh ached deep in the bone. The swim today hadn't done it any good.

"Yeah, but we can't stay here long. JJ said we couldn't all get in a corner and talk to each other."

"Are you saying you're pussy-whipped?" Do-Lord asked, a taunting smile hovering around his lips as he sat on Davy's other side.

"Hell, yeah, I am!" Davy smiled his slightly off-center smile. "As often as I can talk JJ into it. When you're ready for a little something extra, there's nothing like a pussy-whip."

Do-Lord nodded. "Right answer. Me, too. And Emmie said we can't hang out until the party is winding down."

"Lauren's going to come looking for me, too," Lon admitted from across the table. "So talk fast, Lieutenant. Give us a sit-rep."

Garth quickly filled them in on all that had happened, concluding with the story of Renfro's surfacing.

The men whistled silently. "So how are things going with Bronwyn?"

Garth told them about her categorical refusal to consider life as a SEAL's wife.

Lon snorted. "You know, the problem you've got is that you fell in love with Bronwyn at second sight. A decision that sweeping, based on no evidence at all except a feeling, either gives you nowhere to go, because you think you don't get to choose your path, or makes you look like an idiot. Which I am beginning to think you are. Bronwyn at least is attempting to be the doctor she wants to be. You recognize that you're not the SEAL you want to be, but you accept it as the price of doing business."

"Not anymore I don't. Do-Lord, how did you decide it was time to get out?"

Do-Lord steepled his fingers, preparing his answer. "For all the push-the-edge stuff we do," he said at last, speaking to the whole table, "there's a line, you know? It might be a line the navy has drawn for you, or it might have been given you by your religion, or it may just be a line you've set for yourself…"

All the men nodded.

"But there is a line," Do-Lord reiterated with the skill of the natural orator. "A line you have to stay inside. As long as you stay inside it, you're true to yourself, and you're still connected—you know? You're still on the inside. But when you cross that line…" he trailed off.

Garth nodded. He knew how that had felt, not to be connected to himself on the inside.

Do-Lord looked at them all, his hazel eyes unflinching in his rough-hewn face. "I crossed the line," he said simply. "Nobody died, but they would have if Emmie hadn't made me see what I was doing."

Garth nodded again. "I didn't exactly cross the line.

What I was doing was rubbing the line thinner and thinner until I had a hard time knowing which side I was on. But here's the thing that confuses me. I really thought I was supposed to be a SEAL—it was my calling—and that if I could get into the right place, I could do some good, make a difference, make SEALs more effective against terrorism."

Do-Lord gave him a knowing smile. "Come on, Lieutenant, sir. You've studied your history of war. In Iraq we are fighting the same war in the same place as has been fought for the last 4,000 years. Baghdad is where Daniel was thrown into the fiery furnace. In Afghanistan, few invading armies have succeeded, and none has held onto its victory for long." He spread his large-knuckled hands on the white tablecloth.

"Just as there are and always have been an infinite array of people needing healing, so there are and have always been terrorist wars, and there always are the fertile breeding grounds of hatred, lust for power, and greed for them to spawn in. What to do about it? There isn't a one-size-fits-all answer. Or even one answer that will fit one person for a whole lifetime."

"That's true," Davy spoke up. "Remember how I said I never wanted anything except to be a SEAL?"

Garth smiled fondly. "Yeah, and you were a damn pain in the ass about it, too."

"I'm asking for a medical discharge."

There were protests around the table. "I thought you were okay."

"I am. For most purposes. But the hyper-focus thing—it's not there anymore. And occasionally I lose my balance. You saw it at Bronwyn's house that day. I want to stop and smell the flowers. When you're operating, you can't let your attention be taken by the beauty of a sunset or how pretty your wife looked in the shower or your worry about your brother's repeated bouts of pneumonia."

"Do you think the problem is a result of your head injury?" Garth asked.

"It might be. I'm claiming it is anyway." Davy grinned conspiratorially but then became serious. "I'm not going to let any shortcoming of mine endanger other SEALs. If I can't do the job one hundred percent, I want out."

Garth sensed something unsaid and asked, "What else?"

"I ask myself—well, what if the problem of blocking out distractions is that I really *want* to stop and smell the flowers? And I also ask myself, how many brain cells am I willing to lose? Now that I'm able to read again, I've done some research on trauma sufficient to cause unconsciousness.

"The person might seem all right after a couple of days to a couple of months, but they have some scarring. With every loss of consciousness, the damage is cumulative. Add that to the natural aging process and exposure to toxic substances, and you get early onset Alzheimer's and other dementias. They are more common in special operators.

"You know what they say about why SEALs, dedicated as they are, get out. Officers get out when they want more. That would be you, Garth. You don't want more money, power, or prestige. You want more life with Bronwyn than you will have as a SEAL. Enlisted men get out when they'd had enough. That would be me. I've had enough of having my brain shaken, and I want more sunsets."

Chapter 42

SHE WAS BEAUTIFUL. HER HAIR GLOWED DEEP RED, A silken cascade that just touched her collarbones where white skin gleamed and glowed as delicately pink as the inside of a seashell in the hollows.

She was so alive. She was life and light and warmth. He couldn't remember why there was anything else he wanted, anything that was an obstacle or would take him away from her.

He heard the words of the marriage ceremony and knew that was what he wanted—not a poised hostess, not someone with the right political instincts, not a household manager who would make him look good.

He wanted to love her forever. In sickness and in health. In good times and in bad. Whatever else came with it, he would take.

He took her hand. "Come with me."

"Let's not start anything here. Tonight let's just be happy for JJ and David and let it go at that."

"Come." He drew her out one of the French doors and across the flagstone patio. When she saw he intended to go down the steps that led to the boat landing, she hauled back on his hand. "Wait. Where are we going?"

"Someplace we can talk—someplace private."

She had talked for what seemed like hours to people she had little to say to. Everyone seemed to know who she was and had had to exclaim over the novelty of what she was doing. One thing for sure, by the end of the evening, everyone in eastern North Carolina would know who and where she was. Maybe building a practice wouldn't take as long as she thought.

But it had exhausted her—as having to meet so many people and being unable to connect to them always did.

At the end of the long dock, the excursion boat hired to taxi those who wanted to come by water lay moored, the gay lights stringing its canopy over empty seats. It puttered to itself, a deep-throated idle purr. A boardwalk led to another dock, going off at an angle that widened at the end into a screened gazebo.

"We've said everything we have to say."

"No, we haven't. I haven't."

"Garth, we've been over this. I'm not going to be in a relationship with a man whose life I don't share. I don't need a relationship to distract me from my life. I don't want and I don't need a man to be my fix, my empty thing that keeps me from focusing on all the other emptiness."

"I hate long good-byes."

He slipped his hand beneath her hair. He stroked the tender, sensitive nape and then cupped the back of her head. With cool competence, he held her in place for the slow seeking of her mouth. "I'm not saying good-bye."

And there it was. Warm, dark-bright, as if she had walked into an electromagnetic field that expanded the energy of every cell in her body. Always familiar, always new. She inhaled the scent of him that was like desert nights and tall green grass, salty warm and earthy. Civilized scents of starched cotton and the clove and sandalwood. She opened her mouth to let him plunder.

He took her acquiescence as his due. With inexorable skill, he set about inflaming her.

Without releasing his control of her head, he held the screen door open.

Bronwyn understood that he needed to dominate her, just a little. She couldn't claim she didn't love him, and at the same time she had frustrated him repeatedly. She moved. But just to make the point that the frustration went both ways, she grabbed his tie and tugged him along with her. Inside the gazebo it was deeply shadowy. The screens rendered everything outside indistinct. A world with no edges. It smelled of treated wood, sunshine, and rain, and always the salty, marshy smell of the Waterway.

From the outside, unless they happened to be silhouetted against a patch of moonlight-brightened water, they were invisible. Inside, it was like the outdoors had been encapsulated. They had all the expansive freedom of being in open air with the protection of feeling enclosed. Bronwyn made a mental note to find out what it would cost to build a gazebo like this on her dock.

The rumble of the excursion boat's motors would cover any sound of their voices.

"This connection we have, it means something," Garth said. "Did you know I feel a buzz every time I touch you?"

"A buzz?"

"A hum. Something. There's an energy. Nobody else feels it but me—I've asked. It's because I get you. I know you can't—shouldn't leave here. You're where you're supposed to be. I thought I needed someone who could go anywhere with me, since there was no telling where my job would take me. Then I realized I'm the one who can live anywhere. If I can live anywhere, I can live where you are."

"Having your mail delivered to my house won't change anything."

"Pay attention. I said I want to live forever wherever you are, Bronny."

"And not be gone all the time and not have secret compartments in your life I can't go into?"

"I want to be married to you, to live with you. You want me to share my life?— You've got it. I'll share everything I have and everything I am."

She wrapped her arms around his neck as far as they would go, which wasn't very far, but he was always ready to help her out. At the bidding of her tiny hand on his nape, he bent to take the kiss she offered.

In seconds, the kiss turned incendiary. Fire spread through his veins so quickly that he was surprised his hair didn't light up. He lifted her higher and pushed at the straps of the green evening gown. He palmed the treasure he had sought and groaned to feel the already budded nipples.

Bronwyn's soft, oh-so-intelligent hands sought his fly.

"I didn't intend this—" he started to say.

"Don't talk." She went for a different angle on the kiss, emphasizing her point with a sharp little nip.

"—to get out of hand—"

"I don't care." She had him unzipped, his balls nestled in her palm as her thumb stroked his penis.

"Slow down."

"I don't want to slow down."

He pulled up fistfuls of her dress. He palmed her derriere a moment and then pushed her panties down. "Step out of them."

She did, and he knelt to pick them up and tuck them in his jacket pocket. Still kneeling, he said, "Now put one leg up on the bench. Put your hands on my shoulders."

Bronwyn's legs almost buckled when she felt the hot slide of his tongue against her most tender flesh. He steadied her with his large hands on her bottom.

The air was cool on her legs and bottom. The contrast made the heat of his mouth and hands almost burn. The tension gathered and coiled, and each increment seemed to draw off strength from the knee that held her up.

"Hold your dress out of the way," he instructed and lifted her. She instinctively clasped his waist with her legs and then positioned him at her entrance. He drove into her. Drove home.

"Mine," he said.

There was no time for refinements. No special technique. There was only pounding and the surging seeking of flesh to flesh in the ancient rhythm.

They came almost simultaneously.

"Excuse me. Lieutenant Vale? Would you come with me, please?"

The flunky hadn't caught them in the act, thank God, but Garth wasn't ready to sacrifice the afterglow. "Why would I want to do that?"

"Admiral Stephenson would like you to join him."

Bronwyn meant more to him than any retired admiral, no matter how powerful. Admiral Stephenson no longer had anything he wanted. "Tell him I'm busy talking to the lady."

Bronwyn laid a tiny hand on his arm. "Go talk to him."

Garth checked out her face. No question, Bronwyn picked up on things he didn't. "You're sure?"

"I'm sure."

He kissed her. "Don't leave. Promise you won't leave!"

Chapter 43

It is essential to seek out enemy agents who have come to conduct espionage against you and to bribe them to serve you. Give them instructions and care for them. Thus doubled agents are recruited and used.

—Sun Tzu, *The Art of War*

THE BLACK-SUITED MAN DID NOT INTRODUCE HIMSELF when he admitted Garth to the upstairs meeting room. Instead, after an instant of sizing Garth up, he simply stepped to one side.

Admiral Stephenson stood at the window—the very picture of a powerful man relaxing. The cut-crystal tumbler in his hand held whiskey on the rocks. Though he gazed out the window at the lighted courtyard, he inclined his ear to the middle-aged man with Colonel Sanders white wavy hair who stood beside him doing most of the talking.

"Admiral Stephenson, sir?" The door-answerer interrupted his boss. "Lieutenant Vale is here."

"Ah." Stephenson turned, showing long, white teeth in an intelligent smile. He was a study in shades of gray—probably a clue to his personality. Deep pewter-gray hair swept straight back from a high forehead. He had a long, thin nose and eyes the color of hammered steel. He wore a gray suit and a lighter gray shirt. Even his voice was gray, dry and dusty. Nothing he said would ever quite be the truth, nor unequivocally a lie. "Thank you for joining us, Lieutenant. Have you met Senator Calhoun? Vale has a bright future, Senator, very bright."

"I'm always glad to meet a young man with a bright future." Calhoun offered a large-knuckled, manicured hand. "I understand you're a SEAL."

Garth took the senator's extended hand. *I used to be, and apparently, according to the admiral, I am again.* He didn't allow the cynical humor he felt at the senator's remark to show. "Yessir."

Politician to the core, Calhoun smiled in delight. "A dear friend's daughter who is like a member of the family to Charlotte and me married a SEAL last year."

"Yessir. Caleb and Emmie Dulaude. I attended that wedding."

"Did you?" Calhoun looked disconcerted but recovered instantly. "You should have come over and introduced yourself! We've become very fond of Caleb. He treats my daughter Victoria like a little sister."

A signal passed between Stephenson and his aide, and in a moment, Calhoun was drawn away.

"Close the door, Vale," Stephenson directed after the other two men had left, "so we can be private for a minute. But first," he motioned toward drink setups on a table, "what can I fix you?"

"Whatever you're having."

Stephenson splashed whiskey over ice and handed it to him. "Sit down. I understand, a couple of weeks back, you took charge of an unscheduled delivery." His thin lips slipped a little sideways at his own pun. "Good work. I would like to see the child well cared for. Since you would, too, I thought we should confer."

What the hell was going on? The Great Man offers to confer with the lowly lieutenant? The implied honor was a little hard to swallow. Renfro had indicated that the admiral had acted almost relieved that Julia had disappeared.

Garth accepted the drink but continued to stand. "Why should I confer with you at all? I've taken care of her so far."

"I have a reputation for being generous to those who cooperate with me."

"Admiral, I've gone to a lot of trouble to keep Julia alive and off the grid." There was no point in denying that he had the baby or in hiding anything about her. Stephenson *knew*. "Why should I believe you have any more right to her than I do or that you will guard her as carefully?"

Stephenson smiled slightly, a tiny twitch of his lips. "They said you thought for yourself and had a habit of questioning orders. You questioned being sent into that Afghan village. Did you suspect a trap?"

"If I'd suspected a trap I'd have been behind the insurgents, not in front of them. But I did think searching the village was a waste of man power and time, and I said so."

Stephenson had just as good as confirmed MacMurtry's story that Garth's platoon had been set up. And added credence to Renfro's implication that Stephenson might have had something to do with the false intel. This might be the only chance Garth would ever have to get some answers. "Did the orders to send us into ambush come from you?"

Stephenson swirled the ice in his glass as if he was weighing several answers. He took a swallow. "No."

"I feel like that's only half an answer. Sir."

Stephenson's aide slipped back inside the room. "Let's return to the topic of the service you did me recently." Stephenson smiled genially at Garth. "You have done well to care for the child and to keep her out of hands I wouldn't have wanted her to fall into."

Garth refused to be charmed or flattered by the VIP's praise. "First of all, whose child is Julia?"

"Julia?" Stephenson sent a questioning glance to his aide.

"Estelle," the man supplied.

Stephenson nodded. "Ah. You named her Julia. She is the child of an American serviceman and an enemy combatant, also an American, who was a double agent and sometimes a triple agent." Pain, regret—*something* flickered in the older man's eyes, before he added, "She's dead now."

Not *She died* but *She's dead now*. It sounded like Stephenson had played a part in Freytag's execution. Had he been trying to help her, or had he set her up? "The serviceman. The father. Are you entitled to act for him?"

The admiral smiled frostily. The aide's lips moved slightly, too, like they shared an inside joke. It suddenly occurred to Garth that American serviceman could be used to describe Stephenson himself. "No one—*else*"—Stephenson looked pointedly at Garth—"will question my right. There is no family. That is all you need to know."

And that, apparently, was all the admiral was going to say about that. He took a sip of his drink. "Now, about you. I can see to it that you are reinstated and that you get the promotion that's coming to you."

Garth allowed himself something close to a snort. "Right. And I'll be shipped off to the Aleutians to monitor Russian trawler radio traffic for the next ten years. I'm credited with being a yellow, lying, fuckup."

Again, the almost nonexistent smile. "I think you'll find that my cleaners will be able to remove all stain from your reputation. It will be best to transfer you to a West Coast Team. However, I can assure you, your future there is bright."

Stephenson was a most unlikely Santa Claus, but he seemed to have read everything on Garth's wish list and was set to deliver. The future that had seemed shut down from the moment he had awakened after surgery suddenly had the lights on again and was inviting him inside.

Not for a minute did Garth doubt that the admiral could do everything he said. In fact, the arrogance within Stephenson's very soft, understated voice told Garth he could fulfill every promise and more. But no matter where Garth went, he would be Stephenson's man. And *the line* would get blurrier and blurrier.

"No."

Stephenson swirled the ice in his glass. "What then? A Pentagon slot could be arranged, or maybe you'd like an embassy liaison." He studied Garth's face. "No? Money?"

"I want a discharge from the navy. No stalling, no paper-fucking, and no kick in the pants. A nice honorable discharge—oh, and you can throw in that reputation cleanup."

"You surprise me, Lieutenant. Frankly, I'm disappointed. I understood you were a dedicated career man."

I'll just bet you're disappointed, you old sidewinder. You had my career all planned and every way you would use me all figured out. Garth showed some teeth of his own. "Not so much, anymore." He paused to let that sink in, and then added, "A discharge isn't all. I want Julia."

"You want the child, Estelle?" The aide spoke aloud for the first time since he had returned.

"Julia, Estelle, whatever you want to call her. Free and clear. With every 'i' dotted and every 't' crossed on every single piece of documentation that makes her indisputably mine forever."

Stephenson lowered thick pewter eyebrows over hammered steel eyes. He swirled his drink. The only sound in the room was the clink of ice on crystal. "Is that all?"

Garth smiled crookedly. If he was asking, he'd might as well ask for everything. "You can expedite Petty Officer First Class David Graziano's medical discharge, making sure he gets full benefits."

"Did you get all that, Franks?" Stephenson asked.

"Yessir."

Stephenson crossed the room to the window, where he stood looking out as he had been when Garth first saw him. "Franks, maybe Lieutenant Vale has the answer. I was prepared to take charge of the infant, but she can't live with me. My… situation would not be good for a child," he said pensively. His shoulders under the fine gray wool of his suit were as square, his back as straight, but he looked a little bit older. He swirled his drink. The ice had melted.

"Let me refresh your drink," Franks said.

Franks took the glass Stephenson handed him and clinked two ice cubes into it. Then he added a teaspoon of whiskey.

"More."

Franks almost smiled. He obligingly poured in enough to darken the ice.

Stephenson nodded his thanks. "Thinks he can fool me into believing I've had two drinks if he adds ice to the first one."

Franks's little affectionate game had worked, though. The admiral had his composure back.

"Now for my conditions regarding the child. I do care about Estelle... Julia's welfare. Allow me to send her presents and enquire about her from time to time." His voice was dry as crushed bones. "If she needs anything... call... um..."

"Me," Franks supplied. "I'll be happy to assist."

Chapter 44

"Look who I found!" Mary Cole came through the crowd, leading Carole by the hand. As when Bronwyn had seen her before, Carole was beautifully dressed, but the businesslike pantsuit didn't match the formal dresses of the other women guests.

"I'm party-crashing," Carole acknowledged as soon as she reached Bronwyn, "but I knew where you would be tonight. I couldn't call. I had to come in person. I had to thank you."

"Did you go to Sloan-Kettering?"

"I told that oncologist at Lords, if time was of the essence, he'd better get us an appointment fast. Since the testing was all done, all we needed was a consult. We flew up to New York and back the same day. The pathologist there looked at the slides and knew right away what it was."

"Don't keep me in suspense! What was it?"

"A sweat gland. It's extremely rare, and if we'd gone anywhere else, they might not have recognized it. Here's the good news. It probably isn't a metastasis. It's probably the primary site. Since the lymph glands around it were clear and the tumor was still contained and had clear margins, they don't recommend any further treatment."

"They don't even recommend radiation of the site?"

"Radiation isn't effective. It doesn't help a bit.

Bronwyn, you saved his life. He didn't want the radiation, and I'm convinced it would have killed him."

"Give yourself the credit. Your intuition told you it was the wrong path, and you listened to your own inner knowing."

"How did you know to send us to Sloan-Kettering?"

"I didn't know. It's good, but there are a lot of good hospitals. Lords is good, for that matter. My main concern was that the doctors there were pushing a treatment that neither your husband nor you were on board with. You didn't trust what you were being told. Give yourself the credit. You followed through."

"Now, speaking of following through." Suddenly Carole wasn't the supplicant; she was the one giving advice. "You should have a consultation room that's more informal than most doctor's offices, but you can't keep seeing patients on the side porch. I'm taking over the renovation of your house. I'll only charge you material and labor."

"That sounds wonderful, but I've heard about what you do. I'm not sure I can afford even that."

"Don't worry. We'll come up with a figure you can live with. Do you make house calls?"

"I would, under some conditions."

"It's Spud. He hates going to the doctor, but I think if one came to the house and would sit and talk to him, like you do—I don't think he would mind as much."

There she was! Garth finally spotted Bronwyn's tiny form, almost hidden by the crowd. He quickly made his way to her and pulled her from the noisy room to an outside patio.

First he kissed her. Then he told her. "Julia is ours, forever. Legally."

"I don't get it." Bronwyn objected after Garth had finished telling her what had happened in his meeting with the admiral. He had left nothing out. "What's *his* claim to her? Is he Julia's father, or isn't he?"

"I'm guessing that he is. He's either her father or her mother's father—which would make him Julia's grandfather."

"You think Christine Freytag was his daughter?"

"He doesn't officially have any children, but you never know. One way or the other, I believe Julia's mother meant something to him. But, I think Julia is more of an abstraction. You know how you told me that to some people other people aren't real?"

"I'm sorry for ever thinking that of you."

"No, you were right about me. Meeting Admiral Stephenson tonight was like seeing an older, more charming version of what I would have become."

"But you're not that now."

Garth dropped a kiss on her lips. As long as her faith in his goodness lasted, he would never go back. "Back to Stephenson. He was willing to help the baby into this country for her mother's sake. But really, she was a problem— and if he didn't have to deal with it, that would be okay."

Bronwyn shook her head in consternation. "The fact that the man he sent to meet the plane knew nothing about Julia being aboard says it all, doesn't it?"

Garth tucked Bronwyn under his arm. "Stephenson left the door wide open for something to happen to her at the most vulnerable point. He's too smart for that to be poor planning."

Bronwyn absorbed that for a minute and then went on to the part that interested her. "So Julia's real name is Estelle."

"Estelle means 'star,' but I like Julia better."

Bronwyn thought, then said, "So do I, but names matter. We can't take her name away from her. We'll call her Julia and make Estelle her middle name."

Chapter 45

THE NEXT DAY GARTH ARRIVED WITH A RED CANOE ON A rack on the back of his truck.

Bronwyn met him in the drive. "What's the canoe for?"

"We're going on a picnic. Everything's arranged. The sitter will be here by the time you put on lots of sunscreen and that lacy skirt I like."

In thirty minutes they were paddling down the dark, mysterious river. Bronwyn sat in the bottom of the canoe, propped against a strut. Over her shoulder, she said to Garth, who was wielding the paddle, "I've been thinking about your meeting with Admiral Stephenson last night. You didn't ask for a discharge because of me, I hope. I don't want you to sacrifice who you are. I tried that in my own life. I tried *so hard* to shave off all the pieces of me that didn't fit so I could live in my parents' world. It didn't work."

"Yes, because of you, but not what you're thinking. I've come to realize you're doing what I want to do. You're making one spot on earth a little better just because you're there."

"Oh. That's sweet."

He huffed. "Practical, too. I'm needed here. I'm needed by you and by Julia, and for myself, I need to be here. Do-Lord told me last night he wants to open a teaching lodge for men. To teach them the confidence to open themselves to life. I'll run it, do river courses and, of course, work for the volunteer rescue squad. I want to raise tomatoes, children. I want to go to PSA meetings and church picnics, eat barbecue."

"And hunt?"

She might not like it, but they might as well discuss it. "Yes."

"Okay."

He laughed. He leaned down and dropped a smiling kiss on her crown. "If I could fall in love with every woman in the world, I would still want you. I want to live with you. I want to be here *with* you, and I want to be here *for* you. These days, I am the man I want to be, and that man wants to be with you." He steered the canoe out of the current and toward shallow water, where they would drift slowly. He stowed the paddle. "Move over. I want to be beside you, right now."

"Wait! How do we do this?"

"Very carefully," he said counterbalancing her movements. "But a flat-water canoe like this is actually very stable. No sudden movements, and we'll be okay." He let himself down beside her, tucking her under his arm. "Isn't this nice? I've been wanting to kiss you. Now I can."

In a minute, Bronwyn pulled away, satisfyingly breathless, Garth thought.

She stroked his face. "I'm glad you're the man you want to be. You're also the man I want you to be."

"You mean that? You're not repelled by... the things I've done. They come with me, you know. I'll live with them the rest of my life, and so will you."

"I would take the pain of the past away, if I could. I would put my body between you and it and hold you safe.

But I will tell you right now, I do not regret any road you ever traveled—since that path brought you to me."

No woman had ever declared her desire to protect him. He was a man, so he pulled away from how that made him feel. He tapped her nose, smiling. "I don't want to look a gift horse in the mouth, but what changed?"

"You know what? My parents refused to help me down a path they thought I was sure to fail at, and one that would possibly destroy me. All this time, I've held onto the hurt of that—the sense that they rejected me, had so little faith in me."

Garth fought down his knee-jerk rage. It wouldn't help her.

Bronwyn sighed and snuggled deep to his chest. "I've long since acknowledged that *they* knew what I was up against—and, trust me, I didn't! They were trying to protect me. But it didn't stop the hurt. But you know what I realized last night? If my parents *had* paid for my medical education, I would have quit med school. Sooner or later I would have said, 'This is too hard.' If there had been a position to retreat to, I would have retreated."

Garth squeezed her. "No, you wouldn't have. Being a doctor means too much to you. You would never let it go."

She cupped his cheek and smiled into his beloved face. "Because I had to do it on my own, to accept every bit of the cost myself. Let's be clear, because it was *my* money—my *future* money—I was spending, I stayed strong, even when I was discouraged. I'd be tempted to quit, and I'd think about all that money that I would have to pay back whether I was a doctor or not, and I'd put one foot in front of the other and keep going." She chuckled at herself in the way he loved. "Noble ideals may have motivated me, but what made it happen was needing a way to pay back all that money.

"Today, I understood that no harm was done by my parents. I don't know if I finally saw that because I didn't want the pain anymore and so I decided to forgive them, or if forgiving them made me able to see it. All I know is that there is no more pain, and forgiving them is easy—because there's nothing to forgive."

"It sounds circular, paradoxical," Garth told her. "Is this an 'It's destiny and *everything happens for a reason*' line of thought?"

"I don't know if *everything* happens for a reason. I'm still a scientist, and I don't have enough data to make a sweeping statement. I'm not even saying I think this happened for a reason. And again, without data, I don't know if forgiveness is possible in all circumstances."

Garth kissed his little scientist with the magic hands. He kissed her until she began to make the hungry little sounds he loved. "Let's lie down," he whispered. "I don't want to limit any spontaneous movements, and the canoe will be more stable."

They scooted down until they were like peas wrapped in a canoe pod. In their ears was the wet lapping of the water; overhead they looked up into cypress trees millennia old.

The sun was warm, but the water kept them cool.

Bronwyn felt Garth's erection against her hip. His shorts were unzipped. Suddenly it all clicked. The canoe, the baby-sitter. "You planned this, didn't you? You planned the whole thing!"

"Hoped. Let's say I hoped."

"Hoped! Pooh. You're so full of it. You lured me out here to have your way with me. You're trying to ruin my reputation!"

She squirmed against his arousal to show him she was playing, but he said, "Hey! Does that still bother you?"

"Really? No." She squirmed again, trying to get her hands on him. They were squeezed so tight there wasn't room, but thinking about that hot, hard velvet in her palms made her willing to try. Finally she managed to circle him with her fingers. "Why shouldn't a doctor have a hot stud, ex-SEAL lover?"

He began bunching her lace skirt and skating his hands over her bottom. "Lover? You're not taking any lovers. You're making me an honest man."

She stretched to land a kiss on the underside of his chin, reveling in his hot, potent musk. "Show me what you can do. We'll talk about it later."

"Just one question. Should I infer anything from the fact that you have on no panties?"

"You should infer that I am not stupid. And I was hopeful, too."

"In that case, turn on your side," he whispered. "I'll show you."

Bronwyn turned on her side, her head pillowed on his arm with Garth spooned behind her. He slid his hands under her white tank top to cup and play with her breasts, while, devil that he was, he alternately kissed and nipped at her neck.

She loved the freedom, sexual and emotional, she had found with this man. When she was moaning and reflexively arching her pelvis, he slid into her from behind. He thrust, and the canoe began to rock.

"Uh!" She dug her fingers into the arm he held around her.

"Relax." She could hear the smile in his dark voice. The sound traveled straight to the place they were joined. "The canoe won't tip." He slid his hand under her skirt and unerringly found her clitoris. "Relax." He moved within her in gentle nudges. The canoe began to rock in time with the rhythm he set. "We're going to let the canoe do most of the work."

It was like making love with nature. The sun, the breeze, the water sounds that added to the wet sounds of their bodies together. The slow, gentle piling of sensation on sensation.

Bronwyn slowly became aware of the most luscious, heady, thick, powerful, sensual, drunk-making scent she had ever smelled. She drew it deep in her lungs. It blended perfectly with the scent of the river, of Garth and sunshine, of earth and sex. "What *is* that?"

Garth kept up the slow, inexorably gentle rhythm. "I hoped we would come across that." His voice was as thick as the steadily increasing scent. "It's swamp rose. They bloom in May. Unless you're in a slow boat, just drifting, you hardly notice the smell. Breathe deep. Don't work for the climax. Let it come to you."

And that's exactly what they did until the ripples started deep within Bronwyn and she knew the climax would come, no matter what she did. She breathed deeply and let the day, the canoe, and Garth take her to the top of the peak, and let them push her over.

In the lazy aftermath, Garth kissed her ear and said, "Last night, Do-Lord said something."

Bronwyn was too relaxed to open her eyes. "Hmm. What?"

"He said, 'Some things are for a season. Some things are forever.' He was talking about how you know when it's time to get out of the SEALs. But I think he was talking about the kind of love we have, too. This is the kind of love that is forever."

———

Much, much later, while they still lay spooned together, the rough rumble of his bass voice vibrating in Bronwyn's chest, Garth said, "I'll never know if you married me for myself or to get your hands on my baby."

"The baby, of course. Getting my hands on you was easy."

"I was easy?"

"Oh, yeah. Thank God."

Acknowledgments

Whenever I sit down to write my acknowledgments for a book, I'm always blown away by the sheer amount of generosity encountered along the way.

I wouldn't have had the courage to attempt a medical heroine if I hadn't known I'd have my friend Elizabeth Vaughan, MD, always at hand. She talked me through the medical scenes and then checked them for accuracy.

Jennifer Lohman and Elsa McKeithan read the manuscript and offered suggestions and dug me out when I got stuck. VK Powell was always on hand for another plotting session.

My editor, Deb Werksman, and my agent, Stephany Evans, stayed with me—and after me—through thick and thin.

To all of them, and to all the people whose work you hold in your hands but who go unsung—the copy editors, the cover artists, and people like Susie Benton, Danielle Jackson, Sarah Ryan, and Skye Agnew—my thanks.

About the Author

If you don't count a thirty-seven page novel written when she was twelve, then *SEALed with a Kiss* was not merely Mary Margret Daughtridge's first published novel, it was the first novel she ever wrote. She wrote it for fun—just to prove to herself that she could.

Since she was writing only for herself, she had one guiding principle: she put everything she liked into the book and left out everything she didn't like. She likes dogs [check], children [check], heroines with a sense of humor [check], and strong honorable men who are doing the right thing—by their lights. Check.

And since she really likes a romance and a happy ending, she made them fall in love, learn their lessons, make sacrifices, and be stronger and more whole in the end.

A graduate of the University of North Carolina at Greensboro, Mary Margret has a BA in speech communication and an M.Ed. in speech pathology and audiology. All her professional life she has been a therapist of one kind or another, desiring more than anything to empower people to reach beyond whatever limits them. As her alter ego, MM Holloman, she is a landscape artist whose paintings of North Carolina rivers, swamps, fields, forest, and coast hang in corporate and private collections across the state.

She's between dogs right now, so she's thrilled when Fergus, a West Highland terrier, can come for a sleepover, even if the resident cat, Crystal, gets in a snit. Born in Ahoskie, Mary Margret still lives in North Carolina and visits places like Wilmington, Elizabeth City, Scotland Neck, and Topsail Island as often as she can.

SEALed

with a
Promise

BY MARY MARGRET DAUGHTRIDGE

NAVY SEAL CALEB DELAUDE IS AS DEADLY AS
HE IS CHARMING.

Professor Emmie Caddington's quiet intelligence and
quirky personality intrigue him. When he discovers
that her personal connections can get him close to the
man he's vowed to kill, will their budding relationship
be nothing more than a means to revenge...or is she
the key to his salvation?

Praise for *SEALed with a Kiss*:

"This story delivers in a huge way." —Romantic Times

*"A wonderful story that will have readers experiencing
a whirlwind of emotions and culminating with an
awesome scene that will have your pulse pounding."*
—Romance Junkies

*"What an incredibly powerful book! I laughed and
sniffled, was turned on and turned inside out."* —Queue
My Review

978-1-4022-1763-0 • $6.99 U.S. / $7.99 CAN